GW01086994

The Live with Gusto Fund

Mary Moloney

Published by Mary Moloney, 2024.

THE LIVE WITH GUSTO FUND

First edition. May 19, 2024.

ISBN: 979-8223877790

Written by Mary Moloney.

For Tim, Michael and Maureen

CHAPTER 1

It was the pebbles that did it in the end. Neither Ron - Veronica at a push - nor Joe heard the rapping at the window.

"Let me in. I forgot me key. I'm bursting to go to the loo. Ma open the door."

Joe continued sanding down the old kitchen presses. Hearing loss was an occupational hazard when a person had been doing carpentry on building sites as long as he had. Ron having shaped her eyebrows, was filling them in at the kitchen mirror.

"*Not bad,*" she thought. They did say thick eyebrows were sexy. Joe thought his daughter might meet a nice man down here in Leitrim. Culchies weren't her style, not really, despite what she might have declared to the contrary. A few guys down at the pub had been eyeing her since her arrival. She knew she wasn't bad looking; sleek black hair, fringed and parted to one side, fell to her waist over an oval- shaped face. She'd inherited her mother's olive skin. The small, sculpted nose and generous lips were all her own. Her eyes were charcoal and warm. A very polite man she'd met once in an English pub said to her,

'My dear, those eyes are very alluring, like delicate spears."

The rapping came again louder this time.

"For the love of God, will youse let me in or I'll wet me pants."

By now, Joe had taken out his earplugs and set them down on the countertop. He turned to her and frowned, inclining his ear towards the front room.

"Did you hear anything, Love?"

"No," she said puzzled.

Then she heard it too, the abrasive sound of pebbles, like a cool shower on the front window pane.

"I'll kill him - No key again. He has lost his memory since he moved from Dublin."

Joe smiled. "Go on, let him in quick; it's cold outside."

She gave him a look on opening the front door. He stood there jiggling his feet on the step, hitching up a half slid down school satchel.

"No key and no phone credit I'm guessing."

"Sorry Ma, 'scuse me Ma." He knifed past her, bolting up the stairs.

"This is the country Brendan; there's no Hegartys to let you in," she shouted after him to a deaf bathroom door.

"That's better," he said two minutes later on entering the kitchen. "I seriously thought I was going to have to go in the bushes."

"Well I suppose that wouldn't disturb the sheep too much," she said, fielding the corner of her right eyebrow in his direction , suddenly aware of a nervy pull where the tweezers had been at work.

"No Ma, the sheep wouldn't give a bleat."

"Right so, I'll be off now. I'll finish tomorrow Ron," her dad said, exiting the kitchen, giving Brendan a quick squeeze on the shoulder on his way out. He had to stoop as he always did under the lintel of the kitchen door. She followed him into the hallway, handing him his brown cord jacket with the white fleece rising above the collar. "Thanks Love," he said softly as she opened out the armholes of his high- vis jacket to put over the one he'd just squeezed into. "Brendan?" he shouted into the kitchen, putting his large hands through the holes, "bring out me bicycle helmet and clips like a good man."

"Will do Grandad." Brendan handed him his bicycle clips and canary yellow and black safety hat.

"I think I'll do now," he said finally, clipping the straps of his helmet in two places. "It's a PA I need to keep me on track." Ron said smiling, "That would have been Ma." She paused, "or maybe Sally now? me new stepma." He gave her a small shadowed look.

2

"God, Da, you know how cool we all are with it." Her voice reflected the truth. She was happy for him, and so was everyone else really.

Ron and Brendan watched him pedal down the small ribbon of roadway with ditches sequestering primrose patches in the already long grass

He raised his left hand back over his shoulder in salute.

"Right, now," she said ."I'll put on the dinner and you can help me set the table."

"What culinary delights are we having tonight Ma?" her son asked cheekily.

"I'll have you know it's Coq au Vin."

"Cock o what?"

"Means chicken in wine.We have at least some of that wine to use up that Sally brought."

"And there was I thinking an old cock was ridin' in a van from the chippers."

"Funny! Sally was really good to give it to us, but she didn't understand much about teenagers and drink."

He flashed her that cocky "Oh really" teenage look.

"A fresh start here Love, and alcohol is to be taken very seriously."

"Message received," he said, opening the wall mounted press to the right of the kitchen sink to take out the dinner plates.

The smell of the chicken infusing in the casserole filled the small kitchen, giving her a heady sense of tension oozing out like butter on hot toast. Table set, Brendan beat a retreat to the sitting room to watch the last Netflix"On My Block" episode on his phone. She prodded the boiling potatoes with a fork; they were cooked. Straining the heavy saucepan at the sink, she wondered what Sally would make of their use of her merlot -Sally, who had changed all of their lives. If it weren't for her and Joe, she and Brendan wouldn't be making this fresh start. She was the best thing to happen to her Da

3

since Ma's death eight years ago. Joe met Sally from Manchester on a dating website *www.anyoneoutthere.com[1]*. They teased him endlessly about it. He said they were cut from the same cloth, the kind that makes a tight crease under your armpits. When he started corresponding with her first, four years after Alice -Ron's Ma- passed away from breast cancer, Brendan would go out the front door of their terraced house on Patrician Road and shout,

'Anyone out there?'

"Get in you little gurrier, or I'll eviscerate you"

"What's a vistarat Grandad? the boy asked, dodging a clip behind the ear. He was eleven.

"It means I'll take all the cheek out of your insides."

She had to have a word with himself then, and warn him to tell no one about Grandad on the website.

Sally, a plump woman of fifty- four, with unruly blonde hair brought to heel by a straightener, and startlingly blue eyes housed in a small, round face, began to fly over and back regularly from Manchester. She was staying in Shanahans, a three star hotel near the airport, Joe said. Once when she came to visit, her overfull clutch bag toppled from the kitchen counter as Brendan running in, brushed against it accidentally. Its insides spewed all over the floor. A mad scramble began, to pick up her lipstick, diary, car keys, tissues, purse. Loose coins she kept for the parking meters scattered treacherously. Ron was pursuing a rolled away 50 cent coin, lodged under the fridge when she spotted it out of the corner of her eye- a white room key pouch with a gold Wi-Fi symbol in one corner and in italics *'Shelbourne Hotel'*. Just as she was reaching out to handle it, the older woman snatched it, leaving her confused hand hovering above the empty space. She didn't tell her father. He always felt Shanahans was a bit on the grotty side, especially for a woman. In fact, he admitted to Ron, he thought it surprising alright that given Sally's

1.   *http://www.anyoneoutthere.com/*

4

late husband's high profile, she'd pick a place like this. He wasn't one to pry however, given he lived in a council house himself.

In ways she mused, he was an innocent and in more ways maybe not? In his twenties, a block of anger from his own upbringing sometimes writhed in his fists. Their independence from his head mirrored the violence his quiet mother, his brother Alfie and himself endured at the hands of a man who was either amiable or instantly violent, depending on how much he had gone on the batter that day. Joe found himself barred from a couple of pubs in Kilburn in his twenties. Then a week after the last ejection from Moriartys on the corner of The Kilburn High Road, he met Alice at a dance in the Irish Centre. She was working as a nurse's aid in a hospital in Camden. She rescued his good underbelly.

"Like the part of a hedgehog, he can't afford his predators to see," she said once.

"Except he's not a hedgehog?" her daughter said, not getting it.

"Me point exactly. I brought him back to Dublin, soft and chastened."

The other great thing that saved him was his boxing. The house was full of medals, plaques and trophies. His photo of "Best Boxer Award 1993," presented in London, was framed on the wall behind the telly. It was his *"Mount Olympus,"* Alice said, which always meant a smile found a soft landing under his eyes. Boxing drew him and Sally together, her husband having managed many big English names: Barney McGregor and Tom McCullough amongst them. The relationship between them deepened thanks to Skype and the newly emergent WhatsApp. Ron encouraged Brendan to show him the technology, needing an excuse to keep him in the house. She disliked lads calling to the door - almost all older than him - inviting him down to the soccer pitch as she thought, but really to hang out around a local disused hall. The curate, Father Dempsey had once attempted to set up supervised pool here. The older parishioners were upset when the bishop transferred him abruptly on the grounds of ill health. He confessed to Joe his idealism had been rolled over by the drug dealing. The day he refused Tom Hutchinson, the big crime boss's cash donation was the tipping point. When the notes were strewn at the foot of the church altar in front of him, and the other man walked out shouting, "You'll pay for this yet Dempsey!" he knew he had to leave.

She was later to walk around that disused hall after it had been the scene of her child's wounding. Its splintered door banged in and out when a hard wind blew. Some window panes were jigsawed, others completely shattered. She peered inside and quickly withdrew her head in fright and disdain. Shards of glass floating on water gathered in gouged- out spaces in the wooden floor. There was a strong smell of damp and black mould fingered the cement walls. Back outside, she stared hypnotically for a full five minutes at the long fingers of grass poking their way up through the gaps in the mossed paving slabs. Flattened crisp bags and dripping empty cigarette packs shored up the drains. Empty beer cans formed a mound outside a disused latrine where discarded condoms sank into wet cement. This was no place for any child, let alone her only one.

Initially, she let him go out with the lads who came calling nearly every day, as his friend Eamo was in the group. Eamo's brother Trigger was training they said, with the soccer team. He needed supporters. He and Eamo were blood brothers, he declared one evening coming home late from school. When asked why he was so late, he just shrugged his shoulders in a new and developing insolence. She returned to peeling the potatoes at the sink, her chest tightening.

"Why blood brothers anyway?"

In answer to her question, he moved to stand beside her, dropping his satchel on the kitchen chair. To her horror, he slowly unwrapped a dirty bandage loosely wrapped around the ring finger on his right hand. A deep gash, visibly suffering, snaked its way down the three digits to the tip. He gave her a smile, laced with daring and fear.

"Eamo and me mingled our bloods today."

Already it looked septic. Instantly, she dropped the potato peeler. "*Out now.*"

"Where?" he asked, his eyes revealing shock and more fear, his face paling.

"Where do you think, you stupid child ? *A & E!*".

Grabbing her car keys from the hook in the hallway, her coat and purse, she thought ,

'I'm a dumbo! I grew up here. Did I think it would be easier for him?'

On the way to Tallaght, a frightened Brendan sat in the back seat, head bent, shivering. Registering his coldness in the driver mirror, she told him to get onto his grandad pronto. Her tone, hard and bleached, he mutely did what he was told.

"What will I tell him?" the child whined.

"Tell him we're going to A & E, but no panic. I can't talk; I'm driving."

"Hello, Grandad." He paused.

"That you Brendan, everything OK?"

"Ma said to tell you we're going to A & E."

"What happened?"

"Wait a minute- we're at the lights. She's going to talk to you."

He handed his mother the phone. She noted the encroaching black and purple stain under the hot skin of his finger, and heard the small wounded cry of him when his hand touched hers in the handover. She rolled down her window for some air.

"Hi Da, no panic. Our boy has had a small cut on his finger. Getting it checked out. Can you meet us there?"

"I'll be down in ten minutes. Just in from me walk with the dog."

"Ok, thanks."

The lights had changed to green and she hadn't noticed. They were stuck on red again. The guy behind her with the stereo pumping out the half- open window gave her the two fingers. She recognised him from the new estate gone up behind their road. His passenger, a guy of about twenty- five, flicked the ashes of his cigarette with his left hand out his window. The spark reddened in the sharp breeze and drifted away.

"Jaysus Missus!" he shouted out,

"Get your bleedin' brains out of your arse." The lights were green. Are you f*ckin' blind as well as dumb?" She heard a puking sound from the back seat. She observed him in the rearview mirror, head down, spewing. The lights turned green, and the brown brick of the hospital rose in front of them.

"Keep the head Brendan, you'll be just grand Love," she said softly, steeling herself not to turn around as she glimpsed his wan face coming into view when she rechecked the mirror as she drove on.

The security man raised a hand. She rolled down the window

"Everything okay here?" he asked, his head already in the car. He took in Brendan in the back.

"Sick child and black, purple finger," she said, looking up at him appealingly. She recognised him from Da's boxing club in Darndridge. He must have recognised her too.

"I saw those fellas down at the lights," he said now. "Just pull over here, where that car is moving out. It's a disabled space, but I'm taking down the details, so no worries." What made you sick?" he asked the child, stifling the urge to put his hand over his mouth to stay the stench of the puke. Brendan stared woodenly ahead.

They got through A & E with only a five hour wait, and an extra hour in the Medical Assessment Unit to administer iv antibiotics. Adam had told them tales of people being there for twenty- four hours.

"We were lucky Da," she said. "If it had been later, we'd be competing with the drunks. Remember Adam used to talk about the frustration of that?"

Joe just gave a cursory nod. Then he went silent, his face the dial of a still wound- up clock.

She took a deep breath and exhaled slowly into her cupped hands.

"Anyway, your brother doesn't have to deal with that anymore," he said brusquely.

"Thank God he's going to be alright, and you got the repeat prescription for the antibiotics didn't you?"

"Actually, I forgot it," she said, and waited for the effect.

"Better make sure Ron." His furrowed eyebrows were maxed out.

"I'm only messin' Da." She got up off the sofa, and proceeded over to the little pine bureau -bookcase she had bought on Done Deal. She turned the silver key in the roll top desk cover and slid it up. She pointed to the small keepsake drawer under the letter holders.

"It's safe as houses." Then she turned a second silver key and opened it up.

"*Jaysus*," he said, peering in at the folded edges of the crisp white prescription sheet. "You're nearly as good as your mother."

"Oh, nearly?"

"What did the doctor say again?"

"He said the tendons are inflamed, so painkillers, anti-inflammatories and most likely physio to regain full movement. He said he was a lucky boy not to have his finger amputated. He's seen it before."

Joe winced, baring his teeth in that way he often did before going into the ring. "What the hell was he thinking?"

" Trigger put them up to it- said it was a rite of passage. He did it at their age. Then he produced his penknife and cut hard all the way down their fingers. The knife was rusty Da. God, it really freaked me. You remember his meningitis as a baby? He's out cold now. I gave him half a sleeping tablet and Nurofen drops. I can give them to him again they said if he wakes." She sighed, and with her two hands pushed her long hair back up the nape of her neck right to the crown of her head. She held it in place for about two seconds before it claimed grateful release on her taut shoulders. Suddenly, tiredness ransacked her. "You know what Da, I'm bunched. I'm going to hit the sack."

"I'll head out for a bit," he said. Since her childhood, she remembered him doing this, if things got tough. He moved to kiss her on the cheek. Instinctively she pulled him close, and leaned her head sideways across the top of his chest. She could hear his heart speeding down his torso, causing a slight lift in his shirt fabric. He let her tears flow, and because she pinioned him, he couldn't wipe away his own trickle. She could feel their damp on her face. Finally, he released her gently, picking up his car keys from the pine coffee table. He put on his black, padded Puma jacket, and headed into the hallway. It was early February and a galleon of stars mingled with a film of cold air, lifting his breath out of him. She followed him outside quietly, shivering in her green hoodie, stamping her runnered feet up and down on the pavement.

"I'll just get a jug of hot water for the car Da."

The sleeping roadway had that settled look. The cars bunched up on the footpaths gave the night world a metallic emptiness. One pup left outside yelped piteously.

"Bloody bad dog owners," he muttered now, blowing hard into his hands when she came back out. The warm water slid over the iced windscreen. She watched from the open doorway ,moving her feet again up and down on the tiles, as the old fluence puttered off into the dark. She hoped his heater would work this time.

CHAPTER 2

At 5am she checked on him again. His dark curls fanned out against a white pillowcase were a counterpoint to the still ashen face. He stirred softly and moaned in his sleep. Anxiously she gripped the door handle, eyeing the Nurofen drops on the bedside locker. She bent over his inert form; he didn't open his eyes. Her breathing sank gratefully back down. That's when she saw the blue revolving siren in the window. An ambulance was heading down the formlessness of the early morning estate. Her heart strangled in her throat; her tongue chafed against the roof of her mouth.

They were stopping outside number 36, *Eamo's*. Two paramedics disappeared inside the house carrying a stretcher. She peeled her eyes to the doorway, until she suddenly realised how cold she was in her thin, brushed-cotton, pink dressing gown. The linoleum pushed coldly up into the soles of her bare feet. After what seemed an eternity, the two men wheeled someone out onto the roadway, loading them up into the ambulance. She could discern five figures gathered on the pavement, two older adults - a woman and a man - a younger adult male - Trigger, she guessed - and two children. After a short discussion, the woman hopped into the ambulance. Suddenly its siren was the only sound reverberating through the estate at 5.45 am. Streetlights poured a commentary on the shadows dispersing and converging on the open doorway. There appeared to be a heated argument going on between the two males. She saw the older man raise a right hand and strike the younger one on the left cheek, just under the eye. By now, the children were screaming. Neighbours' lights went on. She saw Jack Hegarty from next door and Joxer Flanagan from across the way open their windows. She put her hand to her mouth as the younger man struck back, knocking the other to the ground. The children's screams were frantic now.

"Stop, Trigger, stop, you'll kill Da!"

She heard the creak of the window opening in the front bedroom. She turned to see Joe standing on the landing. He stood there in his pyjamas and bare feet, running his fingers through his wire-brush hair. He looked at her for a minute before turning away and heading for his room. "Don't Da, please don't." He stiffened. "For Christ's sake Da, haven't we had enough of that family." She touched his arm lightly.

"Let someone else go down to the kids."

He gave a short wooden nod; his chest, concave, vacated a long tenured sigh.

'You're right. God what a bloody mess. That Trigger fella is off his head on speed. The Barons are the cause of all this, and the bloody guards are useless.'

'It's not their fault, Da.' That's when they heard raised male voices.

"Trigger, Jesus, leave him alone. Stop it, stop!" They both ran to Joe's bedroom window. They saw Trigger drunkenly throw a punch at his father, Mick and miss. Jack Hegarty and Joxer Flanagan were running hard down the estate. Jack grabbed his flailing arm and both men pinned him from behind. Mick stood up, dazed, from the cement path. Trigger twisted his hard sinewy torso, eel-like and head-butted the sky. Police sirens rent the air. Two squad cars promptly pulled up outside the front door. The children's mouths were arrested in a gaping oval of terror. Ron gripped Joe's big right hand. He squeezed it. After a heated exchange, which they couldn't hear, Trigger was pushed roughly into the back seat of the blue and yellow striped car, his spittle hitting the pavement first. The older of the two guards returned briefly, to speak to Trigger's father, who had got up from the ground. Now he repeatedly shook his head, and put up his hand placatingly. Mick Fagan was a decent enough skin, old school tough, Joe said. His son's scaffolding on the other hand, had poison in the marrow.

The doorbell woke Ron at nine. She pulled back the covers, sitting up, slowly rubbing the last of an unsettled sleep from her eyes. She hauled her feet onto the bedroom floor. Wearily, she belted her dressing gown and felt under the bed for her slippers. A frightened knot bunched up her stomach. The bell rang again three times in succession. Before heading down the stairs, she checked on Brendan. He was awake, his bandaged finger exposed on the duvet cover. She pushed out a quick smile, as he looked at her confused. "Back in a minute Love. Go in to Grandad, he's.awake in there." She'd heard Joe's slow movements through the walls. The bell rang again. A new found anger turned up a dial in her body." What in God's name now?" She saw the outline of Mags Dillon from number nineteen about to push the bell once more before she released the security chain, and opened back the door. Wordlessly, Mags entered, as Ron stood in the hallway, her eyes tiredly questioning and challenging.

'Ron, Ron, did you hear all the commotion?'

She allowed herself a wry smile.

"The whole estate heard it Mags." Everyone knew Mags and Trigger had been an item. She also knew rumour had it, that Trigger was the father of Mags's baby

"They've arrested Trig."

Mags began to cry. A stale indifference cemented Ron to the floor.

"Mags, Trig cut Brendan's finger with a rusty knife and then cut his own brother's- said it would make them blood brothers. I spent six hours last night in A & E and then the commotion down at Fagan's woke me at five."

Mags looked stunned, the fingers of her right hand clamped to her upper lip.

"Oh God, Ron, I didn't know- I swear to you. All I heard was that Trig cut his own brother's finger. I didn't know about Brendan. How is he?"

"He's fine; they caught it in time. I'm guessing Eamo isn't good though. Did you hear anymore?"

"No, I haven't heard."

Mags's voice levered itself down into a frightened whisper. Ron looked at the girl in the corridor, her plain makeup-less face full of freckles, her ginger hair falling tousled onto her shoulders. What age was she, eighteen, nineteen? At twenty-seven, she suddenly felt very old, a pack mule being saddled up again on her own doorstep with someone else's mess. Mags began to light up a cigarette, as she stood there, longingly eyeing the kitchen. Ron sighed hard, jerked her head briefly in the direction of the open doorway ahead.

"I'll put on the kettle. Brendan will be up in a while. You can't stay long Mags; I want to tell him about this meself."

The girl blinked hard, then swallowed some tightly knitted emotion in her throat.

"Don't judge me Ron."

Ron turned back to look at her from where she stood at the sink, kettle in hand.

"I'm the last one in the world to judge, Mags. Half the neighbourhood has been talking about me for years."

"Well, they're talking about me now." Mags' eyes began to well up.

"And they'll talk about another girl, and then another one next year. That's the way round here. Here, have a chocolate biscuit."

Ron pulled a Mikado tin from the top press and plonked it on the table.

"The tea is made strong," she said, bringing it over now along with two white enamel-ware mugs. "Milk and sugar on the table."

Mags issued her a lost bird-like smile. "You've a good heart. Me and Trig... well I guess you know about the baby?"

Ron nodded. "It's an open secret."

"We're not together anymore, and I've given him back his jewellery-well most of it," she said, looking down at a large garnet ring on her right hand, and stroking a thin 24-carat gold neck chain.

Ron had a flashback to last November when she babysat Mags's baby for a day. Mags had a job interview. Her reward was a Swarovski necklace and matching earrings. Joe cautioned her to accept it.

"I can't Da, it's drug money."

'Take it Love. Mags will run with stories to Trigger. We want no trouble." At the time she remembered, she thought Joe was exaggerating. Trig was always so polite to her, eyeing her up even, offering her a lift home from the supermarket in his van, until he bought the Saab. That's when Mags began to feature in his life, preening herself down in the pub, wearing Dior necklaces, Ralph Lauren trousers and matching white shirts. She said Trig was working for important people now, doing good, by keeping down crime in the neighbourhood. There'd been no break-ins in Dobbinstown for two years, she crowed.

" More like keeping out ordinary criminals, so the guards don't get into the area," Joe said when she told him. She still had found it hard to believe about Trig until right now. She focused her attention back to Mags.

"He lied. He didn't want the baby-said it wasn't his. Everyone knew we were together. I would have stood by him if he hadn't been such a louse."

Ron saw a crumpled vision at the foot of the stairs.

"Excuse me, Mags,"she said, her knuckles whitening on the hard back of the kitchen chair Mags was sitting on.

"Brendan, Love, shouldn't you be in bed?" She caught his eye; his could barely meet hers.

"Me hand's a lot better," he said stonily. "Why is Mags here?"

"Go into the sitting room, and put on the TV. I'll get your breakfast. Leave Mags to me."

Mags had another chocolate wrapper peeled off, and was pouring herself a second mug of tea when Ron returned. She looked up, suddenly scared at the fury in the older girl's eyes.

"Mags, leave now. Listen to yourself, "I would have supported him if... yeah, you'd support suicide, drug running, finger amputation, drive-by shooting, children screaming, all for some lousy jewellery and a good time. Trig's brother went off in an ambulance; my child could have been the same. I was here when he came home. Eamo had an empty house, and a brother like a zombie from street valium, speed, you name it and you'd support that rat? Get out, just get out now." Her voice was a low treacherous wave. Children had big ears. Joe suddenly stood barefooted at the bottom of the stairs. He looked at his daughter, before his eyes swivelled coldly over to Mags.

'What?"

"Don't ask Da. Mags is just leaving."

A stunned Mags, her chin smeared with chocolate, dropped the bar on the kitchen table and trembling, she stood up slowly. She looked at Joe with mute appeal.

"Best to leave Love. We've been through a hell of a time."

Joe held the door open. On the doorstep, she flashed Ron a look of disbelief, tangled up with the birth of hatred.

"I just came down to get me shoes and socks." Joe looked at her searchingly after the door slammed.

"They're under the stairs, Da. You put your slippers on downstairs last night."

"Oh God yeah, I did that because the bunions on me feet were killing me." He paused. "Should we?" He looked questioningly in the direction of the sitting room. They went in together.

"We need to talk, Love," Ron said, turning off the telly. She faced her child head- on.

"I don't care if the Dali Lama, or Jesus Christ himself comes to that door in future; you're not to go out without either Grandad or meself with you, clear?" Her cut glass voice punctured her own head. Suddenly she felt shaky all over, and gripped the edge of the couch. Brendan looked startled.

'You OK Ma,?

"I'll go get water." Joe headed for the kitchen. Shakily, she sat on the edge of the two-seater, and told him in a voice, not quite her own, about Eamo. He said nothing, his silence augmented for a long time by the sympathetic ticking of the gold carriage clock on the mantelpiece.

"Trig's friends wanted to sell me one of those for half price," she said, pointing at the clock,

" but I waited until I had the money and I bought it on "Wish."

"You know, Brendan, why it was "half price?" Joe said entering now, with two glasses of water. He plonked one down beside his grandson, and handed his daughter the other. Ron took two large gulps. Joe motioned to Brendan to drink.

'They were "half price," because they were stolen, stolen to sell on, to feed a drug habit. You know the amount of plasma screen TVs in this estate is no accident, with two- thirds of the people on welfare."

Ron added, "Welcome to the real world, Love."

Eamo was apparently in ICU. Trig wasn't giving him any preferential treatment, so he cut down on two fingers, even harder. Ron heard in Centra that Eamo had his ring finger on his left hand amputated and the first digit of his middle finger.

"His wedding finger," Joe remarked. "Some souvenir for his new wife and himself, Ha."

Ron turned to her father, her voice shaky, but threading now with conviction.

"I won't let him be a victim like Eamo. I swear I won't, Da. His teacher says he's so talented, he could do anything."

For months after the incident, Ron made sure no one called to the door looking for her son. She and Joe accompanied him to the soccer pitch, knocking around an old ball between them belonging to Adam. Eamo had returned to school. He refused to look at his teacher or answer when she spoke to him, casting sly, grin- infused glances at some of the other boys. When Brendan approached him on the playground, he shuffled off, awkwardly nursing his wounded left hand in its sling. His lowered eyelids policed angry thoughts.

Joe was keen for Brendan to keep out and not hide him away. But he was by his own admission, becoming over protective. Both he and Ron were at a loss as to how exactly to proceed. "I think we should just keep it up, you know what we're doing now," he said to his daughter one evening after tea when Brendan was watching sky sport in Hegartys next door.

"He's gonna get bored Da, and pretty soon."

Her father looked at her, annoyance walking across his features.

"And what better idea do you have?" So they continued to go to the soccer pitch with Brendan at least three evenings a week before Ron had to head to work. Finally, Joe conceded defeat.

"You were right Love," he said one evening, watching his grandson heading off around the perimeter path on his own, a lonely football left in place centre field. He is bored stupid."

Ron grinned."I'm all out of practice at football, and you're too old".

About a week later, Joe got a phone call from the boxing coach in Fettercong.

"God, I'd forgotten I'd agreed to help Jack Daly months back with the underage boxers," he said when he'd gotten off the phone.

"Well, you are a registered IABA coach Grandad,"

Brendan said, turning around from the telly.

"They couldn't just let you go to waste."

"Why don't you come with me?" Joe tried to make the proposition sound like it had just been born. Brendan said nothing for a while, and then looked carefully at Joe.

"Grandad, I don't really want to."

"I know we've covered this ground before, but I don't get you." Joe swallowed hard in one last final bid. "You're damn good with the punch bag. You've better glove technique than a lot of them and you love the rope work."

"Yeah, Grandad but I don't like the sparring. I mean I'm not a sissy or anything."

Joe smiled. "No, you'd rather be doing your drawings in the manager's office." He left the house shaking his head.

"Grandad, have I got news for you," Brendan gushed one evening, a big grin splitting his cheeks open.

"Mr. Doyle is going to set up an after school soccer club in a week's time."

Some boys were already in after school soccer, but further out like Rialto. There wasn't much enthusiasm for setting one up in Dobbinstown. Too many teachers' cars had been vandalised after school hours if the caretaker wasn't around.The CCTV camera could only pick up the nebulous form of a fleeing boy in a hoodie, his face carefully turned away from the cameras. Only one teacher, Mr Doyle, was willing to give it a go. "Doyler", as the boys called him behind his back, walked everywhere. He only lived two fields behind the school on Ragmount Drive. He once tried out for Celtic Rangers, a fact which wasn't lost on Brendan and Eamo. He always said to parents, "No gurriers can throw stones through the old shanks' mare".

Joe liked him instantly. She had only met him herself on the sidelines of daytime school matches and had run into him in the supermarket, as he taught the other fifth class from Brendan's. Joe had gotten into the habit on a Tuesday evening of putting on his red fleece lined Puma jacket, old baseball cap with the peak reversed and big boots with woolly socks before turning up to Brendan's training sessions. Then he promptly helped the young teacher out. Brendan was a really decent footballer, Mr Doyle said.

"Great to have the soccer for the lads and I can help out more with the boxing," Joe said.

.

She didn't remember much really about the time Joe was manager of the boxing club in Fettercong. Brendan was only three. Alice and herself preferred to head down to the shopping mall (which Joe said was a posh name for "The Square") in her mother's blue Fiesta rather than worry about boxing. Alice could get around well, now that her cancer was officially in remission. Sometimes, she would get a gleam in her eye, and tell her daughter they were going out to do some retail therapy.

"That's what me and the governor of Hong Kong have in common", she told Ron and Joe one night, watching an old documentary on Hong Kong after its independence from Britain in 1997. Joe snorted, "The difference between you and the governor of Hong Kong is ... he's buying Rolex and you're buying ...

"I'm buying for me grandchild." She cut him off tartly. "Now how much of that does the governor do?"

Amused, Ron glanced over at her father, watching his mouth opening and closing, like a goldfish swimming around in his wife's clever fish tank.

"*Ah here*," he said, "I'm off to Flannerys for one."

Listening to the tuneless whistling on the drive outside, Alice asked, "Is that the Whistling Gypsy Rover?"

"Couldn't tell you Ma. He's battered it too much to identify the body!" Alice began to smile to herself.

"A penny for them?" Ron said.

"Just remembering, thinking to meself about when Joe and I went out first. Must have been the singing that triggered it. I had to dig him out of Flannerys to get him to go to the plays with me."

"At the Gate?"

"Yep, the Gate."

Ron was idly flicking through the channels on the telly. There was never much on a Monday night anyway. The index finger on her right hand pressed down on the red button and the screen went blank. She'd heard all about the Gate before, but her mother had a mounting urgency when it came to recalling the past. "Yep, we used to go on a Wednesday," Alice said settling herself back on her reclining chair. Joe had bought it for her for her birthday, so she could rest up her feet. She loved it for reading mainly. Her taste in books ranged from Maeve Binchy to Paula Meehan's poetry - a real Dub she was fond of saying - to Sir David Attenborough.

"Put me shawl around me there Love, would you?" Ron draped her blue and yellow wool shawl around Alice's shoulders. Her fingers brushed off her mother's shoulder blades. She realised with a shock they had become bony promontories on a landscape, where flesh barely showed up any more. Then she banked up the fire.

"Want a cuppa first?"

Alice waved her hand dismissively."We always went to the Gate on Wednesday nights".

"Half- price?"

"Got it in one! Arthur Miller "All My Sons." We saw that twice, then O'Casey's ..."Shadow of a Gunman," they both said together and laughed.

"You're a great daughter to pretend you never heard these stories before. Your Da's favourite one was... you know what it was don't you?"

"No I don't remember that." She selected her most innocent face.

"Brian Friel, "Dancing at Lughnasa." Actually that came out around 1990, well after we were married. Your Da did a great take off of Fr. Jack down at Flannery's. Should have been on the stage, Jack Flannery told him. Missed his calling, the lads said, except of course, he made an awful eejit of himself sometimes. The drink and the applause were too much for him and the other eejits buying him rounds. I had to stand hard on his toe one night to make him sit down."

"Did he give up the amateur dramatics after that Ma?"

Her mother's face birthed a smirk. Suddenly Alice turned to her, "Put on the kettle there now Love. I fancy a cuppa after all."

While the kettle was humming in the newly tiled kitchen, Ron put a teabag in her mother's china mug, unscrewing the coffee jar for herself. "You hear anything from Adam?" she shouted into the sitting room. The double doors to the kitchen were wide open, but Alice didn't hear her. Chemo had affected her hearing. She poured the boiling water from the kettle over the teabag. She barely glanced at the drunken black lettering on the mug.

"Ah thanks Love, you're a star." Alice smiled as Ron handed her the tea.

"Milk and two sugars just the way you like it." Ron retreated to the kitchen, retrieving her own coffee from the counter top. "Just wondering Ma," she said, sitting down on the small settee in front of the fire, placing her mug on the pine coffee table. "Did you hear anything lately from Adam?" Alice went silent. The room froze around the edges.

"Put a bit more coal on the fire Ron."

Ron grabbed the coal scuttle, tipping the coals in over the edge of the black grate. The waning fire was dumped on and the light temporarily extinguished.

"It'll redden in a minute," she said apologetically, returning the empty scuttle to the chipped hearth. Still her mother said nothing, cradling the mug in both hands.

"Best Mum Ever," she read aloud after a while, looking down at the black ornate lettering. The M was giant sized and staggery.

"Adam bought that?"

Her mother dropped her chin staccato like. The gold carriage clock ticked loudly, punching above its weight in the room. She put a small log on the fire now, raking over the coals. After another minute's silence, there was a small seismic shift in the log as the flames engulfed it with a loud popping sound. The two of them were swallowed whole by a boa constrictor of memories .

"He's a good lad," Alice finally said , sipping her tea very carefully. "He's not answerable for what happened. Sure who could keep that fella in check ? Your Da should have been more patient. He has his father's temper Ron." Ron watched the tongues of flame scale up the back of the chimney. It was early November and the rads needed bleeding. She moved over to the front window to pull the blue green curtains closer together. For those who cared to see it, a full moon was iridescent over the whole of Dobbinstown. No one was stirring except a young couple in matching grey hoodies, passing the end of a lit cigarette from one to the other as they hurried along the footpath under a dim streetlight.

"No one much out tonight Ma," she said, "but a gorgeous moon."

She pulled back the curtains on a whim, then turned off the big overhead light. The moonlight swamped the two women. There were tears slicing through Alice's false eyelashes. Ron grabbed the box of tissues from the nest of tables under the window and handed her one. Her mother rubbed her eyes with the tissue and blinked hard at the sudden violent stinging.

"You're like a woman with a bad head cold Ma." They both laughed. Alice closed her eyes. Ron watched as the moonlight flickered over her face, softly pirouetting around her eyelids.

"Firelight and moonlight," she said.

"Why wouldn't your Da have made peace with him? There are all kinds of families."

CHAPTER 3

Ron could hear Joe's voice now. "Bringing his fancy man here, the two of them upstairs in the bedroom. I was a laughing stock down in Flannery's."

She knew the real reason for his ire wasn't Adam being gay. Nearer to the truth was that none of them liked his lover, George O'Reilly. They had met in Rutland.

" At least both of them have been through the methadone programme together," Alice consoled Joe in bed at night. "When Adam gets back to nursing, then life will probably split them up anyway."

In the meantime, George took over her mother's kitchen every morning from 7 to 8.30 when he cooked a fry for Adam and himself. Then he didn't even wash up. The greasy smell clung to the walls, making them damp. The mould poked itself out from the wallpaper tiles behind the cooker. Adam was always running around, washing up after his more flamboyant other half. Things came to a head one morning when George decided to cook Vegetable Samosas in the unwashed deep fat fryer. He left the plate unattended, while he went out for a fag. It was Ron, out for an early morning cigarette and stroll with Brendan to quieten her head, who smelled the smoke first. She was hauling the stroller backwards through the open hall doorway, up over the front step, when she and the child began to cough violently.

Luckily, the door leading to the kitchen was closed. The fire alarms in the short corridor and over the stairs went crazy. Within minutes, there was smoke everywhere, insinuating its way out under the bottom of the kitchen door, snaking the bannisters, the walls of the hallway, the stairs, the landing. George, coming in finally from his smoke, had to beat a hasty retreat as the flames had already begun to engulf the kitchen. They were licking the columns of grease and tearing at the thin billowing kitchen window curtains. He liked fresh air in the morning, he always said.

"Fire!" he shouted up at the bedroom windows. "Evacuate!".

Joe, barely dressed, with no shoes on, grabbed Alice from the bed and made for the stairs. Ron instantly propelled the buggy back down the front step. Minutes later, a sweating Joe almost fell on top of her into the garden with his wife in his arms. He promptly dropped Alice beside the overgrown fuchsia bush in their small 6' x 4' front patch of grass. John Hegarty, next door, called 999. For good measure, the neighbours reflected later that day, there was a new fire station on the next road.

The entire kitchen was burned out. The corridor, stairs and landing all had smoke damage. The sitting room walls were black. Ron watched John Hegarty's face settle down into waves of pure relief once it was all over. His house was untouched. The fates were on their side the day of the fire. The sun emblazoned itself on a blue canvas on an early June morning. Alice eventually was placed on a wheelchair across the road from the house. One of her neighbours, Ann McLoughlin brought it over onto the dividing patch of grass between the houses, which was kept in check by two piebald ponies who had gone AWOL now with fright. Her own mother had passed away three months earlier, and she had always meant to return it. Alice gratefully accepted an arm each from Ann and Joe as they backed her carefully into the chair. She looked around anxiously for her son.

"Where is Adam, where is he?" she asked repeatedly to the by-now gathered knot of onlookers.

"We don't know yet for sure," Ron said, her eyes doing a 180 degree sweep of the houses. She was distracted by a fractious Brendan, who repeatedly threw his soother out onto the dew-soaked grass.

"Where is he?" Alice worked her hands up into the air, drawing down the sky. She shook her head helplessly at her mother, before picking up the soother once more. She placed running water from John Hegartys water bottle over it for the tenth time before she placed it back in the child's mouth again. Her mother's cry blended now with the penetrating wail of two fire engines. Thick black acrid smoke flowed nebulously across the roadway, carried on a light wind. Joe took out his big grey, faded, linen handkerchief which he always carried in his pocket.

"Put that over your nose Love," he said to his wife. Ron felt a tug on her arm. She turned around, releasing her grip on the buggy, to see John Hegarty's grandaughter, Sue at her elbow.

"Will I walk Brendan down to me own house?"

She was a kind young one, Ron knew. She was only thirteen and was already rearing two babbies, as she said, belonging to her two older sisters, Molly and Claire. She took one look at the girl's big soft brown eyes before saying,

"Would you take him? I'll be down in a short while."

She paused, and suddenly remembered.

"He'll be hungry soon now, Love."

"No worries, sure we have all the pandy and sausages in our house all the time for the babbies."

Sue and the stroller had barely disappeared into the folds of the terrace around the corner, when Adam emerged into view. He carried a sliced pan and two cans of beer in his arms. Tesco down the way opened at 8. "*Jesus Christ,*" he shouted to the winds, dropping his load instantly. The cans rolled onto the roadway, careering down the hill to an abrupt halt at the kerb outside their house.

The fire crews on arrival had begun unrolling the long hoses all the way to the back, pouring gallons of water from two hydrants. The chief came over to the grass margin, soot making a soft smudge beneath his eyelids. He lifted his mask, "Anyone still inside?" There was silence; no one was sure where George actually was. *Had he gone back in?* Alice wondered aloud.

"Who is missing?" he repeated above the roar of the engines. Ron took off at a run across the grass, ignoring the fire chief shouting something after her. That's when they all saw the figure crisscross its arms as it got nearer. There was no mistaking George with his cerise open necked shirt and bronze medallion glinting in the light.

"We're all out thank God," Joe said to the fireman. The chief nodded and headed back across the road. The flames had dampened now, but smoke still poured out as if from the underbelly of hell.

It took some time to get the full story out of George, but it appeared the oil in the dirty chip pan had been left on at high. The cooker was beside the open window.

"I only went out to take a call from Tallaght FM about the DJ's job," he said feebly. "I thought it was on a low heat."

Ron could see her father's jaw tightening, his fist in his pocket begging him for the release of a fight.

Two days later, they were given the all-clear to re-enter the house. The O'Donovan's down the road had finally put them up. The Hegartys offered their couch, but Joe declined.

"God help them," he said to Ron. "They have such big hearts, but they have the son and his partner. They take in those grandaughters' babbies every day. We'll find a Bed and Breakfast for tonight anyway."

The O'Donovans, who did contract work with Joe wouldn't hear of it. They'd only recently finished off a granny flat for Eilish O Donovan's mother, Emma. The lady was being kept in hospital, for what looked like another couple of weeks at least. The red- roofed extension was spanking new, freshly painted inside with cream walls and lilac borders. It had its own entrance with a three - windowed mint green door and there was a disabled toilet to boot. All the family squashed into the one bedroom that night. Ron nipped down to Woodies in the Square in Alice's fiesta for a futon. Then she and three -year -old Brendan hunkered down. Oddly enough, tomorrow's troubles had drifted further from them than even the fire smoke, now embraced high up in the atmosphere.

A week later, they were given the all clear to re enter the house. Joe and Alfie were rummaging through the debris, when Ron pushed her head in the doorway. Brendan was at Hegartys. Her eyes roamed over the desolate kitchen. Her lungs, suddenly hit by stale acrid smoke pushed her to cough violently.

"For God's sake Ron, put on a mask and wear gloves. Wear something with long sleeves and get out of those runners too," Joe said.

"Don't touch any electrics whatever you do," Alfie added.

She retreated to the O'Donovans, and returned half an hour later with high boots, a mask, a long sleeved shirt and gloves. Joe barely looked at her. His eyes wandered aimlessly around the black garish kitchen. He kicked at a mountain of rubble on the floor.

"Oh God, the new Belling cooker." He pointed to the melted hobs. "That was your Ma's pride and joy." He buried his large hands in his face.

"We'll be all right; we'll sort it out."

Alfie put his arm out to touch his brother's sleeve. Joe remained in his hand cave. Then Ron glimpsed something on the floor, a charred photo still in its heavily tarnished gilt frame ,the glass, a splintered mosaic. She stooped to pick up the burnt picture, hastily dropping it again. It burned through her cotton gloves causing raised blisters immediately, on each of the two fingers of her right hand. The faces were all but wiped out in the photo as the grey crisped paper curled in on itself. She recognised them though; it was Joe and Alice in Funderland back in the eighties. Her mother was eating an ice cream cone. She should have made a copy.

It took months for them to move back again. Alice filled in all the insurance claims forms. They put down accidental fire. They didn't mention that George was on his mobile. It took several weeks for the claim to come through. The O'Donovans got stuck into fixing the house straight away. For a month, there was nonstop hammering on the roof of number 45 Patrician Road. Bags of cement arrived in a continuous stream from the co-op. The cement mixer churned for its supper that last week in June and all of July. Joe contacted The Hanleys in Dalewood Green, the second next estate beyond the traffic lights. They were painters and got cracking when the new walls were plastered. Joe did the carpentry and Alfie the electrics. Alice complained about how Joe arrived home that first week with smoke, limpet- like on his clothing and soot camped out on his face and hands.

Eilish O'Donovan's mother was in hospital for a total of ten weeks. Alice insisted that they go see her every week and tell her that they would be out of the house as soon as possible. She was energised by all the commotion.

"It's the adrenalin," Ron said to Joe.

"I don't care what it is as long as she stays that way."

Adam and George decamped to Number 1, Dalewood Green; they didn't visit; they didn't phone. Alice appeared to relapse at the end of July. More chemo was considered, but she herself asked the oncologist to hold off on more treatment.

The end of August saw a clear blue sky and a stiff , business-like autumn day finger the breeze when Ron went out the back door of the O'Donovan's extension. Across the way, she could see the new kitchen extension roof tiles. They were a Tuscan shade of burnt orange. Two new roof Velux windows poured light into the larger space. Joe had the builders add on a downstairs toilet for Alice. Brendan had settled well into the new arrangement. Eventually she and the child slept on the futon in the small kitchen- cum dining area at night. Sometimes she woke to see the light going on, and then being extinguished again in her parents' room. Alice needed to get up at night. Quite often, she made herself a chamomile tea, and stood by the back window looking out at the small patch of grass that straggled the back garden, almost engulfed by the granny flat. She wasn't the only night prowler. Ringo, the cat from next door with his explosive green eyes often padded down the thin rim of the garden fence. She envied him his high-wire lifestyle and the freedom of his domain. Her own feral streak cruised the night with him. Nursing the warm rim of the mug between her hands, she glanced back at her sleeping son. He was curled up under the duvet. Chubby hands lay joined under his left cheek. Unruly black curls fell, curtain - like over his face. Closed eyelids revealed exceptionally long dark lashes. People regularly remarked on the " pretty little girl." Fresh air bubbles rose from his breath with every new exhale. She loved the little popping sounds they made. Right now, her universe was her sleeping parents in the room next door, and this small crumpled boy sleeping the lost sleep of the innocent.

CHAPTER 4

They could have been forgiven for thinking moving back in day would blow resolution on the wind. Alice had had a gleam in her eye all morning until the disturbance. Her last bloods had graced them all with a remission. A strong, fresh breeze funnelled down from the mountains. Its gust took a swipe at her frailty when she got out of Joe's white Renault van. Ron and Joe held her steady. Brendan looked out wide- eyed from his child seat in the back.

"We should have walked across," Alice grumbled, her eyes fixed on the dirty brown crack, gaping at random all the way to the manhole cover four doors down at Dalys.

"Ma, you know your walk is still scatty," Ron countered. "To hell with the neighbours, haven't we had enough drama for one day?"

She was conscious of the net curtain corner being lifted at Hegartys. A tall figure stepped back into the shadows.

Adam had turned up at O'Donovan's earlier with a bunch of red roses for his Ma, but Joe ran him. She peered out the bedroom window, where she'd been doing some last- minute hoovering, watching her brother angrily throw the bunch on the doormat. Some petals violently disintegrated; a tug of war ensued with the rising breeze. Adam's retreating back was erect and angry. He could be handy with his fists like Da if he chose to, she thought. She prayed, "Dear God, not today, just not today." Alice limped to the door.

"Who was that?"

"Just your son the arsonist," Joe spat back at her.

"Ah here Joe, it wasn't his fault"

Ron watched the blood drain from her mother's face. Alice's prettiness was legend . Ron had her olive skin and almond eyes. But now the olive skin refused to reflect light anymore and was a cold grotty yellow. The circles under her eyes were steeped in early wrinkles. She watched as her mother pushed brusquely past her father, took a couple of steps outside the front door.

"Adam, Adam Love," she shouted to the retreating figure, his head bowed and hands buried in his green quilted jacket, hunched around his ears. His head and shoulders merged in one defeated stoop. He turned at her voice, just as she fainted. Joe caught her before she hit the cement.

"Dear God, why do you never listen to me?" Ron piled her grievance ceiling high before she rushed to the front door. Brendan was racing with his dinky cars up and down the small corridor of the extension. Hearing the raised voices, the child looked up stunned. Seeing the high wire tension in his mother's face, he began to wail. Soft, oily teardrops spread heavily across his cheeks and she picked him up to soothe him. His fractiousness lulled for a moment, he called out,

"Gaga, Gaga," I wanna go to Gaga," horsing himself out of her arms to run to his grandmother on the pathway outside. It seemed as if everyone was bearing down on them from all directions suddenly. Adam brushed past his father and grabbed Alice's pulse. She was coming round. Jack O'Donovan's wife Ailish driving back from Tesco's after her weekly shop, jammed on the brakes outside her own front door. The last of the builders closing the back of his van dropped his helmet on the ground, and legged it across the road. By this time, Alice was propped up against the low uncapped stone wall between their front and Murphys which mercifully had been handed back to the council three months earlier. Eilish O Donovan had placed two massive red print cushions at her back and brought her a glass of water. Adam was taking the pulse on her right hand. Brendan had flung himself into his grandmother's lap, and was enjoying the kisses she unexpectedly planted on top of his head.

"I'm fine," Alice declared to her growing audience.

"Ye don't have to worry. Just a little shock, that's all."

Joe stood there, a muted bear. He refused to meet his daughter's eyes.

"We'll just get her inside now." Adam was unexpectedly in charge.

"I'll run back to Greendale and get my bag of tricks."

He returned twenty minutes later to check his mother's BP.

"You'll live. Not bad actually, 110 over 70. You taking all your meds, yeah?" he asked in his most professional manner as he put away the sphyg. Joe stood around , hopping from one foot to the other as if his irritation had scalded the soles of them.

"Stay for a cuppa love." Alice's brown eyes were liquid with entreaty. Her son turned to his father, his eyes saucered with rage. I can't Ma, I'm running late already. Remember, I'm gaining work experience with the district nurse until I start back in the hospital next month. I've other patients to visit." The plausible lie lingered on his face. Still Joe wouldn't meet his eyes. He had that red rash back on his chest again.

Finally by 6pm that day, they all piled into the white Renault van. Ron was the last to leave, popping into O'Donovan's with the key. Then she closed the door for one last time, opened the back door of the van and sat in. Joe drove down to the intersection below the houses, did a U turn and pulled up outside their newly refurbished house. The Hegartys had a welcome hamper on the mat. Joan Hegarty had popped it in one afternoon just before the builders left. Alice read the small card on the cellophane wrapping."To all the O'Connells, may your cooking be trouble- free forever more Amen."

"Ah God, isn't she great; Joan was always handy with the pen."

" Like yourself," Joe.said. A small smile dammed up all day, danced its way to freedom across his fierce blue eyes and curled up at the corners of his wide set lips. Ron, with Brendan by the hand, headed straight for the new building. No one had been allowed even a sneak preview on Joe's orders. The floodlit kitchen with its two Velux windows, sparkling granite white countertops, smoothly muted fawn kitchen tiles and white walls enveloped her. Could this rising tide lift all boats after all? Brendan too, caught the magic. Small dust motes floated in the evening light, and swirled over his head in the open doorway. She imagined them ambassadors of good will. She hadn't noticed Alice at her shoulders.

"Angels"

"What Ma?"

"Angels," her mother repeated, pointing to the dust motes. Ron smiled. Alice had a thing about the angels. All of Lorna Byrne, the angel lady's books had been on the kitchen shelves the day it was burned down. She and Joe between them had replaced them over the last couple of months.

"Well, I guess your angels didn't stop the kitchen being burned down Ma, but they sure sent in better quality workers to fix it up."

For the first time that day, Ron toned down her facial muscles when she looked in her father's direction. He was standing in the doorway now, watching his wife, his face unmasked, satisfied even. For now, she had no option but to relinquish Adam to George and to his work in the community in Dobbinstown. Alice too seemed to have released him. She marvelled at her husband's good taste. She exclaimed even more at the new lavender walls in the downstairs bedroom and the chrome fittings on the taps in the en suite. Ron had helped Joe fill in the forms for the government grant. The insurance money had been more generous too than anticipated. Joe and his brother's handiwork had kept labour costs down.

The days immediately following the move back had a slow cinematic feel, the projectionist focusing on every nuanced moment in the faces on the screen. Adam's name was not mentioned. Joe and Alice orbited each other respectfully. Ron couldn't remember her parents being this polite ever to each other. She too didn't mention the emotional elephant in the room. They seemed to spend most of that autumn in their extended kitchen. Joe purchased a small 20" Nordmende TV for a ledge high up on the wall. Alice's bloods stayed good. Their son stayed away.

There was time now for Ron to apply for jobs. With having her son at sixteen, she'd had to forego her Leaving Cert, something much lamented by Alice.

"My girl should have had the same education as my boy," she said to Joe one night after Brendan's second birthday. She tilted her daughter's chin upward..Her eyes pierced Ron's with her resolve.

"We'll get you there yet, I promise."

Two months later, she got her diagnosis and no one mentioned the Leaving again. Ron had begun to investigate night classes at the Tech. She was signed in for the autumn schedule, but kept this to herself for now. She sent a number of CVS around to local restaurants and bars, with Flannerys being a notable exception. She'd had a pristine Junior Cert, thanks to Alice's night-time supervision. Eventually, she got a call from Guiney's pub in Dobbinstown, not far from her dad's watering hole. Her interview went exceptionally well. She was aware of Jack Guiney Junior's eyes on her display of cleavage all through the interview. She'd even put a bit of Egyptian bronzing powder on her exposed breasts. Now she wished to God she hadn't. She felt a full body flush- which didn't discount her face, spread over her, and grabbed at the glass of water left out at the side of the old heavy mahogany table dragged into the snooker room for the interview.

"Your Junior Cert was very good," Jack Guiney senior commented, surveying her critically over the rim of his dropped down glasses on the end of his nose.

"Pity about ..." His voice trailed off and he coughed awkwardly. "Bloody dust in here." His son said nothing, but continued to stare.

They gave her the job, but required, as she half expected, night shifts. It'll do for now, her da assured her.

"Your mother and I can mind the lad. Sure he'll be in bed."

She posted a bland smile on her face and headed upstairs on the pretext of checking a banging window frame in the bedroom. Once inside the room, she closed the door quietly behind her. It was 10 o'clock, and there was the usual calm around the place before the midday storm with mothers and toddlers congregating outside the windows. Brendan was at play school, and soon she'd have to meet and greet as she did every day, women like herself, but more battle- weary. She hated it. Now she sat on the bed, grateful for its springiness, exhaled slowly and re-read the printed off email from the tech. Classes would start on the 29th September in a week's time. She brought over the paper bin from the corner, handled her cigarette lighter, whirled the little wheel with her thumb and flicked softly down on the spring of the metal head. She held up one corner of the crisp A4 page and watched it briefly burst into flame. She dumped the page very carefully in the bin, and witnessed the fiery cremation of her dreams.

CHAPTER 5

Brendan was seven when Alice passed. After the fire, she got close on five more years in remission.When the cancer did return a month before she died, she refused all chemo despite Ron's and Joe's entreaties."I've only an outside chance, the doctor told me, so I'm not wasting time I can spend with all of ye," she declared fiercely, her eyes flaming over the nagging tiredness which lurked in them all the time these days. The cancer free years were punctuated by two things: her weekly visits to 1 Dalewood Green and the systematic spoiling of her grandson. One Tuesday evening towards the end of the November after moving back into the house, she handled Elsie the Jack Russell's lead at 6pm and said:"I'm off for a bit of a stroll."Ron and Joe exchanged glances. Ron was about to head out for her shift."Won't be long," she called out over her shoulder as the excited dog ploughed out the front door before her. When she hadn't returned within the hour, Joe rang her mobile.

"I'm here with our only son," she said tartly on answering.

"He's doing nicely thank you, even if he is living alone."

After that, the weekly visits became a regular occurrence. Joe never asked her where she was going again. Ron exchanged glances with her mother over his shoulder, the second night she headed out. Alice raised her eyes, irritation cemented in them. Eventually, Ron picked up the courage to call to Adam on Sundays with Brendan in tow. George had slung his hook four months after the disastrous fire. He'd found new life and love in Amsterdam. Ron sensed the worm of resentment turning in her brother. Along with his mother, he gifted his nephew a series of frequent small gifts. Joe never asked where the latest Shrek DVD came from or the new burly companion for Action Man. He just kept his head down and applied an emotional pliers to his jaw. His son's name was never mentioned. Her parents never rowed in front of Ron or Brendan, but she knew by the extra visits to Flannerys and the night he came home mouldy drunk, their relationship was burning at the edges in small growing silences.Joe and Alice didn't share a bed for the following month after the drunken episode. "For the love of God Da, can you not park your pride?" she said to her father one night. "He is your son." Her father,scaffolded in silence, exited the room. Alice continued her weekly rambles to Dalewood Green.

One night Joe met her in the hallway, tears wetting his shirt collar.He stood before her "half-baked," she told Ron the next day. "He said, "Im sorry." "Bit late," I said." Then he said no more, just made me cocoa, said he was nothing without me, but he just wasn't ready yet for Adam. So what was I to do Ron?" After that episode, she noted the bedside light in the sitting room was no longer on when she mounted the stairs coming in from her shift. Sometimes at 1 am, occasional conversation drifted onto the landing from her parents half-open bedroom door.

One Tuesday evening about six months before Alice passed, Joe handled his van keys.

"Here let me drive you, your walk has gone staggery again."

His wife's face held shock at first, followed by a tell tale widening of her eyes. "Better bring Brendan so," she said in a curiously level voice. "Ron will be at work." Ron watched as her dad's van turned right onto the main road; the second next exit off it- Dalewood Green. Next morning when she surfaced late, her parents were sitting side by side at the kitchen table. The air had lost the hard knots in the spaces between them. Joe's face had a wound down ease. The crags under her mother's eyes had softened and folded until some of her old prettiness had nestled under them again.

When Alice's death came, it annihilated Brendan's world. He adored her. He wrote about her all the time in school, in his news, his teacher told Ron. "My Granny is very funny. Me and Granny are the best of friends. We do play together and she buys me nice things."

The very evening that Alice took a turn and was rushed to Tallaght, she passed in Intensive Care. They didn't allow him in. He kicked and screamed for days after, she remembered. He shed tears of rage, his child mind grappling with the new tyranny of his world. He just sat in the funeral home, legs swinging on the long hard bench and clung to his mother, both hands wrapped around hers now. The sympathising throng touched the top of his head softly, unable to find a free hand of his or his mother's to press. Adam and Joe sat side by side. After the burial next day, Adam refused to go for the meal in Guineys, saying he had a headache. His straggling grey/ blond hair fell over a long ashen face, whose eyes had retreated from view. Joe didn't press him.

Eventually, they all returned to a duller world, where every leaden sky made Ron summon her mother's smile. She'd been working in Guineys for over five years now and Brendan had got used to her heading out before he went to bed. She managed most of the homework with him before heading out to work. One thing that could never be accomplished by either Joe or herself was the bedtime story. Alice had been so dramatic. She'd had the lead in musicals when she was single, and so could do an impression of all the heroes and villains from the pages of the storybooks. Sometimes she made up little ditties about them and sang them to the boy in the bed ,whose upturned face shared the music of the night with his grandmother.

Joe became more taciturn over the next number of months. The house was a mausoleum. He refused to remove any of Alice's clothes from the wardrobe. Instead he pushed all her garments to the right side and made space for his own stuff on the left. Even her shoes remained on the rack he'd made for them, as if she would somehow step back into her black spangled high- heeled sandals with the pinching strap and totter to the annual GAA dinner with him.

In the end, it was the counsellor who got them all out of the quicksand. Her name was Margie O'Kane, and she came originally from nearby Fenstown. Ron was the first to go see her; she'd never done counselling before. The O Connells weren't the type of people to go to counsellors, Joe said.

"And what kind of people would they be Da?" she asked him saucily one Saturday morning in the kitchen after they had finished the weekly fry up of bacon, egg and sausage. The kitchen was beginning to steam up. She got up to open out the entire lower part of the window and stuck her head out for some air. "Well Da," she said speaking to the garden. "I'm going to be one of them people who go to counsellors." There was silence from her father's broad back as he combed the spread out racing pages, seated at the granite topped kitchen island. His right leg dropped from the bar stool's chrome foothold. He bent to lift his trouser leg and itch it. His varicose eczema was acting up. "Have we any of that steroid cream left?" he asked.

"Da, I'm going to be one of them people," she repeated carefully, pulling her head back in and turning around slowly to face him. "Ma would want you to release her, but you're holding on."

"Bloody hell, why wouldn't I?" he countered furiously, knocking over his coffee in a sudden agitated move off the stool. The brown rivulets trickled out furiously across the newspaper, and dripped in a waterfall onto the grey matte floor tiles. Joe headed for the hallway. The overturned mug reproached her sideways, lying on its belly with the black words "Best Husband" rolling around the perimeter.

The appointment was for Monday at 10am. Margie lived in the next estate. It was late January,and initially a faint flurry of snow had begun to descend from a pregnant sky over Dobbinstown. Ron put on her red fleece- lined ankle high boots, grey sweat pants, dark red wool jumper and thick green puffer jacket. She put on her black felt hat with Alice's silver salmon brooch pinned on the rim. Her hair was tied with a scrunchy and a pale makeup- less face with flat eyes, stared back at her from the dressing table mirror. She pinched the folds under her cheek bones, giving them a little rub. Soon an obliging redness crept obliquely in the direction of her ear tips. The snow came down fast now in soft fat flakes, melting instantly on her jacket and trouser legs. By the time she reached Margie's cheery red bricked two story with an amazing assembly of life- sized angels guarding the front door, her jacket was thoroughly soaked. Heavy white tubular wind chimes caught the breeze with sci fi like music, as they hung from the front porch. Margie pulled back the double-glazed sliding doors. She was a plump woman in her early thirties with blonde ringleted hair on the top of her head. She was wearing a flowing red and green kaftan, loose grey trousers and large silver hooped earrings.

"Saw you coming up the path," she said, with a very white toothed smile, framed by bright pink lipstick. Her dark thick foundation was muted by a smear of white dusting powder high up on her cheek bones. Large silk blue curious eyes, a flattened button nose and two chins overlapping over a soft fold of neck completed her. She glowed .

She ushered her client into her small front room with an eclectic mix of ornaments. A framed Japanese Buddhist temple ran the length of the chimney wall, dominating the space. There were two winged back armchairs with purple and pink throws on them respectively. A small lacquered table stood over to one side of the room. A Buddha, a statue of the Virgin Mary and a circle of interlocking angel figures guarding three night lights stood on it. Sitting on the cracked white marble hearth was a Tibetan copper bowl with a thick round wooden stick resting in its hollow. Margie's counselling and psychotherapy diplomas were arranged in a straight line on the back wall facing the front window. After the preliminary enquiries for the family whom Margie knew of, she took a few details in her A4 ring binder, white writing pad. Then she smiled disarmingly as she flipped the cover back over. "Now we'll dispense with all these ould formalities. How are yeh at all today Love?"

The session went by like a blur from a speeding car window; the journey was comfortable, a bit rocky in parts, but with a feeling of acceleration and destination. There were at least four sessions before she brought Brendan. She'd watched him warily this last six months. He had her thin skin, and Joe's sudden black moods kept the child at bay. Her father's silences and swift eruptions disturbed her too. In school Brendan was doing well academically, but he provoked at least two playground scuffles in the last three months. Joe uncharacteristically refused to meet the teacher with her. She promised both Miss Daly, his teacher and Mr. Horan the principal, who taught herself too, she would have a very serious chat with him. Mr. Horan had known Alice from parent-teacher meetings, and had also recommended her for the Parents' Association when Ron was in sixth class.

"Give the lad time," he said sympathetically, squeezing her shoulder as he walked her out to the front gate. She smiled warmly at him, noticing the crags that appeared under his wide blue eyes. His skin was a little motled, either side of his broad nose. He looked defeated. He stood by the area when other teachers departed overnight, she reminded Joe later.

"You always liked him. Ma was mad about him too. You should have shown an interest. Remember, it was his wife Aggie who got Adam into Rutland that time when I was pregnant. At least he got back to nursing eventually, even if he took the scenic route as opposed to the homeless one. Think about that Da."

He ignored her, walked into the hallway, grabbed his bicycle helmet hanging from the end of the banisters, and took his grey fleece lined jacket off the hall stand. She heard the door slam and saw him unchain his bicycle from the grey metal railing at the front of the house. Then he was gone rapidly, a disappearing figure in grey. She slammed one fist into the other and bit down on the quick of the nail of her right hand until it bled. There was silence between them for a week after that, but oddly it didn't cut her to the marrow. Margie patiently explained Joe's uncharacteristic behaviour as "acting out." "He's angry with the world," she said. "Don't forget his world has been taken away."

"But we're his world," Ron protested.

"I know, I know, he can't see that yet. Just give him time."

By the time Joe came round, she had decided to bring Brendan to Margie. It was late February, and they had shy snow drops obliquely paying homage to a cold wind just under the front window. "Brendan Love, pick a few of them for Margie," she said.

"We can put them in tin foil and give her a little present." In the kitchen, Joe lifted his head from the *Irish Independent*. You going to see Margie?" he asked casually. "We are," she said in as level a tone as she could muster. "Come on Brendan, hurry up." She helped him put on his black bomber jacket, and handed him his ear muffs. Neither said a word to Joe. The child looked at the tight set of her jaw. He shot a sideways glance at his grandad, who promptly buried himself in the pages of the paper, where only his thoughts were headlining.

Margie and Brendan hit it off instantly. The counsellor had given Ron a brief outline of what she hoped to do. "Best to leave the two of us undisturbed," she'd said. When Ron returned to collect him, he had a shiny grin on his face, and thrust a rolled- up A3 paper into her hand. "It's a picture of our family; I put Gran in as an angel." Later she unrolled it in the bedroom, before going to work. Brendan was doing his homework in the kitchen, and Joe was sawing logs he'd brought down in the trailer from Heavey's farm up the Dublin Mountains. The scroll showed all of them standing at his favourite place, Tayto Park. She and Joe had a hand each on his shoulder. Alice wasn't standing behind him, but there were a few images of her flying around in her Savida grey and blue summer dress. She even had on her favourite pink lipstick. Then she did a double take, as she recognised the black spangled sandals with the pinched strap on her feet. When she asked him later why so many Alices, he looked her straight in the eye, a frown on his forehead, and said in a slightly irritated tone, "Don't you know Ma, angels are everywhere. Gran can be anywhere she likes at the same time now." Brendan went for two more sessions. She didn't ask him what went on, as he explained to her in a very adult sounding voice, " it's cofidenshul Ma." However, there was a new light around him. Mr Horan himself signed his "Pupil of the Week" cert for school. "Now when had he brought that home last?" she wondered. Joe noticed it too, though he said nothing. She felt his mood had lightened. She actually heard him say to the boy, "Good, you're taking a piece of Granny's jewellery to Margie. Take the pink brooch. She loved that one, and by the way, tell Margie I said hello. I knew her Ma, Eileen Herlihy, going to school."

After the third session, he returned with a photo of Alice, that he had brought with him and a letter he'd written to her.

Dear Granny,

I know you're in Heaven now. I wish they'd told me you were going to die. But that's ok. I know you're all around me. I know you're minding Ma, Uncle Adam and Grandad too. Please make Grandad not so cross anymore. I miss you all the time, but I'm getting better now.

Lots of love,

Brendan. XXX

They agreed to burn the letter in a little ceremony in the barrel for burning rubbish out the back. "We'll hold onto the photo," she said, "And I'll set a match to the letter so Granny can get it in Heaven. Not a word to Grandad," she cautioned. "It might upset him." Her da wasn't home from work yet, and they'd get it done before he got back. Then finally it was Joe's turn. Mags helped him get out his anger, he admitted to Ron later. She gave him a punching bag, and told him to hit it hard to let all the hard bottled up stuff out. He felt lighter then he said. He told her Mags had gotten him to write a letter to Alice. She told him about Brendan and the burning in the barrel ceremony. He looked taken aback. "But why?" he began.

"You weren't ready then," she said softly. All three of them did the barrel-burning ceremony this time. The white smoke funneled its way around their short patch of cement at the back on a strong breeze. The smoke carried over the garden wall, and trailed off, mingling with the billowing plumes from the chimneys all around.

"Ma's on her travels again," she thought.

CHAPTER 6

Ron drew closer to the fire. She watched a gush of flame leap up the chimney as the dried-out logs surrendered another piece of themselves. The early May evening stretched out like a half-open palm. Its still cold air crisped inside the cottage walls. Brendan was staying over at his friend Lorcan's house. In Dobbinstown, she never allowed him to do anything like this again after the day of the septic finger. In the early years after the incident, she'd made him come home straight from school. He became the target of cat calls:

Jesus mother licker

Witmo

Dick head

Prick

It continued into his early teens when they found even worse ammunition as he walked home with new friends in the Youth Theatre. He was a set painter for "Grease". She began to meet him along the way, and they walked the rest of the way home together. Whenever he and Eamo crossed paths, Eamo dug his left hand into his pocket and moved off.

In front of her on the coffee table was a Leaving Cert Maths book. Maths were a mystery. Eanna was helping. Thanks to him these days, X and Y in algebra had become friendlier variables. Of all the places to run into Eanna, Mister Doyle (Doyler) again, the farmers' market in Manorhamish! Andy Moynihan was selling her some of his organic produce. She was trying to decide whether to buy two or three lots of the spindly carrots, still crowned with their flowering tops. Holding up one lot and fingering down their dusting of earth, she heard the Dobbinstown accent in her ear.

"You'd need three times that amount to feed that hungry young fella of yours."

She spun round, and at first didn't fully register him standing there on a pinched, cold, late April morning. He had on a full-length brown wax jacket and beige, wide-brimmed hat with a daredevil chocolate ribbon trailing down the nape of his neck. It was his green eyes and the glint of a smile that transfixed her. Trance like, she dropped the carrots.

"Mister Doyle!"

she said so loudly, she felt everyone turned at her Dublin accent.

"Don't mind your Mister Doyle," he said softly, his eyes expanding and beaming down on her hard.

"What are you doing here?" she asked.

"Well, I'll tell you over a coffee if you like, and I can get someone to mind me stall for half an hour."

He gestured to the chrome topped tables and chairs in the middle of the little quadrangle around which all the stalls were laid out. Not many brave souls were having coffee at them today. The market was winding down, and some vendors were closing up their respective stalls early. An increasingly nimble wind tugged at Aloe Vera products, knocked over geraniums, and sent lightly knitted baby grows flying across the cobbles. Doyler was gesturing towards a table with a large green parasol above it and weighted down with sandbags.

"Just in case you're blown away on me," he said laughingly.

She looked at him head-on. He was shouting now above the noise of the rising wind and the penetrating sound of a van's reversing sensors.

"OK, will I get some coffee or would you prefer tea?"

"Coffee is grand," she shouted back.

He smiled and gave her two large thumbs up.

She scarcely remembered what the coffee tasted like or the cold pinching through her light fleece. She didn't even know the circulation had been removed from her toes until she got to the bar later. All she remembered after, was a window in time, the two of them like in a painting, captured by some visiting artist to an Irish country market.

"How are you?" he asked again, holding her gaze unashamedly.

"Grand," she said cremating the back of her throat with a barely whitened slug of hot coffee.

"Shouldn't you be in school?" she finally managed, once the pain in her throat subsided, and he had paid for a bottle of water from the meat vendor's van behind them.

"No," he grinned. "I used to be at school, but I'm on a career break, slumming it in County Leitrim. And look what the wind brought in from Dobbinstown today. Did you drive down specially for them carrots? I used to grow them, you know, in Mickser Daly's allotment in Fettercong. You didn't have to come all the way."

"I'd stand on me head for a carrot," she answered saucily.

"Seriously though, you're living down here now?" She fixed him her most questioning look. Suddenly the rain sloshed down hard into the Styrofoam cups. The green parasol began to contort furiously above them.

"Come on," he said,above the noise of the wind and the expletives of some of the traders.

"I'll have to pack up now. I'll show you me stall, will I before we go. Have you a lift home?"

Her key fob felt knobbly in her pocket. She was tongue-tied for once. He seemed to waive a reply as he pointed in the direction of his empire. His stall had a sign above it which she later slagged him for not laminating and he a teacher and all. She could just make out the woozy lettering where the runny black ink had dribbled the words close together, "Herbal Medicine".

"You a doctor or something?" she asked.

"No, just a white male witch. Wizards, they call us in the coven I belong to."

She stood there stunned until the early lines on his face all met in a point around his big green eyes, and then she knew he was laughing at her.

"I'm good at storytelling, can't you tell?"

" Sure isn't everyone in Dobbinstown, isn't that the trouble?"

"Tell you what, if you've time, maybe we'd find a coffee shop down the town, and I can tell you all about it. I can run you home then."

Almost apologetically, she pulled out her car keys.

She thought fast. Brendan wasn't due home for hours yet. Joe and Sally were going shopping to Fermanagh. She had more groceries to pick up for later, but that could wait.

"Yeah, I'd murder a fry up this minute," she said aloud.

"What about Bradys on the corner of main street, you know the three-storey pink house - does good hot food."

"Grand, you go on and order for the pair of us so, and I'll pack up here. Meet you there in about twenty minutes."

"But what do you want me to order?" she called after him.

" I'll have a fry, just the usual," he shouted back.

He trailed off into the wind, grappling with big pot plants rolling sideways along the stones. and silver foil-wrapped teas scattershot with raindrops. Two dark brown glass bottles had crashed to the ground, and Doyler cursed as thick brownish liquid coursed along in rivulets blending with the rain-filled puddles.

She parked easily in the town square, and thought she'd love not just a fry-up, but a fag. Since Alice's death, she'd given up the cigs completely. Her mother had smoked all her life. Passing Simmon's Newsagent beside the hotel, she paused and waved at Sharon, the girl behind the checkout. She was a student in her Chakradance class. She could scarcely believe she was a Yoga teacher now and the latest notch to her belt was Chakradance. She mimed through the window, taking a long drag on a cigarette. Sharon grinned back holding up a packet of Benson and Hedges enquiringly. She didn't hear the footsteps behind her.

"Got that lot loaded up and tidied up quicker than I thought with the help of Larry and Lorraine on the burger van."

Embarrassed, she turned around. He'd witnessed the entire performance.

"Used to be a big smoker meself," he said pointing to the cigarettes still in Sharon's outstretched hands. Her right eyebrow vaulted at Ron and mouthed, "Who's your man?"

He opened the shop door a fraction, and leaned his tall frame through the open doorway.

"I can lip read you know. And I can't speak for the lady, but I'm off them for good this time."

"Well fair fecks to yeh," an old man in an ill-fitting grey serge suit said at the counter. Then he took a packet of Benson and Hedges out of his pocket, and rammed one between his lips, displaying crooked, gapped, yellow front teeth.

The rain was pelting down when they ducked in under the low lintel of Brady's hotel. Inside in the Voodoo darkness of the worn bar stools and darkly polished counter, copper lamps glowed eerily above the long-handled draught taps. A roaring turf fire to their left spat out a welcome into the room. A couple had just vacated the seat around the fire.

" Is it a full Irish so ?" he asked, removing his wax jacket and shaking out his long drenched red curls as he removed his hat.

"Grab that table there," he said. pointing to the fire seat.

"Yeah, a full Irish and a coffee please, " she said, wiggling her stockinged feet in front of the fire once she had sat down.

"Great, we'll make it a double so."

He headed over to the young girl with the white ruffled shirt and pencil black skirt behind the hatch at the end of the curved bar.

"She'll have the order in about ten minutes," he said when he returned.

He looked behind him to see eighteen-year-old Joanna Brady promptly bring a tray of two milky coffees, napkins, and cutlery which she deftly laid out on the table with her right hand. Putting the empty tray in front of her white apron, she looked first at Eanna and then at Ron, her eyes a sea of questions.

"You know that girl?"

he asked, as they watched her head over to another customer,opening up her pocketbook to take their order.

"Oh yeah, Joanna's in my Chakradance class."

"Your what class?" he said frowning .

"Too complicated," she said ,shaking out her wet locks and hoping they could shield her face's crimsoning as she slowly brought the hot cup to her lips.

"I don't even know your real name Mr. Doyle," she began

"Mr. Doyle is for twelve –year- olds Ron. Me real name is Eanna. Me gran was a bit of a republican and thought Padraig Pearse's school had a nice ring to it -St. Enda's. She liked the Irish version better though- Eanna."

"Oh fierce posh," she teased "Bet you didn't tell the lads that in Dobbinstown."

"No," he said, cleaving the beer mat in two neat halves between his hands. "Doyler was good enough. Most fellas thought I was christened that. "Dial the Doyler," they used to say when they were stuck for a sub on the football team." She laughed. He was good-looking in a way, she thought. Ma would have said long hair was for women, but he tied it back now with a large thick elastic band once it dried out. He was quite freckled with high cheekbones, a thin long nose, and two long sideburns running in parallel down past his ears. She decided he had a cheeky smile and she found it attractive when his gaze retreated from her scrutiny. The fry turned up sooner than expected, and between mouthfuls he told her his story.

"Actually your Da had a small part to play in my coming here," he said swirling a bulky burned sausage around his runny egg. She gulped, and hoped he didn't hear the belch.

"Really?" she said biting hard on her own piece of fried tomato. Its succulent tartness assuaged the dryness in her mouth. "How so?" She studied the geography of the fry. With a stab of her fork, she moved her rasher a fraction to the left.

"Well, after he left the soccer club at the school - You know he used to help out didn't yeh?"

She nodded.

"Well... he told me he was moving to Leitrim, so I texted him, and didn't hear back for about a month, but then we got in touch." He cleared his throat and continued. "I was hoping I'd run into you at some stage." He paused, sneaking a sideways look at her. "Well anyway, maybe.....

She smiled at him and repeated his last word, her inflection teasing."Maybe....?.

He grinned. "Yeah, well, I was moving down this way anyway and maybe... maybe I thought I might just run into you. You probably heard me and Kelly Ann broke up." He avoided her eyes

"No, actually," she said quietly. "Sorry to hear that." Kelly-Ann Lynch had been four years behind her in school, a quiet girl, clever, but she was always taking time off to mind her sister's baby. Her sister had colitis and she and her boyfriend shared a room in the Lynch family home.

"She's with someone else now," he said.

Ron said nothing.

"Well then, Joe was telling me about his new partner Sally, who already had a holiday home here." He paused ,running his fingertips up and down the table. " He mentioned how you were moving over here too. It got me thinking. I didn't want to be in Dobbinstown forever either, so I applied for a career break and looked on Daft for a house to rent in the Leitrim/Fermanagh area."

"Does Da know all this?"

Oh yeah, we've had a few calls and we text."

" I'll crucify you Joe," she thought. "Why the hell didn't he ... ?

"And you, what's all this Chakradancing?" he asked, his fine lines meeting up at a needlepoint again.

"Oh, I'm a Yoga teacher and now I've qualified on line as a Chakradance teacher. You know ..."

"No I don't," he said leaning in. So she patiently explained the work of Natalie Goldberg and the seven energy wheels of the Chakras in the Hindu tradition.

"When I studied the herbs, we did a bit about that in Ayurveda."

Then it was her turn to probe him. He'd spent four years studying naturopathy and herbal medicine part-time in CNM (college of naturopathic medicine) in Griffith College, South Circular Road.

"Natural what?" Now he was flushed ."It's naturopathy, no stress."

"But why?"

Why did I, a lad from a deprived area go to college to study naturopathy and herbal medicine? He'd obviously been asked this question before, and more than once she guessed. Me ma was plagued with asthma after Da died suddenly seven years ago. The meds weren't a great help, except for her inhaler. So I began to research online, thinking I could help me sister Ailbhe too. She's Down syndrome, he said by way of explanation, and they have heart and lung problems. I read all about using natural remedies, so I began to dabble in them. Ma was so desperate, she took the herbs I bought for her. In fairness, we have a very good doctor in Darndridge and he said to give it a try".

"It must have worked I'm guessing?"

" Like a dream, so off I went to study the Green Pharmacy."

She loved the way he talked, intelligent and dreamlike. She'd never met a man like him before.

She was enthralled as he gave her the rudiments of tincture making and promised to show her his herb nursery. He'd found an old two-storey house about fifteen miles from her, with two and a half acres of land. "Would you believe rent is only €350 for the month and I can grow all me own herbs. I order a few from Shandruid in Tipperary, but I grow as many as I can meself to cut down on costs."

He was still teaching, he said, three days a week - a wandering learning support teacher between two national schools in the county, Belturbit and Loughnasigh

Two and a half hours later, the lunchtime trade had filtered out to a vacuum. Joanna Brady was busy stacking dirty dishes on a tray across the way from them. She kept a beady eye on the seat by the fire. Just once, she caught Ron's eye and dropped a curtain wink .

"She doesn't half make it obvious."

"Who?" Ron feigned ignorance.

"Miss Brady," he said, inclining his head sideways in the direction of the hatch which she'd just disappeared behind.

"Oh!" A painful awareness of closure was sinking into her.

"I've a dinner to put on for Brendan," she said suddenly with an anxious abruptness. "And Sally and Da are coming over tonight too."

"Oh God, sorry I didn't mean to keep you."

He got up suddenly, all six foot of him. He craned his neck downward. There was an unexpected silence. She felt as if they had driven along a road full throttle, and suddenly met a speed bump.

"Well, nice meeting yeh Eanna," she said as nonchalantly as she could manage. Her car keys sweated down the oily palm of her right hand. He coughed and looked over his shoulder before grabbing his coat and hat from the back of his seat. The bar had emptied. The hour hand of the clock on the blue wallpaper behind the counter was at three.

"God, look at the time," Ron said. He followed her gaze before turning around suddenly. "Would you like to meet up again, maybe somewhere else?" he asked.

"Sure," she said smartly, feeling her body leave her for inside his.

"I'll ring you," he promised, pushing open the swing door to the porch outside. He gave her a staccato peck on the cheek in the doorway before he ran out onto the street. Then he was gone, rushing ahead of the pulsing, dark, rain clouds. She looked after him, wanting to call out, but he had already pressed on the key fob of his Skoda Octavia and was battling the driver's door in the high wind. She watched for a while after he indicated and pulled out into the traffic down Main Street.

CHAPTER 7

The letter was on the mat when she got home. Dropping her shopping bag in the small hallway, she stooped to pick it up. It had been readdressed from Dobbinstown. Puzzled, she held it up to the chink of light coming in through the window in front of the stairs.

Kensington mail office- London 30/3/'16.

"Who in God's name?"

Her phone rang at the bottom of her handbag. She placed the letter on top of the bannisters beside her. Her rummaging fingers found the mobile.

"Hi Ma, I'll be home late this evening."

"Ah, Brendan, you know Joe and Sally are coming."

"Yeah, and I'll catch 'em later. Just getting this new trainer from Dublin of all places. He wants to give us a pep talk. Keep some of the nut roast for me."

"Will do Love." She sighed down the phone."So much for the support," she thought, already weary. She picked up her shopping bags and headed to the kitchen. She was quite organised really. A heap of last night had gone into cooking this nut roast. It didn't taste half bad if she said so herself. She was out to impress. Brendan had looked up Jamie Oliver's recipe on YouTube. Together they chopped and fried and stirred. Sourcing the ingredients saw both of them frantically steering their trollies like demented rally drivers around Dunnes Stores, or so her son said.

"New beginnings Ma, even new posh food." He grinned at her, as he buttered and grease-lined the loaf tin.

"Well, remember we have the same palate as the rich and famous."

"I'll keep that in mind."

She realised now she was quite tired and hungry. She checked the time- 6.10pm. She told them to come around 6.30. She popped the nut roast in the oven to reheat for about 15 minutes, while she covered the dining table with a blue, lace tablecloth her friend Amanda had brought from Ios. She remembered how to fold the napkins and set out the cutlery from her waitressing when Guineys opened up the small restaurant next door. Yes, the linen napkins were fitting. The wine glasses and white dinner set she'd bought online should impress Sally. She folded Doyler into a neat back pocket of her mind, sealed with his staccato kiss. Now she lit two slender white candles in her Newbridge candle holders. Sally had given them to her for her birthday in October. Outside, the growing darkness enveloped the cottage. She'd been so scared of it all at first -the mountains, the trees everywhere, forests, lakes. It left her naked inside. Would she hack it? Would the loneliness drive her back to Dobbinstown? But very gradually since their arrival in January, and especially since moving in here, she'd found her solitude gene. She never really knew she had one in Dublin. Initially, she missed the street lamps a lot; they lit your steps for you. She missed the houses, the walls which had held her up since birth. Cement paving always carried the ring of passing feet. The countryside was boxed in a safe patch of grass for the horses to graze under the mountains. But here, here was ... her reverie was broken by the deep ponging of the doorbell resounding in the kitchen.

Feeling the drawstrings of a little anxiety around her solar plexus, she went to the front door. Joe and Sally stood outside under a small string of porcelain carriage lamps she'd bought on "Done Deal". Diminishing the shadows, they patterned themselves on the walls above and around the doorway. Sally, beaming, carried a pavlova in a thin white cardboard box. Her father held a bottle of Chianti tight under his arm. He drank the odd beer at home quietly now.

"Come in, youse are welcome." She beamed at them, hoping her voice had obliterated her nervousness. Joe looked ten years younger these days, she reflected, as he removed his new moleskin jacket and mauve chenille scarf which she took from him. Sally handed over her own Burberry full length wax coat and matching hat. The entire weight of the garment dropped through her outstretched hands. She inclined her head towards the sitting room to her right. "There's a nice fire roaring inside. I'll just take these things into the bedroom." They expressed disappointment that Brendan wasn't home yet. It was something, she told them, to do with the new trainer."He wants to give them a pep talk."

Joe coughed. "That's probably Doyler. He's actually only standing in tonight for the new manager. But I don't think the lads know that." She looked at her father, her eyes tracing an arc of bewilderment. She was dimly aware of her stirred up annoyance.

" And now you think to tell me. I ran into him today you know." She hoped the casualness in her voice rang true. It was Joe's turn to look stunned. An embarrassed flush advanced up his neck.

"I meant to tell you Love."

You meant to tell me did you? I had a good chat with him actually, at the farmers' market." She didn't mention Bradys. Sally looked from one to the other.

" Who is this Doyalller chap?"

"Long story Sal, I'll tell you over dinner or on second thoughts when we get home." He wasn't blind to the steel-tipped arrows firing from his daughter's eyes. She had left only candlelight in the kitchen. She could see Sally was impressed.

"Hope you didn't go to too much trouble, Love?"

"Not a bit of trouble." The cheerful lie velcroed on the roof of her dry mouth. The meal was a great success and even Da could go vegan he said if he was eating this kind of stuff every day.

" Would you really Joseph?" his wife asked. She sometimes addressed him formally when they were in company. Ron cloaked her amusement ." I just need to use the bathroom," her father said, getting up suddenly and disappearing through the open doorway.

She found herself anxious talking to Sally. Old insecurities rose up again like the deck of cards in "Alice in Wonderland."

"More wine?" she asked.

"Oh, just a little bit more for me Love. Your dad is driving." There was a small silence. The candles flickered in the dusk.

"Lovely to run into Brendan the other day in the sports shop."

Ron said nothing for a minute. "Yeah, yeah, he told me."

They both looked up as Joe came back into the kitchen, holding the letter in his hand.

"Found this on the bannister.Is it an English postmark? The Hegartys re-directed it.

" Oh God," she said running her hands tightly through her hair." I forgot all about it." She left it on the countertop as she doled out the pavlova for dessert. Joe turned on the main light.

"Now you can read your letter," he said.

Finally, over the coffee, she slit open the white starched envelope. The cheque slipped out between her fingers. Joe and Sally looked at her astonished face which had gathered a deepening cleft between her eyebrows.

"I've been gifted a cheque," she said in a questioning monotone.

"That's great news Love," Sally said

"How much?" her father asked.

"Five thousand pounds sterling," she said, her voice flatlining.

"In God's name who's giving you that kind of money?"

"No idea." She handed him the letter in a daze. It's dated three weeks ago. "It says it's from a London solicitor, and the benefactor is to remain anonymous." Ludicrously, this bizarre windfall was the final straw. She stood up from the table, walked over to the sink, and held back the tears she didn't know she had kept in check. Concerned, Sally got up from her chair, walked over, and stood beside her."And you've no idea who it's from?" Suddenly the day deflated in her; her caged distress escaped.

"Please don't tell me it's *you* Sal?" The other woman looked shocked and took a step back. Joe scraped his chair back on the floor and stood up, banging his arthritic knee against the rusty nail on the side of the table. "Ah here."

"Well, you are always offering us money. How do I know it isn't you?" Sally's body stiffened. Her quiet eyes flared.

"Because in the first place, I no longer bank with the London bank where this cheque was drawn down. In the second place, I wouldn't be stupid enough to give you a cheque for five thousand pounds sterling, knowing well you would have to pay tax on it after my demise. If anything, I would give you a drip feed of cash, which I know you would be too proud to accept."

"Well then why did you give Brendan seventy euro to put towards the Nike Air runners he wanted when you met him in Elverys?" As the words left her, the worm of regret turned. Sally dropped her head and stared at the tile cracks. "I know I shouldn't have done that."

Now it was Joe's turn to step to his wife's defence. "You were only looking out for the lad, Love. And if you can't accept a gift, Ron O'Connell, then you're not the girl I thought you were. And furthermore, you need money to fix the hole in the roof, to cut back them bushes in the garden. Sally nearly tripped on your paving stones tonight. Maybe if you spent less money on those websites "Wish" and "Done Deal," you wouldn't need handouts or gift cheques," he spat out . "You should be damn grateful to whoever it was." Nobody heard the tortured sound of the key in the lock. Suddenly Brendan was in the middle of the kitchen floor. He assessed the freeze frame before him. He stared at them all, then threw a dwarfed "Hi" into the air.

"Hullo love," Sally said quietly. Joe nodded in his direction.

"We had Mr. Doyle," he said, trying to squeeze the good news into the chasm.

"I know son," Joe murmured. I think it's just temporary."

"By the way," Joe added, looking at his daughter head- on.

"Better check that out for tax."

"But how?"

Her question floated on a silent airway.

"Brendan Love, would you fetch our coats from the bedroom please?"

Sally moved towards the door. Joe followed. Ron,with her back to them stood at the sink, hands clamped on the worktop. Felix the cat next door had slunk down into a crouched position under the fence. She'd thrown stones. They'd grown into a boulder. She was trapped underneath. As if in a dream, she heard her father and stepmother bid goodnight to Brendan at the door. She heard Sally say, "Thank your mum for a lovely meal."

He came back into the kitchen, his eyes a swivelling accompaniment to his bewildered splayed palms.

"What the hell?"

"Just bottle it, Brendan. I've had enough for one night." She moved to clear the dinner table, avoiding his eyes. He turned on his heels. His angry tread on the stairs was lined with hurt as he went up to the bathroom. Methodically, she cleared every crumb from the table. Then she moved the dishes to the sink already filled up with running water and suds. They could steep there for the night. "Bloody Jamie Oliver. Who the hell wants to go Vegan anyway?"

Next morning she set the table, and made the porridge with a huge flavouring of silence. Brendan could take it no longer. "We need to talk."

"Do we?" She hadn't slept. The farmers' market and Bradys were the past. They did things differently there.

"You know we do. What in God's name did I come into last night?"

"Sorry Love, you didn't deserve that."

"Bloody right I didn't. Now tell me what's goin' on?"

Reluctantly she produced the cheque. He looked at it for a long time, then he kissed it and looked back at her. "Ah Ma, this is MEGA! Suddenly, a **eureka** moment blew across his face

"Is this what you were fightin' with Joe and Sally about?"

"Kind of."

"Ron O'Connell- you're some feckin' puzzle. Speak to me woman." She told him everything, except about Doyler.

"We might have to pay tax."

" So what, it's still feckin MEGA. Ma, that was low about the runners."

"I know, I know. I just wanted you to keep saving."

"Life doesn't have to be hard all the time you know, just 'cause we had it hard in the past." She nodded quietly. He was right really.

He lit the fire, made them cocoa, and they sat in silence for half an hour.

"You have to make it right Ma. Do it today. Go on, do it now. I'm going to go outside to put the logs in the shed. Do it while I'm gone."

Several times she brought up Sally's number. Several more times she brought up Joe's. Joe would have been the cowardly option. She slid her fingers back down the contact list until she could hover over her stepmother no more. She blurted out her apology, thinking it probably sounded like a hollow beer can rolling around the roadway on Patrician Avenue after midnight. "I don't know how to make it up to you for being such an eejit. I just had a long day, but that's no excuse." There was a fractional silence. She bit her nail, as the shift took hold on the line.

"You were over-wrought love and I imagine Mr. Oliver's recipe took quite a bit of doing.

"Ah, Jamie can take a hike."

" Yes, tell him that".

A tide of relief sucked the dammed-up misery out of her. Joe was gone fishing. Sally would pass on her apology to him also. She sat back in the chair, eyes closed. The fire was beginning to die down. When Brendan came back in with the logs, her mobile rang. She gave him a smile that pulled in the world as she headed for the stairs.

CHAPTER 8

His voice sounded a little crackly. The reception wasn't great. She reflected briefly to herself that now with a bit of money - she was beginning to accept the strange benevolence - they could get Wi-Fi installed.

"How are yeh?" she finally heard through the static. She moved closer to the window.

"Now that's better," she said. "I thought you were on a desert island there for a while." His short barreled laugh made her forget the cold upstairs. "You need Wi-Fi," he said. "They've a great payment plan. Oh God sorry, that came out the wrong way. I didn't mean to …"

"No worries." She laughed. "We're definitely thinking along those lines."

"I hope Brendan didn't get too big a fright last night."

"He was thrilled to see you." She could hardly tell him he was off the menu when he should have been the main course.

"Just wondering if you fancy meeting up in Dalys in Manor Hamish tonight?"

"Yeah, that should be good," she said, delight minced inside her.

"Will I pick you up?"

"If you like." She hoped she sounded casual. No one had ever picked her up.

"OK so, say around 9. I know your cottage."

"Yeah, it's outside Drombawn, about half a mile. Turn right up at the old rectory. We're on the Manorhamish Road."

"Perfect, see you then."

"Ok, bye, Ron."

Brendan found her making the bed in his room downstairs, smoothing down the duvet, her fingers a crisp energy machine. She was humming tunelessly to herself.

"Someone's in a good mood," he said.

"Now, Don't Tell me I can't sing."

"Wouldn't dream of it Ma. Why the singing?"

"Well there's the money for starters and..."

"And what? You have that cat thing on your face."

"What cat thing?"she asked horrified, raising her right hand to her chin.

"Well you know, the cat and the cream kind of thing."

She smiled.

"You've big slabs of cream on now."

"Meow," she said, making a big face and clawing her fingers in front of him.

"I just came in to tell you I'm goin' over to Lorcan's house to watch the Man United and Sunderland match. They have Sky. Ma, can we get that now?"

"Seeing as I'm in a good mood, maybe." He hugged her then with firecracker eyes. "You're the best. I'll be back around 7."

"When you come back, I'll be here still, but I have to go out around 9. There'll be a cold salad on the table for yeh."

He looked at her, said nothing, paced up and down the bedroom, his hands behind his back. Then he pivoted on his right heel."I smell a date. You were talking upstairs a long time." She didn't reply.

"Ha ha," he said with a flourish."I'm right.Who is it?"

There was an extended pause while she fiddled with the buttons on her blouse and pursed her lips in a tight reluctant line. Then he had his second Eureka moment.

"Mr. Doyle said he met you at the market. He was doing fierce askin' for you. Is it him?" She nodded mutely.

"I was right, I was right," he said, jumping around the bedroom."Me Ma's got a date with me football teacher."

"Shh, close that window,"

"It's only the curlews here Ma," he said mockingly.

After he left for Jack's house, she began planning her outfit. Sally would be the one to give sartorial advice. She was always so elegant. She had a Louise Kennedy powder blue two- piece for her wedding in April last year, which she and Joe told no one about. They said they were going over to Manchester to visit some of Sally's family. Joe said they told no one because they didn't want a fuss, but then Adam and his new partner Miguel might have flown in from San Francisco for the wedding. When she accused her father of this, he handled his bike from under the cottage window and pedalled furiously down the road, his sullen silence flung into the wind behind him. "You'd think Sally would have gotten him to do the right thing," she thought. But Joe was a hard man to shift. That woman did work magic though. She was the one with the holiday home on the shores of Lough Melvin just outside Killindara. It was a massive two- storey which she and her late husband co-owned with a number of his siblings. After his death, she bought it out, fancying a quiet retreat in her grief. She hadn't reckoned of course on meeting Joe. Ron was amazed when her dad announced they were both going to live there. What was more amazing to both herself and her family in Dublin was she'd chosen to follow him to Leitrim. Rural resettlement in County Clare had been on her mind for a while, but that scheme had ended. Alice's two sisters Kat and Tina were aghast.

"You'll hate it Love, and then you'll have no place to come back to."

Joe, for some reason, had never bought out their Council house. They continued to pay the nominal rent over the years. In a way now she was glad. The Council could take it back and she could cut all ties. Joe's brother Alfie didn't hold back either. "You're a Dub, you'll never settle love. Your lad's roots are here." He paused, "Even if they don't want to know... the other crowd, they might want to accept him someday." At this, she clenched her jaw and resumed a childhood habit of lifting the skin on the back of her hand into a little tight pyramid. "That's what I'm afraid of," she said quietly. The pinch fell flat down again forgiving the hot burden of her anger. She remembered her friends Jenny and Amy's unhinged jaws when she told them down in the pub. Jenny took a long swig from her Bulmers, riveting arthropod eyes on her. Amy's hand was frozen in her crisp bag, and her swan neck tightened as she clenched her jaw. Tears sprang up until she had an eyeliner crisis. Ron handed her a tissue. "Youse'll have forgotten all about me this time next year." They shook their heads in determined unison.

Doyler came at 9pm on the dot. She had taken manic care with her hair and makeup. She pinned up her long mane on the top of her head, leaving stray wisps dangling seductively from behind her ears. She layered on the Bobby Brown foundation which Amy and Jenny had gifted her before she left and applied a Boots shimmer blusher. She then combed down her black mascara assiduously over each eyelash in turn, finishing off with a deft upward flick of the brush. A careful thin stroke of navy- blue eyeliner, a shimmer of pink and gold eye shadow, Summer Pink lipstick and she was done. She stopped to appreciate the effect in the mirror. She rummaged through her earrings until she found the winter- white globes on thin gold -plated sticks. She pulled her loose emerald green tie-dyed silk shirt (a present from Adam) over her head. She had black loose-leg trousers from Penneys which Amy always said looked designer. Black pumps were good underneath. Lucky she was five seven she thought.

Brendan got to the door before she did. She stopped on the top steps, hidden by a slight bend in the narrow stairs. She heard her son's awkward "Howya Mr Doyle?" There was what sounded like banter, then, Doyler's laugh, suddenly a descant above that of his former pupil. "Poor lad," she thought as she appeared into full view of both of them. She noticed their appraising looks before Brendan reddened and looked away. Doyler didn't. He combed her whole body, not once allowing his eyes a bashful retreat.

"You look stunning," he said, as she smiled nervously, making a grab for her silver clutch bag which she'd left on the bottom step of the stairs.

"I'll just get me coat in the kitchen," she said. Brendan had retreated inside. His geography books lay scattered on the small dining room table when she entered. She grabbed her long black raincoat from the back of the chair next to him. His dirty dishes were propped to one side of the table. Following her gaze, he gushed "Don't worry Ma, I'll turn into Cinderella when you're gone."

"Do that Cinders," she said, kissing him lightly on the top of the head. He conceded a space there usually.

There was a porcelain full moon.Doyler commented on it.

"Full moon," he said, pointing at the sky as he held the passenger door of the Skoda open for her. The moon appeared and disappeared in turn behind the trees, while they drove. A couple of stars peered through the inky blackness over the rushy fields ahead. The mountains were running a bulky shadow, as the car headed down the small side road, past a couple of desultory cottages just before the stop sign at the main road. He asked if she was warm enough, and in a studious fashion fiddled with the dials of the heater.

"Your car is lovely," she said.

"Thanks.I suppose the shanks' mare wouldn't do for Leitrim."

"No, no I guess it wouldn't," she laughed.

"Will I put on a CD?"

"Oh I don't mind."

"Okay, then you choose."

She chose Taylor Swift. The seamless tones of the singer comforted the silences as the car hummed comfortably on the main road to Manorhamish.

"So?" he said to her when he came back from the bar, having ordered a Bulmers for himself and a Bacardi and Coke for her. "In the name of Jayus, how did you think of following Joe here?"

"Well," she said reddening slightly, and bracing herself to retell a by now well told narrative. "It's a long story."

She took a look around the bar. The crowd were so different from Dobbinstown with what Brendan called their culchie heads on them.

"Like yourself, I'm here with the culchies," she began. "I'll tell you me story. Then you can tell me yours. I saw an ad online where they wanted to up the population in Killindara. They were looking for families to move here. They were offering a couple of houses at very low rent and all, but the snag was they wanted to build up the number of children for the primary school."

He nodded knowingly. Then the penny dropped. Of course he knew the story, being a teacher . Sure everyone in the place knew the story. "You probably know this," she said suddenly self -conscious.

"No, no," he declared a little too vigorously. "Well just a bit," he conceded with a grin. She laughed. "Well I'll keep it short, seeing as the whole village knows all about me. I was even in the local paper." He looked at her with a twinkle and nodded.

"OMG, he knew it all. Oh heck, coming from Dobbinstown, what the culchies thought was the least of her worries. She was used to people talking about her either in Dublin or Leitrim. If her hide wasn't thick, she wouldn't be here in the first place." She took a deep breath in. "Ah here, you know more about me than I do," she said, suddenly seizing on a pile of peanuts and stuffing them into her mouth

"Alright, while you're digesting them peanuts, I'll talk, but then you have to finish the story. I know all about the school's repopulation scheme, and I know from me own staff that it only netted them one new child, God love them. But then, didn't they tell me a certain Dublin girl emailed them. Said she'd been googling quiet places to live down the West, and found a bit from the Leitrim Observer about the Killindara project. Now her son was fifteen at the time, and was too old they explained. But being a true Dobbinstown girl, what did she do, but email them a second time explaining she was a young healthy woman who might meet a nice Leitrim lad yet and settle in the area. She might even produce a child for the school."

She blushed furiously."Me Ma was a chancer and I got it from her," she said quietly, studying the Heineken logo on the beer mat." Anyway," she continued at warp speed, avoiding his eyes, "Didn't they bring me here for a kind of chat last December. I had me CV updated ; they said I had excellent Junior Cert results and great work experience. I told them I had Brendan at 16. They were very nice about it all actually. Then they said the cottage was going a begging anway, so I could have it. Next thing, they added if I wanted to come back the following September, they would be holding interviews for an SNA post. They didn't guarantee anything."

"Great stuff," he said taking a handful of her peanuts without permission."Special Needs Assistants jobs are hard to come by. There's a girl with severe dyspraxia starting in Killindara in Junior Infants in September. It's a developmental coordination disorder, he explained seeing her frown. You could have a job there for the next eight years if you want."

"Oh I'm not looking that far down the line really. Might want to do something else by then."

"You're a free spirit aren't you?" he said, eating her peanuts again.

"I'm a generous woman too," she said. "Finish up them peanuts. I'll get us two more bags."

Despite his protestations, she bought the next round and two more bags of peanuts. Closing time whistled by them. He told her about his ma and Ailbhe. "She can be a right handful at times. Ma isn't able for her I think, especially when her asthma is bad."

They realised they knew loads of people in common. He told her his ex, KellyAnn was with Brendan Gleeson now. She didn't comment. Brendan Gleeson had been in school two years behind her. He was a quiet steady fellow, but his home situation was fairly troubled.

"Is his auld fella out of jail yet?" she asked quietly.

"Not yet, but soon." Suddenly a tonsure of silence fell on their heads. She felt a little overwhelmed by his physical nearness.

"I really like you," he said, breaking the skin of the silence. "I always fancied you when you came to the matches. You're gorgeous."

"Would you go away out of that!" she said reddening. He was looking directly at her; her body was leaving her again. A sensuous tingle ran the length of her. She had to make a bolt for the loo. As she walked away from him, she risked a comment over her shoulder. "By the way, I fancied you too." A quiet smile laddered itself gratefully up the sides of his cheeks.

When he dropped her home, they kissed in the car. She realised no one had ever kissed her in this way before. She felt her whole body unfurling in his presence. She cringed when she remembered, how at 18, she had embarked on a number of one –night stands to outrun a shadow gaining on her in her dreams. Each encounter was to set her world right way up again. But then the shadow didn't know the right way up. It was the wild shame in her mother's eyes at 6am one morning and her father's pacing the landing with a feverish infant in his arms which put paid to it all. After that, she gradually leaned into motherhood ,with a small sigh she never even nodded to. She never again stayed away at night. Jack Guiney Junior, assuming her bronzed cleavage was a signal for sex, got slapped hard into his box .She began to get a reputation as a "stuck up cow" in her twenties. The longest relationship she had in Dobbinstown was with Matt Danagher, the security man she'd met the night of Brendan's emergency in Tallaght. He was divorced and fifteen years her senior. They got on reasonably well, and he was good with Brendan. The earth didn't move, but what could she expect? Many a girl in her situation would have jumped at a nice, steady, unimaginative fella like him. Joe didn't object to him either "He's a decent sort and a good provider Love. You could do a whole heap worse." When he wanted to move in after a year ,which was a very long time in Dobbinstown, she stalled and stalled until in the end, she refused flat out. Maybe it was all Alice's fault, all those fairy tales she was so good at telling. Last she heard of him, he'd had a baby with a girl five years behind her in school.

.

CHAPTER 9

The next morning after her date, the second letter upended her, almost. Standing at the sink, she heard the metallic sound of the letter box spring in the hallway, then the slap of a letter on the floorboards.When she picked up the stiff crisp envelope, her breath held itself from her.There was no denying the postage stamp. She inhaled sharply, walking back into the kitchen, reading slowly. She read as if she were watching a foreign movie with no subtitles, and yet bizarre good vibe interactions on the screen.

Walker and Hamilton Solicitors,
100 Greys Inn Road,
London WGIX8HB,
United Kingdom,
22/4/2016
phone 00442078314033,
email info @walker and hamilton.com.
Dear Miss O'Connell,

We wish to inform you that you are deemed a beneficiary in the will of our client, the late Mrs Jean Ahmed of 101 Palace-Green, Kensington Palace Gardens, West Central London. SW10. The amount you inherited from her estate subject to probate is £300,000 Sterling. You will have by now received a gift cheque from the said party, who prior to her death, wished to remain an anonymous benefactor. This amount of £5,000 does incur inheritance tax. This may be sorted by A, our firm, B, your own solicitor, C, direct dealing with HMRC (UK revenue). We will be in touch in due course. Any further queries, please contact this office, either by phone or email.

Yours sincerely,
Andrew Hamilton.

An apologetic handwritten note was attached overleaf, apologising for the long delay in forwarding the gift cheque. A clerical error was cited as the cause. A small square envelope was enfolded within the main letter.

Room 16,

St. Andrew's Care Home, Kensington.

September 2nd 2015

My Dear Ron,

It's been many years since I met you with your beloved mother Alice. I was so sorry to hear of her passing. I remember a very fine lady, though we met but once. I apologise for not replying to your kind thank you note, and that of your little boy. Life has a habit of sweeping one up, until one day, one realises that it's not correct to allow oneself to be taken out in the refuse of time, without some more meaning to the whole drama of life. I've never forgotten that night in November 2000 when you and Alice were a beacon of hope in Ireland when I was all alone and distressed. Brendan must be a fine young man by now. I would like you and your family to receive this token of my gratitude. Say a small prayer for me when you think of it. I will be watching over you and Brendan the Navigator, as will your beloved mum I'm sure.

Love and gratitude,

Jean.

Suddenly a flat pack version of herself stood there. There was no breath left to fill out her old 3D self. Jean! She remembered her now, the lady from The Gate- OMG. Paralysed by her inability to contact Joe or Sally after the fiasco on Saturday, she looked up Cian O'Grady Solicitors in the phone book. Her voice landing on a foreign shore, she made an appointment for 11.30 that morning with his secretary.

She knocked on the blue door of Cian O'Grady's large office under the eaves of the three- storey grey, limestone building on Main Street,Manorhamish.

"Come in," a muffled voice said from inside. She pushed in the heavy timber door gingerly. It squeaked. "Come in, come in." He was on the phone and gestured liberally to her with a wave from the back of his right hand. Timidly she sat on the chair which he pointed to.

"It's Ron, is it?" he said once off the phone, looking at her over the rim of his glasses, slightly tipped down his nose. "Yes, how can I help you?" Cian O'Grady was about 60 with what her mother would have referred to as "Einstein hair." He had a big frame which accommodated itself badly to the swivel chair he was sitting on. Now his grey- blue eyes engaged hers uncompromisingly. She twisted Alice's sapphire ring round and round on her left hand before she could raise her head to look him in the eye. "Howya Mr.O Grady, me name's Ron O Connell," she said, swallowing a gobstopper of anxiety - at least that's how she described it to Brendan later, (Oh Lord, sure he knew her name - best give it to him again anyway). Her throat was closing in. He scrutinized her more now, his eyes blinking a meticulous analysis. God, she couldn't even swallow; where was saliva when you needed it most? she wondered faintly. Wordlessly, she produced the solicitor's letter from her bag, also the letter regarding the gift cheque and laid them on the table before him. To add to the torture, he took forever fixing his glasses, giving them a small wipe before his eyes lowered themselves towards the stiff embossed page in front of him. A small oily slick formed on the palms of her hands. Her chest was burning. He read slowly. Her heart ran along cobblestones. After all the seconds in the world had finally run out, he looked up, then down again at the letter before him." Extraordinary inheritance!" Then his eyes again met her anxious ones. " Tell me, how do you know this lady?" She cleared her throat."It's a long story Mr. O'Grady."

"Call me Cian."

"It was a good turn me Ma and meself did for her in Dublin when I was only seventeen. I'd be here all day if I was to tell you the whole story." His face frowned to keep up with his puzzlement.

"Must have been some good turn. And what exactly do you want me to do?" he asked.

"Well I'm worried about tax. The £5,000 cheque needs tax paid on it, and maybe the whole thing does. I still can't believe it's real."

"And when did you get the £5,000?"

"On Saturday."

"And this today?" he said, sounding incredulous.

"The first letter was over three weeks late being forwarded from Dublin." She blinked as a twist of sunlight bounced off his silver pen and into her right eye. He swivelled on his chair and typed something on the computer to his right. The silence stiffened in the room. She looked around and felt eaten up by the cardboard boxes on the floor with large brown files in them. On the shelves behind him, she dimly made out the title on one of the book spines "Layman's Guide to Irish Law."

"Did you read all of them?"

"Pardon?"

"All them books."

He laughed ruefully. "To tell you the truth, No Now, back to you and your tax. Good news is, your friend knew what she was doing. You don't pay tax under English law until an inheritance is over £320,000 Sterling." Ron looked puzzled.

"But why?"

"Yes?" he encouraged.

"Why did she give me the £5,000?"

"I suspect this lady- Jean, knowing you were in her will, but not knowing how long she had to live in the nursing home, wanted to tide you over for a few years. I've been in touch with the London solicitors about the bit that you told my secretary. It seems the £5,000 should have come to you eight months ago after she went into St. Andrews. However, the senior partner in the law firm has recently died, and let's just say he left the affairs in a mess. It only came to light a month ago that your cheque hadn't been handled. The other partner, Mr. Hamilton has taken charge of everything, including her will. That's why you got two letters so close together. Any amount of a gift cheque over £3,000 is liable for tax at 40%, so ..." His fingers tapped expertly on his calculator. "That's £800 you owe the UK Revenue. Just drop a cheque into the office whenever you can and we'll sort it."

She felt a sigh of relief fill the mummified air of the office. She needed life. She headed to the window. A small boy was eating an ice cream cone on the pavement below. It went splat. He wailed. His mother took out her tissue to scrape it off the ground. She patted her son on the head. Then he was beside her at the window.

."Come away from there Ron," he said gently,"Take a pew."

She sat down feebly."I haven't found me sea legs yet Mr. O Grady." He patted her on the shoulder, going back behind his desk."Probate should take about a year to a year and a half and then you'll be a wealthy woman."She didn't dare ask what probate meant.

He took her to lunch. She'd never been in a golf club before. They found a seat overlooking an artificial lake and a garden seat where two golfers were relaxing after a game. Cian O Grady waved at them."I know those ladies from the club", he explained. She squirmed on the chair. The plush dark interior of the bar felt uncomfortable. Alice in Wonderland's deck of cards rose up to attack her again. She took the black gilt edged menu from the bar boy with a soft smile. Cian ordered coffee for both of them, a toasted sandwich for himself and salmon salad for her. A bottle of sparkling mineral water lay in the middle of the table. He poured from the bottle into both their glasses.

"Well, here's to Jean," he said raising a glass.

"To Jean," she said quietly.

"Now tell me the whole story," he said easing back awkwardly into a black leather chair and sugaring his coffee which had just arrived. She glanced at him nervously before she plunged in and began to elaborate on the poor little woman, as her mother and herself referred to her on the night in question. The strange lady was fleshed out again so clearly now, she could scarcely believe the clarity of her own remembrances.

"I was just seventeen. Brendan, me son was three months." She flashed a smile. "We have 'em early in Dobbinstown, Mister, eh, Cian." She took a hard swig from the glass. "I wanted a night out from nappies, you know yourself." He nodded sagely, his blue eyes engaged in a long vacated memory. "Ma was a great one for the plays at The Gate." He raised his unclipped eyebrows, surprised. An urgent need to defend her mother's academic pursuits dragoned in her.

"Ma was cultured," she said defensively. Just because they were from a deprived area didn't mean they wouldn't enjoy a play. The prickly heat on her chest was in full agreement. He nodded encouragingly. "Well anyway, she was mad about Yeats." His eyebrows lifted just a twitch, before he was smiling again.

"We got the bus into town, all dolled up. Da had won a few bob on the nags, horses- like" The solicitor's smile was on cruise control now. Encouraged by this, she decided to keep on talking. She'd been so afraid of coming to a real- life solicitor on her own. Somehow, retelling the story of the little old lady after all these years was opening a torrent she didn't know was there, let alone needed release. "So he gave us a bit of extra cash. We'd enough to buy ourselves a mineral for me, a couple of G & Ts for Ma and maybe a taxi. The play was really good I think. We both liked it anyway. It was "The Plough and the Stars."

"O'Casey," he chimed in.

"Dead on."

"But I thought the play was Yeats?"

"Hold your horses, I'm comin' to that. At the end, didn't they announce that there would be two short Yeats plays in a small theatre downstairs. Nothing would do Ma, but to go down. I had to ring Da and tell him we'd be late. He wasn't best pleased mindin' the baby. But Ma was the boss."

"So is my wife," he said with a dry smile around the corners of his mouth.

"The two plays were about half an hour each, "Cathleen Ni Houlihan" and " The Dreaming of the Bones." Ma was lappin' it up and I was snorin' me head off with havin' to get up for night feeds. Then there was a bit of an intellectual discussion at the end, with people askin' questions from the audience. Then this little auld wan (I mean old lady) piped up at the front and said very poshly," Wouldn't Mr. Yeats be gratified with the night?" The crowd took a good while to get back upstairs. The lift was out of order. The little old lady was holding onto the bannisters, and dragging her left heel. I asked was she okay. We were right behind her. She looked back at me, and gave a small smile." At this juncture, she turned to thank the waitress for her salad, which had just arrived. Wild horses couldn't hold back her story now; she was quite enjoying herself. Taking up a knife and fork, she cut carefully into the soft meat before continuing. "Out in the lobby we could all walk finally side by side. The little old woman sidled up to two of the Hoi Polloi from the discussion downstairs. One was that fella with the curly, blonde hair, well it's grey now, the long nose and big lips. He's with the *Irish Independent*.

"Manus O'Siochru," he said.

"The other was that fashion designer, Margaret O'Shea. Now, she did her best to talk to them about the play, but they were terrible rude. Ma was shocked. They just kept talkin' to their friends and ignored her. That's when she looked back at us; we were comin' up behind. She smiled. We smiled back. Ma said it was great that she liked the plays. She said she'd come from London to Holyhead that morning specially for the Yeats festival, and then she'd caught the ferry to Dun Laoghaire. She was only in the country a few hours, and it was windy and pissin' rain, sorry, piddlin rain."

"Did ye help her out of the rain or something?" he asked. His coffee was going cold. He'd only taken two bites out of his sandwich.

"Yeah, we all walked out together. Her poor umbrella was all bent from the wind. Ma had to steady her. She was stick- thin. We thought she'd fall over. Then I said "why don't we take a taxi Ma, and we can give the woman a lift?" That's when Ma asked her her name and where she was staying. We were surprised when she said The Gresham. Again the solicitor raised an eyebrow. He pushed away the coffee and the sandwich, his jawline propped up with his left hand and elbow on the round-topped table. "We waved down the next taxi and let herself into the front. We all got out at The Gresham, just to see her in safely. Ma was takin' out her purse, when she waved it away and paid for us all. Then she treated us to a drink downstairs in the lobby. The woman, Jean, ordered a 7 up for me, a G & T for Ma and a brandy for herself. We were all smilin' and no one knew the blazes what to say next." Out of the side of her eye she caught the amused twist of Cian O Grady's lips. However she was on a roll, and as her Da used to say when she was about twelve, "When our Ron has something she wants to tell you,her breath gets left behind." She was suddenly compelled to get the bit her school girl self had no compunction about telling off her chest. "I remember her asking me what year I was in school. Ma got all embarrassed. I piped straight up, said I'd had a baby, so I couldn't finish school."

"And how did she take that?"

"She said nothing for a minute; then she smiled and patted me on the shoulder. "Boy or girl ?" she asked. " Boy," I said. I remember dropping my head, and she lifted my chin into her little bird hand. "What's his name dear?"

" Brendan," I told her.

"Brendan the Navigator," she said, " the one who is supposed to have really discovered America." Ma muttered something about there not being too many navigators where we were from. As she spoke, a lightning shaft of memory brought back her mother's flustered demeanour. "Poor Ma," she thought. Suddenly she had a visceral connection with the awkwardness her mother must have felt in front of the posh lady. It must have been so hard explaining what was commonplace in their lives to someone from such a different world.

"And what did the lady say to that?" he prompted, unsure how to interpret her lengthy pause.

"Oh, she didn't say anything to that. Then she asked me how old I was. I said seventeen. We couldn't understand, but she started to cry." "Oh, I do beg your pardon," she said. " I've never heard anybody say that except on the telly. She wiped her eyes with the tissue she had up her sleeve before she asked Ma would she accompany her to her room, as she felt wobbly. She enquired if I'd be okay in the lobby. Ma was a bit worried about that, but Jean called over the manager. Over he came all smiles. She ordered tea and cakes specially for me."

"You'll have to look after this beautiful girl for a little while," she said to him. As she told this part, she noticed her words expand more fluidly in her head space. It was all coming back to her with that strange cinematic feel she'd been experiencing from the time she started to tell the story. "I remember thinking he was seriously friendly with her, like he knew her."

"Probably from several visits," Cian remarked.

"Ma came downstairs after nearly an hour. She was all smiles. I finished munching a cake. I was thinking I'd love to stay the night with the rich people. When I asked how she got on, all she said was we'd missed the night link, so Adam my brother - he's in San Francisco now- had to come in and collect us. She never told me what they talked about actually, and I forgot all about it then. About a week later, didn't we get a lovely thank you letter from London? She had asked specially for us to leave our address with the hotel manager. Then the next time we heard from her was Brendan's communion. Ma had died at this stage. I didn't write back for about a year. One day I came across the Holy Communion card she had sent Brendan, in a drawer. I felt so guilty, I wrote back and told her about Ma's death, and got Brendan to send a thank you note. She had sent him £20 Sterling and a rosary beads. We never heard again. Don't know how she knew about the Communion?"

"Probably the internet or a PI." At this stage, he had begun scanning his mobile with a frown. "She's on a number of websites. This is her death notice from the *LondonTimes*.

Jean Ahmed, wife of the late Tariq, passed away peacefully in St. Andrew's Nursing Home, Kensington. Deeply regretted by her loving children: son Tariq and daughter Sofia, grandchildren: Tariq, James, Elizabeth, Sandra, nephews, nieces and extended family. Pre-deceased by her daughter Ava in 1981." Then it just goes on to give you details of the funeral service," he said with a wave of his hand, not looking up from his phone."There's another bit about her in *The Guardian*. She was a seriously wealthy millionaire. Her husband had extensive shares in shipping and aviation both in the Middle East and the Gulf States. He was from the Emirates. Her daughter Ava apparently died in a car crash at just seventeen."

That's when he looked at Ron head- on. A distance had passed through her and moved on. He registered the subtle rocking of her body below the waistline. A tear flew down her cheek for the little old lady who lost her daughter at the same age as she had been on the night they met.

CHAPTER 10

Brendan wasn't best pleased when she turned up half an hour late to collect him from school. Her heart missed a turn when she saw the crumpled -up figure of him sitting on the dry pavement, landing wave after wave of frowning concentration on his phone. Oh God, she'd forgotten her phone was still on silent. She'd felt self-conscious answering it in front of the solicitor. She beeped the car horn. At first, he didn't hear her. He sat there, his stillness in the dry April evening, a figure cut in relief out of the blue mountain behind him.

She hit the horn louder. He looked up. She waved, and got a small indifferent flick of the wrist back. She saw him turn, and give a thumbs up to the caretaker, who was finally locking up. God, she felt guilty. He sat in, giving volcanic vent to the door handle. She was taken aback. "I'm so sorry Love; I had business in town and me phone was on silent." He didn't answer, just looked out the side window. She rolled down her window. "God I'm terrible sorry Johnny; I got delayed in town." The caretaker nodded and flashed a concerned look over at Brendan in the passenger seat. The boy kept his head in the footwell. "No worries Ron, mind that young fella." He returned her wave as she reversed in the school gateway before heading right onto the Sligo Road. When they got in the door, she busied herself getting the dinner. Unwashed plates lay piled in the sink."Would you give us a hand Brendan?" she asked as she took the lamb chops out of the fridge. He took down his apron from the back of the kitchen door, and silently boiled the kettle to wash the delph. As he waited for the kettle to boil, he just stood there stock still, looking out the window."Jaysus Ma, I thought you were dead. I f*ckin' texted and texted. Christ, don't do that to me anymore."She was about to reprimand him for language when she saw the squashed misery on his face. Angrily, he fielded a trickle down his cheek with a vicious swipe of his right fist."Sit down," she said prizing his hand loose from the chrome- handled tap. He shook her off. She stepped back alarmed."God Love, I didn't think I was that late."

"I was shittin' meself with worry. I thought you were dead. Why the f* ck didn't yeh leave on your phone?"

"OK, no more bad language." She knew she was deflecting him, but it needed saying too. She raised her hand to silence his mouth; his lips ringed in an oval of protest. "Now no bad language. Your gran always said we didn't use it, and that's what set us apart in Dobbinstown. I've a lot to tell you, so tell you what, why don't we forget the chops? The delph can steep. We'll order a takeaway from McAdrews. The fire is set in the sitting room, so go on in and put a match to it." He shrugged, his face squirming out of his rage."I'll ring them so."

They used an emergency fire log and some kindling to get a good whoosh up the chimney. In the enveloping windfall of light, she sensed his wound- up body loosening. They both sat on the sofa, something she used to do when she had to give him what she referred to as a "Ma talk." " Been a while since we did this Love." He looked at her questioningly. "Sat on the sofa together." He nodded. She could see the memories nudging him."Well, before the takeaway arrives, I want to tell you what I did today. You remember the cheque obviously?" He stapled his eyes into her now with more alertness."Well I had to go to a solicitor about that today, and about something else."

" God, not the free legal aid?"

"I want to show you something," she said, ignoring the comment, taking Jean's letter out of her bag. He read slowly. She gave her mother's ring another twist. Suddenly he turned his eyes to her wonderingly."Is that the little old woman who sent me the Communion card with the money and the rosary beads? You made me write back to her."

"And a very good thing I did too, in more ways than one," she said.

"You mean that's the one who gave us the cheque?

And there's more; we're in her will as well.

His body embraced a new startle reflex; he sat bolt upright.

"Jean , Lord rest her – though not religious, she automatically blessed herself as she had seen her parents do when news of someone's passing was announced- was a very kind lady to think of us. We should be so grateful Love."

"How much Ma? *How much?*"

She refused to tell him what they had inherited until she had first told him the story of the night in November 2000. He listened, his body leaning in her direction as she grew more dramatic. When she'd finished, they were both missing,discovered eventually along the crazy paving of their old lives. Then they heard the doorbell.

"Take away," he said jumping up.

"I can see McAndrew's car outside. Go get the plates Ma."

While he was taking in the food, she made a quick decision. How much did he really need to know she wondered .What if it went to his head? Rags to riches and all that. God, they were just above the poverty line last week, and that's all he'd ever known. She remembered the barons and their money. She felt an invasive body chill warning her off. As he was spooning the chicken and noodles onto their plates, she told him the amount her instincts told her to relay. "We got £20,000 Sterling."- about €24,000. He dropped the spoon with a clatter. He had lost his outline of grief. He stood tall; his head swivelled excitedly towards her.

"Now who's the cat that got the cream?" she said mockingly. They ate in silence. She tended to the fire, and slipped her arm around his shoulder.

"Sorry for the bad language."

She rubbed his hair. "You know I'm here for you always." Under her fingers, she uncovered the tentative loosening of his muscle fibres. She listened as he enumerated plans for the money. Darkness stole across the room, hiding them from one another. Still, they didn't light the lamp or draw the curtain. Outside the curlew cried.

Next morning, she rang Sally from upstairs. There were still fences to mend and a confidence to release from its hiding place. Joe answered Sally's mobile. Guilt made her stomach queasy. She couldn't tell him yet. A third party needed to oil the wheels of this disclosure. "That you Ron? Everything Ok?" It was still only 8.30. His voice had the quickened inflection of a practised worrier.

"Everything's great Da." Her voice cruised on a feigned ease. She could hear Sally in the background,"Is that Ron?"

She heard a whispered conversation before Sally came on. "Has sum at come up Love?" She took a deep breath down into her base chakra before answering. "Sally, can we meet in Mandys today? It's me day off." She'd been working in the coffee shop in Drombawn for the last two months. She imagined Joe's face making gyrations in the bedroom and Sally's calm, murmured assurances. "Right Love, no worries. What time?"

"Say eleven."

"Perfect, ok, see you then." One small hurdle down.

Eanna had left a long message yesterday. She texted back, "Can't talk today," then posted a red pulsating heart. Downstairs she heard the ache in the timbers of the old front door."I'm off Ma." She looked down and glimpsed his disappearing back. "Remember, not a word in school about the inheritance, even to Lorcan." He fired a friendly thumbs up over his shoulder, and went racing down the path to catch the purring bus below at the crossroads.

She found a window seat in the café. She was texting Doyler when Sally entered. She put down the phone. Sally stood before the table for a moment, her eyes scanning the black hollows under her stepdaughter's eyes. "Looks like someone didn't get much sleep."

"A bit tired," she said, with a battle weary smile. "Here take a pew Sal." Sally tentatively eased her ample frame onto the unforgiving chrome chair before resting her large Michael Kors handbag on the table. The large diamond and garnet rings on her left hand added a benign sparkle in the sunlight. Ron kept her voice low, denying it a quivering rise. "Sal, I'm desperate sorry again."

Sally nested Ron's sweating palms in the centre of her own large ones. She felt the garnet ring wedge not unkindly into them. Sandra, the waitress who was on took their order. She eyed Ron with a hooded jealousy. She'd taken care with her makeup and her sleek black hair parted on one side fell in a clear cut line over her left eye. "I'll have a cappuccino," she said.

"I'll have the same." Sally smiled disarmingly at the girl. "And add some chocolate sprinkles would you, and a little love heart shape on the top?" The girl looked panicked. Ron smiled, giving Sally a large wink."A heart on top is all the go in Manchester?" Sharon's alarm was mounting. The older woman placed her hand on the girl's sleeve and said "Plain is perfect Love." Ron was deconstructing the napkin when she felt a hand on her wrist.

"Come on, you didn't come here to fold napkins. Tell me what's really going on with you Love. If you like, after we leave here, we can head to my house for a proper chat. Joe's gone fishing and I have a coal fire set in the grate."

"Sally, I got money," she blurted out.

"You told me that already remember?" A faint caustic wave rippled through her stepmother's tone. Her palms got hotter than hell now. She buried them in the softness of the serviette before bunching it finally between her two hands."I mean serious money."

Sharon dropped over the coffee. Sally smiled graciously. Ron fell silent and didn't look up. Sharon gave an inscrutable backward glance as she headed to the counter to take payment from the only other lady in the café, "Serious money Sal." Sally let the words fall under their own weight as she echoed slowly, "Serious money."

"Oh Sal, just drink up that Cappuccino fast and we'll go back to your place."

"What! and not savour the chocolate flakes, not to mention that she got the heart on top," the English woman teased. The intrigue in her eyes was headlined behind the banter. Ron sprint drank her coffee. The acidity hit the back of her throat. God, she'd excoriated it too many times. Sally sipped quietly, but with some urgency.

CHAPTER 11

Joe and Sally's place on the shores of Lough Melvin was very modern, all grey cut stone, floor to ceiling double- glazed windows which sparkled in the reflected light from the lake. Their private apartments were upstairs. Downstairs had been given over to the community. The Manchester woman got a quiet satisfaction from seeing the living room host the Country Market on a Friday, the Lake Writers and Comhaltas on a Wednesday. Tuesday mornings before Easter had been given over to Ron's back- to back- Yoga and Chakradance classes.

Sally was waiting for her in the spacious apartment upstairs. Back from his fishing, Joe had been sent to Flaherty's pub to watch a replay of Aston Villa versus Real Madrid. "He asked no questions," she told Ron, "or at least I didn't answer any." Ron was fascinated by the quiet English woman's obvious command of her father's new life. It was a faint breath of light years across the universe from his old one. "OK, tell me everything before you fall asleep on the couch." Ron had surrendered graciously to the pull into an ocean of soft brown leather. Sally plumped up the cream Harrod's cushions behind her back. She took off her black Skechers and circled her toes deep into two small white and blue patterned Persian rugs at her feet. The Texan -style fireplace with its low beamed mantelpiece crackled with light as a volcanic amount of turf and two small fire logs ignited.

Ron took one of the cushions, and pulled it around her chest for a hug. Then she launched into her story, starting with a small wound up selection of words and growing her tale from that. When she'd finished, with Sally interjecting occasionally for clarity, there was silence in the room. Through the open window, they could hear the relentless lapping of the waters, punctuated by the moaning of the wind which disturbed Joe's small boat at the jetty. The high- pitched cry of a wild duck penetrated the room. Sally and Joe had noticed her nesting in the weeds on an island in the middle of the lake. The fire had begun to die down.

"Have you discussed all this with Brendan Love?"

"Yes," Ron said with a huge sigh. She mangled the cushion until the corners folded into the middle, "He's fine with it,"- well € 24,000 of it anyway- she thought to herself. "Have I ever told you about Brendan's birth?"

"Hang on," Sally replied. She emptied the creel of turf into the fire, adding on a couple of more small logs. Then she disappeared into the dining room, returning with a blue cashmere throw. "I'll ring Joe and tell him to collect Brendan from school. We'll have the night to ourselves."

Sally fed her before they started into the heavy stuff. For a woman of ample frame, she ate lightly, but well. Joe liked a good steak, but Sally was limiting the red meat. They had tuna salad and boiled potatoes. She relished the food. She exhaled silently the exhilarating and simultaneously terrifying waves her mind had been surfing since the news of the inheritance. Over two cups of chamomile tea and flapjacks for dessert, they fell silent. An epiphany of evening light poured into the room. Ron noted the large white lilies draping themselves over an alabaster vase on an antique table by the wall next to the door. "What type of lilies are those Sal?"

"They're a peace lily Love. I get a regular order from Bretts in Sligo."

She said nothing for a moment. "Kind of a spider's web," she said finally. Sally looked at her.

"That's not something I would have associated with them."

Ron flushed. "I mean the kind of good web that draws you in."

"Ah, I get you now. I love their energy and so does your dad." She thought back to all the drama of their lives and nodded. Da was pouring the softness of these lilies into Brendan. She focused on them as she unlocked the door to her past, and allowed the woman her father had met online to pass through. It took nearly three hours to tell, allowing for rounds of weeping, banking up the fire, and Sally insisting she catch her breath."Breathe Love. I'll join you. I've been doing a little meditation myself online." At intervals, when the story became too rocky, Sally prompted her to just allow the breath to flow, whilst calmly rubbing her back. Gradually, her ragged breath merged with Sally's in a new softness. They used two full boxes of Kleenex between them.

It was Halloween 1999; she'd just turned sixteen the week before. Adam was almost twenty. He had announced he was gay. Joe took it hard. Adam taunted him. "You're not modern, I've lots of gay friends. Their parents are cool with it, but then they're more upmarket than you aren't they?" She remembered her da's anger hardening his eye muscles, the rhythm of his fists opening and closing and her Ma begging him not to react. He acted out instead. Her father got on his Honda 150 roaring off down Emmet Road leading onto the N7. He failed to merge with the traffic; it was 4.30pm and quite dark. Mercifully, the oncoming drivers saw the reflective armband Alice had sewn onto his sleeve. But there was still a collision and an ambulance call out. Ma had left the house that night, her face bleached. Her last injunction to Adam was, "Keep an eye on Ron and only give sweets to the trick -or -treaters before 8." Joe was in the ICU. Ron opened her eyes, and glanced up at Sally's face; Sally was suffering."Did he tell you much of this?"

"Oh, something of it Love," the other woman said, her voice trying to maintain a neutral tone against a counterpoint of edgy distress. "He still feels guilty to this day. But he didn't fill me in entirely. I want to hear your side."

She didn't know what it was that started her off on her first dismal sexual encounter that night. The mood in the house had been black for months. Adam was coming home most evenings from his first year nursing course slightly drunk. Alice told him he either quit the drink or get out. For the week leading up to that night, he appeared sober. But what nobody realised was, that he had a stash of vodka under the bed ,waiting to tip him into a nicely calibrated blurry world. There was also a line of white powder along his dressing table, ready to be combed out by the edge of a letter opener. When the doorbell rang, it was "Pablo" Mangan from Ballydun the next estate, barely divided by a wall from Ron's. "You comin' out?" She took one look back into the darkened house, grabbed her coat and headed out. Adam was snoring on the bed upstairs. Pablo, not his real name, was fifteen. James Mangan was nominated by the chief youth worker from the community centre to be the lead painter of a mural on the dividing wall between Patrician Avenue and Ballydun. All the kids had worked on it the summer before last for three weeks. Though he was only just fourteen at the time, even the drug dealers and the pimps stopped their Mercs to stare at his handiwork."Hey Picasso," one of the pimps shouted out the window one day. "Like your style!" After that, they called him "Picasso," but he said, "Make it Pablo."

Even now, heading out towards the bonfire, she could see the mural to her right in the glow from the fire on the waste ground ahead of her. A large, grey -bodied lion with a thick black mane and haunting slit eyes stared menacingly from the top of a dustbin lid. The wall behind him was bathed in a violet sky. There was an incandescence of planets, moons and stars around him. Lines of thick black paint dripped from the animal's underbelly. Just above the blackness, a padlock and key had been painted on his shanks. When she asked Pablo why the lock and key, he shrugged. Then she remembered his big brother Jacko was just out of "*The Joy.*"

The bonfire was sprinting flames into a mushy night sky, emptied of stars. The weather was mild. She could pick out individual silhouettes as she approached. Jacko was there. He was nineteen and very good- looking. Her friend Rosita from number 38 was there with her boyfriend Johnny. Others, she didn't recognise. Most of them were in their twenties and thirties. Rosita made room for her on a long wooden bench that Johnny had found in the schoolhouse skip. He was on a work placement there. Jacko, standing over at the other side of the fire, was throwing the last of a dismembered table onto the flames. "Jaysus man, watch it for f*cks sake. It's too high," a male voice shouted. Jacko ignored him. "He's just a bad tempered cock sucker," Johnny whispered to Rosita. Already, two flagons of cider were being passed around the circle. When it came to her turn ,she shook her head. Suddenly Jacko's eyes fired full on into her. "Go on Ron, afraid of your Ma are yeh?" His gaze swam the length of her hypnotically. She felt the heat rise in her alongside a small thrill of burgeoning sexual pleasure. "You don't have to," Pablo said quietly beside her. Still under Jacko's gaze, she accepted the flagon, and raised it nervously to her lips. The cold sweet rush of the alcohol burned her with courage, and she took a longer swig. "Ah da girl," he said encouragingly.

She felt rather than saw Pablo shift on the seat beside her. She lost track of time after that. Someone passed around a white powder on a silver foil chocolate wrapping. It had been raked into fine lines. Pablo looked at her enquiringly as she handled it. Floating on a heady tide, she beamed at him. Hesitantly he did a line, before handing it awkwardly to her. Jacko's eyes were riveted on both of them. Initially, the powder irritated her throat. She spluttered. Then she closed her eyes. A sudden surge of confidence swept over her. She knew Jacko found her physically attractive. She became aware of the pertness of her breasts, her thighs. Excitement flooded her. She left them all behind. The mural on the wall to her right grew a new streak of blood. The purple sky shimmered in the firelight. She rose out of her body, and but for Pablo would have stepped into the fire. "I'm coming over to you Jacko," she shouted. There were heated cries around her now. She was carried on a tribal stream. The cat calls and whistles grew to fever pitch. Walls of people parted before her; whispers had a goblin- like clarity. The fire crackled intensely in her eardrums. Jacko stared at her with glazed eyes as she reached her arms up to his neck. Then cupping her breasts, he began to move his body and hers together in a blended sensual rhythm. Suddenly she was acutely aware of his groin. Male nearness was new to her. Alice had kept her away from the more forward girls in the area. Then without warning, he threw her backwards. A pile of dead leaves sashaying in the wind became her bed. There were more cat calls and hoots of laughter. The birch trees absorbed her humiliation, spinning around her. She stumbled from the flames. She didn't hear Pablo's feet resound on the pavement. She heard no voice, until he caught her as she almost tripped over a lat that had been left out for firewood; his breath was on her neck. "Let's get out of here. I know some place we can go."

He took her to a squat not far from his house. He threw stones at an upper window. A light came on; a voice shouted out, "Who is it?"

"Pablo Mangan."

In answer, they heard feet on the stairs and a key turn in the lock. The door opened an inch, and a boy of about seventeen looked out at them. His thin blonde hair was limp and his eyes were unfocused. When he saw Ron, he paused and looked over his shoulder into the dark hallway. "Who's outside?" a voice called out.

"A couple of me friends from school," the boy answered. An older man in his forties came to the door. He looked surprisingly well dressed and clean- shaven.

"You should go home Love," he said to Ron.

"She has nowhere to go," Pablo lied .

The man looked at Ron searchingly and then thought better of it. His thin shoulders gave a battered shrug. Then he turned his back on the teenagers and retreated inside. The lad beckoned them in. He took them straight up the carpeted staircase which somebody had hoovered. The threads on the red carpet were untangling at their feet. Ron almost tripped on the landing. The boy, not seeming to notice, showed them into a front room with five mattresses on the floor. Only one wasn't made up with sheets and pillows. Light came from the low- watt bulb dangling naked from where the plaster was peeling away in the middle of the ceiling. There were a couple of broken chairs at either end of the room with clothes heaped in a scrawny mess on top. She averted her gaze from the pile of dirty male underwear on the one nearest the door. There was a sour unwashed smell in the room. Wardrobe doors hung to one side, as hinges had given away at the top. She barely remembered afterwards noticing labelled tin boxes on the floor.

"That's for our personals," the lad said following her gaze. "There's a padlock on each one; Nico, that's the guy downstairs, made 'em; he used to be a metal worker. You've privacy in here anyway," he grinned, pointing to the grimy roller blind, which flapped loosely against the window. "Springs are broken," he said, lightly touching it. Seeing the teenagers' petrified look , he said, "Don't worry, most of them are out. They won't be back 'til near morning." Then the boy said suddenly, struck by his own one- off pleasing inspiration."I have the honeymoon suite if youse'd like." They looked at him blankly. Ron was still finding it hard to come into focus. He seemed to be swaying. Then she heard her own voice say, "Go on show it to us."

They followed the boy into a box room, piled high with cardboard boxes.

"I could take these out and put the spare mattress in for youse."

Ron looked for the first time at Pablo. He looked scared too. She squeezed his hand."That's fine." she said. "Go on do that." The boy motioned to Pablo to help him.

Alone in the box room with the bare mattress, they looked at each other unseeing. Ron pulled the ragged, grey curtains, coughing at the thick nicotine smell from them. For a while, they sat on the mattress, helpless, unsure, feeling the drug beginning to wane. Ron felt a heaviness grab hold of her limbs. Suddenly Pablo was pushing white powder against her nose. "Jacko gave it to me," he said in a tight voice that had lost its owner. He snorted it first. Then she took it in her hand and did the same. Its whiteness glowed in the darkness of the room. They didn't put on the light. A glimmer of reflected street lamps pushed needles of wintry light in through the half -pulled curtains.

She barely remembered afterwards reaching for Pablo and drawing him on top of her. He responded awkwardly at first, then hungrily. She felt the sharp pain, as he came and let out a small vixen - like cry. Afterwards they just lay there, not daring to face one another. He felt for her hand in the darkness and they slept.

It was the call of male voices shouting downstairs that woke them. They heard as if through a fog, a pounding up the stairs and banging on the door. Morning light was fingering the bedroom. Ron sat upright, her head pounding. She couldn't discern if the pounding were outside or inside."Ron,you in there Love?" It was a concerned male voice, her Uncle Alfie. His son John was with him. She stumbled to the door to open it. Then she remembered too late. Her jeans were scrambled up at the end of the mattress. Pablo was sitting up wide- eyed, super alert now and frightened as hell. Before she could get into her trousers, the door was pushed in hard. She grabbed the bedspread to kill her nakedness from the waist down.

Alice was at home waiting. Her face was sepulchral, her eyes hollowed out orbs ringed with shadow. She met her daughter's eyes and emitted a soft cat- like wail before she took her hand and kissed her repeatedly on each cheek in turn.

"Will I get the wife over?" Alfie asked. Alice didn't reply. Instead, she led her daughter up the stairs like a very old lady, one step after another. It was the longest procession of their lives.

CHAPTER 12

"Joe told me what happened to Pablo," Sally said softly looking over at Ron on the couch. Ron didn't hear her as her body moved in a wave under the blue cashmere throw. Sally had persuaded her finally to lay down half way through the narrative. She covered her tenderly. She was about to repeat the question when a tiny, shadowed voice emerged from under the covers.

"Yeah, he died."

The grandfather clock in the corner of the room ticked ponderously before it struck. By the time it had finished, Ron was looking up at Sally. Tears were frozen high up on her cheekbones. "He was out joyridin' down the Ballymount Estate a week later. The guards were chasin' a group of them. He was in the front, when they ran into a big industrial wall round the old steel factory. The driver was paralysed. The other two guys in the back had to have several operations in Tallaght. Pablo was in the front. He was dead by the time the paramedics got there." Suddenly Sally knelt on the ground in front of Ron. "Come here to me Love." Ron found herself swept up fiercely into the other woman's embrace. Sally's ample breasts brushed against her flushed cheeks, and she drank in the motherhood. The murmur of the lakes infiltrated the room. There was a soft hurrying sound of evening traffic in the wind outside. The raggle- taggle of birch trees around the lake were lonesome outlines through a crack in the floor to ceiling wool curtains.

"He never knew he was a dad; he was killed before I found out I was pregnant." She ovalled her index finger round her belly button. Then she stretched both arms up, pushed back the throw, swivelled sideways and dangled her bare feet on the floor. "Ma wanted the morning- after- pill, but Da wouldn't hear of it. So we crossed our fingers like they all do in Dobbinstown."

Sally smiled, "So it didn't work?."

"Nah, Brendan decided he'd like to have a go at living on Planet Earth, so he popped into me womb just to say "hello". Then he settled down." There was silence as the fire logs began to hiss and split. The evening light was waning; it was time to light the lamps.

"A month after the funeral, I missed me period. That's when we found out. The evening Ma and I came home from the doctor, I told her I had to go out again to visit me friend Sharon and I'd be back soon. I ran like a mad thing out the front door before she could ask any questions. I went straight over to Pablo's Ma and Da. I wanted them to know a piece of him would still be around.

"What happened?"

Ron's eyes moved into the middle distance.

"They said I was a cheap little trollop and a dirty bitch." She was crying again quietly now to herself. She felt the placenta of a dead energy ooze from her body.

"And I believed it; I thought I was cheap and dirty until I talked about it with Margie - you know, the counsellor we all went to. Did Da tell you?" Sally nodded sagely.

They sat by the fire for the rest of the night, barely speaking. Words could find no outline to fit their shared sorrow. Brendan and Joe were another world away in the cottage. Sally made more cocoa; Ron sipped it gratefully, but refused any more food. Then she slept on the couch. Sally brought out more blankets and slept in the big recliner chair next to her.

It was after nine next morning, when Sally began to stir. Ron vaguely wondered where she was at first, pushing back the heavy layers of blankets. Brendan raced across the canvas of her mind. "Oh God, Brendan," she murmured.

"Joe and Brendan stayed together last night," Sally said. "Your Da rang late, but you were out for the count."

Sally headed out to the kitchen to make breakfast. Ron hauled herself off the couch, and looked at her sunken eyes in the gilt-edged mirror over the fireplace.

"Take a shower Love, if you like. You can use the ensuite," Sally called out. "There are fresh towels on the bed."

The water from the hot shower splayed itself over her body. She soaped her breasts gently, the breasts of a once sixteen-year-old mother and now those of a thirty-two-year-old woman. She touched her private parts tenderly, once the portal through which her son came. It was Margie who told her never to feel her body was dirty. She bunched up the five fingers of her right hand, kissed their tips, then touched every corner of herself with them, sending tactile blessings to her womanhood as the counsellor had encouraged.

They didn't turn on the radio. Cleopatra (Sally and Joe's black Labrador) laid her big haunches between their legs. Ron placed her palm on top of the dog's head, feeling her silent empathy. Sally had made pancakes. They realised they were both starving. A generous helping of maple syrup was lined up on the side of each plate.

"My girth is expanding," the English woman said smiling. "And you're to blame Miss O'Connell."

Her mobile rang on the kitchen table."It's Joe," she said. "Do you want to talk to him?" Ron nodded.

"Hi Da, sorry for landing Brendan on you last night."

"That's no problem Love. How are things?"

"Things are great," she said, casting a glance at Sally. "Things just couldn't be better."

There was a silence at the other end,"Are you still there?"

" Yeah, yeah."

She couldn't be sure, but it sounded like he had a head cold.

"Got to go here now. That young fella of yours got the bus anyway. He'll be home early this evening."

Sally was beaming a full headlight of tenderness on her now. A shaft of sunlight caught her in a headlock as she sipped her coffee at the broad pine table. She was approaching sixty and kept her ample figure under control by what she called her "slime diet" and walking.

"She drinks that green chlorine," Joe said to Ron one day. Sally had spat out her coffee when he said this.

"Chlorella Love. I don't drink chlorine; that's for swimming pools."

Ron looked at her appraisingly now. She was about 5'5" in height. A heart shaped face framed two large frank blue eyes and a strong straight boned nose. She had a slight double chin and a mild rosiness across wide cheek bones. Her unruly blonde hair fell disarmingly around her ears. Wednesdays, she had it styled in Sligo. Sally was real modern with her black leggings and high boots under a loose sway- tailed, black pinafore. Alice would have loved her. Suddenly aware of Ron's scrutiny, she began to fussily collect the plates. Reaching out in her confusion to collect a cup, Ron stayed her hand. Then she said so softly that Cleopatra asleep under the table stirred understandingly.

"Thanks for being so good to us. I wish you could'a met me Ma."

Sally looked at her. The two women's eyes plumbed each others before either of them spoke again.

"It would have been an honour to have shared a brew with the woman who reared this fantastic daughter." She squeezed Ron's hand so tight, that her ring finger pressed once more with a fierce kindness into the palm of her hand, leaving a small red weal for days after.

Brendan was home early that afternoon; he decided not to study at Lorcan's for once. He gave his mother a "tell- all" look with his eyes.

"You alright Ma? Granda never stays over now since Sally moved down."

Then lightning struck.

102

"You and Sally have a big girlie thing going on or what?"

Ron smiled.

"Yeah, definitely a big girlie thing Love".

After they'd washed up together and were sitting at the kitchen table, she decided to tell him about her LWG. fund idea. It had kept her awake most of the night. She began by bringing in the large globe from the small side table in the sitting room.

"Twirl it around," she said to his astonished face, "and close your eyes."

His body, parcelled up in a strange scrutiny, he did what he was told. He twirled it first; then she tried it. He turned it again.

"That's the power of three," she said. "That should be enough."

They stood there for a moment,seeing where his fingers had landed and both promptly burst out laughing.

"Ma, we're in the bleedin' Atlantic."

"That's us, always up the creek without a paddle, but no more young man, no more."

Next, she asked his permission to take one of his school copybooks out of his bag. She looked at it, before writing across the cover in capital letters LWG.

"That's me essay copy! The guys will slag me."

"We'll cover it. It's the perfect copy though."

"What are the letters for?" he asked, frustrated now.

"LW G. means "Live With Gusto"- you know, give it socks, give it welly. Really enjoy life."

A snarl of thoughts congested his features. The comedian in him began to lift his large black eyebrows up and down, Groucho Marx style.

"OK Groucho, I get it. Now let me explain."

Then she began to lay out the bones of her great idea for her only son. They talked about it for over two hours - how he would ask three important people in his life where he should go in the world with his mother's money. Then, hopefully he would take their advice and go to those places. She would meet up with him in his final destination, if he had no objection. The time frame was hazy, but Ron suggested either straight after Leaving Cert or taking a gap year out of college perhaps.

"That's if I go to college," he said.

"What do you mean if? The English teacher says you should get an A in your Junior Cert and the other teachers are following on the same lines. What did you tell the principal again in first year?"

He blushed slightly at the memory. "Ah Ma, I told you this before."

"Well humour me Love. I forget some of it".

She actually remembered it word for word; the story was silhouetted in every dark corner of her mind.

" Mr.O Halloran took our English class one day. He made me and Eamo sit together up at the front. Then he wrote on the whiteboard the title of an essay, "Where I see myself ten years from now".

"And you wrote?"

" I wrote I'd be a fella in Trinity like John O Heaney down the road in St. Ita's Park, that Gran used to tell me about."

"And Eamo?" she prompted softly, after he'd gone silent.

"Eamo wrote he'd be in *The Joy.*"

"Jail isn't too far off for him from what we hear from Dublin."

She wasn't sure why she inserted that piece of information, but maybe subconsciously she needed an extra deterrent, especially given their new status.

" Anyway, Mr. O Halloran took up the essays, and said to me next day when he handed back mine, after keepin' it til last,

" Nice one O Connell, but it's a "Fellow" of Trinity College. Come back and speak to us when that happens".

Yes indeed, she thought; she was already mentally picking out his suit for the occasion.

" Now," she said with a sudden briskness, getting up off the chair.

" Fellows of Trinity College had to study a lot, so get to the bedroom."

He emerged twenty minutes later; she was in the sitting room.

"I can't study Ma. You sure you won't need all this money for yourself?"

"Don't worry Love. I'll hopefuly get the SNA job by September; we'll manage."

"God forgive me,"she thought.

" I'll work me way around Europe anyway."

There was an awkward silence; he began to crack his knuckles. He sat on the edge of the armchair beside the fire, studying the blackened ruts in the floorboards.

"All this money got me thinkin'; we'd never have been able to do this before."

"Do you miss Dobbinstown?" she asked, screwing down her breath a fraction.

He shook his head definitively.

"I was just thinking, you know, about the other crowd - Da's lot."

She'd never hidden who his father was. She used to tell him as a child how they called his da "Picasso." When he went to school, he told his teachers he was so good at art because his father was Picasso. That took a little explaining to his Junior Infant teacher. Over the years of his growing up, she had never given him the details of his conception, and somehow he never asked. Joe in particular was never comfortable with the rawness of it. Now, finding her base chakra, she decided this was the opportunity she had been waiting for to finally tell him about the Halloween night she and Pablo got together. He already knew about the squat. Trigger had filled him in. When he came home upset, Alice's reaction at the time was to tell his seven- year- old self a fairy tale version in which Pablo and Ron were the heroes and he, the marvellous appearance on Earth nine months later. Now she gave a more honest account, unsure exactly how much he had heard in the estate. She omitted the sordid bits, still presenting it with a veneer of respectability.

"We were young and we were kind," she said looking into the fire. She sensed him stirring on the chair opposite."Your Da was lovely and a little unsure of himself. We didn't plan on getting pregnant, but now I think I got the most amazing gift when I look at you."

She dared to look him in the eye. He fed her a quiet candid look; his body had lost its caged hardness. Then he jumped up.

"I'll just put more coal on the fire."

As he tipped the coal scuttle over the grate, he said, "The guys on the road used to call me "squat baby" the time all the jeering went on, and you started to pick me up. I punched Mikey Green's lights out over that. They didn't mess with me again"

The strong set of his jawline was an inheritance, "handy with his fists too," she thought, in a justifiable war.

"I didn't listen to them; I'm listening now though, and I think me Da was really a genius from what you tell me."

"Now let's hit the sack; you still have school tomorrow," she said smiling.

There was a crescent moon marbled with a very bright light when she looked out the top landing at 2am, unable to sleep.

"Pablo and Alice," she murmured. "You're out there somewhere. Watch our backs."

The moon retreated behind the cloud, and then she watched it return with a strange luminosity. The dark sky was blessed by it and morning rain hovered on the wind.

CHAPTER 13

She realised she'd never finished the text she'd been sending to Doyler. This week the gospel of her life to date had been seriously edited. On Thursday night she rang him. He answered instantly.

"Thought you'd gone off me. Was it something I said?"

The heat rose in her chest again. She scratched at it irritatedly. "Oh no, you were perfect."

Her last word exploded onto the phone like her breath had detonated it.

"Well that's a relief anyhow. So if that's how you treat your perfect boyfriends, I'd hate to see the poor fellows who don't measure up."

"They're all dead," she said in a lightening monotone. He emitted a low hoot of laughter. She forgot to scratch.

"So are you free tomorrow night? I could pick you up."

"Yes please. Sorry for the mix up. I can explain. It's complicated I warn you."

"I'm used to complicated," he said.

The date was dreamy. They went to the Peony Court in Manorhamish this time. Doyler had made reservations.

"So?" he said when they got to the coffee.

"What's going on that left me poor self-esteem in tatters?"

"Eanna, I'm so sorry." I can explain, honest to God."

"Honest to God? It must be serious."

She loved when the green fleck of his eyes invaded hers interestedly. His eyes were very interested just now. She began with her mother's love of poetry, and her days with the *Young Tallaght Actors*. She moved her narrative skilfully through the night at The Gate and fast- forwarded to Brendan's Communion.

"So she sends £20 and a rosary?"

He sipped his latte very slowly, brushing his upper lip with a thin white line of cream. She giggled.

"You've a moustache."

His eyes never left her face.

"Go on, the rosary and the cash."

"OK, I'll speed it up."

So she launched into the letters from the London solicitors: Number one, the initial gift cheque and two, the final shocker on Monday.

"She left us ..."

He put his hand up to her lips. "Ron, you don't need to tell me; I didn't ask you out for your money."

At this, he coughed and looked away a little embarrassed. She felt the fire rise furiously in her cheeks. A little overwhelmed, she pushed her chair back and studiously watched the door as a young couple came in. The guy held the door open for the girl.

"Ron, I'm sorry. That didn't come out right. I didn't mean to upset you. You've had a hectic week and I just want you to deal with all this in your own time. You don't owe me explanations you know," She turned back to him, tears spattering her cheeks.

"I never expected any of this in any lifetime."

"How many have you had?" he mocked gently.

"Dunno." she smiled.

"Anyway," he said more breezily,

"All this because of a woman and her seventeen- year- old daughter taking pity on a stranger on a dark night in Dublin?"

"I guess so."

Then she paused."I don't know, but if it's karma, maybe me Ma might have passed it on to me sooner rather than later." His smile was a hot sunrise burning off the fog that had arisen from her fears.

Afterwards she worried should she have told him so much, but she was like that. Alice often scolded her."You're just like your da -

can't keep a secret." She had sworn him to secrecy, and loved him for not wanting to know how much. She needed to befriend the amount herself for a long time to come. When they parted at her door, he refused to come in, pointing to the light in the downstairs bedroom window. She felt a small relief invade her, and a tingle of regret too. Instead, he moved under the stoop of the timber porchway to kiss her. The circling forest of white carriage lights around their faces cleared the shadows. The depth of her feelings caught her off guard. They kissed again, their lips, each a stairwell of the other. When they finally broke off, her ears were ringing and her body ached in an unfamiliar way. "I'll ring tomorrow and answer me this time," he said.

Then he ran out into the night onto the roadway where his car was parked. As she watched his greyhound figure with the tied- back red hair and the green, belted coat disappear down the gravel path, he turned and waved. She waved back slowly and thought to herself, "He's bloody gorgeous."

She rang him early next morning."I couldn't start the day without chattin' to yeh this time," she said. She heard his chuckle down the line. They agreed to meet up Monday evening after he'd finished his day's teaching. "Ma and Ailbhe are here for a couple of days, so I'm tied up, he said by way of apology. She paused before she said, "They're lucky to have you. Me and Adam... well he's in San Francisco now, but things are improving between us." Suddenly she heard the dulled sound of water splashing and press doors closing downstairs. "Got to go here Eanna. Have to get that lad of mine fed before training."

"He's a brilliant goalie, well worth feeding."

"His football boots will grow wings down at the pitch when he hears you said that." She sensed his smile as she slid the phone icon across.

While Brendan was at training, she rang Joe to come over. She saw the compassion pooled in his eyes as soon as his 6' 2" frame ducked under the kitchen lintel. "Always have to do that," he said dramatically, patting the top of his head. "Can't damage the little bit of sawdust that's left in there now, can I, after all the years of boxing?"

She made him coffee, and a chamomile for herself. She played around with the tip of the teaspoon, stirring her tea exaggeratedly.

"I suppose you're wondering why I told Sally first and not you?"

To her surprise, an expansive smile coursed through the furrows on his cheeks.

"I'm glad you did Love. Sally is a good un." She raised her eyebrows mockingly.

"Oh Manchester speak is it now these days?" He grinned at her, and placed his large hands on the table, before coyly sliding them across to cover hers. She felt their strength infuse her. "Sometimes women need to talk to each other," she said. He paused. She knew he and Sally had discussed everything last night.

"She told me you had a long night. Sally's not a talker, so you can always confide in her Ron. I'm here for you too you know and I'm sorry, sorry for being such an immature eejit that night." His shoulders caved onto his chest until his confined breath escaped tiredly. Suddenly she stood up and placed her hands on top of his head. Her fingertips touched the damp sweat forming on his bald patch. "Some things turn out for the best don't they?" she said quietly. "The best thing that ever happened to me is down there on the football pitch. And it's good to know I have me da too, me rock of Gibraltar nowadays."

Without saying another word, she opened the kitchen drawer to take out something she never possessed before.

"This," she said airily, "is a cheque book. Take note."

He looked at her curiously. "It's me first one ever. I'm going to write you a cheque for €1,000." Before he could protest, she continued, "It's a down payment on €20,000 for a new boxing club in Kilindara."

"But you haven't got anything yet."

"Yes, I have €5,000 remember? well 4,200 to be precise and that's Sterling. I know you want to start one here and many lads need it. It'll keep a few young fellas out of trouble. The culchies do drugs too, you know."

"But you're going to need the money."

"All £300,000 Sterling?" she mocked.

He smiled a quiet acquiescence, and opened his palms in a deferential gesture."Maybe." She wrote the cheque at the kitchen table. He sat there in silence, twiddling his new tweed cap in his hands. "This money could change you and the lad," he said suddenly." Just be steady with it." Then he bolted off the chair to empty the washing machine for her. "Where's that basket of yours for the clothes?"

"Da, Da stop," she said putting one arm around his comforting belly from behind, and nestling her face into the broad of his back. With the other hand she placed the cheque on the draining board beside him. He pocketed it and planted a kiss on her forehead.

"I won't let it change us," she said simply. "Before you go," she said, sensing he was heading for the doorway. "I have something to ask you." To his surprise, she brought out the wooden globe from the sitting room and placed it firmly on the table.

" Now," she said to Joe, "close your eyes and twirl it fast." He gave her a sceptical look, but obeyed. This time, with the delicate precision of the two forefingers on her right hand, she steadied the turntable twirling that Joe's hands had initiated . Joe opened his eyes and followed the downward trajectory of his daughter's.

"It's America," she said flatly.

"That's a big continent Love. Who's going there?"

"Your grandson ... we hope."

She refilled his coffee mug, and helped herself to another chamomile. Slowly she elucidated her great plan, her LWG fund.

Joe had trouble afterwards remembering just what she called it when telling Sally.

"He's going to ask three people where he should go. Mind you, he thinks I only have €24,000 euro, so not a word. I was afraid if I told him the whole amount, he mightn't handle it too well- you know, given our former life. I didn't actually tell Sally that bit, that he doesn't know the whole amount." Joe's face shadowed uncomfortably for a moment, but then he nodded slowly.

"Gotcha. For what it's worth, I agree. Let him get used to it in small doses. Big money can be heavy medicine at his age. Let him get used to making his own way in the world first"

"So, where should he go then, because he will ask you? You'll be number one on the list." A smile creamed off the edge of her father's eyes.

"I've only ever been to London and Manchester Love, and I wouldn't tell him to go there. Tell you what though, I'll ask Sal. She'll probably say Rome or Paris. I'll pretend it's me own idea," he said excavating the furrows in his forehead again.

"I've more news for you as well," she said, wincing as she burned her upper lip with the hot tea.

"Oh yeah?" he said suspiciously, as if expecting some kind of deflation in the good news finally.

"Yeah I'm eh, I'm eh... going out with Doyler." She lowered her eyes and blew slightly over the rim of the teacup. She lifted them in response to his hand on her shoulder. She looked up; his eyes were a cocktail of relief and pleasure.

"Ah the girl," he said; "he's a good un."

She giggled."I'll tell him that Da."

"You do that Love.You do that," he repeated slowly to himself.

"Now I better be off. The missus will be lookin' for me."

Their silence was comfortable, as she helped him put on his grey fleece and then slip on his High -Vis jacket. She handed him his bicycle clips from the top of the bannisters. As he pedalled off down the ribbon of a road, she thought, " how much better than blasting his way onto the N7 on a Honda 150".

Brendan returned that afternoon. She barely remembered to light the fire before he came in. So much was buzzing around in her head, she felt her thoughts would crack her skull open. Once exposed, they'd lay on the floor in front of her son buzzing around like bees in a honeycomb. When she described how she felt to Doyler on Monday, he laughed appreciatively."Not a bad analogy at all," he said. She didn't like to ask him what an analogy was. Looking at her son now, she could see he was all fired up. He was pacing the kitchen floor, like the soles of his shoes needed a good wearing out, before finally turning to look at her.

"I just rang me old primary school teacher Mr. Devlin. He was big into geography and cool places in fifth class."

"How did you do that?" she began baffled.

"Had his number when I left Dobbinstown. You remember the party they held for us in the boxing club?"

"And he was there?"

"Yeah, do you remember, he coached under 13 and he knows Grandad?"

"Oh yeah, I remember him now."

"Anyway, he gave me his number in case I ever needed it."

Seeing her mystified look, he grinned, his brown eyes electrified. "I didn't tell you in case, maybe... I don't know... maybe, I shouldn't have a teacher's number."

"C'mere." She pulled him in for an awkward hug. "Where did Mr. Devlin think you should go?" she said on releasing him, enjoying his discomfiture.

"Machu Picchu."

"Machu where?"

"You'd love it Ma," he said earnestly.

"It's all about women power. Will we google it?"

They spent two hours online and let the fire go out. They got dinner for a second time from McAdrews. Their heads emigrated from Leitrim to YouTube before they hit their pillows.

CHAPTER 14

Looking back, she wondered where the last eight months had flown to. Hard to believe they had reached December and not just accommodated themselves to Leitrim, but actually settled in.This county seemed to have settled them, maybe for the first time ever she thought. Brendan had soared in his Junior Cert. "An eagle whose eyrie was destined to be on the cliff top higher than all his friends," Eanna had said. Ron sighed. She couldn't keep up with clever analogies (now that she knew what an analogy was) or brilliant sons either. Brendan's head would require a new hat at the rate his grandfather was boasting about his 6 H1s and 2 H2s down in the pub. That's when she discreetly inquired in Flannerys would they have any weekend work for him. He needed to change a few beer barrels in a damp cellar.

Cian O'Grady had been on the phone last week. After making enquiries from the London solicitors, he expected the inheritance to come through by March or April in the New Year. Even though the portfolio was very extensive, Jean had had her will filed with the Probate Court before she passed. She had already put the will to the back of her mind and packaged it somewhere in there. Once life held the tip of a teaspoon of promise, she was content. Presently, every morning when she thought of Eanna, it offered her a tart sweetness. There was a near perfection to their relationship. Just one thing was lacking yet.

He became part of the family. Joe had probably supplanted Adam with him, she thought ruefully. Speaking of Adam, she would Skype him in a few days time. They'd built up quite an extensive email correspondence in the last four and a half years since he moved to San Francisco. Skype had crept in too. She had planned to call for Christmas Eve. This time she insisted that her father be present.

The cottage glinted these mornings in the raw early December light. The hefty frost of this last week had bleached the window panes and clamped down on the door handles. A new yellow door had been installed only last week. Eanna said they should break open a bottle of champers just to christen it and give a decent send off to the rheumatic piece of oak which had shuddered in the doorway for so long. Sally swung a bottle of champagne off the old door before Eanna and Joe took it off the hinges. The fitters stood by grinning. Then they swiftly began installing its perfect, canary yellow, PVC replacement. Ron poured champagne from a second bottle into glass flutes she'd bought on Done Deal.

"No need to change old habits just yet," she thought.

"Here's to the new door and all who sail in her."

Sally's broad north of England accent carried across the roadway, startling the Healy's sheep who'd wandered close to the stream in front of the cottage. The installers accepted a glass of Schloer apple juice in the kitchen. Brendan just stood there with a big sky face of happiness.

The kitchen wall clock registered 3.30pm. On a weekday, she'd normally be coming in from school at this time. She'd secured the prize of SNA-Special Needs Assistant- in October finally. When she got the job, she told Eanna they were both academics."Whatever you say Professor," he said, selectively removing a maths book from the dining room shelf. He'd continued helping her with her maths since May. She'd only one other Leaving Cert subject under her belt, English, which she had completed in Dobbinstown. Words were music to her ears, as to her mother's. Maths just brought out the pugilist in her. The doorbell rang; it was Eanna with a bunch of maths books under his arm. After an hour of theorems still rumbling through the corridors of her brain, she realised the Eureka moment was elusive. It probably always would be. Finally after the last "But I don't get it," Eanna deluged by her frowns, pushed back the maths

116

books on the kitchen table. A thunder storm was brewing on their shared wavelength. He massaged his closed eyelids, stretching both legs out on the kitchen floor and lifting his arms high above his head. She knew he had been up since six for the farmers' market. A two minute prolonged silence between them was textured with irritation.

"Well I can't help it if numbers aren't me thing!"

she said eventually, more peevishly than she meant.

He began fumbling in his pockets.

"What are you looking for?" she asked exasperatedly, already knowing the answer.

"The last of the fags," he said wearily. "I'll just go outside and have one."

He'd started to smoke again in the last few months.

" You were off them things when we met.

"And you a herbalist," she chided.

He grinned ruefully at her, popping a Benson & Hedges in his mouth and said, "You're bleedin' right Ron."

He was outside so long, she worried he'd catch his death. The December damp was a second skin on the air these days. An emergent fog flowed across the denuded birches around the perimeter fence. She went outside, shining her phone torch. He was standing over in a corner of the garden on a mobile call. He was obviously waiting for someone to get back to him.

"You have availability," he said finally.

She went inside, feeling the cold air tighten around her. A sudden splurge of misery forced its way through to the back of her eyelids. It blew tears in its wake. God, she was so thick and of course he was "Mister Clever School Teacher". Then she heard the sound of his feet on the gravel. She pushed the tissue out from up her sleeve and wiped her eyes in small agitated circles.

"Ron, you alright ?" He sounded concerned.

His tone lowered the drawbridge. A thermal spring pushed up from inside her. He moved to the sink where she was standing, kettle in hand. Gently he untangled the flex from her hands, which she had grabbed onto reflexively.

"Come on Love" he said guiding her to the table. "What's wrong?"

"You and your bloody maths; you're a teacher and I never finished school. Just another Dobbinstown single mother, another barmaid that's all."

He went silent for a moment; then he took her hand softly.

"Now listen Veronica O'Connell; you are some woman: feisty, brave, intelligent, kind. I'm a teacher, because the aunts and uncles in England paid for everything in college for me. I'm lucky I'm a man, so I couldn't get pregnant in Dobbinstown, now could I?" She looked at him, cautiously beginning to shed the high wire tension in her nerves. She could feel the damp splodges of her mascara half way down her cheeks now. He kissed her tenderly on the lips. She closed her eyes; he kissed her eyelids too. The mountain outside advanced into the kitchen lifting her to the summit.

"Why don't we leave the damn maths books and maybe you know...?"

he said, pointing in the direction of the stairs. They'd never made love, which her girlfriends in Dobbinstown couldn't credit.

"The time isn't right yet," she always said a little cattily, "and he's prepared to wait".

"Brendan!" she said suddenly.

"Can he stay with Joe and Sally?" he asked anxiously.

She picked up her mobile.

"Da, can you pick up Brendan off the bus from Sligo? He's been Christmas shopping. Me and Eanna have to em... go some place."

There was a moment of silent configuration from Joe at the other end.

"You and Doyler have a lovely time love. We'll collect Brendan, don't worry."

She turned on the night light in the hallway, before they headed up the stairs. The fire was roaring in the sitting room and the back boiler was on. She forgot to draw the front room curtains, leaving everything to the shadows from the table mountain outside. He helped her undress in the darkened room. She felt the wobbly heart beating in her chest again, but it was friendlier this time.

"I haven't ..." she began, suddenly self-conscious, as they saw each other naked for the first time. He said, "We'll take it slowly." He caressed her in ways and in places she never thought anyone could, before reaching inside her. She arched her back when he came, touching the lean sinews of his arms. They were two in one now; an illuminated space had gathered around them. Her fumbled encounters in Dobbinstown over the years were a crude imitation of this. The love she didn't believe in,was suddenly made flesh.

They slept eventually, exhausted. When they awoke, he reached for her again and she melted into him. Then they lay there for a while, side by side. His breathing got softer and softer and suddenly she heard a little convoluted snore. She threw back the covers, pulled on a dressing gown and padded barefoot to the small sash window, which was shuddering now in the newly driving rain. The racing clouds in the early night sky held a garish menace as they drove in hard. Nothing stirred outside. The red night light downstairs fingered through the gap- toothed timber bottom of the doorway. It reminded her of the Sacred Heart lamp in her Granny's house as a child. She pictured him then, Jesus with his thorns, his luminous love and his heart on the outside. She imagined him smiling at her. He had lots of thorns. Heat had deserted the room. She shivered and slid back under the covers. Eanna was turned on his side, away from her. She touched her fingers lightly off the small of his back. Then she pulled up the warm duvet around her, touching his bare feet with her own. They woke again at 10pm.;she rang Joe. Eanna left through the front door. Maths books were strewn all over the kitchen table.

He rang her the next morning. Brendan was still in bed. Oddly she felt a little awkward. Unplanned, they had each stepped over an unexpected threshold of the other.

"How would you like a weekend back up in the big smoke?" he asked.

Sensing a certain alarm in her, he said

"We don't have to visit Dobbinstown at all if you'd rather not. I thought it would be very appropriate to stay in a certain hotel."

"What hotel? OMG you don't mean ..."

"The very one."

His voice in her ear was an arrow landing on a distant shore.

"Yep, The Gresham. I have a confirmation email."

"You mean it's booked?"

"Well, only provisionally; I was on a cancellation list for ages."

Hesitancy now climbed into his speech.

"God, I'd love that. Just think what Jean would have to say about it!."

"Jean would be delighted, and she'd probably say, "it's entirely fitting, my dear."

His uncannily accurate upper class English accent was a 180degree flip from his normal Dublin drawl. She chuckled appreciatively.

"Oh Ma would have loved this."

"Then we'll do it in both their honours," he said.

The booking was for three days before Christmas Eve. Timing was perfect; she'd be back in time for the Skype with Adam and Da. She wasn't aware of Brendan in the kitchen until he tapped her on the shoulder. She skyrocketed at his touch. He looked at her wonderingly.

"Good news?"

She nodded, propelled in a new synergy forwards and backwards to The Gresham. He was chuffed at her news as he handled the frying pan and took out the rashers for the Sunday morning fry up. Turning the bacon, he asked over her shoulders with a studied intonation,

"And how was the pictures?"

She looked at him baffled.

"That's where Grandad said ye were going."

She blushed hard, moving the furniture around in her capillaries. Oh God, she'd just made love in the house, under his roof. In Dobbinstown, Joe preferred her to stay over in her boyfriend's house, probably a throwback from the days with Adam and George. Would he judge her? Should she have cleared it with him first? He was sixteen, but maybe they should have sat on the couch and had one of their chats. Then she cleared her throat and said in a strange third party voice,

"Eanna may be coming over a lot more Love. He am might ,might....."

He gave a hugely knowing grin, running his cheeky brown eyes over her flushed cheeks.

"Sure that's mega. He's really cool ...well for a teacher."

Her cheeks moved the furniture back the right way in her capillaries as her skin visibly paled.

"So you're **OK** with that? Sorry I didn't ask you first."

"Ma you don't need my permission; it's cool I swear."

When Eanna came over that afternoon, Brendan let them both off the hook.

"Any night youse'd like to go to the pictures, I can stay over with Grandad."

Eanna looked at Ron, his face a map of rising anxiety.

"It's ok Eanna; he knows."

Her voice was buttered with relief, which she was spreading liberally around her.

Eanna's embarrassed look faded rapidly. He emitted a loud sigh.
"Well, that's good Brendan."
he said, studying the "Man of Aran" print on the kitchen wall above Ron's head.

Neither he nor Brendan made eye contact for the rest of the night, but Brendan made the tea and brought it into the sitting room on a tray.

"One sugar, Eanna, the way you like it," he said, before heading into his room to study.

Just as Eanna was heading out the door round 10pm, Brendan called after him.

"Eanna can you text my email onto your contacts in the Bronx?"
Eanna had long ago suggested to him his second port of call should be New York. Joe had already suggested Rome. Brendan cheekily asked him to thank Sally for that one. He sent his courage to his tongue, not long after his old teacher had become a regular caller at the house. He said little one evening, but produced the globe, as the older man feigned surprise.

"If there was one place in the world you think a young guy like me should visit, where would it be?"

"Are you visiting on your own?" Eanna asked innocently.

"Well maybe, maybe not. Maybe somebody else might like to come and visit in the last place I'll be."

He shot a glance at his mother on the fireside chair, assiduously watching the logs dismember. She continued to watch.

"New York" came the unequivocal reply.

Brendan's eyes lit in a sudden conflagration.

"Cool, I was hoping you'd say that."

Then he poured out his plans for his three world destinations at the feet of this incipient male role model in his home. Eanna listened for the next hour or more and spoke only to interject occasionally with his own experience of living in the Bronx each summer on a J1 visa. Ron made the coffees, creamed with gratitude. The talk flowed.

"You'll love the "Big Apple. It's made for young people and they sure can party. The Bronx has to be experienced. Think NYPD, Blue Bloods, you know- all those dramas. They just touch on it, but man it's raw; it's alive. *New Yorkers*, they walk with you. They have their own story to tell, especially now since 9/11. You can take your Ma to Broadway."

At this Ron cleared her throat,

Ahem.

"I'll be going to Machu Picchu."

"Alright. Well, if you decide to go to New York as well ...just kiddin,"

he said, seeing Brendan's alarm. New York was tossed about and googled. By the time Eanna left at midnight, it was the place to experience. He reminded Brendan he still had two more years in school. Brendan stared at him unseeing.

"Night Ma,"

Brendan said as he closed the stiff bedroom door behind him.

"Night Love," she replied, mounting the stairs holding onto her old hot water bottle with the smell of Joe's talcum powder still on it.

'How did all this come to them? And hadn't he turned out alright, her boy? Yeah, he turned out fine. Jean did call him "Brendan the Navigator" after all, and she would make sure he lived up to the title.

CHAPTER 15

Ron must have packed her suitcase at least four times, putting in outfits then turning them out again.

"Ma, you're not goin' on a cruise,"

Brendan said, putting his head around the bedroom door. "You're going for two nights. I'm heading over to Joe and Sally's to watch the Sky Sports."

She had promised him a Smart TV for Christmas with Sky Sports as an add-on. He was more than happy with that deal.

When he was gone, she caught a glimpse of herself in the long wardrobe mirror.She giggled aloud at the image she made in the midst of scattered waves of dresses on the bed. She was wading through a thicket of jeans and tops at her feet. On impulse, she took a selfie for Instagram to send on to Amy and Jenny. They knew she was coming up. She had conquered her demons around Dobbinstown, talking up a hurricane with Eanna well into the night a week earlier. He often stayed over now a couple of week nights. On alternate weekends, he headed to Dublin to visit his mother and sister.

"You need to have the two worlds spinning around each other," he said, before his breath moved softly over the hot cocoa in front of him.

"It's like the planets, isn't it?"

she said, allowing her fingertips merge gingerly with the steam along the rim of her own mug.

"You have to let each planet follow its own pathway. They're in their own orbit in Dobbinstown and we're in ours. That way the planets don't collide.

"Well, we hope they don't anyway," he said,his voice burrowing into the kitchen floor.

"And what about you and Kelly Ann?" she asked softly.

124

She had stopped cosseting her fingers. Suddenly now the steam bit into them. She withdrew her hand instantly, spreading out her fingers along the tabletop, feeling the cold hardness beneath.

"Will you be able to let that planet stay in its own orbit?"

He looked at her sharply. The wobbly heart dance rose up unexpectedly.

"That's well over Ron; she and I have moved on and are with other people now. You and Brendan are my other people," he said, sliding his hand across the table, twining her fingertips around his in a tight lock. She closed her eyes to feel the granite reassurance in the grip. The tiny LED Christmas tree on the ledge above the telly seconded everything he said, with a halogen glow all along its fake spines. Suddenly Dublin beckoned, a city with a soother in its mouth. Lions with padlocks, and guys with white powders were cruising the nurseries, but just not hers.

She caught her breath as they approached The Gresham. The heavy city traffic had been flowing staccato like in a murky sea of rain and dipped headlights.

"You know, I never thought I'd hear myself say this, but I miss the mountains and the forests already. I feel as if I've been shaking hands with trees for so long now they're talking to me."

Eanna relaxed his concentration and turned on the six o'clock news on the radio. He flashed her a smile. She liked his face immersed in concentration, she thought just then. He gave her a look over the top of his driving glasses which he had angled towards her.

"Well that's one for the books, Veronica."

The hotel frontage appeared before them. It exuded an unobtrusive grandeur with a string of wide arches at the base of the five storey building. Almost giddily, she registered the pure white buds of light pouring down the walls in a sinuous stream from the roof tiles. She closed her eyes; Alice would have loved this. They parked in Thomas Lane car park behind the hotel. She refused point blank to let him drop her off outside the door. At least the rain cried halt as they trundled the luggage to the front door. Once inside, she abandoned all trepidation.

The crystal chandelier above their heads and the beaded fairy lights on the floor to ceiling tree spun Rumplestiltskin's gold. The marble foyer tiles danced away from her with their fluid brown and cream patterns breaking up the contoured shapes beneath their feet. She stood frozen for a moment. She remembered the chandelier now from before. It was the same explosion of light and cut glass that had mesmerised her at seventeen.

"You OK?" Eanna touched her hand lightly.

"Just remembering," she whispered. "I'm grand now."

Then impishly, she pointed at the tree in the middle of the space.

"Do you think we could bring some of them pine cones home for our own tree?"

He gave her a look of mock horror.

"Veronica, please!."

"I bet it happens; even posh people have their little strangenesses you know."

Then, catching a glimpse of a hovering porter looking at them, she suddenly felt a prickle of heat all over. She began to scratch through her jumper. "Should we let him take up our luggage do you think?" she asked, suddenly engaging the young porter in an ice-melter of a smile.

"Well we could, and he might even nick a pine cone or two for us as well"

Eanna said now with a big grin. She gave him a playful push.

"Go 'way you bleedin' eejit."

"We'll be expected to tip you know, if he does take it up."

"No problem," she replied airily. "I'm walking in Jean's footsteps now, remember? and anyway that young fella could well be from

Tallaght. A nice tip could help him buy a Christmas present for his girlfriend."

Light filtered through the long folds of the tulle curtains. Ron always liked to leave a little bit of light shining so the angels could peer in while she slept, something Joe had passed on to her as a little girl, from his own mother. They had slept past breakfast time. Eanna reached for his phone on the bedside locker.

"Oh God, no breakfast - We're too late!" he moaned.

"Never mind," she said groggily, turning over and reaching for him.

They snuggled there for five minutes, each absorbing the room around them bathed in a muted winter light. They'd made love in The Gresham, she thought dreamily. Suddenly she giggled.

"What's so funny?" he said as he bent his lips down to kiss the top of her head.

"I'm just thinking, what if Jean can see us now or Ma? You know Ma went up to the room with her that night?"

"We've probably had better sex than Jean ever had," he said, pulling back the bed covers and disengaging his right arm from around the back of her neck.

Whilst he showered, she lay still, a gift of her new mindfulness practice, listening only to the waterfall drumming on the enamel bath behind the closed door. The traffic was hotting up beneath the windows. They were on the top floor. She felt a sumptuous peace take hold as her arms and legs parlayed with the white cotton sheets. Reluctantly, she pulled back the covers on her side, her feet hitting the fathomless grey carpet pile. She moved over to the curtain rail, pulling down on the side cord to watch the effortless swishing apart of the heavy green brocade drapes. Grey clouds rolled in over the city, encumbered with rain. She noticed a tiny rent of blue in the sky. Maybe the day would open? Large raindrops suddenly splodged on the white double- glazed window. People ran for shelter as the momentum of a squall built up. Some, she could see were standing under the archways of the hotel. One man in a navy- blue suit and impeccable, white shirt held a newspaper above his head. She wondered if it was "*The Times.*" It was her first ever hotel break, she realised and she was thirty- three. Her eyes atavistically took in the lacquered dressing table, with its swivel mirror, the writing table to the side with a neat baize chair discreetly rounded at the back. She toyed with the idea of writing a note to Brendan on the headed notepaper, residing in a black gilt- edged folder. She sent him a photo instead of the Picasso prints on the wall. All he texted back was,

"Weird Ma, seriously strange."

In the end, they had breakfast in the hotel bar- full Irish. She had a mad impulse to walk barefoot across the heavily polished oak floor and into the conservatory. Of course she didn't, and merely ordered sausage, bacon, egg and fried tomato instead. Eanna buried up to now behind the "*Irish Times*" raised an eyebrow at the sudden rounding of her tone.

"What?" she asked a little peevishly.

"Nothin," he said evenly, his face fading back into the newsprint.

"Am I trying too hard, do you think?"

He put the newspaper down on the glass table top, and meticulously folded it; then he creased it again before looking up.

"Love, we don't need to impress these people. I love you for just being you."

The waiter was standing beside them now with two coffees and some cutlery.

"Thanks Love," she said quietly as he placed them on the table.

When he was out of earshot, she said, "I just wanted to do meself justice, that's all."

The sting of tears was back venomously behind her eyes. She closed them. She heard his quiet insistent voice from far away.

"Ron, open your eyes ; you're a gifted woman. You have a charisma all your own. People want to be around you." No one had ever spoken like this to her before. She wasn't sure where to file it. So many changes were happening all of a sudden, she scarcely recognised herself in the mirror these mornings. Which version of her was in the Gresham anyway ? her seventeen- year- old self maybe, who was totally in awe of that chandelier downstairs, and the gilt edged notepaper in the bedroom? Or was it more likely to be Ron from Dobbinstown, sent here by her fairy godmother, AKA Jean Ahmed, and that Ron was only faking it, waiting to be found out. What was someone like her doing here at all? She looked across at her boyfriend. He was so damned secure in himself in this environment. Yet their worlds were the same, weren't they? except of course he was a teacher. That set him apart. Teachers could stay at the Gresham or at least the Gresham would accept a teacher, but not her.

"Where did you get that palaver from?" she asked edgily.

His smile opened up the green fleck in his eyes.

"I don't know; I grew up same as you. When I went to college, I took some psychology classes, and then I did private psychotherapy. I heard things that we were always told were just sissy before, but no Veronica, we have to express our feelings."

"I believe you," she said softly now, reaching for his hand.The thaw of a new belonging had suddenly set in.

On the N7 out of Dublin back to Tallaght, they fell silent. Suddenly she said

"Would you mind if we visited someplace on our way to the families?"

"Sure," he said, as he neatly overtook a Guinness truck, moving deftly across the inner lanes following the filter arrows for Fettercong and Dobbinstown.

"I'd like to visit Pablo's grave."

She'd told him all about Pablo by now. She told him the story one night over a shared bottle of wine by a roaring fire. Brendan was staying over with Jack his friend. They'd spent the day hiking on the local mountain "Little Ben Bo." He listened attentively like a midwife attaching a stethoscope to her belly, needing to hear every minute turn of the story she was birthing before him. When she finished, he took her hand and said softly.

"Ron, you'll never walk a journey like that alone again, while I'm around."

Her tears were as usual full throttle. They joked how her rivuleted mascara had become a badge of honour.

"If that's what you want Ron, I know the graveyard is in Tallaght village."

The car glided silently past the high stone wall to their left. The graveyard's church peered above its jagged caps. There was a heartbeat of suspended rain.

"We have to come back to find the Hawthorn behind the wall when it's in bloom," Eanna said. "The flowers are good for broken hearts you know."

She didn't answer. The car had turned in the open gateway to the car park, facing the old church head-on and the random selection of bent slabs half buried in the clay.

"He'll be in the new graveyard won't he? Do you know where the grave is?"

"I have an idea," she said. "I got the bus out this way with Brendan in the stroller. Da was amazed I was bringing the child, said he would have given me a lift, but I kinda needed to do it on me own, you know?"

As they got out of the car, the rain began to spill in large wind-blown drops now. Suddenly it gathered speed as a strong wind gusted towards them.

"You'll be soaked," he said, as she stood there rooted to the spot. Her eyes squinted against the downpour, as they combed the stones. Eanna reached into the back seat for his black "Mr. Steed" umbrella, as he called it."Come on so, we'll nosey around," he said, shouting above the wind.

"I think if I remember right, it was over to the right of the gate. I think we can check online for this graveyard".

She had a flash back to doing it before .Eanna opened his phone.

"You can check St Maoliosa's Cemetry Memorials. Include his nickname,"

she said helpfully, lifting the vaulting umbrella from him while he checked .

It came up at once.

ID NO.10665113, in the newer section.

They scanned the 106651s painstakingly, gradually scaling up the numbers.

Suddenly Ron exclaimed,

"It's this one!" The wind tore the umbrella down from their faces. Eanna attempted to raise it again, but it pulled frantically away from him, baring its prongs as it reversed itself. Defeated, he slipped it back down. Neither of them felt the driving rain seep into them as they stood there bare headed.

"It feels like he died just last week," Eanna said, pointing to the headstone with carefully arranged pots of cyclamen and fresh roses laid on the pebbles. A chipped photo of a boy with thin fair hair and blue eyes was inserted between two arms of a granite cross. He read the inscription,

"In loving memory of James (Pablo) Mangan, beloved son of Oliver and Simone. 1984 to 1999, aged 15 years. Paint in Heaven young man."

The rain drummed steadily off the tin pots on the grave. Ron bent down and dropped her voice low over the stones.

"Next time I'll bring a rose Love. Our son is doing just fine." She straightened up at the touch of Eanna's fingertips on her lower back.

"We must get back now," he said gently. She nodded a faraway compliance.

They raced back to the car. As the Skoda wheeled around in the car park, the sky relaxed its fists. She could see the tent of blue again; her heart rate slowed physically down as she watched the roadway for oncoming traffic. They said little as they headed back to Dobbinstown.

"We're soaked," Eanna remarked.

"Yeah, I'm a bit shivery, now that you mention it," she said.

The skyline of the estates came into view. Wind-blown trails of grey smoke drifted erratically above the houses. Eanna turned down the radio. The wipers moved hypnotically in unison. What would Pablo be doing now? she wondered to herself. As if he'd read her thoughts, he murmured,

"Poor kid, he hadn't a snowball's chance in Hell."

She closed her eyes, and imagined Michelangelo from the books Brendan had on painting.

"And he could have been touring the world, gettin' commissions and appearin' on the Late Late Show," she said.

Eanna briefly touched her lap with his left hand. "He sure could have been. No doubt about that."

Then they were entering Patrician Road. They passed by Ron's old house. A very young woman with a toddler in a polythene-covered buggy emerged. She couldn't tell if the child was a boy or a girl. The young woman pulled up the hood of a small - waisted grey jacket. She didn't look up as they passed.

CHAPTER 16

The Christmas lights were on in O'Connell Street that night as they drove back up towards The Gresham. Blue and white bulbs trickling from roof tops and garish headlights in a synchronised swim, strengthened her exhaustion. Eanna, bless him, was still battling it out as she slunk down in the passenger seat, grateful to be carried on this frantic tide of people and expectations. Family members were swimming in her head, their faces a jigsaw blur. Amy and Jenny had both cancelled. Amy had the flu and Jenny was in Dromoland Castle with her new fella.

"Don't ask," she said to Eanna when his pupils expanded . Her voice was coming through to her in a type of static fog.

"I think you've caught something in the rain today," he said.

"How come you never catch anything?" she asked, a little irritation filtering into her voice. Her eyes were pouring small streams into tissues she'd found in the glove compartment. A headache pounded her temples.

"It's me magic bullets," he said, arching an eyebrow as the car finally turned into the car park.

"You mean them herbs?"
she said

"Well, you can load them into me now mister."

"Will do," he said as he opened the passenger door .

Her teeth chattered as the raw cold turned inside her. He helped her out of the car.

"Lots of grief in there Ron."

"And there was I thinkin' it was just the rain,"
she said, her eyes half closed as she leaned on him all the way into the foyer and upstairs to bed.

He opened his dark bottle. He had many formulas that Brendan and his friends had christened "Jungle Express."Every half hour, he spooned a mixture dissolved in boiling water into her. For a number of hours, she tossed and turned. Sweat cascaded from her. He found a change of nightie in her bag. About 3am, the magic happened. Without warning, sleep drew her down into itself.

When she woke again, the full morning light had inveigled its way into the room, unshadowing the corners. She put up her hand to her eyes to shield herself from the glare. Eanna was up and dressed, unshaven and red -eyed. He was reading the *Sunday Times* in the curved- back baize armchair over by the window. Dimly she registered that he had just polished off a breakfast of bacon, egg and tomato from a warmer tray in the centre of the room.

"You're awake Veronica at last,"

he said, slightly pulling the curtains.

"Oh no, don't close out all the light," she said; "or I'll only see a shadow of me man."

He chuckled, and pulled back the heavy drapes until they met the light halfway.

"Well, you slept the sleep of a cherub," he said smiling.

"I'm a bit old to be a cherub," she said stretching her whole body out cat- like under the crisp white sheets. She felt lighter somehow, and her headache was gone.

"What did you give me last night?" she asked.

He began to call out: "peppermint, boneset, lemon balm, echinacea,yarrow."

By the time he'd finished the list, she had fallen back asleep.

She slept all day Sunday. Eanna had booked an extra night on a cancellation. Whenever she woke, he gave her a teaspoon of the mixture again. She went back to sleep. She finally woke properly around 7pm, to see him stretched out on the floor with a pillow behind his head, and a spare duvet from the top of the wardrobe covering him; he was snoring. On Monday she was feeling half human again. They analysed their visit on the drive home. She was apologising for ruining the weekend, when he abruptly wheeled the car up the ramp off the motorway, and into the forecourt of a garage.

"Thought you had enough petrol?" she said, alarmed at the abrupt movement.

"I have some yes, but I just wanted to tell you something."

He shifted in the seat, facing her full on.

"You're the best thing to come into my life in a very long time, so there's nothing to apologise for. It was a privilege to look after you."

She studied the foot well, his Dubarry shoes with the nice stitching. She swallowed hard, her throat closing down over a shaft of emotion.

"I'll just go out and fill up the tank."

She watched him wrestling with the green pump nozzle in an unsheltered spot where he was standing, his light mustard scarf unwinding with the wind. She thought,

'what did I do right in the Universe finally to find him?'

Their visit had been an unqualified success, according to phone calls and texts from family. Her Uncle Alfie was thrilled with that nice teacher fella, and better still he was from the same place. They knew loads of people in common. Alfie's son had been a few years behind Eanna in St. Gabriel's Community College in Jonesboro. They'd been smothered with cakes to bring home. Alice's sisters, Kat and Tina had been invited over specially to meet them. Ron looked anxiously at Eanna as he was tucking into a load of turkey and ham, with scrutiny on the side. The twitch at the corner of his right eye was the only thing that spoke to her. Otherwise between mouthfuls, he was verbally replaying last October's All Ireland football final between Dublin and Offaly. Alice's sisters were eyeing him favourably as he spoke. Kat was always the hard sister to succeed with. Tina usually accepted her take on things. The family often called Kat" The General." Before they all sat down to eat, Eanna held out a chair for each of the women at the table. The two aunts looked stunned, but accepted nonetheless. As the meal progressed, it seemed he worked harder at winning Kat over which surprised her. She hadn't forewarned him.

"Pets," she'd said quickly when asked about them.

Observing the accustomed flint in her aunt's eyes begin to smoothen out, she had to hand it to him. She imagined Alice assessing the scene, rubbing her hands together, creating a kind of static glee which was a habit of hers when she could scarcely credit the outcome.

The late afternoon was for the other side of Dobbinstown.

"One down, and one to go," he said in a tight voice, easing the seat back into a more comfortable position. The car spat into life as he turned on the headlights. It was nearly 4pm, and the wipers were on from the minute they left. Christmas lights running in rivers down the houses, looked dappled through the raindrops. Dobbinstown did Christmas like no other she suddenly realised. An electrified Santa Claus, gnomes and reindeers loomed out from inky wet gardens. Eanna's mother had a discreet tree in her small front window and a small wire sculpture of a doe outlined in LED lights in the front.

"I set it up for me sister," he said to Ron as they hurried past it to the front door.

Eanna's sister Ailbhe was standing in the doorway with her eyes widened to a cavernous smile. Ron felt the magnetism of her pulsing towards them. Inside the hallway, her brother's waist was wrapped furiously in her short arms.

"This is Ron, Ailbhe," he said.

"Pleased to meet you," she said with a sibilance and a pushing out of the word you to the front of her mouth. Without warning, Ron felt the younger woman bear hug her ,almost knocking her over.

"Go easy on the poor girl," a hoarse voice from behind chided. Eanna's mother Aileen appeared out of the kitchen, wearing a Christmas reindeer apron over her white bobble jumper, and navy, denim trousers. She was wearing an additional mantle of stale cigarette smoke. She embraced Ron.

"You're welcome Love; we've heard all about you."

Over tea in the small kitchen, Ron discreetly observed Aileen. She didn't have her son's height, but her laughter chiselled her face in exactly the same part of her cheek bones as his. She had the same honeyed green fleck in her eyes, and his way of deliberating before she answered a question. Ron had always relied on humour in awkward situations, but the atmosphere was a little more circumspect here at first. She knew she was being appraised, and more than likely compared. 'No pressure,' a voice said in her head distantly, almost comically. She realised with a slight voltage of unease pricking her, she had never actually met any of her other boyfriends' families before, (well except for Pablo maybe, and that didn't count), even Matt Danagher, as his parents were dead, and he was an only child..

"I love the decorations Aileen," she said suddenly, grabbing at a conversation opener.

"We go to the sales in Marks and Spencer every January to buy more decorations for next Christmas," Eanna said, giving his sister a large wink.She went slightly crimson.

"I like your hair and your jewellery and your shoes and your red dress," she said to Ron without once looking up from the floor. She formed her tongue slowly, carefully, around all the words. She pronounced her vowels in a loop, lengthening her sentences. Ron directed the rays of an intense smile her way, reaching out to touch her.

"And I like you," she finally declared triumphantly. "You're gor-geous."

At the explosive cleaving of the word, they all laughed. Ron flushed. Eanna gave her an amused look. She began to scratch her chest with her right hand, whilst trailing the fingertips of her left along the reindeer patterns on the kitchen table cloth.

"You're gorgeous yourself," she countered now, looking up. All eyes were trained on her. She flushed more deeply. Aileen's eyes poured a soft gratitude into hers.Before they left, they handed the two women their presents.

"I know it's early," Ron said apologetically, "but we wanted to deliver in person."

"Like Santy," Ailbhe said delightedly. Another barrel hug left Ron standing this time.

"I saw this one comin'," she said. She judged the laughter now to be more on tap somehow. Ailbhe ran to put the presents under the tree in the front room before they left. Finally the rain had subsided. In the doorway, Aileen drew her in for a hug.

"You're great for him," she whispered into her ear as Eanna went to fetch their coats from the stairs.

Ron whispered back, "And he's great to me."

They both stood there a little adrift in this "new world order." Returning with their coats, Eanna looked from one woman to the other, clearing his throat, and handing Ron her short black jacket.

"No wonder your family had to give you a towel to dry yourself off," Aileen commented, eyeing the light jacket, finally happy to find something to hang a sentence on. Before leaving, Eanna turned to give his mother and sister a big hug. Ron followed with a lightning kiss for each. As they stepped outside, the starless black dome appeared to mercifully have finished drowning the world for now.

"We'll have presents for both of you for Christmas," Aileen shouted from the doorway. Ron turned back briefly and gave a final short wave as Eanna and herself splashed their way to the car. The two women's features were emblazoned on the doorstep by the full spread of the headlights once the car started up. Aileen placed her hand across Ailbhe's shoulder, gently rubbing her daughter's left arm affirmatively. Wordlessly, Eanna reversed onto the roadway of the estate. Ron closed her eyes, exhaling the tension of her first milestone with his family.

CHAPTER 17

The night sky was cloudless with a kind breath among the alder and fir. She gazed up at a water colour blue and purple pallet - an unspoken thunderclap above the canopy. Using the light on her mobile, she viewed the jagged uniform limbs of each tree recently cut by the forestry. It gave them a spectral look this time of year, but they were her friends by now. They made her feel safe. Only last month in mid- November, Brendan , back from a field trip with his geography class to Valencia Island, had taken her out to show off his new found astronomy skills.

" That's Orion the hunter, Ma," he had enthused, pointing out a large cluster to their right in the clearing beyond the copse."You'll see him easy. Mr. Cotter says a mid- November starry night is a very good platform from which to view the old warrior."

She crunched her boots through the limp undergrowth well wrapped up this time, as she was still shaky. She remembered how she had gasped at the cluster. The outline was exceptionally clear

".Look Ma, his club!" Brendan pointed out. She could see the red star the *Betelgeuse* pulsating clearly

"Look further down now," he said in a half- whisper. "It's his belt."

The three linear stars put on a performance for her, glittering a language she couldn't speak.

Now she wondered just what on earth she was doing out on a star- blind night on Christmas Eve. She was like Da in that way, taking to the road or the hills before an event.She had just reached the clearing when she saw the time on her phone. God, she'd lost track. How could she forget the Skype? Da and Brendan were at the house. She invoked the old hunter.

"Come on Orion old man. Even if I'm blind to you, I know you're there. Give me a bit of that battle courage of yours," she shouted to the elements. Startled sheep moved their fetlocks in closer to the blackthorns. She laughed, "Ah youse don't need to be afraid of me." The wind picked up now, and they huddled closer together in the lee of the ditch. She took one more deep breath, and tore down the pathway until she arrived at the cottage door, breathless. It was 8 o'clock. The Skype was scheduled for 8.15pm. Lights were on all over the house. The mountains above silently blessed her as she fumbled for the key and let herself in. Joe was anxiously pacing the kitchen floor. She entered, removed her coat and hung it on the hook behind the door. She asked softly, "Everything OK Da?"

What the hell were you out in the cold for after just being sick.?

Stunned, she was pointing a verbal arrow in self defence, when suddenly he bolted for the stairs. Shortly she heard the toilet flush. Da always had a weak bladder.

"Skype is up in 7 minutes," Brendan called from the small front room. Joe ran down the stairs. He'd just come from his second-ever boxing match in Killindara. It wasn't a win, and she knew he'd gone for his usual drive to clear his head. He'd arrived in to find his daughter gone AWOL. Brendan had been at the match. He had texted her with the result. The promising lightweight Mat Lynch from Drombawn had lost on a knock out.

"Sorry about the poor result Da," she offered when he came downstairs. Her father didn't answer, but his fists were balled up in his blue Nike sweatshirt pockets.

"Come on," she said, softly touching his arm. She put the redundant arrow back in its quiver

"Let's go inside to the fire." She could feel the resistance and unease in her father's huge shoulder muscles.

In the front room, her son was seated on the two- seater blue couch, laptop on the glass table in front of him. He patted the couch for his grandfather to sit beside him. He had lit a blazing fire. On each of the four small windowsills of the room was a blue ceramic lamp, with red lampshades casting a soft focus around the cream walls. A hand -picked Christmas tree from the Drumshanbo market stood wedged between the two corner windows. The minuscule forest of white lights draped across it lent a halo to the fireside. Brendan had decorated it with fresh pine cones and gold hand-painted Christmas crackers which stuck out at odd angles from the branches.

'Not bad,' she thought, 'Not bad at all.'

The logs had burst into a full- blown wind song, and were licking the chimney breast sensually. She loved the dried -out smell of the cut timber. "Now for the great show down," she thought, looking over at her father's glum face. At least his hands were cut loose from his pockets.

On cue, they heard the high pitched, deep- throttle music of the Skype. Adam's profile loomed on the screen. Brendan tapped on the dancing green icon. They were in. Adam appeared before them seated behind a writing desk. In the background, she could make out a window sill with an ivory elephant and a pink azalea on it. She glimpsed a grey counterpane on what seemed a very modern futon.

"I'm in the guest room." He grinned at them before anyone had a chance to speak.

"Thought you'd be like Ma Ron, taking in the décor."

She felt a fluttering in her chest. Prior to this he'd done Skype with her a number of times from his friend Rod's house next door; his own connection was too poor. From now on with the new broadband connection, he and his partner Miguel would be in more regular contact he promised.

"Howya Uncle Adam, Happy Christmas," Brendan chirped.

"Thank God for young fellas," she thought. She sensed rather than saw the hard block of Joe's physical body, sculpted in the past.

"Happy Christmas Brendan," Adam replied warmly. He sounded different, more relaxed. A black shadowy figure bobbed into the room, and then sort of slid out the doorway again.

"Is that your partner?" Brendan asked.

"Oh?" Adam turned round and then turned back to the screen.

"That's Miguel. He's Mexican, and he's disappeared. He's shy. Happy Christmas Ron."

Before she could reply, his eyes taking on an emergent worry, he said

"Happy Christmas Da," in a smaller voice. She could just see the bitten quicks of his nails as he scratched his jaw absently with his left hand. Joe said nothing for a few seconds. The fire in the chimney cried, rattled by the wind. Brendan looked across at his mother. She was about to intercept the menace of the looming silence, when her da shifted on the couch.

"Happy Christmas son," he said in a short flat voice. "What's the weather like?"

"Oh it's so pleasant here Da at the moment. I miss the cold sometimes though."

"You must be out of your tree, you bleedin' eejit," Ron countered.

"Come to Leitrim to the rushy lands and sheep, and that'll sort yeh."

They all laughed. Then Adam's face was contoured differently somehow. His big blue eyes bore down on her softly like they once did when he shared the sweets he got in Tescos on a Friday night with his little sister or he held one of her hands as he took her to school with Ma her first day. She was relieved he was so amiable. Their own Skypes had grown gradually warmer over the last year. When he had told her about Miguel, she had a gut feeling this was the one. Now that they both had strong relationships, the winds of cocaine had pretty much blown themselves out. Now she wanted Da to relegate the drug- damaged years to the past.

He asked about Eanna. "Where's Mr Doyle tonight?"

"He's gone back to his Ma and sisters for Christmas. We'll see him in a few days."

"You never met Sally," Brendan chimed in. "She's at home skyping her sister in Manchester."

Adam's eyes travelled slowly across the screen to his father's.

"I hear she's a lovely lady Da. I think ... I think its right you know, you found someone."

Here he fumbled with a qualification.

"You know,... well someone after, well, after Ma. I'm sure she wouldn't mind."

"She's given him her blessing wherever she is," Ron said softly.

"Sure you couldn't let Da out on his own."

Adam laughed properly for the first time, his eyes trained on his father's face. Joe grinned sheepishly.

"Your sister's right. I do need mindin' or so they tell me."

"When can I meet her?" Adam asked. At the surprised look on all their faces, he added hastily,

"On Skype I mean. We're saving for something at the moment. It could be a while before we get home," he said, dropping his chin a tad. Ron recognised the characteristic chin drop from childhood, usually when her brother had hidden away some of Ma's Queen Cakes in a biscuit tin in his room or told a fib about having no homework. There was a lot about this new life of his they didn't know yet.

"Well, Sally and all of us would like to meet Miguel on Skype too."

"Maybe after Christmas," he said lifting his chin up to the screen again, his eyes moving onto Joe once more.

A lot of the hour went on family tattle. She told him about her visits to both sets of relations in Dobbinstown.

"Nice one," he said meditatively."

He told them they were having their friends Alan and Jack and their baby daughter Eva over on Christmas Day. She saw a small piece of flint striking in Joe's eyes, but Da was still cruising, she thought.

"And work is going well," he said with a bright brittleness. He cleared his throat again, finding Joe's eyes."I got a promotion. I've been made Clinical Nurse Manager in my nursing home.

"Way to go Uncle Adam," Brendan enthused, his brown eyes rocketing.

"Fantastic Adam," Ron said "We're proud of you."

His lips registered their gratitude. He was hard locked on his father now.

"That's a very responsible job you have there," Joe said slowly.

"Are you saying I'm not up to it?"

Ron held her breath."Oh no, he's saying no such a thing, he's ..."

Joe gave her that look from childhood when she knew she couldn't mind her own business to save her skin.

"I'm saying," he said with a cool edge to his voice, "I used to worry about your sense of responsibility, but Rutland and your Ma helped a lot with that I know. You didn't have the best influences either."

Adam moved a fraction in his chair. The lanky shadow hovered in the doorway again and appeared to gesticulate. Adam shook his head slightly at it and turned his attention to the screen.

"You're right Da," he said slowly, treading on familial stepping stones over a weir.

"I was like that, and Rutland saved my job and my life. I've had more counselling here. I've made peace with the past. Have you?"

There was a long pause. Brendan looked anxiously at his grandfather, vestiges of old fears in his eyes. The fire went very low in the grate. The clock ticked warily in the silence. The wind picking up outside, tore hard down the chimney, sweeping up around the gable end of the house. Joe stared out the window at the lower limbs of the trees moving to keep balance in the gathering storm.

"I have son," her father said finally. His gaze met his son's frank one.

"I'm proud of you. You turned into a ....; here he paused, "a good man."

The shadowy figure had left the room, Ron noticed. Adam's face had visibly lost its hollowed anticipation. Despite herself she interjected again, but her father seemed oblivious now. She saw a long exhalation leave his chest.

"Manager sounds very good. What does that mean?"

"I'm Assistant Director in The Star of the Sea Nursing Home," her brother said modestly. Joe closed his eyes for a moment.

"Congratulations," he said quickly, on opening them.

"Thanks Da," Adam murmured.

"Well, I guess I'd better go here. Miguel is calling me. Happy Christmas everyone again."

Collectively they murmured the greeting back. As Adam turned from the screen, he lifted the bedroom window blind. Champion sunlight flooded the room. He gave a little wave before the screen went blank.

CHAPTER 18

She found it hard to credit when she woke up the next morning that it was the first Christmas they weren't actually in Dobbinstown. Later they would have dinner with Joe and Sally. At 8am, her mobile belted out "I'm Dreaming of a White Christmas." Eanna's profile picture flashed on the WhatsApp screen. Brendan was still asleep; it had been a late night. She had sat up with him until 2am, long after Joe had gone. He plied her with questions about Uncle Adam. She'd answered truthfully and carefully, including in her narrative the time he had spent in Rutland Clinic to help with his addiction.

"If it wasn't for your gran, he wouldn't be where he is today for sure. Adam has come home to himself Love".

They opened a bottle of wine.

"Give the lad a drop," Sally had encouraged when she voiced her fears.

"One glass of wine won't do any harm. I'm sure he's had it before somewhere." Sally's eyes held amusement. Ron knew right well, he'd been offered the vino, not to mention heroin, and plenty more in the mix besides in Dobbinstown. If he'd tried any of it she couldn't be sure, but the lectures he'd received from his grandad were legend in the family. She herself encouraged him to google every sordid side effect there was. In fact, the drugs and cider parties which he was banned from attending were only half the battle. Older lads he didn't know had started waiting for him outside the school gate at thirteen, giving him the chance to be a runner. Someone called Murph had apparently singled him out, a big lad like him. All she knew was Trigger had been delivering for them before the 'Crack Squad' picked him up. That was another reason either she or Joe began picking him up after school. It was enough he said to have a son who had done drugs, let alone a grandson carrying crack cocaine halfway across the city for the barons. Between them they watched

147

Brendan like a hawk. When he began to kick at the traces and said he was a prisoner, she knew that if they didn't leave, things could soon be out of her control.

"Happy Christmas Love." Eanna's voice sounded excited as she answered, sitting up in bed shivering. It was still dark outside. She put on the bedside lamp.

"Hang on a minute Love," she murmured groggily.

Quickly she hopped out of bed, casting around for her chunky green jumper and black leggings. She laid the phone on the bedside table. Breathless, she picked it up again now as the warmth of the clothes against her skin offset the early frost.

"Another minute now before I put the duvet around me back," she said.

She sensed his amusement at the other end.

"Happy Christmas to you too Love- I miss you."

"Me too," came the wistful reply, then -

"Ailbhe, out of me room now. No, you can't talk to Ron."

Ailbhe's voice stumbled carefully over the words down the line.

"Happy Christmas Ron," she said in a breathy tone.

"A Very Merry Christmas to you too my love."

"Put me back on again," a voice inside her insisted desperately. Instead, she said

"Thank you very much for Cathy Kelly's latest book and the PJs. I'm wearing them already and thank your Ma too. Did you open your presents?"

She could hear Eanna poking the prompts his sister's way in the background.

"Thank you for my Princess Diary,"

she said now, her sentences finding more pace with her breath.

"You're very welcome Ailbhe."

Ron smiled to herself as she heard another argument on the other end of the phone.

"No, ask her yourself."

"Ron,"- the breathless tone again,

"Will you come up here next Christmas?"

She pinched the folds on the back of her hand to stop her usual spontaneous acquiescence.

"That's a lovely thing to ask me," she said slowly, carefully.

"I might have to stay with Brendan and me da, but I'll let you know next Christmas. Sure I'll see you in the New Year and your Ma and yourself must visit us in Leitrim."

There was a pause. "Oh God she'd hurt her feelings now."

She tented the duvet around her then. The breathy rush was back on.

"Ron, is Leitrim nice?"

She could hear Eanna's hoot of laughter on the line.

"Leitrim is divine Pet."

There was a fractional silence before Eanna came back on.

"I finally managed to clear her off. The smell of a fry sent her off to the kitchen."

"Did you open my present?" she asked, suddenly shy. There was a significant pause.

'Oh Lord God help me,' she thought. She realised she was freezing.

"One minute," she said into the lengthening silence.

"I must put on me second- best bed jumper -You know, the Aran one."

Still no reply.

'Mother of Jesus, he didn't like anything. Where was the bloody jumper?'

Just as she laid her hands on it at the bottom of a pile of ironing on the bedroom floor, there was a crackle on the line.

"Sorry, Ma asked me to empty the big pot of water that the ham had been boiling in. What did you ask me?"

A tide of relief flooded her marooned self-esteem. She went back to bed, the duvet fully over her this time, burrowing underneath, her mobile in her right hand. She didn't need the Aran somehow. She hurled her breath into the question this time. He told her later she'd been shouting.

"Did you like my presents?"

'Please God, please God, he mustn't pause.'

"Bloody brilliant, how did you know?"

She sat bolt upright, duvetless. She remembered how the girl's foot popped in the princess's diary when she got the right kiss. A slight tingle in her right foot would have to do instead. She was awash with giddiness.

"Well, I've heard you on about the cost of buying them herb books, the entire Matthew Wood collection. And I knew you wanted that registration to the online plant lectures for twelve months. I knew you were wishing on stars Mr. Doyle."

"Yeah, herbal ones," he said laughing. "Me very own good fairy."

"Now you know you'll have to teach me too."

"You will be my perfect student."

The anxiety shifted places on the line now. A sudden clearing of his throat led to a hesitant opening.

"Did you em... did you like my gift?"

She fingered the moonstone pendant softly now. Its opalescence slipped through her.

"It's connected to me sacral chakra," she murmured.

"Sacred chakra?"

"Sacral," she corrected, laughing.

"I'm wearing it Love. I'm wearing the bit of magic and me bit of you too."

The silence on the line stretched out lazily.

"I bought it on O'Connell Street," he said. "I knew you loved the bit of mysticism and the crystals and stuff. Do you like the book on rare gems?"

"Sure aren't I one of them meself?"

A chuckle stitched itself onto the airways."A rare gem indeed I have found."

"Seriously, I love it; it tells me of stones I never even heard of before. I'm more intimate with me crystals now."

"Mmm, nice words," he said, his voice trailing off. "I can't wait for us to be intimate when I'm back."

What began as a flush in her, became an unapologetic sensual storm. To cool herself down, she told him they were going to Sally and Joe's for dinner. She told him about Adam and the Skype, and how he was asking for him. He told her his mother's two sisters, Jackie and Connie were coming for dinner. At this point he said

"I'm going here love - more crises in the kitchen. Ring you tonight.

Ailbhe wants to put the turkey in the oven all by herself."

The lake at night had an alert presence. She was walking with Joe by the water's edge. They could hear the restless sucking in and rebound slurp of the water. Ron watched the urgent eddies and swirls of the grey white foam on the surface. A small boat tethered at the jetty moved uneasily against the half- submerged buoys. There was a melancholy out here under a watered -down black sky. She stopped suddenly, placed her hand on her father's elbow.

"Did you hear that Da, a kind of cry?"

"It's a vixen Love; there must be one of them out on the town."

At the mention of town, she smiled. He'd rung her before she came out, said he missed her, missed the woods.

"Woods are lovely, dark and deep, and I have miles to go before I sleep.

"And promises to keep," she added.

"I'm impressed," he countered..

"I love that poem by Robert Frost," she said.

They both loved poetry. Alice would have eaten him up, all that education.

"Penny for them," Joe said, turning his phone torch on her. Startled, she jerked herself back to the moment, turning to face him. She raised an eyebrow; a slow smile fielded itself across her face.

"Ah, true love," Joe said softly.

In the shadows, she could just make out the loosened contours of his jawline. Now it was her turn to shine her torch full on him. His smile was lifted on the high beam.

"I'm happy Da, are you?"

"I am," he answered simply. "It's been a brilliant day. I never thought ..."

"You never thought you'd find love again."

Ma used to finish his sentences for him; now she was doing it.

"It's different with Sally you know, but... good different, like today, our first Christmas Day together."

"And we'll have lots more Da, lots more."

She linked her arm through his as they picked their steps on the gravel pathway back to the house. Her touch relished the new release in his muscles. Before going in, she held her pendant in her right hand.

"There isn't a moon tonight, but I can feel it in me bones," she said.

Her father exhaled slowly, his breath returning readily to the night.

"I've no doubt you do. I've no doubt you do Love," he said with a small chuckle.

When they got back into the warmth of the upstairs lounge, Joe was blowing hard into his cupped hands. He had Raynaud's syndrome as long as any of them could remember. Sally quietly produced a facecloth and a bowl of warm water with a slick of ginger oil droplets on top. She left them on the coffee table in front of him before asking if anyone wanted hot chocolate. There was a little chorus of "Yes please." Ron offered to help. On entering the kitchen, as usual she admired Sally's good taste. A bare branch from Glenevan Woods stood in an empty peat-filled beer cask, underneath a large window framing the lake. Crystalline pear drop lights wound their way around its nudity. Crocheted snowflakes dangled between twigs. Beside it, over on the worktop space was a small glass crib. Slightly to the right of the crib stood a silver framed photo of a man and woman at what appeared to be a function. It took a moment to realise it was a younger slimmer Sally, and a sharp faced man with ginger wispy hair, and tinted glasses. They were both grinning, the man's arm circling his other half's waist.

"That's me and Sylvie-" Sylvester- "No one called him that though. Didn't we look well?" she said, handling the frame pensively. Ron realised this was her first ever glimpse of Sally's first husband. Selfishly, she realized she hadn't given the older woman's previous life much thought until now.

"Do you miss him?" she asked gently.

Sally nodded. "I used to miss him so much. I imagined I'd hear the clink of his car keys in the ashtray on the hall table in the evenings. I imagined it for a long time after he died. There were times I could barely breathe. I could feel him on my shoulder, his kiss on my neck, but I couldn't touch. I'd walk around our empty white kitchen; I'd call him to his tea; I'd call him louder, but there was no sound of him taking off his big boots in the hallway. I always made him wear slippers in the house. In my ear, I could hear his big North of England accent,

'Hullo Love, did you have a good day?'

I swear I heard it time and again mocking me, and then I'd turn my head to the empty hallway. The stairs held his shadow on them for at least a year. I thought he'd come back again, plant the evening paper down on the kitchen table before washing his hands at the kitchen sink. He was very clean, very fastidious in his ways."

"Was it sudden?"

"Yeah, an aneurysm," Sally said, her voice loosening on the word.

"I texted him two hours earlier to bring home milk. He sent me an emoji of a cow," she said in a choked- up whisper. She wiped away a tear adrift from its mooring after the day. "The last of my history is in that tear Love - forgive me. It's just Christmas does strange things is all."

Joe pushed his head into the kitchen.

"Can we men do anything?"

His eyes trailed across the room to the photo in his wife's hand. He looked at her keenly before he cleared his throat. Then discreetly he dropped his large frame back under the doorway, turned and headed inside to the fire again.

"Sorry Love, we were talking," she called after him, setting the frame back down on the worktop.

"Life is different now," she said to Ron, her eyes pulling up a sparkle.

"But it's bloody brilliant too."

All smiles, they brought in the hot chocolate and Madeira Christmas cake on a tray. Ron watched her father's eyes navigate Sally's body as she set the tray down on the coffee table. They were alert, suddenly watchful.

"Move over on the couch Love," Sally said sitting down beside him. She picked up her hot chocolate in one hand, and rested the other on his large lap. Joe relaxed a little, but the shadow of watchfulness remained. Ron considered for a moment. Then she heard herself say quietly, holding up her mug.

"To Alice and Sylvie."

Joe and Sally looked at each other, a little startled. Sally was the first to her feet. Joe followed sheepishly. Brendan stared at his grandfather first, then his mother, comprehension rising in his eyes. He jumped up. Ron was the last to her feet. The shadows of four mugs touching swam in the firelight. Joe put his face down to his wife's cheek and kissed it. She nestled against him, closing her small chubby fingers around his own stiff large ones.

CHAPTER 19

February 2019 (Brendan has begun his travels)

Ron turned, startled in her tracks. He was calling her,
"Ron, Ron!"

She was halfway across the large interior floor space of the Farmers' Market, carrying two plates of chickpea and beetroot salad in her hand.

"Sorry, I didn't realise you were serving. There are folks here looking for your Brazil Nut Smoothie."

She sighed, "What was it with men?" She'd shown him already how to make the smoothie.

"Be back in a minute Love," she called out, and then headed in the direction of the stairs. She was serving from 'Ron's Kitchen' to the new open- plan seating area upstairs under the Perspex roof. She smiled generously at the young couple with their one- year- old in the buggy. She liked to remind Eanna that these were the customers they should be courting now: young, upwardly mobile, earth- conscious.

"Think of young Greta Thunberg,"

she said, "standing up the big fellas in politics to prevent climate change. Green is in. Vegans are cutting the carbon emissions."

" I'll warrant you cattle do account for 14% of methane gas in the atmosphere, but on the other hand only 2% of carbon emissions" he replied wearily, "and some vegans don't get enough protein."

"And what about all them air miles transporting the beef and the lamb?"

she said a little tartly. " Young Greta wouldn't even take a plane."

"Vegan is here to stay."

He looked tired these days she noted, with dark streaks nestled in tired folds under his eyes. He had a lot on his plate. Tiredness birthed combat in him. She noticed her own belligerence too.

"You're turning into a cynic."

"I'm not sure what I'm turning into," he replied.

"General dogsbody - that's what I am these days. I do care about the environment; It's just me carbon footprint isn't high on me agenda right now.

Aileen hadn't been well with a post-Christmas bout of asthma. She'd been in hospital for a week. Ailbhe wasn't being looked after properly. Now that they were both more involved with the farmers' market, it was hard to find a weekend for him to sort them out. He had decided last September, while Brendan was still planning his big journey for 2019, to take a year out from teaching. He planned to develop his organic centre which he had christened "Green Pharma." He hadn't anticipated his mother's illness. He told Ron that at least he was flexible mid-week now to go up and stay a couple of nights. She looked at him as she returned to her timber- framed log hut. She was proud of 'Ron's Kitchen,' where she had a hot plate out the back for cooking and electric sockets installed to plug in her smoothie maker. The admonition she had prepared perished on her lips. That dog- tired look which she was now familiar with haunted his eye sockets. He hadn't shaved in two days. A flutter of a by now familiar sadness suddenly came to perch on her again unexpectedly. She knew she was missing Brendan badly, so she kept herself manic busy, as she told Joe.

She had just handed the smoothie out the open window of the cabin and was rummaging for change, when her mobile rang. She could see Brendan's head showing up in the little porthole picture on the Whatsapp screen. She tapped on the screen phone icon and she was in. As usual, she was catapulted elsewhere immediately. A small clearance of a customer's throat made her turn around.

"Oh sorry Love, your change."

She handed him €3.50 from a tenner and wiped her greased hands on a roll of kitchen paper. Now, holding the phone in her left hand, she said, unable as ever to conceal her glee, "How are yeh love? Just give me a minute to get out of here. I'll put you in me apron pocket."She lifted the hatch door of the cabin, made her way across the floor, oblivious to the high volume of noise working its way up to the rooftop. She caught Eanna's eye over the far side as he looked at her quizzically. She made the phone handset sign with thumb and finger. He smiled for the first time in two days, she thought wearily. Her retreating back missed his large thumbs up. In her deep front pocket, the call was still on. She was aware she was carrying him around like a young kangaroo.

"They're called Joeys, Ma," he told her when she shared her thoughts with him out the back, once she'd found a quiet place to sit down.

"How are things ?" he asked excitedly.

"Oh you know, same old, same old," she said. "Eanna and meself are at the market today."

"Sorry about that," he said sheepishly."I forgot."

"Don't be sorry," she said. "I love talking to you. If the Pope himself or the Dali Lama came into the market, I'd excuse meself."

His big grin filled the small screen. She touched it wonderingly, drawing him in.

"How's things with you Love?"

Good, yeah," he said animatedly. "I'm in Naples at the moment, just doing the tourist bit."

"Tired of Rome are yeh?" she teased."There was I, thinking you were heading for the seminary."

"Church wouldn't have me," he said laughingly.

She realised with a jolt he had her eyes and Alice's too. The call was only five minutes. He'd been offered a job in a trattoria in Rome which was a kind of restaurant and wine bar, he said .

" It's in a place called Trastevere," he said rolling the sound off on his tongue.

"Nice Italian," she said. "I'm impressed already."

"Grazie Mamma," he said beaming.

"I'm heading back there next week. It's a real tourist area. Cool, young, hip, great vibe, lots of students as well, We're near a university, and I'm about twenty minutes' walk to the centre of Rome. I have accommodation lined up in an apartment just 5 minutes from the restaurant. The hostel I was in was too far away especially for night work.

"Well done you," she said, unable to hide the tide of rising pride in him.

"Now be careful with them little gangster motorbikes. I've seen them in the movies."

"They're called mopeds, Ma"

"I know, I know, just don't be a muppet on a moped Love."

"Ha,ha funny woman. Got to go here now. Love you to the moon and back."

He flashed his moonstone pendant on the screen and blew her a kiss; then he vanished somewhere into Naples for another week anyway.

That night she couldn't concentrate on the telly. After a half -hearted attempt at channel hopping, she turned it off. Her musings were more pressing. The camera in her head panned across the events of their lives since moving here. Eanna and herself had only recently moved in together. He always felt it would be better to wait until Brendan was gone on his travels- more fitting he said. Tonight he was gone to check on the plants in his polytunnels. His dream for

""Green Pharma," where he could grow several plants as medicine and eventually get into tincturing was still in its infancy.

"We could have several therapists there Ron," he said to her.

"You could do your Reiki when you finish your qualification."

She'd been doing a series of weekend courses. Her next one would bring her up to Master Practitioner level.

They pored over his friend Mike, the architect's drawings together.

"It would be gradual, very gradual," he said.

"First, we could extend the polytunnels, and drain some more of the land behind the house that I was living in. We'd need a lot of work on raised beds and digging drainage channels. Then we can do the dispensary, and add on treatment rooms as we go along. What do you think?"

She had to admit the plans looked exciting. Looking at the hazel green fleck in his eyes and feeling the electricity of his body as she danced with his dreams, she thought "yes, yes, Yes!"

He had refused point blank to allow her to invest any money.

"I'm not with you for your cash Veronica. I have some savings and a friendly bank manager in Sligo. I probably will have to go back to the teaching though, part- time."

"Ok," she said meekly."Love you." Then he pulled her in for a kiss, and was gone. Eanna was a restless creature, she had discovered, always on the move. He was pitta in Ayurvedic medicine he told her," fire and water".

He was often out 'til seven or eight at night. Sometimes she waited until he came in. More often than not, the hunger got the better of her, and she kept his dinner over. Life had gotten busy, but good busy. She was working as an SNA in Killindara National School by day for over two years now. Gosh, she remembered the day she arrived by train, and took the bus out of Sligo for the "chat" after her cheeky application on line. She cringed at the memory of what she had told them. Meeting a Leitrim lad and a child for the school,"*Yikes.*" That was the day they mentioned the upcoming SNA post in September. Not bad, not bad at all, Alice would have said. She came to love the cottage here in Drombawn, not the original one offered, mind you. That had needed a lot of dry lining on the walls and roof repair too. Joe was not impressed. Sally had found this one for her, more central actually and near to Sligo. The rent was doable, and somehow she felt she was here more on her own terms. The nest egg had settled nicely between the credit union, the bank and the post office. Cian O'Grady had advised for now against long term investments. He also hinted she might like to build in the area, and settle down, seeing as she was doing what he called "a strong line."

All of this brought her neatly back to Brendan. Last October, she finally told him the full value of her inheritance. She remembered they were walking in the woods. The late sunlight of an Indian summer emblazoned the length of the Alder grove path. The whirr of full- blown thinking was speeding along the highways in his brain, she could tell. He frowned, trod heavily on small dying leaves, parchment- like at the edges and didn't look up for some time.

"Brendan, wait for me!" she called, as he ploughed ahead of her pushing the hard stub of his boot through the dirt. Suddenly he turned to her, framing his whole face into a question mark.

"I told you we only had 20,000 sterling because ...... "

"You don't need to finish that sentence," he said with a quiet anger. She observed his volatile fist tighten and unravel .

"I didn't tell you ,...maybe to save you, and me too," she added, as the quiet afterthought washed over her suddenly.

"What was there to save Ma?" She hung her head.

"You didn't think I would suddenly turn into a pimp with a big ugly head on me did you?"

"You know I never thought that- just I didn't feel you were ready, thats all."

"We are living the fairytale of Drombawn, not the Rocky Horror Show of Dobbinstown. I am never going back there, even with no money.I thought you trusted me."

" I did, but ... The pause swelled out onto the emerging coolness of the evening.

" You made me go out with my friends in faded denim and Penneys shirts."

"Exactly," she said with a crispness that superseded the creeping sting in the air.

"Designer, that's not us. We don't need that"

"Who says?" His tone was belligerent.

" I do," she said hotly, the gremlin of an anger with him, taking hold in her.

"I repeat. That isn't us at all, as you well know."

. "What is us?" he asked peevishly.

"I'm tired of talking about Dobbinstown, me roots in Dobbinstown. That's history."

"Don't you want even the good bits?" she asked despairingly.

"Not even those."

His walled- off voice came from across a chasm; wizened demons on the other side gripped him.

Leaning against a sturdy birch, her breath came to live in her in short waves. He was looking away. Suddenly she was an emotional coin, whose anger had turned flip side. Her love for him tore out of her chest and ran towards him. Their brave new world had fallen out of her grasp. This had all been for him, his future. Who were they really? Where did they belong? Tears filmed her eyes. Turning to run for the cottage, she stumbled over a log. She didn't feel him pick her up nor hear his voice at first.

"Oh God Ma, I'm so sorry. I'm an ungrateful git. Please don't cry. You'll ruin your mascara again."

She took his hand as he helped her up.

"You hurt?" he asked, with a wild penitence in his voice.

She shook her head mutely, dusting herself down.

"Ma, come over here- there's a tree stump we can sit on."

He led her through the thinning grove to a well -circumscribed, smoothed stump. They sat in silence. A sentient wind blew down a sudden gust of leaves. He put his arm around her; she leaned in tentatively.

"God Ma, you know I love you. I didn't mean it, you know about Dobbinstown."

"It was no picnic Love, but we knew good people there."

He nodded slowly."You're right. Maybe I would have gone wild. I just wanted to fit in with the cool kids in a new place, you know, not just ...the blow in from gangland."

" You could fit in without designer gear."

" I Know, I know," he said guiltily.

She faced him then, unsure of herself at first, but she kept going. There was no road map back to the place her next words came from.

"It's not where you're born that makes you, or what you have; it's the decisions you make."

He accepted this. She could tell from the centring of his eyes, the stillness of his hands.

"I have something for yeh," she said softly, pulling out of her coat pocket a black lacquered box with a thin gold rim.""I was saving it for later, but here."

Carefully she withdrew the moonstone pendant. It became momentarily stuck in his tentacled curls as she lowered it over his head. Then it flowed down his neck and chest.

"Same one as you have," he said, his eyes lighting up.

"The very same."

CHAPTER 20

He didn't get to go on his trip without one hell of a send- off. Joe and Sally wanted to hold a party in their house and get in caterers.

Brendan said "Cool Grandad," when Joe mentioned it.

Then he was out the door to football training. She caught a flicker of hesitancy behind his eyes, but she was pretty sure Joe didn't register it. She knew he wanted a night in the pub with Lorcan, Eanna and his school mates ,and some of the guys from the football team.

"Grandad would be upset," he said to her later. "I can't let him down."

"Tell you what," Eanna said suddenly standing in the doorway bringing in bags of dried nettle leaves. "Why don't you have two nights? The first one will be on me and your Ma down in Flemings, and the second one in Joe and Sally's."

Brendan looked from Eanna to Ron and back. His obvious delight sent a riot of pinpricks sliding along her scalp. She had a wild impulse then to leave with him. She could imagine the two of them haring it over the new connecting bridge between the two terminals in Dublin airport chasing the flight to Rome. She would live the Bohemian life on the continent for a while with him. Drombawn could wait.

"You'll probably meet a nice sexy señorita in Rome,"

Eanna was smiling at him now. It was as if someone had stuck a pin in her. The colours of her dream had run badly together. The picture was a mess. Had she never had a youth at all? She pulled on her practised face for all seasons.

"Yes bring back a sexy lady Love," she said softly.

He blushed, and she noticed him scratch his chest for the first time.

Flemings was packed to the rafters. Most people were still home after Christmas. Sean Fleming gave a big thumbs up to Brendan as he entered.

"First one is on the house, seeing as it's your first night off," he said ducking his head behind the beer tap as he levered a stout. Brendan had been working there full time since he finished his Leaving Cert.

"Some of the lads know these guys in a band," he shouted over to her at the bar.

"They're called the *Dirty Nines*. They're coming in later. They can play
in the beer garden."

"Bit cold for beer gardens, isn't it Love?" Sally said from behind.

She turned to her stepmother to explain they had infrared heating out there for the smokers.

"Come on," she said, "let's find a free seat over here."

Brendan had disappeared into the outside. She, Joe and Sally headed for the long monks bench by the white -washed wall. Eanna went up to get a round of drinks. She noticed him making small talk with Sam Ellis, standing sideways at the bar, who kept one eye furtively on her. Eanna was oblivious. He was focusing on the loose change from the bartender, a lad whose younger brother he had taught. She knew this wasn't the first time Sam Ellis had given her the once over either. He was a bit of a local stud, Angela Sweeney, the other SNA. at school said one day in the staffroom when his name came up. He'd gone out with the vice principal's sister, Jenny Delaney for over a year and had a reputation as a womaniser. His hard brown eyes were crawling into her now. She felt goose bumps salute.

"You alright Love?" Joe asked concerned.

She jumped back into wakefulness.

"Grand, grand," she said studying the smooth polish of the cobbles on the dark stone floor.

She made her way over to where Eanna was grappling with two slippery pint glasses.

"I'll give you a hand," she said, grabbing the remaining Gin & Tonic and last Spritzer from the counter.

She could feel Sam Ellis's eyes now close to her breasts. She turned to face him full on.

"Had a good look did you?"

His face infernoed, he moved off at a slow pace, snaking through the crowd to the beer garden. Eanna's eyes held an amused glint.

He whispered in her ear, "that's my woman."

The band came around ten. They boogied through the night. She was aware how a few drinks usually unseated her tongue.

"To my son the jeen- yuss" she cooed into his ear. "My son" (she knew she was slurring her words) "who got H1s in English and Art and French and H2s in, in... I can't remember. Your gran would be so proud. She paused, as an addendum presented itself.

"And I'm clever too; got an O3 in me leaving cert maths. Credit where credit is due, Eanna me love," she said, arching her right eye in her boyfriend's direction. We burned the books after you know in a barrel .

She didn't notice Brendan's chin dropping, or see his mute sideways appeal to Eanna. Then he was at her shoulder.

"Come on Ron, we'll get you outside for a bit."

Her head was spinning. How young they all looked. God she was so old; she was thirty-five for Christ's sake.

"I'm so old Love," she said to him as he propelled her by the elbow out the door into the freezing night, speckled with stars. Lucky the mountains were in shadow, he told her later with a grin.

"You probably would have wanted to climb them."

He gave her Milk Thistle for the hangover the day after.

"Evening Primrose Oil would be good too," he added as an after thought.

"Oh here, don't be complicating me life," she said, her head a sledgehammer on the kitchen table.

"Will I get the primrose now?" Brendan offered.

"Evening Primrose," Eanna corrected.

"I don't care if it's morning or evening," she said wearily, her face still flush with the pine.

"God, she should have remembered she couldn't hold her drink. Amy and Jenny could always drink her under the table."

"Sorry I told 'em all about the funeral," she said groggily.

"You mean the book funeral?" Brendan said ."You invited me and Eanna to the cremation in the barrel".

Eannas freckles met up in needle points as he stood at the cooker heating a little milk.

"Then I asked should we say a prayer and your mother said..."

"Them books are pagans, waste of time." Brendan finished his sentence.

Eanna turned from the cooker.

"Here, hold your head up so I can get some of this Milk Thistle powder into you," he said.

He added a teaspoon of the herb to a little boiled milk and honey in a cup, and put it in front of her. She made a grimace and averted her mouth, as he pressed the drink to her lips.

"Come on Veronica."

"Oh, it's the teacher's voice now is it?"

she said, her tousled hair streaming recklessly over the edge of the table, as she flattened her reddened cheek onto it.There was silence. She cocked an eye up at him. He was still holding the cup aloft smiling. Meekly she took it from him with both hands and took a desperate swig.

"You're too good for me," she said, reaching out to press his wrist when he took the cup away. She could feel his fingers through the strands of her hair when she placed her head momentarily back down. Then she allowed him help her to the wing- backed chair by the range ,where she promptly fell asleep as Brendan heaped half a bucket of coal on top of the two logs burned down inside it. She was asleep by the time he returned from the chemist with the Evening Primrose Oil.

Luckily Joe and Sally's party wasn't for another week. Eanna had suggested she buy something different for herself. She gave him a wary look.

"Well something not too..., not too vintage," Brendan offered in a placatory rush.

"I know you love buying in the charity shop and all that."

He stumbled on through the vortex of gathering clouds on her face.

"Just as well I'm not hung over anymore," she thought or I might clock 'em both."

"And you get lovely".... his voice trailed off.

"Lovely what?"

Her rising inflection baited him.

"Original stuff," he said, the words in a pile up on his tongue.

"You mean me astrological collections,"

she said slowly, looking at both of them through slitted eyes. They nodded woodenly.

"Alright, alright, I surrender. But I'm not buying designer stuff, just 'cause Sally has stuff like that."

"I wouldn't dream of suggesting it," Eanna said, his eyebrows accomplices to his mock innocence.

In the end, she went into Joannas in the main street in Sligo. Joanna, the proprietor knew her from the Farmers' Market. Explaining the situation to a veneered face, she found her Dublin intonations on the rise. Joanna appraised her wordlessly, and headed in the direction of multiple dresses she had wrapped up and sheathed in plastic covers by the back wall. Instantly she loved the royal blue silk offering. Its soft cowl neckline, tightened waist and sleek fit over the hips was made for her. A flicker announced itself in Joanna's eyes behind her, as she studied her reflection in the long mirror.

"Compliments your skin tone perfectly."

There was the slightest serration in her polished tone. A prickle of unease ran down the nape of Ron's neck.

"Do you have something to put over it?" she asked.

"Yes, give me a minute."

Joanna disappeared from view as she headed up the spiral staircase.

"You look stunning."

The voice caught her unawares. It was Una Healy from the farm whose land their cottage was on. She turned around to face the older woman.

"Lord, I wish I had your figure. Don't mind that upstart,"
she whispered loudly.

Relief washed over Ron. God, she loved the country people. She beamed out a nebulae of smiles at the middle aged woman standing there, one foot uneasily balanced behind the other, her torso dropped.

"It's my back- can't stand for long," she said apologetically, heading for the grey sedan chair in the corner. Her brown belted coat swallowed her down to the tips of her square black shoes as she walked. Joanna arrived back with a selection of silver wraps. Slightly embarrassed by the choice, she unfurled the first one.

"That'll do," she said quickly.

Una looked over at her quizzically.

"No need for a fuss," she said quietly. "You're coming to Joe and Sally's aren't you Una?"

She was rewarded with a quick nod of the head. Joanna looked over at the older woman, her face coated with a paper smile.

"Lucky for some," she murmured, her voice a cool current.

"Well, just give me back the other dresses," she said crisply, referring to the grey and red ones still hanging in the dressing room.

"Come to the counter when you're ready."

Mutely Ron handed over the dresses without meeting her eye. She cleared her throat as she exited the dressing room, crossed over to Una, bequeathing a wink and a small shoulder squeeze. Then she faced the counter, emitting an exaggerated sigh. "Sorry", she said to a surprised Joanna. "Just tired - too many preparations for the big night; I'm sure you know from your own social life how these things go." She thought she heard a short laugh dissolve into a sudden cough behind her.

"That'll be €400 for the lot," Joanna said. Her eyes betrayed the smooth curve of her lips. Ron produced her credit card with a flourish which her theatrical mother would have loved.

The party at Joe and Sally's got underway by about nine. Brendan came in with a couple of his friends. He had texted to say they were shooting pool in Lorcan's back garden. Then Lorcan's dad was dropping him off to the cottage to get changed. She nudged Eanna, who was warming his hands standing by the large white chimney breast, and discreetly reading Christmas cards on the mantelpiece.

"Check him out, check him out"

she whispered cogently. They weren't the only ones checking him out she realised. Sally's twenty- year- old niece, Laura, from Birmingham had been staying with her aunt for the last few days. She had competition too, she noted with a mother's triumphalism. Lorcan's twin, Julie was star- struck. Lorcan said something to her. She blushed an indeterminate crimson, then suddenly became intent on studying the arc of the Christmas tree lights spiralling across the wooden floor. Ron caught the word mistletoe. Eanna and half the room caught it too. A ripple of cloaked amusement showed on many of the faces. "Yes, he scrubbed up well," she thought, especially with his Calvin Klein jeans, Tommy Hilfiger white shirt and Hobbs shoes. She noted the moonstone pendant around his neck. She'd given him a hundred euro voucher for Heffernans men's clothing in Sligo. The rest of his cool wardrobe, he had purchased himself. After their chat in the woods, he had asked her if she minded him buying designer gear.

"God, no," she replied.

"I just wanted you to have a bit of perspective Love, that's all".

"Designer clothes will look great on you. Go for it." .

He was beaming over at her from the doorway, oblivious to the stir he was causing. "Still my man," she thought to herself absently."But not for long," an under current in her warned. She caught sight of Una coming in the door. She and her husband Tommy were divesting themselves of their coats when she flew over to them.

"Great to see youse"

Una smiled, aware of her husband's encompassing gaze. Ron was too, but pushed on regardless. There would be no alcohol tonight. This one, she could handle on her own.

"Tommy, great you could come," she said.

"Una was telling me about your livestock when I ran into her in town."

He looked surprised and discomfited by turn. Then he dropped his head and strummed his chin with his fingers, shooting a surreptitious glance at his wife.

"Yeah," he muttered, "got in ten new ewes last week."

"They'll be a great addition to us Ron," Una said. "We can breed from them."

She smiled. She didn't have a bean about sheep, but she'd ask Eanna later.

Sally was beckoning to her from across the room.

"Excuse me, Sally's looking for me. Lovely dress," she remarked over her shoulder as she headed to where her stepmother was standing in the kitchen doorway.

"I bought it in Amys- wouldn't give yer wan the custom."

Ron pivoted a full 360 degrees, and gave her a double thumbs up.

"What was all that about?" Sally asked.

"Oh a bit of bonding between me and Una," she said with a giggle.

Sally lifted her eyebrows and looked in Una's direction.

"Nice woman," she said softly.

"Now Miss O'Connell, I need a little help. Around ten when I give you the nod, I want you to turn off all the lights, except of course those on the Christmas tree. Then Brendan can blow out the candles on the cake."

In the kitchen, the caterers buzzed around discreetly, emptying drink trays, stacking the dishwasher and preparing the canapés. Ron was transfixed.

"My God, canapés and what else?" she whispered.

Sally whispered back, "Only the best for our boy."

Her eyes bore down on the cake then. It was in the shape of a Boeing 747. Typed in alternate silver and gold lettering on the near wing were the words 'Bon Voyage'. Suddenly her composure was hijacked, emotions cutting a swathe through her. Joanne Brady, who was helping her father with the serving, slid a tissue down her sleeve. She handed it over and patted her arm. Gratefully she smiled at her. She wondered idly what her mascara must look like this time.

A quick trip to the loo enabled her wipe off the runaway mascara. She reapplied a touch of her Clarins makeup and lipstick. Maybe she could get the hang of this designer thing after all. What the heck, you only live once, and if you get it right they say, once is enough. She so wanted for him to get it right.

People continued to come upstairs to the large sitting room. It seemed half of Drombawn was there. Aileen and Ailbhe sent their apologies. Aileen had a bout of winter flu. She surveyed them all from the kitchen doorway. Eanna was in chat with John, her school principal. Una was sitting by the tree having a brandy and visibly enjoying some banter with a few of the young ones. Her husband stood alone until David from the local co-op drew him into conversation. The lads were having a few beers standing over by the chimney breast. In the middle of the room, the girls were laughing affectedly, and shooting studied glances in their direction from under heavily policed and painted eyelids.

Sally called everyone to the kitchen for the buffet. Speared avocado and salmon, Quiche Lorraine with some side salads and vol-au-vents with white rice made a welcome change from turkey and ham, everyone agreed. Sally's niece angled her way up to where Brendan was standing. It seemed the Birmingham lass could flick her long black hair over her shoulder at record- breaking intervals. Poor Julie, Ron thought; it was always the same for the shy ones. Well, she never had that problem exactly. Working- class girls in tough areas were quicker per force off the starting blocks.

She took the nod when it was time to turn off the lights. The room was peopled with silhouettes as a galaxy of camera phone lights created a felt intimacy. Smartphones flashed in the dark. Cutting the cake, he looked a little excited, embarrassed, surprised; she couldn't really tell from across the way. As unobtrusively as she could, she edged her way until she was at his elbow.

"Have a fantastic trip son," she whispered.

He stiffened as she planted a long kiss on his cheek. There was a chorus of "Stay in that pose Ron. Put your arm around him. Joe and Sally, get in there too."

So there they were, all four, Dublin and Manchester celebs on show. Outside the window, the winter grey waters of the lake pooled and foamed silently.

CHAPTER 21

Skyping happened weekly in Joe and Sally's. She contented herself with WhatsApp in between whenever either of them could make it happen. They had emailed each other tentative schedules. There were weeks when it seemed neither of them could snatch a free hour. Working in a Roman trattoria, he had quite a few night shifts. Then he was often asleep by day. That's when the long emails began. Late at night, cocoa in hand, the keyboard travelled a journey bearing all of her Leitrim in its hard drive. He never tired of hearing even the trivia. It took him usually until the evening of the following day to reply.

From brendanoconnell21@gmail.com
To ronoconnell15@gmail.com.
February 20 2019 5.02pm
Subject: Brendan The Navigator
Hi Ma,

Blue skies over Rome today, though it is nippy. I'm working four nights a week in Mario Ricci's family- run trattoria here in Trastevere. The Italians don't dine out until about 9.30pm at the earliest, and every meal is a production. I work every second Saturday during the day. I think I'm getting the hang of making a decent pizza al forno now. The culture here is so cool and laid back. The girls are hot and the guys have to be even hotter! Do you like my new profile photo with the slicked- back hairstyle? So no more tentacles. Cool white shirts and chinos make the ladies swoon. Ma, you'd love the Italian women. They'd rather be dead than seen without their makeup on. There was a little old lady died of hypothermia last winter here- no money for fuel and very little for food,but she still went to L'estetista (the beautician) just beside where I work. She was always so beautifully dressed and made up, no one knew she was poor. Everyone was shocked when she was discovered like that.

You were asking me about the two guys in the apartment with me.Well, Raphael is 20, and he's a student of architecture. He gets the bus to the university every day. He gave me a guided tour of the famous buildings in Rome last week on my day off. He seriously knows his stuff about the Roman Forum and the Circus Maximus and all the history of Rome. He has his own car by the way. The other guy is the quiet one, Piero. He's not sure what he wants to be just yet, but he loves to paint. Right now, he's working in the trattoria with me, but he has signed on for some daytime classes in the Accademia di Belle Arti. We just call it the Accademia. I might take some courses there too, especially in painting. I told him my father was a really good artist, but he died before I was born. He smiled and said 'Che triste'- how sad-

I like him; he's from down south -San Vitaliano, only 30 kilometres from Naples. His dad works as a waiter in Sorrento. There are three English girls in the apartment below us. I've only seen them out and about. They like sunbathing on the flat roof, even though at least one of them has red hair and freckles. Me, I like sitting in the shade and eating gelato (ice cream). The guys are mad jealous because I *still get a tan.*

I've been exploring all the sights of Rome. Of course I had to see the Sistine Chapel. Man, *that ceiling"* Way to go Michelangelo. The guard was giving me dirty looks because I sat there so long staring up. There was this ornamental chair just behind a cordon, and I was dying to sneak in there to get a better angle, so I waited until the security guard took a lunch break. Some of the guys in the bar told me the best time to visit is between 1 and 2pm on a Tuesday. They have no relief guard on that day. I was doing some drawing sitting on the nice ancient chair when a shout from a big goliath of a security man knocked the creation scene off the ceiling, well close ! I was hauled out to the guard's office at the rear of the building. I had to follow him down some spooky corridors. I thought I'd be fined or jailed or something. When we got to his office, he motioned to me to show him my drawings. Suddenly his face actually creased into a small smile.

"Non è male," he said over and over. That means "not bad." Then he said,

"bueno, molti bueno."

All this was followed by a big lecture in Italian which I didn't understand a word of. He paused for breath, then looked at me and asked,

'Di dov'è Lei?' (where are you from).

I said," Irlanda."

Then he said, " il Papa, il Papa- è andato in Irlanda."

He beamed at me."Cattolico?" he enquired, raising big wild eyebrows.

"Si, si," I assured him.

"I swear Ma, I would be any religion he asked me. Anyway, he let me off with another Italian- sounding flea in my ear. I must have said "Grazie" a hundred times before I fled back down the long corridor and out a side door."

That's all for now,

Your own Michaelangelo!

Ciao,

Brendan.

She had just finished scanning the last sentence when she heard a shout from the kitchen.

"Ron, you up in the bedroom?"

She clicked on the x in the top right hand corner of the screen and put the lid down on the laptop. For some reason she always liked to read his messages upstairs. "Up with the cherubs," Sally said, or the swallows she thought under the eaves .The mud nest clinging to the side of the wall was empty now. He was in the kitchen on the mobile when she came in, a mug of steaming coffee in his left hand, sipping it whilst listening to Auntie Nora. He was saying now,

"Phew, that's a relief. Woman you're a trooper - can't thank you enough.

Bye, bye."

He turned to face her slowly, almost gingerly touching the red handset icon before placing the phone down on the cream countertop. His eyes had a new register of faint bewilderment.

"Everything alright?"

He nodded carefully, still weighing up his words. Then he beamed a wide ranging smile on her.

"I'm off the hook for a while anyway, assuming they don't kill each other."

Her eyebrows arched into a large question mark.

"Auntie Nora is going to take in Ailbhe and Ma for a while, just 'til Ma gets back on her feet."

Relief expanded his shoulders and released his chest.

"Sit down Love," she said taking the coffee from him. "I'll make up a refill."

She filled up the coffee machine again, changing the filter as she spoke. She was aware, glancing at him sideways, that he sat slumped in the chair. The last couple of months had aged him. The crevices under his eyes had slid down towards his cheekbones. The fleck in them didn't dance anymore.

"That's really good news," she said, carefully putting the lid on the machine before flicking down the switch. "Does this mean?"

"Yes," he said emphatically.

"Yes,Yes, I can stay here and know they're going to be fine."

She said nothing, just grabbed a chamomile teabag from her exotic tea box blend and popped it into her favourite lavender mug. Waiting for the kettle to boil, she looked out at the garden. The speared daffodil buds shivered in unison in their patio boxes, afraid to open in the prolonged cold.

"Ron, are you happy?" he said, his voice a lost shoreline "I know it's been tough with Brendan gone and everything."

She exhaled an imprisoned sigh before turning around. She crossed over to him and kissed him on the top of the head. He pulled her down with both hands. Their kiss grew deaf to the sudden whistling of the kettle.

'Oh God,' she thought as tears blinded her in a headlock. "Oh Lord, I'm at it again,"

she said, helplessly fumbling for a handkerchief in her green cardigan sleeve.

"Well," he said finding his own tissue first, and dabbing her face, "at least no mascara today."

She laughed, perching bird like on the edge of his lap and kissing him again. The chamomile and the coffee sat flatly waiting .

From ron oconnell15@gmail.com

To brendanocconnell21@gmail.com

February 21 2019 3.04

Subject Brendan The Navigator under blue skies

Great to hear from you as always Love. I adore hearing about blue skies over Rome. We've had some shocking frost at night and pretty cold days. It's been hard on the vegetables and herbs that aren't in the polytunnels. Anyway, enough gloom. You don't want to be hearing about boring old Leitrim. Be nice to the English girls downstairs. I notice you didn't tell me their names. Courage mio figlio. Invite them in for coffee. Your friends sound like something out of a movie to me. As for the Sistine Chapel episode, as long as you weren't trying to take photos in there, were you? I suppose no harm done. That old chair was probably a couple of hundred years old. You could have knocked the bottom out of it and we'd have to pay the Vatican! Being a true Dub, you got on the right side of the guard. I'm dying to see those drawings. Will you WhatsApp them to me or maybe post them on Instagram? You could be selling movies to Netflix yet, "Brendan in Rome," doing a video diary thing, like the one you put up of historic Rome. That got you 200 followers I noticed.

We've had a long day here. I had to stay back after school to put up farewell banners in the big hall for Miss Bowles' retirement. You met her last year when you called in to me in school for a lift to a match in Derrynaglin. She has taught all the parents here in Junior Infants. Big Mike Hanratty, you know the Cummins kids' dad ? said he remembers winning a lollipop from her. Hard to believe that now to look at him. Some of the parents are going to pop in and surprise her on the night. She'll be mortified.

Good news for Eanna and myself. Auntie Nora is going to take in Ailbhe and his Ma for a while. That gives us all a break, I've been worried about him working too hard and losing money on his business by not being hands- on. Sally and Da send their love. Sally has probably emailed you all the news from their end. We'll see you on Skype anyway Sunday night, that is if you aren't sight-seeing with one of the English girls. I'm dying to hear their names, probably Penelope or Dorothy or Dawn. Are you enjoying your work? How is that new boss Mario treating you?

Miss you lots.

Love,

Ma.

The week flew by with a kind of urgency. Spring always did that to her anyway. But in Dobbinstown it was more about standing at bus queues in skimpy jackets, tight stone- washed denim jeans and two inch high heels, waiting for a bus to town in the raw cold on a day off work. God, those heels; they wouldn't do with the vegetables or the herbs. She remembered the tug on her psyche, or so it seemed as the days struggled to lengthen. Here it was different .Normally she leaned into the days, though of late she felt unease, somehow chafing at the raw edges of the growing season. At times she inched back to the cocoon of winter fireside nights. She held the lemon balm seedlings between her fingers for an instant before transplanting them into the small pots. Already they were infusing the polytunnel.

"Nice comforting little beggars aren't they?" Eanna said over her shoulder.

Smiling, with the seedlings still held in a pinch between her fingers, she asked,

"Any news from Dublin?"

"All quiet on the Eastern front. Seriously they're getting on like a house on fire."

Then he went silent. That's when the gnawing concern showed in her eyes, as they rested frankly on him.

"Well not exactly a house on fire. There were a few mutterings from Ma. Nora can be a bit of a control freak."

She packed more of the earth into the small pot, her breath not quite waiting for her hand to catch up.

"Ma says Nora doesn't understand Ailbhe, and not just her speech."

Here he took a long pause, as if wondering where the steering wheel was in this communication.

"She's been into boys for a long time really; there's this fella- a supervisor I think- in the workshop in Fettercong"

181

"The place where they make the cards?"

"Yeah, all the proceeds go to Down syndrome Ireland. Well he's Downs as well, but more advanced than her. Ma thinks they're getting way too cosy."

"Ah, God love her. Is she on the pill?"

He looked at her as if she had just asked him for an abortion, she thought. Slowly she put down the plant, brushed down the soil from her apron.

"All I'm saying love," she said, keeping her voice even, "is, you've got to stop treating her like a little child." She looked up at him now slowly. His face was uncomprehending.

"She's twenty- eight isn't she? I know Santa Claus and sex; It's a tough one for your Ma. Just don't count on Santa Claus alone, is all I'm saying."

"She'd never..." his voice trailed off.

"Come on, finish up here," she said gently. "There's no never with baby making. I ought to know."

He exhaled a spent sigh.

"God I'm bushed; I need a coffee and a fag."

She injected a double -strength question into her eyes.

"Okay, I'll stay on Lobelia- you know the herbal nicorette I told you about."

"Perfect." She realised her tone sounded satisfied even to herself. He realised it too, and touched her shoulder lightly.

"We're going good Ron aren't we?" I know I've asked you that already. It's just that these days..."

"We're going just fine."

She linked her arm through his as they stepped across the unlit gravel path around the polytunnel. There were clouds of dark rain granules gathering as they got into the Skoda. As he started up the ignition, she said

"I know I'm a bit shirty these days-female hormones and all that."

He gave her a sideways look.

"Oh nothing like that." Her reply cruised on the wing of a speedy inbreath.

"I'm taking those little pills in the box, remember?"

The corners of his eyes lifted a tad as he smiled faintly.

CHAPTER 22

From brendanoconnell21@gmail.com
    To ronoconnell15@gmail.com
    March 4 2019 12.10pm
    Subject Brendan The Navigator got lucky.
    A smile stretched out her lips languorously when she read the
subject line."What made him so lucky?" she wondered. The Ides of
March hadn't affected him obviously. The month had come in like
a lamb. She worried about the lion part in the tail though. Anyway
she was always treading on eggshells around fate. Time to relax her
vigilance. And here was her boy navigating the streets of Rome.
    Well Ma, how are things?
    Are you and Eanna still having a bit more time to yourselves?
I hope he hasn't had to go back to Dublin. I finally did what you
asked, well not exactly, but a version of it anyway! I knocked on the
British girls' door yesterday and introduced myself. Piero was too
shy and Raphael already has a girlfriend. I plucked up my courage.
You'd have been proud of me. I did that "we're out of coffee" trick,
standing with a big soft head on me at the door. Anyway, this real
nice girl, Sarah, no not Penelope or Dorothy invited me in. She
seems to be the eldest of the three. As it turned out, they were all
at home. Well it was 7pm, and I had a night off. I have to admit,
I kind of enjoyed myself with them; they're all from London. But
wait for it, two out of the three have Irish relations. Sarah's parents
are from Sligo, but have been living in Richmond in London for
over thirty years. Elizabeth's grandmother is from Donegal. As it
so happens, there is a Dawn. She's from Islington and her parents
are from Yorkshire. They're all so nice and down to earth. Two of
them are being funded to study for a year at the American University
of Rome. They're law students from UL (University of Limerick)
who want to work in an international law firm. Those are the ones

with the Irish heritage. Dawn is actually a newly qualified nurse, who is friendly with Sarah's younger sister in London. She and her boyfriend have kind of broken up, and just want some time on their own for a while. She just wanted some blue skies to cheer her up. (Don't we all, Ron thought, a sigh vaporising from her breath). She got a job in the Roma International Hospital, which is close by. They're always looking for English -speaking nurses there because it's privately run. I stayed for over an hour. Raphael opened the jar of coffee when I came back upstairs. He took a whiff of it, smiled at me and said "I smell romance." Those Italians Ma, always so full of amore- you would love them, but they'd be too dramatic for Eanna. The girls are going to be invited up to our flat next week for a coffee. Watch this space.

I'm enjoying work a bit more now. They are thinking of sending me on a barista course, but I'd have to stay longer for that. I said I'd think about it but "The Big Apple" awaits and of course *Peru*. Mario, the boss can be very temperamental. One day I spilled some olive oil all over the countertop in the kitchen and he went ballistic. I was told later it's a superstitious thing here, like spilling salt. Another day, we were toasting George, an English guy who's been working here for six months; he was leaving to go to Africa to do volunteer work. They had run out of wine by the time I got to the kitchen so I filled my glass with tap water and raised it. There were looks of horror all around. I looked back at them with shock. Suddenly I was persona non gratis. Should I crawl into a worm hole and come out in another century? I wondered. Piero explained afterwards about the superstition; I was bringing bad luck with my glass of water. And I thought we were bad in Ireland with walking under a ladder! These crazy Italians are way worse than us. They're funny, but so drammatico. One more thing before I finish- I have to send some drawings into the Accademia to be accepted even on only a four

-week course. I haven't heard back yet, but the guys here think they're seriously good. So fingers crossed .

Must go here now,

Ciao ,

Brendan

PS, I like the idea of selling a movie to Netflix - might do a post grad in media studies. Watch this space.

From ronoconnell15@gmail.com

To brendanoconnell21@gmail.com

March 6 2019 5.05pm

Subject: Brendan The Navigator and women!

Hi Love,

Lovely to see you on Skype last Sunday night. Your grandad gets all teary- eyed. Don't tell him I told you that now. His arthritis is acting up in his knee and lower back these days. Sally wants him to see a consultant surgeon in Sligo General, but you know our Joe! Eanna and I are still having full weeks together, but I do wonder for how long more. Auntie Nora is a pain in the ass, and Ailbhe has discovered boys. His Ma finds it all hard to cope with. She's off the fags to help with the asthma. Eanna says the humour isn't the best with her as a result. The business is coming on well, now that we can both be here all week. The new polytunnels are up. Eanna has applied to the Department of Agriculture for a grant to erect two greenhouses. He approached Aldi for a contract to grow culinary herbs, and they're going to give him the green light. Their marketing manager and commissioned horticulturalist were very impressed with his organic vegetables and all the herbs. We have so much beginning to come on now, though still not flowering. He has increased the herb space for yet again more yarrow, chamomile, marigold, lemon balm , hyssop ,borage (which he says is for the courage). There are small hawthorn and lime trees by the back wall, not to mention the dandelions (piss a beds literally!} and a serious nettle and ribbed plantain patch. Last count, he s growing 30 herbs and rising; it's so exciting for him. In time, the teacher in him hopes to give classes on growing your own herbs. Aldi could mean serious money for us in the short term. I know, I know, I don't need it, but he does. He won't be a kept man he says, and I say, what woman would be daft enough to keep him anyway only me? He plans to get into tincture production eventually down the line. But I said glass houses first- "padam, padam," one step at a time as they say in Sanskrit. I learned that line in my mindfulness class a few years back. Tincture production is a big outlay between steel vats and casks, not to mention a bottling operation. I remind him we are young yet. He has such big dreams on the holistic medicine front, and again I remind him good things come to those who wait. Our Green Pharma Centre will be a flagship for natural medicine centres all over Ireland. Those are his words, not mine. In the meantime, he's selling the dried herbs at the market along with the organic veg. Our herbs are in much demand from the herbalists around the neighbouring counties. It seems they're more potent than from some of the other suppliers. He sees patients at night after seven, on Tuesdays and Thursdays. Then we have the Farmers' Market on Saturdays. I help make up his tinctures, that is his phyto- defence formula -winter tonic to you and me - which we often bring to sell at the market.

Now back to those girls, I knew you would have an impact there. Which one of them do you fancy the most? Will it be Sarah or will it be Elizabeth or will it be Dawn from Islington as they say on Blind Date? The art course is a shoo in. Joe and Sally loved your drawings on Instagram. Your Grandad laughed mightily when I told him about the guard and the Sistine Chapel.

"Alice all over," is what he said. That's a compliment by the way. Don't mind that Mario fella and his superstitions. If Italians were only discussing the weather, you'd think Vesuvius was going to erupt. I must fly now; I've dinner to make. Eanna will be in shortly.

Ciao mio figlio,
Mamma Ron.
"Brendan the Navigator has been on I see,"
he said, coming up behind her unexpectedly.
"Yes." She quickly shaded her yet unsent reply from him, turning down the laptop cover a fraction. She didn't want him to read what she had said about Auntie Nora- pain in the ass or not, she was still his Auntie Nora.

"Yeah, he's doing well, even on the women front! She bolted a fixed smile onto her eyes. He kneaded his own eyelids with the backs of his fingers. That dog- tired look was in them again.

"Great stuff," he said quietly.

"I thought you'd still be on the farm?"

Guilt stole a ride across his features. His eyes flickered warily.

"Ron, I was thinking- no need to cook tonight. Why don't we go to Vie de Chateau in Manorhamish for a treat instead? Its midweek, so they can easily take a booking."

"What ?" he said, seeing the question teetering and falling off the cliff -face of her eyebrows.

"Are you buttering me up for something?"

The kitchen drank down the moment's silence.

"Come on, spit it out Eanna."

"I have to go back to Dublin for a while- well not til around the 20th. I might be able to delay it til the first of April at the latest. Some of the Dublin gang are gonna manage Ma and Ailbhe until then."

She said nothing for a while. The kitchen wall clock ticked harshly. His hands spoke in an agitated arc as he clasped them above his head, then unclasped them, finally flattening them to his sides. He rolled out his shoulders slowly. She couldn't muster up the will to give them a massage.

"God, Eanna of all the times when we need you here. By next month, the building will be taking off properly, and there will be more work in the nurseries.

"I know, I know. It's just they have no one. Things aren't working out with Nora.

It'll only be for two to three weeks at most'til they sort out something.

I'm so sorry Ron." He studied the floor tiles at his feet before looking up at her with mute appeal.

"Can you understand?"

"I bloody don't," she thought .

"I'll cook," she said, her voice sandpapered."You can't buy me off with Vie de Chateau."

She reheated the stew from the previous day, and waged war on the delph as she took it out of the press, refusing all offers of help. Eanna seated miserably at the table, made a play of reading *the Independent*. At the sound of the heavy clattering, he turned around. Suddenly he headed out to the back for a smoke. She wiped away the viper tears that stung her eyes. It just wasn't *fair*. No fancy restaurant could fix this mess.

CHAPTER 23

She stared out her bedroom window. An early morning nubile sun slid sensuously over the brow of the drumlin beyond the thistle field. Healy's sheep grazed undisturbed. Their hallmark wool droppings were left along the wire fence dividing the field from the house. Dew drops necklaced in- between them. She pulled up the collar around her red Candlewick dressing gown, her feet uninformed of the cold floor beneath her. Hard to believe it was two weeks since "All Fools' Day." Who was the fool this time? she wondered. He had gone on cue- March 20th, couldn't even wait 'til April. Damn those two in Dublin. God, why couldn't things have worked out with Nora? No, her knight in shining armour to the rescue as always.

"Why in God's name, she had wailed to Joe, does he have to go now just when the foundations for the new greenhouses have to be dug, and he's got the contract from Aldi?" Joe remained stock still, looking out the front window of the cottage.

"The worst bit of all," she continued, irked by his silence,

"is the architect has just drawn up the plans for the new house. The foundations are meant to be in by early May, and he may not be back by then at all by the looks of it, so what happens now?"

Joe continued to stare, then turned to her, bringing up the full wick of his smile.

"Look over at the stream Ron."

"What has a bloody stream got to do with anything?" she thought, "just 'cause you're content Da."

"See the ripples now. Stand back, and see the wall."

"I never noticed that before," she said flatly, suddenly aware,despite herself of the sunlight- patterned water swirling around the gable end of the house.

"There's a pattern to everything Love. You can't always see it at first."

"Da, me very own philosopher," she said sanguinely, leaning her head on his left shoulder.

She felt scooped out inside these days, a carved pumpkin. Gently, Joe put his big arm around her, and she heard his long slow exhale.

"I'll be off now," he said. He'd taken to calling in around six, a couple of evenings a week.

"See you on Sunday for the Skype."

That's when Ron usually visited them. Sally begged her to come up more often and have dinner. Something in her resisted. She wouldn't cry to them or live on their coattails either.

Today was thankfully a Saturday. She had some time to dream and email. She also had to meet Jack Casey and Mick Brady up at the farm, who were digging out the foundations for the new greenhouses in the back acre. Then she would check on the new polytunnels which had been erected before Eanna went to Dublin. She needed to make sure that the heating in them was constant as the frost could kill off some of the less hardy plants. She enjoyed meeting the men, and they knew she could give as good as she got. But she knew too they'd skived off to the pub more than once when they were meant to be digging out more channels for drainage.

"Bloody Auntie Nora," she thought.

'Bloody Eanna, couldn't you just once have forgotten where you left your bloody shining armour?'

In the afternoon, she drove down the rutted lane to the four acres they were leasing again from Jim Gibbons' adjoining farm. Eanna had added two more acres after the first- year lease had ended. Having lived in the old farmhouse that came with the land for a couple of years, he had had it painted, cleaned out and basic pieces of furniture put back in. Now he used it to see patients at night. Sitting in her car outside its straight up pebble- dashed front and small brown window frames, she tried to envisage it according to the artist's impression that Mike - Eanna's friend- had drawn up for them. Eanna was very excited about the Green Pharma Centre. Poring over plans was one thing, but seeing a drawing on a computer screen made a butterfly emerge from where it had been cocooned in imagination. He was breathless, talking about healing spas, treatment rooms and a medical doctor on board. His very energy was a bird with bright plumage taking the dulled feathers of her own caution apart. She was soaring with him. Suddenly she felt the bright bird had bombed. A fat waddling duck had replaced it. First things first they both agreed, would be the house. Then they would have the next decade to go for their goals. The house couldn't even get started; they weren't yet hitched and she knew that some of her money had to be used. What if he pulled out of everything including the relationship? She had a sudden memory of Alice reading "Daedalus and Icarus" to Brendan when he was seven. Like Icarus, they were soaring close to the sun, and she didn't cherish the idea of damp feathers in the ocean before they drowned.

It had been a long Skype with him that morning. She wanted to see him properly she told him, in person and fairly soon. He reassured her once he got things sorted at the weekends, and carers were in place, he'd pack.

"I cancelled the digger," she said. "It can wait 'til your return."

She was surprised by the length of his silence. The small sinews that carried themselves down his face from the inner edge of his cheekbone began to twitch. He was drumming his fingers softly on the kitchen table. She could just about make out Aileen's figure hovering around the cooker under an open window.

"Tell you what Ron," he said softly, and then paused.

She watched him turn, and saw the entreaty in his eyes when he caught his mother's attention. Aileen's retreating figure disappeared through the doorway. It slammed shut.

"I might be another while here, to tell you the truth. You're well able for it,"

he said to the overt protest he saw forming around her lips.

"I'll keep them on their toes at this end."

From: brendanoconnell21@gmail.com

To: ronoconnel15@gmail.com

April14 2019 11.00am

Subject Brendan The Navigator socialising

Ciao Mamma,

Saluti da Roma,

How are you? You must be missing himself these days. Sorry to hear he isn't back yet. I hope Joe and Sally are keeping an eye on you 'til he is home. As usual, the sky today is your favourite shade, duck- egg blue. We've had molte docce.(many showers) The Romans complain about the weather just like we do. Now I ask you?! How are things at your end anyway? As you know, I was accepted into the Accademia. It will be a dress rehearsal for art college on my return. I got your congratulations card yesterday, Grazie Mamma. We've been doing life drawings, that is nude models. Our professor says if you can draw the human figure accurately you can draw anything in nature. It gives perspective and symmetry. I didn't mention this to Grandad, well, just in case you know... it's all very discreet really. Models change behind a screen, and then they pose at different angles, so we get an appreciation of every aspect of human form. One guy was grinning the first day when a young girl came out before all six of us at our easels. He's banned from the class for the next two weeks. Did you get a chance to look at any of my drawings that I sent on Instagram?

Now I must tell you about the social life that I've discovered. There's a whole Roman youth culture and it's not in the pub like at home or the night club. They use these old municipal buildings with massive empty spaces in them. They're called Centri Sociali and there's one near the old Roman baths. It's a cool hang out, brilliant vibe. I get to go on Sunday nights when I'm off or sometimes I can do a day shift on a Friday as I swap with Benito. He's got a family, and doesn't go out Friday nights anyway. They had an art exhibition there last month. They do plays as well as having live music bands. I wish I could stay a bit longer but I'm hungry for a bite of the "Big Apple. "

Ciao,

tuo figlio,

Brendan.

Her head was in a slow tiresome swing. She was in her favourite pose on her tummy, reading his emails on the bed upstairs under the eaves. The face of the world was rapidly becoming featureless. The pellucid skies of Rome, wistful with vagrant showers, clamoured for her attention. God, she'd love to be there. Did she and Eanna love each other enough? Why had he never proposed? Was it too late now to leave all this domesticity behind and follow her son to New York? She was a free agent. All she had to do was cancel the building work and to *hell* with them all. She was being strangled in a big unwieldy noose while she had an unlived youth to restore.

From: ronoconnell15@gmail.com

To: brendanoconnell21@gmail.com

April 15.2019 11.13am

Subject Sounds Fab.

Hi Love,

I'm mad jealous. I can just see you in that big arty building with Dawn and all your friends. Yes you did mention you asked her out a few weeks ago, though the details have been scarce since. We did Romeo and Juliet when I was in Junior Cert, and I can picture gangs of Italian young fellas on mopeds turning up to a live gig. As for the art, well let's maybe leave Grandad in the dark on that one. In answer to your question, I've been up to my eyes at work and didn't get a chance yet to look at your drawings, but I know they're brilliant.

194

Weather is passable here in Leitrim, but the showers come out of nowhere as usual. No blue skies of Rome to lift a soul .

Sunday of next week is Easter Sunday. Where will you go to celebrate? Eanna will be in Dublin I'm afraid for Easter, so just Joe, Sally and yours truly the spare. Did you get any more messages from Eanna on WhatsApp? I'm guessing he told you the plans for the house may still be on track. I'm supposed to ring the builders and undo my previous cancellation, a tall order from the Boss. The diggers can get in, and the guys can lay the foundations. You will have a palace to return to or at least one in the making if we ever manage to get it all together.

School going OK, I guess. My special needs' kids distract me from all that's going on here. One of them, Grainne, has severe dyspraxia. Remember me telling you about her?; she can't tie her shoelaces, cut paper or do PE. As for Rihanna, my Downs child, she is such a sweetheart. She has made an Easter card for you which I will photograph and send it on WhatsAppp later. Must run now (I'm always running these days.) It can get pretty draining I can tell you.

Ciao mio figlio,

Mamma.

Easter crept up on her slowly, insanely, mundanely. Sally, somewhat concerned about the shadows under her eyes and her unusual silences when they met, offered her a girls' night in on Easter Saturday. Joe was going to the boxing club to do the books while it was quiet. She turned it down, and had already refused point blank, despite their protestatations, to join her father and stepmother for Easter Sunday lunch.

What the hell was wrong with her? Where was her joy in living gone? She hated bloody Leitrim; she wanted a bunker, not a life. She envied Brendan. Did her last email sound morose, put upon? Too late now - she had hit the green arrow of no return, and all her pancake news was in cyberspace. She poured herself a final glass of Merlot.

"God, she thought, "Ive polished off the bottle."

She barely managed to get herself up the stairs at 1am on Sunday morning. When she climbed into bed, she pulled up the covers over her head and crawled into a cave .

The phone rang out at 7, 7.30, 8 and 8.30am. She stared at the ceiling, and remembered her dream chasing Brendan into his Centro Sociale, but he wouldn't face her. Her voice was hoarse from calling him, until out of the shadows emerged a gang of Italian biker guys. One of them was grabbing her roughly saying, "Why can't you see?" The first insistent garrulous ringtone hauled her out of her unfinished dialogue. She had no idea, nor did she care what time it was. She wasn't answering. She turned to face the wall. There was a small spider in the top right- hand corner scuttling into a thin crack. She shut her ears on the intentionality behind each successive call. On the final one she turned and grabbed the phone angrily from her locker. The dial flashed 'Sally'. Oh Lord, now what?

"Hi, she said in a dishwater voice.

"Hi Love." The tone was concerned.

"Sorry, I was asleep and didn't get to hear you the first time."

"Oh well, I didn't mean to wake ..."

"No, no , it's fine."

She knew her unleavened tone was becoming commonplace these days even to herself. A terrible tiredness swept over her suddenly, drunkenly. Swearing, she touched off the bedpost unsteadily, knocking over her coffee mug on the locker.

"What was that? Ron what's the matter? You OK?"

Sally's inflections were rising on the tectonic scale every moment.

"Ah Sal I'm just so **tired,**" she exploded into the receiver.

"I don't know what to do. I'm just spent, that's all."

Then she realised she was crying into the empty silences, and burrowed back under the covers. The mobile slid down the sheet, a dull magpie object that had a shiny front and emitted voices.

The doorbell was sharp and peremptory. She sat up in bed, an unnamed terror clenched between her teeth. Whoever they were, they could go away. Then her phone rang. Oh God, Sally **again**. Why was she being such a pain in the ass? Didn't she realise she wanted to be alone?

" You are alone," her own voice reminded dispassionately, starkly cruel. There was a time in Dublin she craved space. Now space had become galactic, even in a small cottage. She let the phone ring out, staring at it as if from outside her head. Then reflexively, she grabbed it and tapped on the last call.

"Ron, you've got to let me in. If you don't, I'll break a window. Are you listening?"

In silent reply, as much to herself as the older woman, she instinctively grabbed her dressing gown strewn on the floor, and headed for the stairs. She grabbed the key from the hook on the wall to the left of the front door, and met her stepmother in the full glare of a remarkably sunny morning.

"It's Easter Sunday; Eanna is frantic. He's been trying to ring you and he now has rung me."

"So he knows I'm not dead," she said, her voice squeezed through the ringer of a corpsed self.

Sally paused , scanning her intently. Gently now, she pushed the open door inwards, touching Ron's arm softly.

"I'm coming in Love. Now I need a strong brew. Lead on Macbeth."

Both of them surveyed the kitchen mess with the newly horrified eyes of those coming across carnage on a battle field. Sally took charge.

"Sit over there Love, on the chair beside the range. Where is your heating clock?"

Mutely, Ron pointed to the hot press in the scullery which made its way out to the back door.

By 11, Sally had swept, scoured, and rejuvenated the old kitchen. Ron made vague efforts to get off the chair, dimly ashamed of the table crowded with coffee mugs, their caked, unwashed insignias at the bottom. She remembered too late the two empty wine bottles nestled in the black polythene liner of the roll-top bin. McAdrew's fish and chips lay only half eaten and soggy in a black plastic tray on the counter. Dimly aware of Sally heading over to the black bin to dispose of the fish and chips, she cringed at the sound of a late pulled in gasp. There was silence. The wall clock ticked exaggeratedly. Floor dust intermingled with cake crumbs embarrassed her feet.

"Oh God Sally, I'm so ashamed."

"You used to drink chamomile Ron. What's with all the coffee, not to mention the wine bottles?"

Ron nodded, her eyes a full vacant blackness, as her pupils dilated against the light filtering in through the kitchen window.

They made a fresh pot of coffee. The news on the radio came preceded by a number of Easter Sunday requests. Sally moved to turn it off.

"Now," she said, "what to do for you my love? You can't go on this way. Joe didn't mention you were out of sorts?"

"Well, he hasn't been here this past week. I try to do a little clean up before he comes."

The English woman swept a lazered gaze over Ron. She squirmed in the raw transparency.

"You know when my Sylvie died, I needed to get help," she said finally.

"I started with the GP."

Ron looked up alarmed. "I don't like doctors."

"Well, you're coming to my GP in Sligo on Wednesday morning. I'll pull a few strings with the secretary. I'll call to collect you, and we'll start where we should have started at least two weeks ago. I owe you an apology my love."

"For what?"

"I was feeling sorry for myself when you wouldn't stay with me the other night, a bit resentful if I'm dead honest. I know I was a bit catty with you on the phone."

Ron's eyes issued a pinprick of light. Then she hung her head tortuously, swathed in her long unruly locks. Tears landslided down her cheeks. Sally reached for the man-sized tissues on the window sill.

That's when the phone rang on the kitchen table. She looked at the dial, recoiled and moved away. Sally answered.

"Hi Eanna, Happy Easter Love. Sorry about the delay. Did you get my text? Yes she's OK; she's here beside me. Right Love, I'll put her on so."

Ignoring Ron's frantic gestures, she placed the phone to her ear. Her mouth mimed, "talk to him." As if through the drumming of a large waterfall, she heard him say "hello" twice before she trusted her voice with a scarce "hello" back.

"What's up Love? I've been worried sick."

"I can't talk Eanna- I just can't."

Frightened, she placed the phone back on the table. His concerned voice spoke alone.

Sally handled it again.

"Can I ring you back later Love? Nothing to worry about here. Ron's a little poorly, that's all. You have a good day; she's well minded. Talk later."

CHAPTER 24

The doctor was a pleasant middle- aged woman who had very soft skin in a round dimpled face with molten brown eyes. She listened intently to Ron's story, eyeing her steadily all the while. When she had finished, the other woman reached into her desk drawer for a packet of Kleenex.

"Oh God doctor, me eyes are a mess. You should see the state of them when I wear the mascara.

" I'd well believe it."

Dr. Halpin smiled. "I don't wear mascara for the exact same reason."

The two women's eyes found their intuitive meeting place. No wonder Sally liked this woman, Ron thought.

"You appear to be depressed Ron. The doctor's voice was clinical, but kind. "What you describe is fairly classic: bouts of unrestricted crying-sometimes for no apparent reason, a terrible lack of joy, sleeping poorly-you even say it's been affecting your work. Let me write you a prescription for a month, but that's not all." The doctor reached into her top drawer where she kept her writing pad. She wrote out a name and phone number on a page which she promptly tore off and handed to Ron. You can guess what's coming- you've been to someone before. This lady is an excellent counsellor. You need to see her very soon"

"Well?" Sally asked when she rapped on the passenger window of her Ford Galaxy.

"Well," Ron said, exhaling slowly, drawing her safety belt around her before clicking it into the holder.

"She was...oh she was so lovely Sal."

It was the first time her intonation had lifted in the last ten days. Sally reached over and squeezed her hand. She didn't notice the ring anymore. She prescribed some tablets just to get me over the hump."

"That's good." Sally nodded slowly as she indicated right before pulling out into the traffic.

"Oh yeah, and she said I need to talk things over with a counsellor. I told her about Margie in Dublin, so she wrote down the name of an excellent one here in Sligo."

She showed Sally the slip of paper.

"Well, hold on to that my love," she said as they pulled up outside Finnegan's pharmacy on Main Street.

She told Eanna everything on the phone later, no holes barred. He listened in a seamless silence. She asked eventually, fearfully, "You still there?"

"I'm here," he said gravely. "Ron, I'm so sorry Love."

"Sorry for what?"

"Sorry for leaving you. I had no right at all to expect you to take everything on from your end. I've cancelled the digger."

She made no comment. "How are Aileen and Ailbhe?" she enquired, unable to erase the dullness in the dutiful question.

"They're just fine," he replied. "You don't need to worry about them."

"Ron?"

"Yes?"

"I wish I could come home to you right now. I'm biting my fingernails here, but things will improve I promise you. I miss you like hell."

"I miss you too Love," she said, glad it wasn't a video call or he would have seen the tears in freefall yet again.

From brendanoconnell 21@gmail.com

To ronoconnell15@gmail.com

May 2 2019 11.20am

Subject: Brendan The Navigator bites the "Apple"

Ma, I've arrived. I've taken my first bite out of the "Big Apple" last night. Did you get the address I texted you on? I'm staying in the

Bronx. The part I'm staying in is actually Belmont or "Little Italy." Another Universal non coincidence? I'm going to look for work here tomorrow. There's great connections on Facebook. I'm already befriending and following a number of public houses in the area. I'm giving them all likes of course! I've subscribed to the Bronx Mayor's Facebook page too. I'm like you - I don't sit around.

Oh, just to backtrack, the guys gave me a right old send- off in Raphael's Pizzeria near the Trevi Fountain. It's really, really expensive; the wine was three times the price and the coffees too, but, as you say I'm worth it! Oh by the way, I did throw a coin into the fountain backwards, so I can come back with my significant other some day. Piero says he might visit me here in New York- so will Dawn. We've been really hitting it off, even though she is, as she says, a mature woman of 21, and I'm not yet 19, but I grew up fast didn't I ? She hasn't mentioned poor old Islington, ha ha.

How are you? I know I saw you on Skype, mad quiet on Sunday, but no emails and it's Thursday. Not like you Ma. Are you busy with the builders? I tried a video call on WhatsApp yesterday, but you probably weren't able to take it. Let me know how things are at your end, and I'll keep you posted on my job hunt from here. By the way, as luck would have it, one of my house mates, Pedro is from Peru. Can you believe that? The other guy Declan is from home, from Ballina. They're both really cool. I'll tell you more about them in the next email. Please send me all the home news. Hope Eanna gets back to you soon. You need one of your men around at least.

Ciao Ma,

Brendan.

The last innocent statement flew off the page as she closed down the laptop. "Oh God," she thought, "Brendan, I must never let you know any of this." Alice always said one shouldn't guilt trip a child. She reminded herself that she'd fashioned his wings. Now she didn't intend to take a scissors to them. She must email back- no need for him to be worrying. His energy must be on this glorious time in his life.

In the last week with only minimal badgering, she'd moved in with Sal and Joe. Staying with them was definitely assuaging her pain. Their daily business tripped a switch which at least for now, partially energised her. She'd been on the "happy pills" as she called them, for over a week. The doctor cautioned her she would need a couple of weeks to see if things were picking up. Eanna sent her on a tincture of Hawthorn. He said it was for a weary heart. He put in a small note. Hi Ron, found this quote on WhatsApp,

"Your heart is the softest place on earth. Take care of it."

She placed her hand over her heart as she lay on the big brown sofa in Joe and Sally's living room. With her left hand she pulled up the blue and red cashmere blanket Sally had thrown over her. With her right, she crossed over her chest to explore the flutters under her fingers on her heart side. Yeah, it was kind of fast, not too free and yeah, she could feel its trembling.

The first visit with Fiona the counsellor had been yesterday, and she had encouraged her to tune in mindfully to her body, and where she was feeling her emotions. Eanna apologised repeatedly. He spoke in a quiet, constrained way for him, like a man in need of a good holler in an open space she thought. She didn't ring or text every night as he had suggested. The counsellor had said perhaps three nights a week might be enough to allow space for her own heart to unfurl naturally. Well, she must email her boy now- she must, she just must, **oh God**. The large house was empty. Sally was in Sligo meeting a friend, and Joe was out on the lake fishing in his new fibreglass boat which Sal had bought him for his birthday.

"I've me mobile on Love. If you need me, be sure to ring," he had said.

The laptop sulked for quite a while, unwilling to allow her connect her fingertips with her thoughts. Taking a deep breath, she struck the first keys, her fingers hesitant butterflies, preferring the chrysalis of her introversion.

From ronoconnel15@gmail.com

To brendanoconnell21@gmail.com

May 5 2019 6.30pm

Subject Big Apple

Hi Brendan,

Great to hear from you Love. You've finally hit New York. Take a bite of the apple for me. Sorry I didn't email all week. Things are manic busy round here. Some of the seedlings have to be transplanted out, and the greenhouses arrived last week to be assembled. The lads are very busy and I need to be here. Eanna is still with his Ma and Ailbhe, but he thinks another month might cut it to get them up and running again.

What a coincidence that the boy in your flat is from Peru?

I hope you get a job soon. If you need any money let me know, and either Grandad or myself will transfer it online in the next day or two. Great that Dawn will be visiting you and Piero too. Well that's all for now.

Love in truck fulls,

Your Ma,

Ron.

She surveyed the email before she pressed send, aware that it was languid and uninspiring. Would he cop it? He was young and absorbed in his new life; he wouldn't notice. She extended her right forefinger hesitantly, let it hover above the Enter key, and then she pressed down hard. Unbelievable that on his screen in New York, there would be her dull uninspiring words, just hot off the plate.

The second trip to Fiona went better she felt. Fiona made her realise she'd never ever in her thirty- five- years been alone. In Dublin the crowding was excessive with Adam and George and then the young baby. Alice's illness provided a constant duty of care. In

Leitrim she still had Brendan to care for. Even when he was at school or training, she waited for his return. When he left, Eanna supplanted him and finally after his departure, a day came when her thoughts became a current of dissenting voices, in which she might even drown.

Suddenly finding herself alone, was like pulling out all the strings that had tied up her life until now.

"I was always parcelled up with other people,"

she said aloud wonderingly.

Fiona smiled,

"Exactly, now it's time for you to just sit in your own parcel, "Ron's world." Make friends with a little silence."

She realised too that Eanna had been her knight on a white horse, who then disappeared after rescuing her. Fiona was right; she needed a fresh appraisal of herself, and even though she had Joe and Sally for support, they couldn't carry her any more than Eanna could.

"You will grow stronger in yourself Ron," the counsellor said, looking at her squarely.

"From all you've told me, I think you are amazing."

She uttered the last words very slowly and clearly. When Eanna had complimented her the weekend in The Gresham, she had almost run and hidden from the too tender bud of her self- awakening. Now she began to mull over that sentence "You are amazing." That's what Margie had said in Dublin too. Maybe she really was after all?

Before she left, Fiona gave her a small gift.

"What is it?"

Ron asked, her curiosity plunged into the little white box with the thin gilt edging.

"It's a mosaic- framed pocket mirror. I bought a box of them in Seville. I give them to my women clients. My prescription-look in the mirror at least three times a day and say,

"Ron O'Connell, you are an amazing woman. Tell this to your reflection until you believe it. Trust me the day will come."

From: brendanoconnell21@gmail.com

To: ronoconnell15@gmail.com

May 11 2019 12.20pm

Subject: Where have you been hiding?

Hi Ma,

Where have you been hiding on me? No email again from you and you hardly said a word on Skype on Sunday night. You were in bed with the flu on Easter Sunday. Is it really the flu? Now are you going to tell me what's up or will I have to worm it out of Sally? I will ring you, you know if you don't spill. The two of us are a team and if a man is down that's *SERIOUS*.

I'm starting a new job in O' Neill's pub which is only a block away, so you don't have to worry about me getting buses or taxis at night or taking the subway. The interview went very smoothly. I told them about my bar work back home. I had to come clean with them and say I'm travelling on to Peru. They thought the whole idea of the three destinations was mega and joining up with my mother even more mega again. They were all smiles, and the boss's grandad hails from Mayo. He asked did I know the O'Connells of Mayo. Now how on earth would I know them? He must think Mayo is in my back garden, ha ha.

Yesterday I did my first sightseeing with Pedro, you know the guy from Peru that I told you about? He actually has cousins in Lima, so I can look them up when I get there. Now what kind of cool coincidence is that? You must be right about this conscious Universe thing Ma. Well anyway, I digress. Getting back to the sightseeing, we got on the subway and then into Manhattan. You'd love it here. I could see you walking down Fifth Avenue like Queen Latifah. Man- would you *belong*. So now, before you go on about being a Dublin girl and Dobbinstown and all that, remember Julia Roberts in Pretty Woman? You are her Ma, I swear.

We started at Sachs. Next we went on to Wall Street, and you should see the guys in Ralph Lauren suits, scurrying out of huge buildings with their Bluetooth phones even on their lunch break, keeping tabs on the market. They say they're all burned out by 35. I think a spell in Leitrim would do them good, ha ha. Then we went on to the One World Observatory, and we went right up to the top. The view just blew me away. Just to see the entire Manhattan skyline on a clear day makes you feel like you're up with the angels. I had a clear view of the Hudson River, the Statue of Liberty, Empire State Building, Brooklyn Bridge and over in the distance I could see the World Trade Centre Memorial.

We hopped on a bus that took us to "Ground Zero"; they don't always call it that these days; I'm not sure it's PC to use that term any more. We had pre- booked tickets online, so we got into the smaller queue of the two that had formed. When we got to the top of the line, we met our guide, a guy whose uncle had died when the plane crashed into the second tower. They like the guides to have inside information. We did a walking tour which started at St. Paul's church. They brought survivors in here, and on the gates outside they had posted all the pictures of the missing loved ones. The little church was so peaceful, I almost couldn't imagine people crying and congregating there, frantically looking for information. I tried to imagine you and Joe and Sally looking for me. I couldn't even bring myself to do it. The guide said his mother and his uncle's wife put up a recent picture of him. They kept asking everyone if they had seen him. Everyone else was doing the same. They showed us some of the actual photos that were on the church gates later in the museum. Gosh Ma, some of them were only in their twenties. I saw a picture later on Instagram of one young Middle Eastern guy. They had his head floating above Ground Zero. Seemed kind of spooky, but I guess it's like he's just a presence now.

Anyway, getting back to the memorial, there are two stunning reflection pools where you can hear the soft slushing of the water all day long. They have what they call bronze parapets that sort of flank the pools all the way around the perimeter. All the names of the people who died either in 1993 or 9 /11 are inscribed here. I traced my fingers along some of the Irish names especially the two girls from Headford, Co. Galway. Can't imagine how their mother must have felt. Pedro has been to see it a couple of times already, but he hadn't been inside the museum. So in we went. It's huge inside, and all the voices sounded really muted because of the high ceilings. We were both a bit overawed. They had artifacts from the towers: wallets, key rings, baseball gloves ,even theatre tickets- the bits and pieces of lives that ended out of nowhere. Our guide told us there are I phone recordings of people who rang their loved ones just after the planes had made impact. All of us in the apartment asked each other later what would we say in those messages, and every one said to a man "I just want you to know X, Y or Z how much you mean to me. I want you to remember me always."

When Dawn comes to visit, I'm going to take her to the Rockefeller Plaza, and we can have a posh meal there. Then I'll take her up to the Rock Observatory on the top. Depending on how things go she might not even see Manhattan at all, just stars when I kiss her! Lol. Say hi to Grandad and Sally as always. Tell Joe I'll pull the first pint for him in spirit when I start my new job.

Her face contoured a shadowy smile when she read and re-read the email.

" Good job Alice," she said." He is a carer just like you."

A small bubble of pride filled her. On impulse she printed off the email and brought it into the kitchen where she placed it on the island. Sally would be back soon. Almost on cue, there was a scrunch of tyres on the gravel outside. Within minutes she heard the sound of the key in the lock and Sally's cheery "hullo."

"Ron, you in the kitchen?"

"Yeah, in here," she answered.

Almost reflexively, she went over to the sink where she pushed the mouth of the cream jug-kettle under the tap. Time for a brew as her step mother would always say. She turned around from the sink to see Sally cast a cursory glance at the email. She cleared her throat.

"I want to talk to you about that Sal."

Sally raised an inquisitive eyebrow, but remained silent.

"So," she said eventually, as Ron poured out the steaming strong tea she favoured.

"Has our boy done us proud again?"

Ron's lips slid across into one of her rare, un hollowed smiles. Without making any comment, she pushed the piece of paper over in Sally's direction. The older woman scanned it for quite a while in silence. Finally, she pushed her glasses onto the bridge of her nose, and her eyes searched Ron's from across the rim.

"That boy may be young, but he knows your moods intimately. He's the most qualified person to read you. My advice is tell him. I don't want a phone call some night when he comes in a little mowldy (Joe's words) with the drink at 1am New York time."

They both giggled.

"My son? Never!"

"Good to hear you laugh. Seriously Love, give him an abridged version."

At Ron's quizzical look, she explained,

"Just tell him you were feeling lonely and you went to the doctor and you've moved in with us until Eanna comes back, which won't be long. Tell him you've had lots of rest, and you're on the mend. Promise to reply to his emails from now on, even if your reply is a little short. He's a very understanding chap like his mother." Ron mined an energy for another tremulous smile.

CHAPTER 25

For the 19th of May, it was still cold in the evenings. She had taken to going back to the cottage some nights to prepare herself for when she would eventually need to return. She planned on doing this before Eanna came back. Judging by his phone calls, it wouldn't be long more. She wondered what it would be like when he did come back. Would they slip into the same comfortable routine or had it been that comfortable? This was a question teething in her these days. Were they spending enough time together? He was so full of plans, and she was trying so hard to accommodate them. He knew there would have to be changes because she had changed. The counsellor had told her she needed more from him. She wasn't the best supporting actress in his movie anymore even though she knew she did endorse what he was doing. She moved more easily around the house now. The fire was lighting in the grate. She enjoyed watching the circling patterns made by the flames on the old white ceiling above her. Freer in her body, she curled up on the old settee under the big red Foxford woollen blanket- Sally's Christmas present to her.

It was nine days since she consulted Sally around whether or not she should tell Brendan about her depression. His email left her with no option but to "spill" as he put it. She'd gotten off the computer with her head and heart spun centrifugally . She wondered if he'd swallow the abridged version of events as Sally recommended. Perhaps she should drip feed him what was going on? A rush of information around depression might be too goddamn awful for him to digest. She could honey coat the truth, play it down, diminish its significance. Sally had advised a drip -feed. Alice always said it was best to have your head and heart talking to each other. They were both correct.

Her email the next day began more honestly.

211

From Ronoconnell15@gmail.com
To: brendanoconnell21@gmail.com
May 12 2019 11.10am
Subject: Brendan the Navigator and Truth.
Hi Love,
Wonderful to hear all your news. The twin towers are so disturbing aren't they? I know I haven't been there, but from your account, it seems to strike awe or deep sadness into your heart. I'm glad my son is a sensitive young man. I sound like an old lady now don't I? I'm thrilled you're thinking of bringing Dawn over. I'd love to meet her eventually. As for work, you tell that bar man the O'Connells of Mayo are your long lost cousins ha ha, if that gives you a pay rise.

Now onto more serious matters- yes you are very intuitive. I haven't been myself lately. I was hoping you wouldn't notice. I guess I've been lonely and a little depressed. Sally says I should give you the abridged version of events, but maybe I should tell you a little more. I did have to go to the doctor, but she was absolutely lovely and she sorted me out. I took some pills for a short time, just to get the old brain chemistry up and running. Then I moved in with Joe and Sally for company. I've been taking Eanna's herbs. He calls them his hardship herbs; Lemon Balm{ which is just so beautiful and fresh in the herb garden at the moment,} Hawthorn and Lime. I can tell you I'm feeling a lot better these days, Scout's honour. Joe and Sally take great care of me. You will be coming home soon enough I know, but I've had counseling, and even if you weren't coming, I can stand on me own feet much better now. I'm my own woman and I'm stronger than I ever realised. You take care and keep biting out of the "Big Apple."
Love Ma XXX

She was just dozing off, having read the book on mindfulness which Fiona had lent her, when her mobile rang. Eanna's number flashed on the blue dial. She hesitated just a fraction before she swiped the green handset icon across.

"Hi Love,"

she said, her voice a tube she still needed to squeeze brightness from.

He sounded excited, perhaps a little wired too.

"How are you?"

His concern was real, but it didn't evince the response from her that it usually would have. It was as if the butterflies his voice always summoned wouldn't come out to dance.

"I'm good,"

she said, and realised she was beginning to mean it.

"I've good news," he said, and paused expectantly.

"Things are looking up this end. They're finally getting a home help.

Auntie Nora's daughter - my cousin Siobhan - who lives in Coolock has agreed to take Ailbhe to her house a couple of evenings a week.

Fingers crossed Love, that all this works."

"And if it doesn't?"

her head argued frantically. Then she chided herself. Wasn't she always spouting about the universe providing?

"That's good news Love," she said, feeling his brightness dissipate in her.

She slept in the cottage that week for the first time on a Thursday night. It was a spur of the moment decision which surprised even herself. When she awoke the next morning, she realised how much she had missed the view from the kitchen window. The mountains, which she glimpsed through a break in the Alder wood seemed to return apocalyptically like before. She remembered the first rainbow she had seen over them not long after moving in. Da had said the rainbow was God's promise to Noah that the world would never be submerged by flood again. She had wondered was it a sign? Their blue soft folds wrapped around her now like a mantilla. The sun had become a warming disc in a very clear sky suddenly. The weather was on the up. She had breakfast at 9 the next morning on the front patio which Joe had painstakingly laid for her since Eanna had left. He said it was to be his gift to his beautiful daughter. Now when on earth did Da start talking like that? she wondered. She knew she didn't have to look too far and smiled to herself as she feasted on leftover cheese, vibrant red and purple grapes and her cup of chamomile. She was surprised to see Joe's car pull into the driveway.

"Looking for me already are you?" she said jokingly.

He grinned back.

"You're a hard woman to get hold of. Your other half is looking for you.

He's a worrier that lad. Said you weren't answering your phone."

"Phone? Oh, these days I've taken to leaving it in the house."

"Well anyway, he's coming down from Dublin this evening for the weekend. All must be well in Dobbinstown."

"Oh!" she said surprised, and realised her pulses were more a shadow of what they once would have been at news like this.

"What time is he coming?"

"He won't be down until about 7."

"Right, she said processing slowly. "I'll tidy up the cottage, light the fire and do some shopping."

Her father looked at her strangely.

"What?" she said, intuiting into the silence.

"You don't seem that excited."

"Ah Da, I am - it's just..."

"Just what?"

"Today is the 24th May. He left here on the 20th March. I haven't seen him for two months."

Joe came over, easing himself slowly into the other patio chair beside her. His knee was playing up again.

"It'll be just fine," he said quietly.

"Every couple goes through a patch. You know your Ma and me had our moments, don't you? We just forgot the bad bits that's all."

There was silence for a while. The trickle of the stream at the bottom of the garden grew loud in its commentary.

"Well, I'll be off now," he said, getting up slowly.

She made as if to help him get off the chair, but he waved her away.

"Sure you won't have a coffee?"

"No thank you. I'm just after breakfast, and I have to do the garden and then go to the DIY centre".

"If you want a hand with the shopping later, let me know."

"I'll be fine," she said airily. "This will be a test run,"

she thought to herself, aware her voice was a dry riverbed in her brain.

She set the fire for the evening in the grate, swept the red and black tiled kitchen floor, cleaned out the aga, and was washing down the countertops when her mobile rang. She didn't recognise the number.

"Ron, how yeh?" The voice sounded breathless, unsure. "This is Amy from Dobbinstown."

"Amy, great to hear from yeh! How are things?"

"Grand, just grand," the other voice said with a hurried lack of conviction.

" Jason and me are movin' in together next week. We're getting a corpo flat."

"Love, that's brill. I'm delighted for ye"

Amy, three years her junior and Jason had been an item for as long as she could remember. Strange how she hadn't heard from her for so long though. There was an expectant pause.

"Sorry I haven't been in touch."

The voice trailed off repentantly.

"Ron, I rang you, because something's bothering me. Jenny wanted to send you a photo on WhatsApp, but I said I should ring first."

The war drums reassembled in Ron's heart as she discerned the anxious edge in Amy's voice.

"Well, Eanna was very friendly with his ex in Whelan's on a few occasions this last month."

The centrifugal motions of her head and heart began to play out again.

Silence stitched itself onto the line until finally, Amy said

"Ron, you still there?"

"Yeah, yeah, I'm still here."

How do you mean very friendly?"

"Well, I can send you the photos if you like. It's just they seemed to be... cosy, and I thought you should know. Now, I said to Jenny, that's what friends are for."

"Right," she said woodenly, suddenly feeling like a deer in the headlights of a revelation.

"Send me on them photos."

She cursed herself silently. Would Fiona agree with this? But she had to know, didn't she?

"Listen Amy Love, I have to go here,"

she said suddenly.

"I'll get back onto you soon. Say Hi to Jason for me."

A second later, the photos appeared on WhatsApp. They were a little blurry as if taken from a distance, but the two heads were definitely together in what appeared to be an intimate pose. She sighed. She could just ask. There must be a logical explanation, but cosy a few times together in public view? Her anxiety stirred, and she reached for her first " happy" pill in a week.

CHAPTER 26

The day went by all out of focus. She raced around Dunnes in Sligo, filling the trolley with T Bone steaks, pepper sauce, cream cheese, biscuits, a chardonnay wine which she knew he liked. Back at the cottage, she set out the steaks for cooking later and immersed herself in making a cheesecake for dessert. It felt good to be preparing a meal again. As she laid the wobbly cheesecake into the fridge, a part of her wondered was he worth it? She couldn't shake off the photograph. Stick insects of jealousy chewed on her. Rage preceded tears as she fixed herself a small salad. Sanity then returned to the court of her mind. "Not guilty," she pleaded on his behalf, "but what if?" Oh God Amy, why today of all days did you have to ring? She decided to practise her mindfulness and watch her breath move in and out. Slowly the detachment worked. Calm swept over her desert self like a cool breeze. She would get through tonight somehow.

She was listening to her playlist on Spotify, when she heard the scrunch of his tyres on the gravel outside. She checked her phone - 8.05pm. A quick look in the mirror assured her that her makeup was still intact. She applied a final touch of her Bobby Brown lipstick. She put on her mascara for the first time since the doctor's office.

When the doorbell rang, it surprised her. Then she realised he didn't want to use his keys. She opened the door tentatively. The late evening sun shrouded him from behind. He was wearing shades, and his recently acquired reddish beard had grown longer since she'd seen him on Skype. They both stood for a second, frozen in the open doorway.

"Aren't you going to invite me in?" he said with a smile, shifting his shades to the top of his head. There was that familiar big smile. Temporarily, she forgot his infidelity and every fibre of her lurched towards him. Gently, he closed the door behind him, looked at her full- on.

"You're more beautiful than ever Ron."

She didn't reply, but held his gaze uncertainly. He waded into the silence with a kiss full on the lips. Despite herself, she felt a massive stirring in her cocoon of loneliness. Then she remembered Amy and the phone call. Unexpectedly, she pulled away. He looked hesitant, confused, and she couldn't afford to feel his hurt.

"Come in Love," she said, her voice a fine line, petering out .

"I have the dinner almost ready. Just drop your bags there."

Meekly he followed her into the kitchen.

"Something smells really good. I'm starving"

"Yeah, I did the steaks in the casserole for a change. More tender that way."

"Yeah more tender," he said, casting her a sideways look, laced with desire and a new shyness.

Over dinner, he filled her in on Dobbinstown and Aileen's new home help due to arrive in another week.

"She's a grand woman," he said, "and she'll do two hours a day. Ma is getting a lot stronger and I finally persuaded her to start taking the herbs again. Now Ailbhe, I have no herb for. She's still mad into the boys."

He saw her face across the table.

"Yeah, I know that raised eyebrow. And you're probably right; she will have to start taking care."

Then they discussed the house.

"I've got onto Matt Gibbons the foreman on the site, and the digger is ready to start next week."

"Don't worry over any of it," he continued in a sudden gush of anxiety.

"I'll be back down for keeps in a week or more, and Matt will whatsapp me from the site."

She was about to do her usual cartwheel of apologies over the delay with things when Fiona's voice sounded quietly in her ear.

"You need self-care. You're no longer in the old role of best supporting actress."

She met his eyes quietly.

"Good," was all she managed, a little too tersely.

"We can walk the site tomorrow," he said looking to her for approval.

"Right," she said quietly,"we'll do that."

He looked at her with a soft disquiet and a question mark. She studied the white tablecloth and the two red candles she'd lit.

He made a point of doing the washing up and bringing in the cheesecake and coffee.

"Thanks Love" she said, sipping it demurely.

"Nice to hear the rustle of the wind again in the trees. I've actually missed all that silence."

She didn't answer. He tried again

"Ron, everything OK? Have you been back to the doctor?"

"Yeah, I'm going on Monday. I'm doing much better. I just need a bit more time, that's all."

He hung his head, staring into the firelight. She noticed the extra lines on his profile, more granite chippings of stress, she thought. Idly she felt she'd like to tidy up that beard as well.

They climbed the stairs at 11, leaving the banked- up fire to dismember wistfully. Eanna hauled his large carpet bag with him.

"I brought extra," he said to her straight back as they went up.

They undressed in silence with just a chink of light coming in through the drawn curtains. Laying still beside each other, she was aware of her body trembling. The longing was excruciating. His hand reached across, felt inside the inner tips of her thighs, her breasts and travelled to her hair. He stroked it with his fingers. In spite of herself, she released a soft feral moan. But then the photo injected itself into her head. Involuntarily, she turned away from him. She heard his voice through a funnel.

"Ron, Ron, I've missed you so much. Please don't turn away."

She kept her hair buried in the pillow so he wouldn't see the silent, dammed- up tears start to flow.

"I'm not ready yet Love," she said. Her own voice came to her, rolled in from a sea fog. She realized what she wasn't ready for just yet was a confrontation, an explanation even. It was much too soon, and she knew the rawness of a new wound opening up would rapidly become septic. For now, the poison had to sit and find its own exit in due course. She heard him sigh before he said in a strangled voice

"I understand- we'll just take it gently."

She didn't reply, and closed her eyes, willfully imprinting sleep on them which never came until nearly dawn. She heard him toss and turn beside her until his snoring told her he had succumbed to his tiredness.

At 8 the following morning she heard him downstairs rummaging in the cupboards. Sadness knotted in her. She remembered the Sunday mornings when he would go out for the paper. On his return, he'd slip into bed beside her and the newspaper would lay unopened as on second thoughts they made love. That was the last thing she remembered thinking until she heard the front door slam. She looked at her phone beside the bed. Oh God, it was 11. Her exhaustion had gotten the better of her. He was calling her now up the stairs.

"Breakfast ready Love. I went out to get the Sunday papers."

"Coming," she shouted down, pulling back the covers, slipping her feet into her slippers and hastily pulling on her dressing gown. She glanced in the mirror. Dead eyes returned her gaze. Her mascara had streaked badly this time.

Over breakfast, she feigned interest in the newspaper.

"More people died in the Gaza Strip," she said.

"What? he said, looking up from "*The Observer.*"

She noticed the oily slick of the cold sausages on

his plate.

"You not hungry?"

"What?" he said again, absent- mindedly.

"Oh no, not hungry-must have been the steak last night.

Will we walk the site so today?" he said, changing the subject.

"Oh ok, great,"

Her untruthful tongue was sprinting in her mouth.

"What time?"

"Say 3?"

"Yep, 3 is fine," she said, making a play of clearing the dishes.

Over at the sink, she handed him the washing up liquid. He stood with his hand on the bottle for a full ten seconds until she said,

"Would you rather I did it?"

"Did what?"he asked vaguely.

"The washing up," she replied, irritation strangling her tone.

"No, no, I'll do it," he said quickly.

He glanced at her curiously as she wiped and re-wiped each plate slowly. They fell into an unaccustomed silence again, broken abruptly by the ringtone of her phone. It was Sally. She put Eanna on.

"Yeah Sally, all good here. We've just had breakfast. We're heading to the site for 3."

Then to her own surprise, she beckoned to him to hand her the phone.

"Hi Sal," she said cheerily. "Will I book a table in the pub tonight for the four of us? A catch up, you know?"

There was just a small hesitancy at the other end of the line. She caught his transfixed look from out of the corner of her eye.

"Yes, Joe and I would like that very much, thank you Ron"

The building site was just two miles away, near Cowlroe on the back road to Sligo. They took the Skoda. She made a play of turning up the radio. In answer to his sideways look, she said

"They do a request programme on Shannonside FM, and I think Sally has a request in for Joe's birthday."

He nodded slowly, keeping his eyes fixed on the hook of a narrow bend. In silence, they turned into the laneway where a two acre site greeted them. As they stepped out of the car, Eanna swept his hand expansively over the land.

"God, in Dobbinstown we had shoe boxes. Here we have Versailles.

His voice trailed off as his arm swept biblically over string lines,pegged into the ground. Suddenly he grabbed her elbow excitedly.

"Come on, race you down to where the kitchen will be."

He hared off ,shouting into the wind with a tired hoarseness in his voice.

"Come on Ron, we'll race into the future."

She walked into the newly rising wind behind him.

At the far end of where the outer walls were pegged, he grabbed her hand tightly, not looking at her, as they paced the dimensions of the kitchen together. Walking the fourteen foot length, she willed her tense muscles into stillness and lamented the cave her heart was blundering into. Her hand grew limp in his as she began to pull away. His eyes registered a hurt surprise. He tugged at her desperately.

"Will we not pace out the width?"

"I'm going back to the car," she shouted back -"Bit of a headache."

They drove in silence back to the cottage. He had scarcely turned off the ignition before she scrambled out the passenger door, walking briskly up the path to open the front door before him. Once inside, she headed for the stairs.

"I'm just having a little lie down," she shouted to the shadow in the doorway. It was still only 4 o'clock.

He didn't reply, but headed into the sitting room where the fire was set. She could hear the rasping of the tongs and the slosh of the coal bucket as she got to the top of the landing. He would bury his head in the *Sunday Times,* she knew. For a full hour, she immersed herself in re-reading Brendan's emails.

From brendanoconnell21@gmail.com

To ronoconnell15@gmail.com

May 15 2019 12.40pm

Subject I Knew It.

Hi Ma,

I knew it, I knew it; your bubble and fiz was gone. I wish I could lean into the computer and give you a big hug. It must have been awful to lose everyone so fast. You've never been on your own before. I should have thought of that. I'm just a klutz as the Americans say.

No major news from here. I started my new job. Some of these Irish American guys have to be seen to be believed. One fella actually told me I had the map of Ireland on my face. Now how gross is that?! Think of all those jagged curves on the coastline. I'm only 18 for God's sake. Dawn said she'll come over in early July. I'm saving to take her to the Rockefeller Plaza. The guys in the apartment are cool. We get our food from the deli downstairs. I'll tell you about the little Jewish woman that runs it in another email. The Bronx is something else Ma. As you know, Im in Little Italy so it's Roma all the way.

Don't worry about me getting home from work at all hours. Our boss pays for a taxi which drops me off at the apartment. He's a decent skin. Gotta run now. I'm cooking dinner on my one night off. Now isn't that cruel? LoL

Bye for now. You take good care of you. If you need anything at all, just text or holler. I swear I'll hear you!

Ciao,

Brendan.

By 6, she emerged from the bedroom, fully made- up, wearing her black palazzo pants, loose white linen shirt, silver sequined high-heel sandals and gold torc around her neckline. She allowed her long black hair to swing freely, making a small part in the middle. Eanna let out a low whistle when he saw her.

"Pretty woman, you clean up good."

She smiled apologetically this time. "I was reading over Brendan's emails upstairs."

"Thought you had a headache?"

"Oh I lay down first," she lied. "It's gone now."

"Oh," he said, and a heavy silence fenced them in before he added, "He rang me last week."

"Who?"

"Brendan."

She raised a terse eyebrow at this.

"He's just concerned Ron. I am too you know."

"I know, I know," she said impatiently, then added quickly, "I just need some time."

"Time to do what?"

"Just a little more time to meself for a small while yet," she said, not looking at him. The hurt in his eyes broadcast loud enough for her to see it without facing him directly.

They had arranged to meet Joe and Sally in the pub at 6.30pm for the early bird menu. By 6.15, Eanna had pulled into the gravelled front of the old ivy- clad pub.

"I just need to run into the loo," she said ,opening the passenger door to get out of the car. She didn't look behind to see if he was following. Her heels scrunched and sank into the gravel. Grimly she pulled them up. What she wouldn't give to be in New York right now, maybe heading down to the local pub or pizzeria in Little Italy with her son. She spent a good 20 minutes staring at her face in the bathroom mirror. She would be 36 in October, and she could see the lines carving a little dried up bed for themselves high up on her cheek bones. She had stagnant centres in her eyes.

Feeling the drift- wood inside of her, she faced the trestle table where Joe, Sally and Eanna sat, and applied her mannequin smile.

"Seamus just took our order for the drinks," Joe informed her.

"He'll be back in a moment with the menus. You alright Love?"

She nodded, and curved her lips into an agreeable shape. As if on cue, Seamus Mulrooney appeared with black, faux, leather-bound menus. He was a class mate of Brendan's. His eyes lit on her immediately.

"How's it going Ron? How's that fella getting on in the Bronx?"

A smile escaped from its jailer inside her.

"He's playing a blinder- got a job like yourself."

"Really?" he said."Bar work?"

"Sure he's a dab hand at pulling the pints."

"Can you text me his number?"

"Will do," she replied.

"Excuse me," he said, turning on his heels."Got to go back to the bar for a minute. I'll be back to take your orders."

"I'll have a Bacardi and Coke," she called after him.He turned around briefly to give her the thumbs up.

She felt the Bacardi and Coke hit a spot at the back of her throat and then warm her throughout. Half way through the third one, she didn't care about the scampi and chips she was eating- just drowning the numbness was bliss. She was also aware she had taken one of her "happy pills" before coming out.

She knew she was speaking too loudly, bragging even about her clever boy, his great Leaving Cert, his latest plan to do a post- grad in London in Media Studies.

"He's just cruising it over there," she said, her voice getting more slurred as the hands of the wall clock above her head ticked louder and louder. To distract, Eanna said suddenly to Sally,

225

"Did you get your request played on Shannonside FM?"

Seeing her puzzled face, he added, "For Joe's birthday."

Joe's suspended cutting the last of his steak for a moment, and looked at his wife, puzzled.

"You never told me you were getting a request played?"

"That's because I didn't get one played," Sally said mystified. She turned to Eanna. "Who told you that?"

"Ron."

She was helpless before the conflagration in her cheeks as they all looked at her. She poured water from the heavy carafe into her own tumbler, and gulped it down urgently. At that moment the black Liscannor flag stones came up to meet her, and she felt sick.

"Excuse me," she said, feeling the bile rise up in her throat, and dashed to the loo. Getting sick in the toilet bowl was almost the easy part. Her heart pounded insistently in her temples, and she felt the onslaught of a headache. The fluorescent light was blading across her eyes. Her feet wouldn't anchor her. She was a ship at sea. She got sick all over again, but this time there was a steadying hand at the tiller. She heard Sally's voice as if through a fog.

"What on earth is the matter with you Love?"

She couldn't answer, but retched into the toilet bowl a third time. Then she saw Sally's accusing look.

"Have you been mixing alcohol and your pills?"

She lifted her pallid face out of the toilet long enough to register Sally's outline before she fainted. When she came to, Sheila Flaherty, the bar owner, was taking her pulse.

"You'll live." The older woman smiled down at her. They brought in a chair from the lounge and placed her on it. Both Sally and Sheila were at either side of her looking down concernedly. Sheila was a paramedic with the local St. John's ambulance. She handed Ron a glass of water, which she drank gratefully.

They didn't speak on the way home. From time to time, he glanced over at her anxiously in the passenger seat. By the time they pulled up in front of the cottage, she dimly noticed the dead hollows around his eyes. He helped her undress. She slid her jelly legs between the sheets. As he pulled up the duvet cover over her, she muttered

"I didn't mean this to happen Love; it was that photo, that damned photo."

Then sleep grabbed her complete with bad dreams. Ailbhe was running after Eanna down a mountainside. Another woman was waving a flag at the top. Just as she woke, she heard herself say in the dream

'She's bad news Love, get away'.

By 11.30 next morning, he was ready for road again. Neither of them said anything over breakfast. He'd made her black tea and toast, and presented her with Milk Thistle capsules.

"To help me liver I suppose?" she said. He nodded. Mutely she stood in the hallway, as he dragged his heavy bag down the stairs. With one hand on the door handle, he turned around to face her. She studied the red and black tiles at her feet. A small spider was scuttling away into a crack.

"Ron, *please look at me!*"

She lifted her head inch by inch from the spider's endeavours until her eyes were level with his chin.

"What did you mean about a photo?"

Her heart unseated itself. Her speech was a phantom.

"What photo?" she asked finally.

"Last night when I put you to bed, you said,

"If it wasn't for that damned photo."

Her head lied pendulously.

"I have no idea what you're talking about ."

CHAPTER 27

About an hour later, after Eanna had left, she went upstairs to lie down. Her head flooded intermittently. She took some more Milk Thistle capsules, and kept the water bottle beside the bed .There was some pomegranate to suck on downstairs if needed. Just as she was drifting into a light hazy sleep, a blue light flashed across the desktop on her writing desk beneath the window. Struggling out from under the heavy duvet, she picked her dressing gown off the end of the bed and put it over her shoulders. Taking a swig out of her water bottle, she padded across the room in her bare feet. He was on again.

From brendanoconnell21@gmail.com

To ronoconnell15@gmail.com

May19 2019 7.30am

Subject Have I got news for you.

Ma, have I got news for you. Uncle Adam just emailed me. He and Miguel are coming to Queens for a Nursing Home Conference in a little over two weeks' time. It's in a posh hotel called The Arboretum. The two guys will be staying there, and they've asked me to meet them. Lunch will be on them! I have to make sure I get time off as it could be a long night. I'm dying to meet them, Miguel especially. Apparently they did this conference last year too. When they heard from you that I was now in New York, they thought it was perfect timing. Anyway, I will keep you posted. I'm guessing Eanna has come by now, and probably gone back again. Look after yourself, until he's back for keeps. I have my spies in the camp you know, AKA Grandad and Sally.

Gonna go back to bed for a while because I'm wrecked. There was a sing song in the bar last night- the afters of a wedding party; it was all madness.

You take care now,

Ciao,

Brendan.

She sat there stunned for a while. There was hope for this family yet. Only last week, she had finally gotten around to emailing Adam. He had tried to do a WhatsApp video call twice in the last two months, but she had fobbed him off by saying the connection wasn't good, and she would email him. To be fair, he was sorry to hear about her illness. Miguel too had suffered his share of depression. He asked for Joe and Sally and of course, Brendan. She had emailed him on Brendan's schedule, but she hadn't expected this. She was still working on Joe to do another Skype with him. He had begun to manage one at Christmas and Easter, just not this Easter for obvious reasons.

Feeling a little more clear-headed now, she pulled back on her jeans, smoothed down her pink top, and popped her feet into her slippers. She was hungry she realised. There was some left over salad in the fridge, and probably a bit of the cheesecake too. She was just tucking into a large egg and cheese salad with chutney when the doorbell rang. Joe was outside. He took a long look at her from the doorway before entering the narrow hallway.

"Don't look at me like that,"

she said, her body tensing. She looked at her father now, head-on, as he entered the kitchen. The lost place in her started up again.

"What the hell was going on last night ?"

Without waiting for an answer, he suddenly backed himself into a straight chair and sat down stiffly.

"The knee acting up today?"she asked compassionately.

He nodded a weary assent. "Forget about the knee. Are you going to tell me what's wrong or not ? " he said, his pugilistic instincts bear- hugging his tone. She imagined himself and Sally forensically picking over her and Eanna's relationship when they got home. She hung her head. The spiders had left the tile cracks under her feet.

"Ron, Ron," he said softly, the fight dissolved on his tongue.

"You're having difficulties, that's all."

"You don't know anything about it," she said frustratedly.

"Then enlighten me," he said, folding his arms.Without warning, a hot spring of tears gushed from her bedrock of control.

"I'll put on the kettle," he said, getting up slowly, "and we'll talk".

Over a coffee, it tumbled out messily.

"Whoa," he said " Back that colt up and begin again."

So she told him about the phone call on Saturday morning,and then she showed him the photo.

"It's blurred love. It doesn't prove a thing."

"Yes, but what was he doing meeting her three times in the pub?"

Joe shrugged his big shoulders."Why the hell didn't you ask him?"

"We'd only two nights Da. If he was carrying on, I couldn't face it. I wasn't ready."

"I know," he said sanguinely. "Talk to him, you must; I'm sure there's nothing to it."

His voice emptied itself into a small cloud of doubt.

"Now, you know Sally and I will be gone next week?"

Dismay funnelled through her. She'd forgotten all about their trip.

"You're off to Manchester to visit Sally's sister?"

"Yeah," he said wearily. "It's been planned a while."

"You up to it?" she asked.

"Yeah, yeah," he said with a dismissive wave of his hand. "Now Madam, what will you do for the week?"

"Well actually Da," she said "I've been thinking about asking Laura O'Neill from Tipperary, you know the young teacher who started at the school, to stay with me for a few days. She's had to leave her digs and is looking for accommodation. Joe scrunched up his nose which she knew was a sign of approval.

"Nice young one that, sensible."

"Jenny O'Reilly might stay over a night as well. You know, she works in the bar. We might have a girls' night out. She realised she was making it up as she went along, but an idea was forming. This time a furrow planted itself between Joe's thinnng eyebrows.

"That one's a bit mad if you ask me," he said, "watch her."

"I'm a big girl Da,"she said, planting a kiss on the top of his balding head. He placed a hand along the side of her cheek. She nestled in for quite a while, the silence expanding comfortably around them.

After Joe left, she had an idea. She was praying he'd answer his mobile. He was probably back in Dublin by now.

"Ron?"he said, sounding surprised. "I was just going to ring you."

"Did you have a safe trip?" she inquired.

"Yeah, yeah very smooth."

"How is everyone?"

"Fine," he said cautiously.

"Good, I'm glad for you Love. Listen, sorry about the weekend. I will explain but not right now."

She heard his sigh slip down the line.

"What will you do tonight?" she asked innocently,ignoring the tom- tom of her heart.

"Will you go out to the local like you often do for a drink?"

"Yeah, I probably will -gets me out of the house."

"That's a good idea."

"Do you ever meet anyone there?"

"Like who?"

he asked, his inflection tightening around him.

"I don't know, some of our friends from the old days."

There was another pause.

"Ron, I just like to sit in me seat in the alcove and catch up on the news.

I've run into a few school friends from time to time alright. John Lynch invited me back to his house one night. He has three children now you know, all under five."

"Oh I remember him, gas man."

"He's tamed now."

She allowed herself a mirthless laugh on the phone.

"Got to go here," she lied. "Told Joe and Sally I'd call down before they left for Manchester."

"Oh I forgot about that. Wish them Bon Voyage". "Will do," she said trying desperately to filter normality through her strangled tone.

Next morning after the 11 o clock break, she approached Laura.

"Listen Love," she said gently. (She realised she really did like the girl. She hoped she wasn't using her).

"I know you've been looking for accommodation- any luck?"

"No," the girl replied dejectedly.

"Do you know any place Ron?"

"Well as it so happens," she replied "I do. My place."

"Your place? But I thought you and Eanna?"

"Oh, he's not coming for another couple of weeks," she said quickly.

"I could use the company," she added, pushing an extended pause gently.

"You're on," said the girl, a bright finality to her tone. "When will suit you for me to bring in my stuff?"

"Ah, this evening is fine."

"Great," Laura said, her body language issuing a huge sense of relief.

"I'll be at the cottage after 5," Ron said, gathering up the tea things from the staffroom table.

That afternoon, she sped around the local Centra with new purpose. She was having a tenant and a nice one too. Other plans were formulating also, gyrating in her head. The fizz was starting in her. She had lamb chops under the grill when Laura rang the doorbell.

"I hope I'm not bringing the kitchen sink," the girl said apologetically, flicking back her long brown hair nervously. Ron surveyed the accumulated luggage.

"Not bad, not bad," she said smiling.

She looked onto the roadway over Laura's shoulder.

"Have you a bit more in that Yaris of yours?"

There was a brief anxious pause.

"A bit of cardboard," she said with a sigh.

Ron laughed, "Come on, I'll just turn off the grill first and I'll help you bring everything in."

Two hours later they sat ensconced in front of the TV.

"I hope you don't mind using Brendan's room," Ron said. "I took most of his gear down to Joe and Sally's house."

"Not at all - I'm thrilled to have a place to stay. Thanks for dinner too Ron, I was going to get a Chinese later."

"No need to head to China when we have good Irish lamb all around us."

Her little joke was rewarded with a shy smile pocketed in deep set brown eyes. Her collywobble heart sat back in its seat. She had made the right decision.

They got to know each other better over the course of the week. Laura was from Nenagh in Co. Tipperary and had been going out with the same lad since she was eighteen. She was twenty-two now. He was a mechanic, a little older than herself and planned to take over his dad's garage in a couple of years. It turned out she was quite a good cook. She treated Ron to her favourite food, Spaghetti Bolognese on Friday night. Laura sang when she cooked, she told Joe over the phone. She could almost see his nose curling up with approval.

"How is Sally?" she enquired.

"Marvellous," he said.

"She's in her element with the new baby."

Swiping the red icon on the mobile, she sighed a little. Now for the girls' night out. She rang Jenny,whose voice was etched with surprise. They had recently become friendly when Ron headed into the pub for a coffee after school. In the past ten days she had taken to having a small Bushmills or two.

"My Irish Coffee," she joked as Jenny systematically wiped the beer glasses behind the bar counter. Jenny was newly divorced with two teenage children. She had just turned forty.

Laura was in the front room on all fours, making a chart for her Junior Infant class when Ron went back into the front room.

"Number two is it?"she asked amusedly.

"Now don't you start. I've enough grief from Greg.

He slags me no end about my hand made charts, when all I have to do is go on "Scoil net," print off and laminate!

They both smiled.

"Mmm, seductive Greg," said Ron.

"Mmm," the younger girl replied, "very dishy isn't he?"

The beefy Canadian on a teacher exchange worked out every morning, and made all the women swoon.

" I love his jet black hair and his big puppy brown eyes," said Ron giggling.

"I'd say he's no puppy dog somehow," Laura replied.

"Yeah," Ron countered, "more big mastiff wouldn't you say?"

This sent them off into a headlong rush of uncontrollable laughter.

Slipping her voice softly into the aftermath of their giggles, she asked casually

"Are you going to Tipperary this weekend Laura?"

"No actually," the girl replied. "Larry, my boyfriend has the flu. He said I'm not to come near him. Do you mind my crashing here? I mean, if Eanna is coming down or anything...?"

"Oh no, he's not coming" Ron assured her. "That's what I wanted to ask- do you fancy a girls' night out in the pub? They have a trad session on Saturday night lately."

Laura's eyes lit up. "Yeah, cool."

"I've asked Jenny from the pub as well. Do you know her?"

Laura shook her head.

"Great, it's a date so." As she headed to bed around 11, Tom Moran, Eanna's friend from the GAA flashed before her. He played bodhran with that trad group, didn't he?

By Saturday afternoon, Jenny had rung to finalise arrangements. Eanna had rung as well. Their conversation was terse. How had it happened she wondered? Unvoiced reproach was sharpening its sword down the line on both sides. She got off the phone, and made a special effort with her appearance. Her deep purple kaftan with its swirling suns and zodiac signs would do nicely with her white Monsoon jeans. She decided to leave her hair loose. She fingered the moonstone at her throat, and admired her pear drop earrings in the mirror. Then she took a deep breath, "you'll do nicely," she said to herself.

Laura let out a little whistle when she saw her.

"Oh I think you could make Eanna jealous tonight if he were here."

She smiled wanly .

"You look great youself-love the cream jeans and blue top."

Now let's go Miss," she said, aware of a maternal register in her voice.

"You sure you're ok to drive?"

"Yeah, I don't feel like drinking anyway."

Jenny was up at the bar when they entered.

"Makes a change being on this side of the counter," she said. "And at least it's not Flemings."

Ron introduced Laura, who looked around a little anxiously.

"Any chance of a seat in the corner?" she asked. Ron and Jenny exchanged knowing glances.

"Now why would you stay there?" Jenny said, "and hide your light."

Laura didn't reply. Ron noticed a constriction of the deep muscles in her throat. The pub was filling up rapidly. The trad session was about to begin. Tom Moran was in the thick of it. Ron waved over at him from her bar stool. Lifting his bodhran onto his lap, he spotted her and waved his stick airily above his head. Then to her surprise, she saw Greg sporting a tin whistle in the middle of the musicians. She nudged Laura.

"It's the mastiff," she whispered.

They both giggled. Jenny looked at them uncomprehendingly as she passed over a Bacardi and Coke to Ron and a 7up to Laura. She was on the G & T herself. Laura filled her in.

"Not a bad hunk at all," she said, her voice a cool weighing scales. "Is he available?"

"Oh yes," Ron informed her.

"He's been divorced for the last year, has no kids. He's exploring his Irish heritage."

"I wouldn't mind exploring him," Jenny said, in a barely audible voice.

"He's like the Nile," Ron added, "mysterious and unexplored, at least in Ireland, we think!"

They all giggled again.

She decided to have water in between her drinks this time. She was sipping a Ballygowan sparkling when Greg came over after a break in the session.

"And how are you beautiful Irish ladies tonight?" he asked charmingly.

Ron did the introductions. Jenny blushed. She couldn't take her eyes off him. Greg's eyes swept over Ron methodically from head to toe. She felt a small sweat trickle down her back.

"What part of Canada are you from Greg?"she asked.

"Saskatchewan."

"I'll have to google that one," she said with a twinkle.

"Excuse me," a voice interrupted from behind.

"Are you the sexy one whose son is gone on a big trip?"

Greg turned around to face the owner of the question. Irritation made his cheek muscles twitch.

"That's not a nice thing to say to a lady," he said, his Canadian accent getting stronger. Ron felt herself crimsoning. Everyone was staring at her as his slurred voice rose a decibel above the conversation and the music which was just beginning to start up. She recognised Sam Ellis from the night in the bar when they had the first party for Brendan.

"I think you should leave; you're quite intoxicated," Greg said, lowering his voice now.

"I will in my arse," he said loudly.

She realised Tom Moran was staring over at her. John Fox the barman looked up alarmedly.

"Now we want no trouble..."

With that, Sam Ellis put his arm round Ron.

"Where's your fine hunk tonight? Has he fecked off on yeh?"

"That's enough," Greg said angrily.

Tension suddenly roamed the Serengeti of Fox's small bar. She realised with a shock that Greg was about to throw a punch. Luckily he missed his target who ducked. When he went to swing a second time, his left arm was restrained by John Fox who had stepped out from behind the counter.

"I'd like all of you to leave... Now please."

Ron was mortified; tears threatened her mascara again.

"We should leave Greg," she said quietly, putting her hand softly on his shoulder.

All three women shuffled out the door, head down with Greg hot on their heels.

"Wait up," he called as they walked fast ahead of him.

"Ron, Laura, I'm so sorry. I didn't mean to...In Canada, we don't let guys speak to women in that way."

She turned and faced him head- on. His eyes were contrite.

"Let me take you into McCaris in Sligo for a takeaway," he said, "to make it up to all of you."

Seeing their hesitation, he added, "Please, please"

"Laura is driving," Ron said.

Laura let out a small sigh. "Ok," she said. "We'll follow you."

The chipper was jammers when they went in and found a hard-topped plastic table with red chairs to sit at. He gave them his life story in between mouthfuls of hugely cut chips. He'd been divorced for two years.

"Came home one night, and found her in bed with my best friend," he said.

They murmured sympathetically. Jenny's eyes were like copper rivets fastened on him. Ron was well aware how his eyes meandered stealthily in her own direction continuously.

"And you Ron?" he asked pointedly, "What's your story?"

"She's in a loving relationship. Lucky her," Jenny answered quickly.

Laura cast her a sideways look.

"And you two ladies?" he asked with a smile tilting the corners of his eyes.

"I'm seeing a lad at home in Tipperary," Laura said.

"I'm available," Jenny piped up.

"Really," he said, his inflection dropping, as his tone flatlined.

CHAPTER 28

Ron was setting out the mugs in the empty staff room. She sensed Greg before she saw him, standing in front of the window, backing onto the children's garden. His bulk frame oozed a raw sensuousness as he blocked out the sun slanting in behind him. She froze and for a series of excruciating seconds, minutely observed the dust motes that the sun threw up on the mahogany bookcase in the corner of the room.

"I cut class to catch you here," he said softly.

He stepped over from the window and began taking some of the mugs off the tea tray. Opening a biscuit wrapper beside her and casting a furtive glance in the direction of the doorway, he said,

"Ron, I find you very attractive." She looked at him surprised.

"Guys must say that to you all the time," he said.

Before she had a chance to answer, he continued. "It's not just your looks; everything about you is so spectacular." She realised she was beginning to sweat under her armpits.

"Look, I know you have this thing going with Eanna, but I get the sense, you know... So well, the sense that maybe you like me too."

Before she could answer, the staffroom door opened and John, her principal walked in.

"Am I interrupting something?" he asked tentatively.

"Oh, no, no," they both mumbled almost at once.

The principal headed to the kitchen to fetch some milk from the fridge.

"Meet me this evening for coffee in O'Briens," he whispered when John was out of earshot. She nodded, putting her hand up to the quivering light in her eyes, now he had unblocked the sun He put up four fingers and pointed at the clock on the wall. She nodded again, wondering just what on earth she was doing.

The school day dragged on. Eanna did a WhatsApp video call at lunch time unexpectedly. Seeing her surprised look, he said

"Ron, I just wanted to see you. I have some things to tell you and maybe I'll get down on Sunday or Monday for keeps this time."

"Eanna, I've got to fly here", she said. "I need to be on the yard with Rihanna..."

He couldn't deny the veracity of this statement because he knew too well the duties of an SNA.

" Oh Lord," she thought, "What kind of web am I weaving?"

At 2.40 pm she bolted out of the classroom door, waved at Laura through the window who was preparing for next day, and headed across the staff car park to her fiesta. She wanted to get away before he came out of his class. Heading onto the main Sligo road, she pulled down the sun visor. The evening light was spilling down from the mountains above her on the three Jersey cows in the rushy field below. She remembered suddenly her mountain meditation from her mindfulness class."Bloody easy for a mountain," she thought ruefully. Heading into Sligo, she practised what she would say. Deep inside her, she knew there was only one for her, but was it really the same for him? Was his phone call today one of guilt? She found a parking space right in front of O'Brien's and then applied her Bobby Brown pan stick and bright pink lipstick, She gave her cheeks a little pinch, as she'd seen them do in the movies. Then she silently began to rehearse again her "speech of truth."

She finally opened the restaurant door at five minutes past four, having spent the last half hour walking around the town as she stared unseeingly at belted cotton dresses and featureless mannequins in Gill's window. He was over at a table in the corner in front of the seascape mural, his face hidden behind the *Irish Times*. Suddenly he looked up, folded his paper meticulously, placing it on the seat beside him and beamed expansively at her. She fixed herself a small tight smile.

"Hi," she said, injecting a high pitched cheeriness into her voice. "Have you ordered?"

"Oh no," he said "I always wait for the lady to order first."

He studied the menu as if it were the Quran before he finally selected his favourite toasted sandwich. By the time the waitress came to take their order, Ron pointed out the lemon meringue pie on the menu."I'll have a coffee with that please," she said.

"I'll have the triple-decker," he said politely next.

"You not hungry Ron?" he asked a little anxiously. She didn't answer, but shook her head, keeping her eyes level with the place mat on the table. As he chomped his way through a triple layer of bacon and tomato, he began to tell her all about Saskatchewan.

"Man, fields of wheat" he said, his eyes lighting up, "Clear blue sky all the way to eternity, that's what they say.

He told her he and his wife had no kids. They had been planning them, just before she cheated on him. Ron heard the word cheated with a small tight sour lump growing at the bottom of her stomach.

"Tell me about you," he said brightly. "Oh I'm a Dublin girl who grew up in a deprived area, got herself pregnant at sixteen, dropped out of school, and one day woke up to herself and moved down the country."

His chewing slowed to a crawl as he digested her condensed history.

"Lady, you don't mince your words," he said finally, his blue eyes full of admiration and something else she couldn't quite make out.

"Were your family wealthy?" she asked casually, stabbing her fork into the middle of the meringue.

"Yeah, I guess you could say so. Dad was a local GP- my Mom, a practice nurse, so yeah, I got a good education. Didn't have the stomach for medicine though, so I kind of ended up in teaching by default I suppose. When I get back to Canada I'm going to do a Masters in computer science. I'm still only thirty- two. That's where the big bucks are. I know a guy in Facebook who says if I get a good enough Masters, he'll try to wangle a job for me."

He insisted on paying the cheque. Standing outside the restaurant door in the bright sunshine, she averted her eyes, aware of his tunnelling into her.

"Ron," he gushed before she had time to open her mouth.

"I want to see you again." Before she had time to reply, he reached over, took her by the hand and said, "Come on, I want to show you something." Mutely she allowed him steer her down the small alleyway to the right, which intersected the High Street, praying she wouldn't meet any parent from school. Her hand felt as if a large pliers were gripping it.

"What are we looking at?" she asked, as they peered in the jeweller's window. Without warning, he pulled her into the doorway, squeezed himself against her. She could feel his hardness through her skirt, as his lips pushed against her resistant closed mouth. That's when she slapped him fiercely across the face. Then she ran up the cobblestones. When she finally got to the main street, she looked back to see him wincing from the blow, as the right corner of his eye twitched, like a mad locust on a high wire.

She didn't see him in the staffroom next day. Then as she was about to refill her tea cup, she overheard John say that Greg had rung in sick. That explained the older woman with the glasses at the end of the table. She was obviously his substitute.

"He's got gastric flu, poor devil. He'll be out for the week at least." Laura caught her eye, arching it subtly as John spoke. She'd been so upset when she came home from Sligo that Laura took one look at her and said, "I'll put on the kettle."

She tumbled it all out over seven cups of tea, her difficulties and near escape with Greg.

"God, I thought he was going to rape me," she said with a shudder.

"Lucky it wasn't night- time," the younger woman added.

"You know, you're lucky Laura to have come from such a stable background,"

Ron said with her hands blanketing her eyes and hairline. She became aware after a moment of a heavy silence wading into the space between them. Then she heard a hesitant voice saddled with a foreign- sounding angst. "Actually, I'm fostered since the age of four."

Ron looked up. "I thought..."

"Yes, that's what I like everybody to think".

She took her thumb and began to suck it around the inside of her mouth. For a minute she ran the back of her teaspoon along the deep grooves in the wooden table. She dragged it up and down for so long that Ron was about to catch her hand.

"My mother died in prison when I was ten." She dropped her voice. "I know you don't want to ask me what she was there for, but she did drugs and prostitution."

This time, silence did a triple somersault in the air above them ,waiting, as Ron struggled to find words to respond. Finally, she said,

"Laura, I'm sorry. There was I, thinking I had the hard childhood."

"Well you did in a way," the other girl countered.

"I was brought up in the countryside by two amazing foster parents. My Mum didn't get the chances that I got. She told me once before she killed herself, that she had done me a favour by putting me in foster care. I only got to see her on birthdays and at Christmas. She refused any other access. I think she had a fear of contaminating me."

Ron stood up and walked around the other side of the table.

"Come here to me," she said engulfing Laura in a feartight hug.

She could feel the staccato rise and fall of her chest as the girl began to tremble a little. As she released her, she saw the tears find their exit.

"I'm not like you, brave enough to tell people my story."

"Not yet Love, not yet. Wait a while".

"Ron, I'm so sorry, "there was I meant to be consoling you." Ron smiled, compassion finally clearing her perceptions for take- off. She realised she had to try somehow and make good what she had.

He rang her on Wednesday, to say the carer was well in situ. Ailbhe was behaving herself.

"I can come at the weekend," he said, and then paused. Her longing for him vaulted into the silence.

"I can come for keeps," he added weakly.

"Yes, do that," she said, "just come".

CHAPTER 29

She was upstairs re-reading Adam's email when he arrived late. Laura had headed home to Tipperary. She'd arranged to rent a house in Sligo.

"You're not leaving us?"

The question was infused with real loss .

"I so appreciate having stayed here Ron," but it's kind of settled now. There are two girls and a guy moving into a brand new house in the Carrickmore Estate."

Ron issued her that maternal thing Eanna told her she did.

"Don't worry, we've all met in Jones's pub on Main Street. One of the girls is a student in Sligo IT. The other two are nurses."

Before getting into the car, Laura suddenly threw her arms tightly around her friend's neck.

"Spirit sisters," she said fiercely the words burrowing into Ron's ear drum. For a long time, they locked in a titanic hug under a darkening sky, whose clouds were gathering convulsively.

"You're always welcome here, you know that."

Laura disengaged from the hug and nodded. Her eyes ranged over the blueness of the lower mountain slopes east of them.

"It's going to be fine when he comes home. Just ask him... you know."

She threw an encouraging smile over her shoulder as she opened the driver's door. Ron stood staring at the disappearing Yaris for quite some time before she turned, her sandals burrowing deep into the pebbles of the cottage drive. Her front door beckoned lamely.

Adam's email had arrived that morning.

From adamoconnell17@gmail.com

To ronoconnell15@gmail.com

June3 2019 4 30am

Subject Conference

Hi Ron, Seeing as I couldn't sleep, I thought I'd email you. Great to hear from you again. I'm sure by now you know Miguel and I are meeting Brendan next week in New York. We can't wait. The conference should be very interesting. I'm giving a paper on self-empowerment for the elderly in nursing homes. We also have some other business to attend to, but I'll tell you about that later. All is well this end. Brendan tells me Eanna is coming back for good this time.Delighted for you.

Love to Da and Sally,

Adam

Brendan's latest email had come in an hour after Adam's.

From brendanoconnell21@gmail.com

To ronoconnell 15@gmail.com

June 3 2019 7.30am

Subject Exhibition.

Hi Ma,

As you know, I'm meeting Uncle Adam and Miguel next week in Queens- can't wait.I'll fill you in on all the details, I promise. Work is going great. There's a new development also. I'm going to have a small exhibition of my paintings in the pub I work in! It may even be in July around the time of my birthday. If I sell some of them, 80% of the money will go to charity and I get to keep 20%. The charity is a really cool one. It's to help set up basketball courts for the kids in the neighbourhood. My boss John bought a piece of of real estate years ago which he never built on. He's going to be taxed if he doesn't build on it so he's decided to build three basketball courts, a club house and set up a registered charity called HOOPS {help our own powerful students}. There will be a one on one mentoring for street kids, fostering good role models. He'll get a grant from the municipal authorities. He's asking the mayor to come to the exhibition, and then open the basketball courts when they're ready. I'll be gone by then though. Imagine Ma, an exhibition! Good Eanna is coming home today. The two of you are meant for each other.

Ciao,

Brendan

She checked her watch and frowned. He was very late; it was almost nine. She hadn't checked her phone. Perhaps there was a message. Just as she was about to scan for one, she heard the soft crunching of the wheels on the gravel below.

Mindfully she followed her breath all the way in and all the way out as Fiona had taught her. She'd been back for a session yesterday. In the conversation there were no holds barred. The counsellor encouraged her to open up about Greg first, rather than make any accusations, and then take it from there. She'd slept fitfully. At 5am, she padded around the kitchen, making a big pot of chamomile tea. They grew the best chamomile in the west, Eanna always said. She fell asleep with her head on the table, listening to the dawn chorus. Laura found her there just before school. Today she had arranged one of her extra personal vacation days. She waved drowsily at her lodger as she headed back up to bed. By 11am, she was up and running around, cleaning and polishing. Cleaning always gave her a clear head. By 3pm, she'd had a light lunch, washed the tiles in the hallway, swept the sitting room and scoured the bathroom. She hoovered the bedroom carpets like a mad thing, all the time listening to Michael Buble on Spotify. She needed his big brown eyes today.

This time she opened the door before he got to it. He hauled in his big carpet bag and a smile. She had a cooked chicken ready for the microwave and baked potatoes with creamed carrot and broccoli in a casserole dish.

"I'll just go upstairs for a quick shower," he said.

"All the traffic was backed up on the dual carriageway for over an hour and a half. There was a big pile up. I texted," he said, registering the puzzlement on her face.

"It was on the news; I just missed it, actually, by a whisker. One fatality at least they say."

She could see rivulets of tension had skidded off into the corners of his eyes and nestled in the hollowed bags beneath. Her heart lurched out of her. God, it could have been him and she would never have gotten to ask.

"Two squad cars and two ambulances," he continued, "and in this bad weather."

Her head was in a candy floss machine. The thin threads of her concentration crisscrossed endlessly. It might have been all over. She frowned at him.

"This guy hit the crash barrier, overtaking another car. Then he bounced back across the lane, pushing the car he overtook into the hard shoulder.

Loads of cars went skithering into the back of each other."

Listening to him showering upstairs, she felt a dull headache cementing her forehead. Guilt laid tendrils of steel on her as she took the casserole from the oven and heated up the chicken. Having set the table, she turned on the news on the radio.

'A pile up on the Naas dual carriageway this evening has left two dead and five more people seriously injured in hospital.'

Instantly she turned it down, fright jellying her legs. He was suddenly standing beside her in her kitchen again, droplets of water catching the slanting light on his bare chest. She handed him a fresh white shirt which she had ironed despite herself.

They ate in silence for the first five minutes. She could tell he was shaken.

"Did they release any names?" he asked finally.

"No, I don't think so; I didn't hear."

The wind outside gathered itself for a fracas.

"Thunder on the way," she said weakly.

When a large bolt of lightning pulsed into the room, she screamed. The cooker in front of her was suddenly thrust in a spectral light. Reflexively, he grabbed her hand; her damp palm clung to his.

"Let's bring in the food to the front room," he said, "and we can draw the curtains."

She asked him to leave the telly off.

"Information overload," she said, drawing the curtains close. Uncertainly, he placed the remote back on the couch, his hand not on terra firma. By way of distraction, she said.

"Tell me about the new carer."

"Well," he said, breathing more evenly.

"The carer's name is Bridget, and she's a pet. Ailbhe has gotten more hours in the rehab as well so she won't be under Ma's feet so much. My cousin is going to take her more at the weekends too so she can help babysit her twins."

She fixed a small kind smile in her eyes.

"I'm delighted to hear all that."

He looked at her for a moment slowly and enquiringly.

"How are you doing?" His tone was circumscribed with trepidation.

"I'm missing Laura already," she said.

"I'm not talking about Laura."

She picked over her words, stepping stones across a torrent.

"I met a guy for coffee the other day, Greg the Canadian I told you about. He told me he fancies me. He suggested we meet and I agreed."

She didn't allow herself to look at the canyon between his eyebrows. She stared at a spot above him on the chimney wall and continued.

"I don't remotely fancy him. He tried to grope me, but even if he hadn't, he just wasn't you. So why did I meet him?"

His stare was impacted on his face now. He was about to interject when she raised a hand.

"Let me finish. I met him because..."

Here she paused, and looked him in the eye.

"I met him because I was jealous and I need to know if I have reason to be."

She could see the oscillation of his Adam's Apple .

"My God Ron, why are you jealous?" he asked tetchily after a hard pause.

Because...she said slowly and evenly,

"I got a photo on WhatsApp." She pulled up the WhatsApp photo.

"Why didn't you tell me about this?" She sounded more plaintive than she had intended.

The thunder was mouthing outside. Lightning slipped and blinked through the gap in the curtains. Rain hopped off the galvanised roof of the turf shed. Her torso tensed.

"Because there's nothing to tell," he said defensively.

"You've met her at least three times in that same pub."

He looked startled.

"And," she continued, "you lied when I asked who you met. Why did you lie Eanna?"

He got up from the chair, and moved to the window, pulled back the curtains a fraction looking out at the spills of rain in the growing night. He continued to speak with his back to her.

"At first I lied stupidly because I thought you wouldn't understand."

"Understand what?"

He turned slowly, pivoting on his heels, as he did when he wanted to emphasise something.

"I met her because she asked me to Ron, but that was it. I should have told you that from the start, but I didn't want you to get the

251

wrong idea. You caught me off guard with that question on the phone so I lied. But I swear I've no interest anymore."

"Then why were you meeting?"

"Because she split up from Donal Gleeson," he said with a sigh.

"And maybe I'm just a soft touch. That photo was her showing me the solicitor's letter. He's looking for custody of their two- year -old girl."

"And what about the other times?" she persisted. He wasn't getting off that lightly.

"Yes, the other times too, she was looking for advice about her bills."

"She could have gone to the Citizens' Information," Ron said curtly.

"She knew I was in the Vincent de Paul some years ago, and she wanted to know how to get a helping hand from them. I sent her to MABS, you know the mortgage advice and .."

" budgeting service," she said, finishing the last two words of his sentence, allowing their weight to sit on the airways.

"Yes, I think I know them well... as does everyone we know in Dobbinstown, she replied curtly.

"Why did you always meet up in the pub?"

"You look so puzzled. Did your source not tell you the reason?"

"My source," she said, feeling the ruffles of her ire, "was Amy, as you well know."

"I'm sorry," he said dropping his gaze to the floor; "you didn't deserve that."

"No I bloody didn't," she said standing up from the table, and walking over to the window beside him.

"Tell me the whole truth Eanna."

"Yes, she does fancy me Ron, and she wanted to get back with me. The pub meeting was her idea. Her mother has lung cancer, and she said she couldn't get away during the day. Her sister comes in at night to let her go to work. The boss gave her the time to talk to me, but he deducted an hour's wage."

"Are you sure you don't fancy her?"

This time he looked her straight in the eye, took her rigid hand in his and said softly

"We shared a life for three years Ron, so I'm always going to have that attachment. That's just being honest, but I don't love her. I'm not sure I ever did. I have missed you every day like my second heartbeat."

He swiped away a tear viciously from his eyes.

"God I've missed you," he said turning on his heels, staring back out at the bereft night .

Her entire body propelled her towards him then. She put her hand on his shoulders and whispered, "It's OK Love, don't cry. Well I'm sorry I met that horrible Greg guy. You are my second heartbeat too."

She could feel the damp sweat on him through his shirt, and for the second time in a week, someone trembling at her touch. He turned slowly, and said

"I was an eejit, and I'm so sorry, but I'd never cheat on you Ron O'Connell. You're my morning star, my true north."

At this, she moved her face into his until she found the lips that eased her terrible famine.

Their love making was filled with raw honesty and urgency. He traced his fingertips delicately up along the length of her body. He touched her breasts gently, reverently before he kissed each nipple in turn. Slowly, sensuously, he moved his lips up along her neck until they kissed. Her entire body surged underneath him. Every fibre of her being, long neglected, quivered with relief. Each had come home at last.

CHAPTER 30

For the next week, each walked around the other in technicolor. Her senses were heightened around him. Neither of them went to work. Ron had her June break and Eanna told the lads on the building site and on the farm he'd caught the flu.

"It's the love bug you have," she joked.

"Delicious flu," he smiled.

When he got up in the morning, she loved his sexy walk in his boxers, his long tanned legs covered in delicate red hairs. She felt aroused just when he touched her accidentally. She knew she was having the same effect on him. They needed only each other's company. Reality could wait. She snuggled into him early in the morning. Suddenly they felt the delight in their jigsaw that just now fitted .Sometimes they made love first thing in the morning, the June light pouring a fluid commentary on the proceedings. They were hungry to find their way inside each other again. Their responsibilities no longer held them in the old tiger grip. There was no world outside of each other. He read her the "Good Morrow" by John Dunne. Her favourite lines were,

"For love all love of other sights controls, and makes one little room an everywhere."

She closed her eyes, listening. He had a fine speaking voice. Why try to find herself in New York piggybacking on her son's life? All she ever needed was right here in a small sunlit bedroom in a Leitrim cottage.

Reality rang the doorbell one morning in the form of Joe. She flew down the stairs in her dressing gown. Her father frowned,

"God, we thought you were sick. We haven't seen sight nor light of either of you since Eanna came back."

Joe took in his daughter's embarrassed face, dishevelled hair and unbelted dressing gown.

"Things are good?"

"Yes," she said, "very good."

Joe smirked.

"And there was I worried about you."

"No need," she said, her eyes slowly elevating a twinkle to meet his.

"I've had a WhatsApp call from Adam of all people. He's fine, but he wants to Skype us all tonight. Brendan is going to be on the call too."

"Oh God, Da, I'm sorry, I forgot all about the Skype."

Her father's smile was enigmatic.

"What?" she said

"Nothing, nothing."

His lips pursed cheekily "I feel like I've just broken up a honeymoon. I'll be off so,"

he said turning on his heels quickly.

"See you later tonight."

"Bye Da," she said, waving as his retreating back headed for his car.

"Was that Joe?" Eanna said behind her. He'd just had a quick shower.

"You know what?"she said looking at the bath towel wrapped around his loins.

"I could make love to you all over again."

"Now Veronica, that's scandalous."

He pulled her in for a kiss. Her lips lingered on his lightly and succulently for a moment, before pulling herself free.

"We have a Skype call at Joe and Sally's tonight. Apparently Adam and Miguel have news for us.

"Good news, I presume," he said, as he ascended the stairs slowly.

After a very late breakfast, Eanna said he would check on the polytunnels. She thought she would pot hanging baskets for the gable wall and the front of the cottage. As she was firmly bedding down the white and purple petunias, she wondered about Adam's news. His email had been very cagey and Brendan's email this morning which never mentioned the Skype, was effusive in his praise of Uncle Adam. He was also hinting heavily at mysterious things. After the potting, she practised some yoga asanas on the patio. Since his return, she hadn't touched her "happy pills" once, she realised. She kept them on standby nonetheless. Getting in touch with her body through her breathing, she came to realise her muscles had loosened and her colly wobble heart had slowed. She had plans to give Yoga and Chakradance classes again in Joe and Sally's communal space. She reached for her phone now, put on her earpieces and drew up her old tutor's voice from her downloads. For over an hour, her body followed the sensuous rhythms of her heart chakra. Green for harmony suffused her aura. She was embodied freedom on her own patio with oblivious motorists the other side of the high hedge. When next she checked her watch it was 4pm. Hard to believe she'd been dancing for more than an hour. Every sinew in her welcomed home her joy .

Eanna returned at 6, showered and changed before dinner. Ron was already changed, and realised she was starving. She rustled up an omelette and chips for them. They ate in silence and at ease in each other's company.

"I wonder what Adam wants?"

Eanna said pouring himself a second cup of tea.

"No idea," she replied. "but whatever it is, it's got Brendan all fired up."

By 7.30 they were in the Skoda and heading up towards Lough Melvin. The call was for 8.30.Eanna was embraced by Joe first and then Sally. Ron joked

"The prodigal returns."

"Never thought I was going to see that fella again,"

her father said, giving him a friendly punch on the arm. Eanna hung his head, and grinned sheepishly. When the deep reverberations of the Skype call came on, they were seated and waiting in front of the screen. Brendan's head was the first one they saw. As usual, Ron visualised herself hugging him .She closed her eyes.

"You giving him your mental hug again?" a voice said. She opened them, blinked for a moment and saw Adam next. He looked very well, she reflected. He'd gained a little weight. Contentment was catnapping in his eyes. Next on the screen was Miguel. No one had seen him before except as a shadow in the background. A tall man with thinning lank black hair and glasses covering dark- set, kind eyes, appeared in front of them. She noticed a deep cleft in his chin as if it had long ago been stitched up.

"This is Miguel, my husband," Adam announced.

She heard Joe's sharp intake of breath beside her and glanced at him anxiously. His jaw had slackened, but his eyes were smiling.

"Congratulations son," he said quietly. "Welcome to the family Miguel."

"I echo that," said Sally."I'm Joe's wife."

"I've heard all about you," said Miguel happily, " and it's all good."

"Nice guy and a charmer," Ron said to herself. "He will iron out the creases in Adam."

"I was the best man at their wedding," Brendan chimed in.

To a chorus of "What?"and the look on four puzzled, bewildered faces, Adam explained.

"We got married in New York in a civil ceremony. Brendan was a witness and Miguel's older sister was the other one. We'll have a proper party when we get back to San Francisco," he said.

"But why New York?" Ron asked .

"and why didn't you tell us?"

"Well, we wanted no fuss, and we had another surprise to announce. The getting married was a kind of an afterthought," Adam said.

The crevice between Joe's eyebrows collapsed inward.

"We can explain," Miguel continued, looking to his partner for reassurance.

"Da, we're going to have a baby," Adam said breathlessly.

"We do not do things by halves" Miguel said, flashing a gap-toothed grin in very white teeth.

It was Sally who saved the day, after a stunned pause hung upside down in the air.

"My congrats again to both of you," she said, beaming into the screen.

"Joe, that's fantastic isn't it?"

"But how?" Joe asked, ignoring Sally's warning frown.

"Is it surrogacy?" Eanna asked now.

"Bang on the money Eanna."

The relief in Adam's reply rode on his last exhale.

"Now, before I have to talk about egg donors and all that, I can tell you there wasn't one."

Ron wondered if her father had any idea what they were talking about.

"It's my sister who's having the baby for us,"

Miguel announced proudly.

"It will be Adam's sperm," he said.

"Mother of God," she thought, "did they not know Irish culture was a hare which used to be a tortoise, and all tortoises weren't yet *extinct?!*"

"Right," said Joe slowly

"Right you be," he added carefully."I get yeh."

"How far gone are you?" Sally asked now.

Joe stared at his extra- terrestrial other half.

"We are past the first trimester," Miguel said.

Ron could see a small sunrise of comprehension on her dad's face. "Congratulations," he finally said meaningfully. She was proud of him.

"Did you have the surrogacy done in New York?" Ron asked.

This time, Brendan answered for them.

"No, they got married here, but they're going up to Maine to finalise things."

"We can get a pre-birth certificate there," explained Adam, "which would put two fathers on the birth cert. Miguel's sister Roma is a resident. Only New York residents may avail of surrogacy in New York. Maine is one of the best counties in the States for surrogacy and less complicated. We will be adopting, of course, after the birth."

Miguel took up the story.

"My sister Roma has all her family now, and is still only thirty-six. She wants to give us this gift."

Ron's hands fled to the outline of her flat belly. She caught Eanna's eye subtly following the trajectory of their flight..

The Skype ended with Brendan gushing about the fabulous hotel the two men were staying in. He gave them a rundown also, much to Adam's embarrassment, on his uncle's presentation for the conference. Brendan got cut off mid-sentence, as he was explaining how Adam got many of his compos mentis residents to take charge of small jobs like delivering the post, watering the plants, planting window boxes, baking, etc. Apparently, that's what he wrote his paper on. When the screen finally went blank, Joe said

"Clever lad Adam, after all. Wonder where Miguel picked up that chin?"

Sally looked at him oddly, and said, "Anyone for a brew?"

CHAPTER 31

She knew she had to do the housework. The duvet covers were crying out to be changed. Floors needed washing downstairs, and she should really wash down the window sills, but she had to keep reading his emails. So much to savour, so much to revisit. A mist was on a slow crawl down the mountain. A finger of cold wagged in the air. She caught the date on the computer screen, 29.8. 2019.

"Oh my God, where had the time gone?"

Brendan was due to head to Peru in the next couple of days. That's why she was scrolling back through all his emails which she had stored in her file full of downloads. Of course she called it 'Brendan The Navigator'. Eanna had access to it too. Sometimes they both read his emails together. At times she smiled at the hilarity of them. She found now she didn't want to chase him round the globe anymore. Somehow she had her world right here, right now. She scrolled back up the list of emails, until she found the one dated June 10th. It was just after the exploding Skype news, the one that threw a grenade in Grandad's ordered perceptions!

From brendanoconnell 21@gmail.com

To ronoconnell15@gmail.com

June 10 2019 7.00am

Subject a spanner in the works

Well Ma, we really threw a spanner into the works last night, Adam and me and Miguel of course. Oh poor Grandad's face! I had the most amazing day with the guys in City Hall. There was a big queue in front of us for the Justice of the Peace. He only does weddings on a Friday. Everyone was allotted twenty minutes. God, I'd like more time than that when I get married, ha ha. It was kind of moving to see the two guys exchange vows. Believe it or not Ma, they had ordered Louis Copeland suits on line! I borrowed Sean's best suit. It didn't fit great, but Mrs Elliott downstairs got out her needle and thread the night before the wedding, and took it in at the waist. Thank God for Mrs E. After the wedding we went to Giovanni's trattoria on Arthur Avenue. I sort of know the boss there by now as his nephew is the chef at the pub where I work. They put on such a spread for us Ma. I rounded up Sean and Pedro for the meal, and Adam and Miguel invited an American couple they knew - Mark and Sophie who live in Brooklyn. We drank champagne. It tasted a bit funny, but I toasted the happy couple like everyone else. The owner brought out a cake with big sparklers on it. He gave us a cocktail each on the house, and *wait for it,* three guys with mandolin, accordion, and ukulele serenaded Adam and Miguel. I really like Miguel's sister Estrella. She seems really decent, and I know she's going to get a financial settlement from the guys which will help her and her husband pay their debts. Then she wants to study to be a solicitor, so not much chance really of her ever wanting to keep the baby. Adam might have preferred a donor egg, which is what the surrogacy agency recommend all the time, but Miguel was adamant he wanted to keep it in the family, so we toasted modern families as well with the champagne. The guys have gone on to Maine now with their honeymoon/adoption business.

Dawn is coming over for two weeks the middle of July and I can't wait. I've loads of plans and places to take her. It's getting hotter than hell in downtown New York now, so Sean's boss has a getaway, a big log cabin in the Catskills. Everyone who is anyone goes up there in the summer time, and yours truly is invited with his girlfriend! Now what do you make of that? I'm going to take her to the Bronx Zoo when she comes which is right beside us, not to mention the Botanical Gardens. Eanna would love that. I'll send him a link to their website and YouTube videos. We might manage Orchard Beach as well, and have a picnic under the evergreen trees. By the way I've been to my first Yankee Stadium football game. The Louisburgh

Harriers and the Cotton Rollers. Louisburgh Harriers won 10 to 5. The game wasn't great, but I sure enjoyed the experience. Looks like the exhibition I told you about will probably be near the end of August- not as many around then, but hopefully we'll sell enough paintings, and I'll get 20% for myself, yippee.

Ciao for now,

Brendan

As always she read her own reply which was directly underneath his email.

From ronoconnell15@gmail.com

To brendanoconnell21@gmail.com

June 11 2019 1.00PM

Subject So Much News.

Hi Love,

Just a brief email, as we'll meet on Skype on Sunday night. You have so much interesting news. I love the idea of going to the Catskills- very posh! Sounds like Dawn is going to be a very lucky girl, and you're a lucky guy. As for Adam and Miguel, Granda is still not over the shock LoL. Personally I'm delighted for them, and as you say, it's modern families isn't it? We'll have another wedding party for them in Drombawn yet. No major news here. The house is flying up, and they're putting the roof on next week. I spend every waking hour down there at the site. A part of me in truth doesn't even want to give up the cottage. We might give holidays a skip this year what with the house and work commitments. I'll see you in Peru anyway!

P.S. Grandad went to see the surgeon in Sligo General today, and he's got to have a knee replacement possibly around the end of August. Then he might do the other one a few months later. Sally says he'll be a bionic man, and Joe says he'll be a new man.!

Ciao for now,

Ma

She kept scrolling down skipping some of his longer emails in June, mainly about work and the guys in the apartment, until she came to the one dated August 2nd

From: brendanoconnell21@gmail.com

To: ronoconnell15@gmail.com

June 2 2019 6..00 pm

Subject: Mega birthday gift, soo appreciated.

Hi Ma,

Thank you soo much for the birthday gift in my account. I know you say you're a rich lady and all that, but still seriously Ma, 500 Dollars- a king's ransom, as Mrs Elliott said when I told her. Serious apologies for not being in touch. I was, shall we say busy! Dawn has come and gone. Brill to have had her here for my big day. She was too shy to go on the Skype on Sunday when you were all singing Happy Birthday, but I posted all our photos on Instagram, so you know what a smasher she is. There's this old lady in the market who speaks Yiddish. One morning she was watching us pick out the best apples to take back to the apartment.As she checked out our fruit, she kept her head down at the till. Suddenly out of nowhere, without even looking up, she said out loud to herself ,

"Shayna Matel."

Then she caught my eye and winked. Sean looked it up on Google translate, and it means beautiful girl.I can see all the guys are jealous of me. Pedro just kept *staring*. I caught Sean giving her sideways glances when we all went to Giovannis together or even just sitting around the breakfast table. I have a thing for gorgeous women. You're included in that by the way.

Well we did the touristy things. Her jaw dropped at the 9/11 Memorial. I know how she felt. We wined and dined in the Rockefeller Centre for my birthday. Then we went up to the Observation Point and she fell in love with the Manhattan skyline. Of course I was pointing out all the landmarks: the outline of the

Bronx, the Hudson River, the Empire State Building, Queens, Brooklyn. It looked dreamy, a kind of light elegy in the semi-dark. I know I'm being all poetic and all, but I wondered about all those people just like us living in those lit up apartments, and working their asses off by day in the big office blocks. I know that life will never be for me Ma. We also did the Bronx Zoo,(which is *GINORMOUS*) and The Botanical Gardens. You'd love their giant cactus and the tropical rainforest in the huge greenhouse. We didn't quite get to Orchard Beach, but maybe another time. Now for the best bit - the Catskills. Sean's boss drove us up there; it's about a two hour drive. We drove steadily into the cool of the mountains, which was a relief from the heat I can tell you. The cabin is state of the art: jacuzzi, outdoor swimming pool and wait for it, a massive spiral staircase in the downstairs reception room. The steps were made from... would you believe ...Liscannor slate? We Irish get around. More news to follow,

Gotta go here,

Brendan

She remembered he didn't get back for two more days, said his emailing got interrupted by the guys in the apartment asking him if he fancied going out for a beer in Mac's Diner two blocks away.

Over the two days when he hadn't yet got back online, she got involved again in one of her favourite things of all times to do.

"Well better get your head on now girl."

Alice's voice turned itself on in her mind as it did in tough times. This was to be her first back- to- back -Yoga and Chakradance session in a few months. The group filed in. Joanna Brady directed a bunsen burner of a smile at her. In fairness, she had been able to confide in Joanna. The others in the class just knew she had to take time out for family reasons. Also seeing as it was July, they were even surprised any classes were running. But she had posted messages on Facebook and uploaded a video of herself doing her top ten asanas

264

on Instagram. The palms of her hands ran red and she wiped their sweat off on her black lycra leggings.

The group in front of her consisted of three of her regulars and five holiday makers, three of whom confessed to being beginners. They had barely begun the Mountain Pose, when the door handle turned downward. Sally tiptoed into the room in her double layer of man's socks, lycra leggings and yellow oversized tee shirt. Ron glimpsed the lettering D G. The laces of her runners dangled in her right hand, and a blue yoga mat was rolled up under her left arm. She flashed an apologetic smile at the group before claiming a place at the back right, near a large window overlooking the softly dreaming lake under a razor blue sky. Initially, she was a little taken aback by Sally's entrance - her first time ever to come to class - but the calm reassurance messaging from her stepmother's eyes tamed any emerging panic.

The class progressed in a steady flow. She guided them through the floor relaxation at the end. Nimbly she moved around the spaces between the bodies, doling out extra pillows and cushions. She instructed the newcomers to tune into their breathing, by placing their hands on their bellies.

Sally and Joanne were the only two for Chakradance. She explained for Sally's benefit that Chakradance was a dance from the inside out, and it was a free expression of a soul journey. She warned as she often did that it might unleash old emotions and reassured that healing sometimes flowed. This generally took a number of sessions. There were no steps to be learned. Sally, having done Yoga classes in London admitted after, she was a bit hesitant at first, but declared herself a convert. Today was base chakra. Ron had pre-recorded the session, and sent it out now to the two women on WhatsApp. As they moved fluidly in freestyle, tuning into the red core of the earth beneath them, each woman planted her feet on the ground, growing her metaphorical roots in the earth beneath. After that, the tribal music transported each to where their souls needed to be in that moment. Sitting quietly back on their heels when the music ended, the three women did a freestyle mandala which was a private representation of their individual experiences. Outside the window, the evening air was translucent. At the jetty, two freshly painted yellow and blue boats rose and fell with the gentle swell on the lake. The ducks' nest, now abandoned in the midst of the reeds, would soon cave in, but not before autumn.

She scrolled down now to the second part of his interrupted email.

From brendanoconnell 21@gmail.com
To ronoconnell 15@gmail.com
August 4.2019 8.00am
Subject got interrupted
Hi Ma,

Sorry for the interruption. The guys were badgering me to go and get a few beers in Mac's diner. It is hot as hell in the apartment and the A/C isn't the best, so we get out when we can.

Anyway, we all went hiking in the Catskills Park. We followed the main trail and set up camp on one of the ledges that branch off it. The view would take your breath, and you wouldn't even miss it. The mountains hugged us close. The conifers did sentry duty up along the trail, and you could see folks doing a zip line from one mountain peak to the next. I was hooked and I booked one for the next morning. Dawn wouldn't come. She actually waited for me back at the camp for three hours. Sean kept her company. He was a bit too keen I thought LoL. It was the most exhilarating experience of my entire life. Don't worry, we were well harnessed and locked in and we had to do an induction course for two hours. At one stage, we got up to a speed of 50 kilometres per hour. I felt like I was up with the gods. I soared like an eagle. The treeline below just dropped away.

On our last night there, we had a barbecue, and we sat around a small bonfire on a piece of open ground away from the forest. Sean's boss Ian invited some of his friends from the neighbouring cabins. They began talking about their investments and share prices dropping- regular bores some of them. Dawn and I slipped away. We sat on the decking just looking at the mountains above us. Mountains are like eternity come to say Hello aren't they ? They sort of comfort you Ma. They never get tired. Dawn went inside, and fetched her binoculars and some blankets. She said we would have to wait for the pre-dawn sky to see some planets. So we said we would sleep on the decking with our blankets around us. We set our alarms on our phones for 4am, but we didn't sleep at all, just sat there talking as you do. Dawn showed me two planets: Castor and Pollux in Venus. It was such a cool experience. When all the world was between sleeping and waking, there we were travelling the skies, enjoying the company of other parts of the universe. My exhibition is coming up late August; it's a bit late unfortunately for my birthday, but it'll still be taking place before I leave, so gotta get to work on it.

Ciao Mamma,

Brendan

She continued to scroll until she found her own email.

From: ronoconnell15@gmail.com

To: Brendan O Connell21@gmail.com

August 5 2019 5.00pm

Subject What a wonderful time.

Hi Love,

You seem really busy at work these days, and I know the exhibition is distracting you from thoughts of Dawn. Loved the photos on Instagram. I agree with the old lady. She is a beautiful girl. Not much news here. Grandad, as you know is still waiting for his knee replacement, and I'm finally doing my Yoga and Chakradance classes again. Had a really interesting session yesterday with Sally in attendance for both! I was a bit nervous at first to tell you the truth, but Sal is a trooper. She was surprised by how much she enjoyed the Chakradance. By next month, I hope to have a full class. Eanna has quit his job finally in Dublin. He can always go back to teaching, but he wants to try his hand full time at the organic farming and herb growing. He still treats people with the herbal medicine. Sometimes he rings the house here with the prescription and I make up the formulas. We're storing the tinctures{ which he mostly buys in yet} and teas in the shed out the back, which you remember we got dry lined a couple of years back. We still do the Organic Farmers' Market every Saturday morning, so we're up at 6, but do you know I love it. My green smoothies with the Brazil nut milk go down a treat. I've also begun making hand made soaps after watching YouTube videos. My cabin in the market is now called Tigin Ron, (Ron's little house). There is one other piece of news I nearly forgot. Ailbhe came to stay with Joe and Sally. Do you know she's quite a handful ? Now I understand Aileen's dilemma with her. When you come home we'll bring her for a long weekend and you can entertain her, LoL.

Ciao for now,

Ma

She allowed herself a moment to catch her breath. The house seemed so still, and he was so far away, but she felt him around her all the time. Briefly she fingered her moonstone pendant. She hadn't seen it around his neck on Skype lately, but she didn't want to comment. Then her heart flitted back to the weekend when Ailbhe came to Joe and Sally's. She came to Eanna and herself for lunch on the Sunday. Having gone upstairs to the bathroom, she didn't come down for a long time. Ron found her in their bedroom, and cursed herself silently for not having got a lock for the bedroom door. She had her back to the door. She had been rummaging intently through the top drawer of the dressing table, as was evidenced by the number of displaced makeup tubes, lipsticks and cotton buds on the chair beside it.

"Are you looking for something?" Ron asked.

She turned around suddenly, a small slyness settled on her face.She had a pill half way to her lips.

"Put that down at once."

Ron's tone was fierce. Like a small piece of lead, she dropped it on the floor, and hung her head to one side. Her bottom lip went into a tail spin.

"Look at me."

Her head swivelled in denial, stubbornly refusing to make eye contact.

"Not my fault- I'm not bold. Ma says I'm bold,"she said petulantly.

Ron moved over swiftly to her, and gently took the pill, leaving it down on the dressing table.

"You're not bold Ailbhe," she said, putting her arm around the girl.

"Do you want some pills?" In reply, she got a mute nod.

"Well you can't take mine; they might not be right for you, and would make you sick. You'll have to go to the doctor."

"Ma won't let me. I wanna have sex. Darren and I wanna have sex, and we need pills. I want a baby, but Ma says I can't keep it. Darren said I need to get pills; then we can have sex, and when we get our house, we can have a baby."

Ron exhaled sharply; she must talk to Eanna again. That family needed a wakeup call. She shepherded Ailbhe down the stairs, her arms still around her taut rounded shoulders, and shook her head at Eanna when he opened his mouth to exclaim.

She glanced at the clock; it was nearly midday-just time for one more final email, her favourite one about the exhibition.

From: brendanoconnell21@gmail.com

To: ronoconnell15@gmail.com
August 27 2019 5.00pm
Subject Exhibition.

Well Ma, I'm a rich man now. I've just had my exhibition and I guess you saw the photos that I put up on Instagram. Pedro made a short video and we've put that up today. I think it all was a mighty success. My boss Sean opened up the unused dining room to the rear of the pub as a kind of art gallery. I had fifteen pieces for exhibition in all. Some of them, as you will have seen, were my drawings of the Sistine Chapel, and more were from the art college in Rome. I left out the nude paintings, as they can be kind of prudish around here. I had a nice landscape one of the Catskills which I sketched when I was there, and Sean let me use an old shed out the back to make a painting of it. I painted a couple more there of the New York skyline and one of the bar itself. That's my parting gift to him. He was chuffed.

All the boss's cronies turned up: Maguires, McCarthys, O'Neills, and then of course there were the Italians: Fabuccis, Trapatonis, Donatellos. I was very nervous, but Dawn skyped me from Rome at 5am her time. She said she couldn't sleep with the nerves. There was a huge buzz in the bar that evening, with all these well dressed strangers milling around in designer suits, rolexes and glittering cufflinks. The locals were there too by the way. We draped pink silk material over the back wall, and set out long trestle tables with food. We had commercial signs printed for outside the pub. You'll never guess who was there? The boss knows his Dad from Offaly, where his own Dad still lives. It was Mundy- you know the "Galway Girl" He's on tour here in New York, and just happened to drop in. Yours truly had his picture taken with him and an upcoming young fella, a rising star called Shobsy who met up with him, and came along too. They played for two hours after the exhibition was over. The crowd went wild, both Irish and Italians. The pub was jammed to the rafters.

Apologies, I'm digressing a little. I must finish my bit about the exhibition. The local press were invited along with the Bronx mayor which was another photo op. Dawn says I'll be insufferable. Me- never! However, I will require a new hat for my head, ha ha. It was very posh Ma, canapés and cocktails with waitresses in black and white uniforms walking around with trays of drinks. There was an entry price of $100. (Locals were free in) Everybody got a card a bit like a catalogue, with my paintings numbered 1 to 15, and a description of each one underneath. I sold the lot, average price $300. The charity rep made a speech about a talented young Irishman, yours truly LoL. My boss made a speech, and I had to say a few words; you'll see it on the video.

Ciao for now,

Brendan.

Her heart ran along the cobblestones again- no speed bumps this time. Wow! the O'Connell's cruising at a higher altitude. Dobbinstown had receded completely.

She closed the laptop with a deep sigh. She heard Eanna moving around downstairs. The swallows' nest under the eaves was long empty. It was time for them to move on. She now had to plan for going back to school. The bones of an idea was forming at the back of her mind.

CHAPTER 32

Sunday morning, and as usual her first thought was her son. He'd just gotten into Lima International the night before last. He'd made an unexpected WhatsApp video call at ten to five yesterday morning. Eanna nudged her awake and she panicked when she saw his number, until she remembered Peru is six hours behind. It was 10.50pm by the time he had cleared arrivals That's when he promptly rang her, all apologies and a little flustered when he remembered the time difference. He'd been up since 6 and his boss had driven him in to Newark for an 8.30 check in. There had been a three and a half hour stopover in Fort Lauderdale. Lucky he said he had his sketch pad, and managed a call with Dawn, who had just come off nights.

She lay awake staring at the ceiling, watching the light advance into the room with its sloping white ceiling. She got out of bed, padded over to the window in her bare feet, and scanned the sky.

The forecast was good for today, Sunday the 2nd[n] of September. A soft shade of blue elbowed its way through a patchy sky. A high breeze drove off the clouds. The sheep on the lower slopes of the hill were quietening. They were finally taking out the barbecue set. The summer had been so frantic, between the house building, and then Eanna had just dipped his toe into the tincture making. "It is just a toe Ron, I promise," he said when he saw the alarm broadcasting faintly on her face. We will hasten slowly. I've learned my lesson." He had taken on two more people at the herb centre, and just purchased a white Mercedes van for delivery purposes. His organic vegetables were in much demand around the county, and quite often there was a drop off to various herbalists too. There was a range of fresh herbs produced to his exacting standards and alufoil wrapped dried teas, which customers could now order online. In time, tinctures would follow, once he got the hang of the production. Roll on her own trip to Peru. She'd seen the quality of light and the vibrancy of Mardi Gras in Latin America on YouTube. Soon she would be the living sponge for it to moisten..

Today there wasn't time to think about Lima. Joe was in hospital, recovering after his knee replacement surgery. She'd give him a ring later. When she called into him yesterday in Sligo General, he was still quite drained from the anesthetic. Seeing the ridged green hospital bed cover rising up over a protective cage covering his left knee, she felt an instant pang for the man who could ride a Harley Davidson out of Dublin town and into the Wicklow Mountains like a Hell's Angel in thick leathers and silver chains. Her Ma always said the night he had his accident, just before Brendan was conceived, was the beginning of his arthritis

Her thoughts turned next to the barbecue and a wind blowing in from Dublin. Aileen was scheduled to go to hospital for routine tests. She had asked if they could keep Ailbhe through the week. She winced when she recalled the last episode with her. She was a good girl really .All she needed was better management she reflected, yes better management. Her inner voice rang clear with her newfound conviction. When she took on Eanna, he came with this little package, a voice in her head reminded her sagely. Well, worry was a poor companion on life's journey, Alice often said. Why invite it along? Her new inner pilot voice was comforting in its reasoning.

Eanna stirred in the bed.

"A worker's allowed a late breakfast Love," she said to his tousled head, which was just emerging from undercover.

"It's just 9 o'clock now."

Half an hour later, showered and dressed, she was downstairs fixing up some porridge with linseeds and blueberries. The coffee machine was on.

"Breakfast's ready," she called.

He appeared at the top of the landing, freshly showered and still in his new white bathrobe, a left over gift from Christmas, unused until now. She let out a sharp whistle when he entered the kitchen.

"Look at you, Hunk."

He grinned sheepishly, unbelting and belting his robe provocatively.

"Mister Doyle," she said sounding shocked. "What would your former students say?"

"They'd say what lesson is that Mister Doyle?" he said, tilting her chin up, engaging the line of her eyes. Then he kissed her full on the lips. Almost losing each other had frightened both of them. He'd been to Fiona with her twice and things were changing. When breakfast was over, he got up suddenly and went to turn down the radio on the kitchen window sill.

"Ron" - He paused ,

"You know I'm collecting Ailbhe today. She's coming on the bus. I'll collect her in Sligo for 3 o'clock. You're sure you're OK with that?"

He scanned her face anxiously. Taking a deep breath, she lit her dark morning smile.

"Of course it's fine Love; she's a pet."

"Hmmn, a wolf in sheep's clothing more like," he muttered, collecting the breakfast dishes, and slowly stacking them in the dishwasher.

When he was gone to the farm by 11, she checked out everything needed for the barbecue. Lucky, the landlord, now that they had renovated much of the cottage for a reduced rent, had put up a new decking at the back. This made it perfect for their barbecue. Yep, everything was ready to go, she noted: brand new barbecue set, number of easy chairs to scatter around the garden. She would put her blue and yellow fluffy cushions on them later. Sausage rolls were stacked on a black oven tray ready to cook; mixed salad was trussed up in a large perspex bowl. Chocolate flapjacks were cooling on two chairs in the small back porch. Eanna was buying the steaks and drinks in Supervalue. This was indeed the last of the summer wine she reflected. Una and John Healy were coming. Some of Eanna's former staff had been invited: Paul and George from The Leitrim Organic Growers Co-op, her own principal John, Laura obviously and her boyfriend Larry up from Tipperary. Cian O Grady and his wife had been invited by Joe and Sally. For a minute, she stood stock still in the kitchen. An image of Dobbinstown floated in front of her mind. Would they say she had gotten too big for her boots? She had shared this thought with her other half earlier before he left for the farm.

He looked at her oddly, his hand on the front door handle. "Veronica have you learned nothing? If Dobbinstown met Drombawn tonight, would you turn either party away? She considered for a moment.

"No I couldn't obviously."

Would you be ashamed of Dobbinstown ?

A picture of the solicitor and his wife crash-landed before her briefly. To her surprise, she heard herself say,

"Honestly, I might have been six months or a year ago, but now they are all just folk who would have to adjust to each other ."

"Yes Love, the difference is in you now, and that's the point," he said. Then he was out the door, his lightning stride lengthening, as he headed out to the van

Her train of thought was suddenly arrested by the blue flashing light on her laptop, which she had brought down to the kitchen, just in case there was mail. Yes there was mail. She pounced on it. Yes it was from him.

From: brendanoconnell21@gmail.com

To: ronoconnell15@gmail.com

September 2.2019 5.00 am

Subject: Brendan The Navigator in Lima.

Hi Ma,

Sorry about the early morning call. I forgot the time it was at home. Well I'm here in Lima, and up real early as you can see from the time on the computer. It's mighty-un poco loco as they say here. They're all so welcoming, and big into kissing! I've been kissed by Francesco the house owner's aunt on both cheeks! How would that go down in Drombawn do you think? Ha ha. I haven't gone exploring much yet. I'm sharing the whole house with Francesco. He's a 29 year old lawyer, who inherited it from his wealthy Gran. Like I told you, he's Pedro's cousin. Serendipity strikes twice with lodgings. He isn't here much of the time, as he spends a lot of his free time with his girlfriend downtown, but I enjoy the freedom to sit out on the balcony, and look down at the beauty of Mira Flores. I think I've hit the jackpot here Ma; it's real touristy: restaurants, night spots, fabulous shops, a must visit when you come. It's on a clifftop above the beach. You can get out that lovely bikini you bought last Christmas specially for your trip. As for me, I won't be here long. I'm only going to stay a week. Then, thanks to you transferring money to my account, I can go and explore the bigger, wider Peru. Pay you back by the way when I get some bar work at home. In a week's time, I'm going to fly to Cusco up in the mountains. It's at a very high altitude in the Andes.

From Cusco, I'm going to visit Machu Picchu- remember woman power? When you come out, we'll go back there again. After that, I'm going to be what is called an immersion volunteer. I'll be living with a Quechua family with a slow pace of life. I have to be in Cusco by the 10th[th] September for an orientation day with the organisation IVHA,(international volunteer helpers association) so I'll have to fly up there. They have no mod cons in the mountains Ma; it's all very basic. They have running water, but no Wi-Fi alas. My mobile will be ok for a signal in Pisac, the nearest town. The charity provide 24/7 cover for us anyway if needed. The indigenous people have no English, but the Quechuan language has lots of Spanish words thrown in, so we should be just fine along with sign language and the dictionary ha ha. Seriously, the IVHA people can interpret. My volunteer family are Andes and Alyma Amaru. They have four kids. The smallest is a baby I think. Alyma is a weaver in the village, and women need a good strong Leitrim lad to help them. I'll be cutting back the Alfalfa plants in the fields with Andes and the other men. Could I ask for a little more money, maybe 500 more dollars? I had to pay the IVHA 400 dollars up front for more supervision, etc. in addition to the €1,500 programme fee which you already sent on.

Muchas, muchas gracias,

Besos,

Brendan.

She closed the lid of the laptop with a gentle sigh of relief. He was living his dream, God bless him. The dream of the Andes was suddenly displaced by the peremptory ring of the doorbell.

'Who the heck? She thought peering out the sitting room window. She instantly recognised Laura's blue Fiesta. The girl was waving madly at her through the front window. She felt her heart tipsy with a little joy. She opened the front door and surveyed her friend who had a very large chocolate cake in both hands.

"Sorry, wrong house," she said. "We don't like chocolate here."

Laura's grey eyes opened wide, letting in the light; her lips powered into a furnace of a smile.

"Ok, I'll take it back so," she said, turning on her heels.

"C'mere you daft eejit - bring in that cake." She pointed to the kitchen table through the open doorway. With the cake deposited, both women embraced. Laura apologised for coming early.

"I was dying to see you," she said, "just to hear all the news from you on your own."

Ron made coffee, and they had a slice of the chocolate cake.

"You missed your vocation," she said to Laura; "that cake is worthy of Rachel Allen."

Laura smiled, "So how are things now? I mean- really," she said. Ron looked at her hard.

"I wasn't spoofing on the phone; things are really good," she said slowly and carefully."Now where is the man in your life?"

"Oh you'll meet him later on. He took the car into Sligo, to do a little shopping for his mother. What time is everybody coming at?"

"Around 6," but ...and here's the but....Ailbhe is coming this evening. We have her for a week. Her mother is going into hospital for tests."

"I see, the famous Ailbhe."

"Ah she just needs proper management, that's all."

Laura rendered her a look, and echoed very softly, "Proper management - you're right."

The girl apologized for the short visit, but she had promised to meet Larry in Sligo .

"He's hopeless at picking out a shirt for himself," she grinned.

Rons fired a commiserative arrow into her smile.

"Men, like children aren't they? You go on Love. See the two of youse later."

Observing Laura from the window, pull her safety belt across her waist, and check her rearview mirror, she remembered something and headed for her bedroom. Just as she put her foot on the bottom rung of the stairs, her mobile rang on the kitchen table. A WhatsApp video call was lighting up with Joe's head looking a bit oversized and disoriented. She gasped, "Da how are you doing? I was going to ring you later."

Sally stuck her head in at an angle onto the screen.

"Hi Ron, Love."

"How are you Sal?"

"Very well indeed; your dad's coming home tomorrow."

Ron beamed, "Ah the bionic man returns."

"Less of the bionic if you please," her father said.

She cleared her throat, "The new man returns."

"That's better."

Sally promised to pop in later for the barbecue.

"God, I can smell those steaks from here," Joe said.

"We'll send you some on WhatsApp."

"Yeah, yeah, you do that."

Suddenly there was a flash of white uniform beside the bed, and a few murmured exchanges.

"I'll let you go now," she said, and the screen went blank. The hospital world had swallowed him whole.

She barely had time to register the kitchen clock said 1, when Eanna let himself in, lugging some cases of beer and twenty vacuum packed steaks into the kitchen. The wine bottles and soft drinks were stacked in a cardboard box in the kitchen corner from yesterday. She promptly put the beers in the back porch, then opened the fridge door to make room in the bottom drawer for the steaks

Over a lunch of cold ham and chips, she told him of Laura's visit. Eanna polished off a slice of the chocolate cake. "Mmm, that girl can bake," he said, before nervously glancing at the wall clock. She observed the stricture in his throat, the sudden stilling of his features. "Have to be out of here by 2.30." She nodded. A temporary shadow cleaved the sunlight in the kitchen. He cleared his plate. She took a few timid bites out of the ham, and pushed the plate away.

"Too much chocolate cake," she said, her eyebrows lifted on a thin smile.

"Laura's fault then," he said.

She waved him off at 2.30. Her steps sprinkled lead into the gravel path, as she moved back into the kitchen to finish off the preparations. She emptied the dishwasher first, then counted out bags of crisps and peanuts. She began to make her nibbles next: oat cakes with cheddar cheese and tomato. Well, no one would accuse her of not being a good host anyway. The O Gradys made a silent movie again in her head. She had come such a long way since the day in the golf club, hadn't she? Suddenly, feeling ambushed by her traffic jam thoughts, she headed for the sitting room, intending to do her meditation. She promptly fell asleep on the reclining chair. The doorbell jolted her awake, and announced a new presence on her doorstep.

Ailbhe's arrival hadn't discommoded her like she thought. Eanna took charge and served her cold ham and chips at the kitchen table. She had eaten ravenously, sending small nervous smiles in Ron's direction. Ron moved over to where she was sitting, her torso leaning heavily into the wooden kitchen table, her legs spread-eagled onto the floor. She gave her a small kiss on the top of the head.

"Well done Love, you ate every bit of it."

Ailbhe beamed. Eanna's eyes searched hers out softly over his sister's head.

"Thank you," he mouthed silently. He kept his sister busy putting out the peanuts and the nibbles on a few small round patio tables. She fetched the soft drinks from the kitchen, and placed them beside the beakers on the tables. Then she handed her brother the blue and green box of party lights, which with the help of a step ladder, he was stringing from one birch tree to another. She was revelling in her new usefulness, Ron noted.

Many of the guests had turned up by 6.30pm, when the pungent smell of barbecue steak was a forgiveness on the slightly chilled air. Ailbhe was glued to her side, being introduced to all the guests as they arrived. She flicked her long auburn hair back shyly and positively glowed with the admiration for her Laura Ashley party dress. By 7, Eanna's former principal Mark and his son Paul had arrived with their guitars. Ron mingled, offering drinks. Eanna manned the barbeque. Finally, when everyone had queued up for their food, she could relax. She was introduced to Laura's boyfriend Larry. Super nice guy, she thought - able to engage Cian O'Grady on the subject of a new Toyota Avensis, and expressing an interest in herbal medicine, to her partner's gratification. She gave her friend the thumbs up sign behind his back.

She kept an eye out for Ailbhe, making sure her plate was topped up, and walking the garden with her. Sally stopped by when the music was in full swing, and immediately appropriated Ailbhe to herself, dragging her out to jive to "Four Country Roads." Ron felt the soft winds of relaxation finally blow her tangled skein of worry away. After a few glasses of red wine, she began to drift lazily off to a more benign universe.

Sally approached her around 9pm with Ailbhe in tow.

"This one's bushed Love; she wants to hit the sack. Eanna says he'll get her to bed."

Her partner suddenly materialized by her side. "Ten is the latest she goes at home."

"Ok, I'll check in on her in about an hour. Thanks Love."

She turned her attention to the girl. "You must be exhausted Pet."

Ailbhe gave a small martinet nod, and seasawed the backs of her fingers across closed eyelids. Ron turned on her chair to watch the retreating backs of brother and sister as they headed for the house. Eanna helped Ailbhe over the lip on the backdoor, as her right leg hesitated to take the rise.

When she looked at her watch again, it was going on for 10. 45. Fortunately they had borrowed outdoor heaters from Joe and Sally which kept the party alive outside for longer. The night itself was reasonably benign, and the red and yellow light bulbs caped a benevolence over the darkened sky. The musicians were finishing up. A number of the party had made their excuses. She insisted on seeing each of them to the front gate.

As she returned to the garden from seeing Larry and Laura off , she noted the remaining stragglers were heading into the house. Time to check on someone. A heavily snoring Ailbhe lifted the bedcovers into a soft swell when she glanced into her room before heading into the kitchen for the sing song and a final G&T.

At 1am, they mounted the stairs, checking one more time on the sleeping girl downstairs in Brendan's room. She reflected groggily the night had been a startling success.

"Did I do well?" she asked Eanna repeatedly, to which he nodded with his old cat grin, lifting the corners of his eyes. "You were the star of the show Ron, especially the singing."

"Oh God, was I too loud?"

"Not at all," he said, the vowels in his words unfolding slowly in amusement. "Lady Gaga may as well have been here tonight."

She groaned, "Don't tell me... don't tell me."

"I won't," he said, putting his left arm around her waist, as she attempted to steady herself by holding onto the bannisters.

She frowned, trying to concentrate. A pendulum swung at the base of her brain. As Eanna opened the bedroom door with his free hand, she broke away from him. She remembered something. In a not unpleasant, but slightly chaotic fog, she headed for the top right-hand dressing table drawer. The blue pill box was in its usual place. Her fingers felt around inside it, in the dark until Eanna put on the overhead light. She was perplexed; the second last pill in the blister pack was gone, and the last pill was still in its slot. Her eyebrows furrowed reluctantly. But she hadn't taken yesterday's one or had she? Well, she must have taken it this morning; her head was all over the place. A thought crossed her mind - "maybe take the last one anyway." Eanna looked over at her curiously.

"Something wrong?" His voice had a woolly texture, and she squinted in the glare of the strong ceiling light.

"Turn off the overhead light Love; it's too strong. Can you turn on the bedside lamp?"

"The bulb is blown," he said, as his hand flicked the switch.

His eyes flickered over to the box in her hands. Then he frowned heavily, yawning in a huge arc.

"Just come to bed Ron," he said, patting the white duvet cover. The room got a bit out of focus as he turned off the main light. They undressed in the dark, which issued her a certain kindness. She felt her body's hankering for her clean cotton white sheets. He got into bed first, and pulled back the covers. Noticing her pause one more time - considering, he said again,

"Just come to bed Ron."

She swung her legs comfortably in beside him.

CHAPTER 33

Unable to sleep, she sat on the side of the bed, her laptop open in front of her. Hard to believe it was Tuesday the 11th[th]September, over a week since the barbecue. Eanna had taken off for Dublin on Saturday with Ailbhe. All in all she thought, it went quite well. Sitting in her red Candlewick dressing gown, she wiggled her toes in her slippers. Then she did a brief grounding exercise, aware of her feet on the ground, her hands touching the duvet, registering each sense in turn. The day ahead would be busy. Ailbhe had been a model of good behaviour. Eanna had brought her to the herb nursery where she had helped with the harvesting of the plants. He had shown her how to thin out the roots of certain plants in order to have a feasible herb for tincturing. She informed Ron when they returned, she was going to put the leaves of the sage and lemon balm into the deshkitor (desiccator, her partner translated)

"She even helped bag some of the teas," he said proudly, running his fingers through her hair. She creamed off her usual smile when he did this, her surveillant eye looking up at him pleased from under the hem of her fringe, as she stood shyly, head lowered on the kitchen floor. Even out shopping, she'd proven very independent. When she was unsure of how much money to count out for her ice cream at McMahon's ice cream parlour, she wouldn't let Ron take any money out of her Laura Ashley purse.

"No, I do it myself," she said, pushing Ron's hand away. Between them they separated the €6.50 for the ice cream sundae from the plethora of coins she had put out on the counter. Then she put all the extra coins back herself in painstaking fashion, elbowing Eanna's helping hand angrily away.

"I do it myself," she repeated vehemently.

"Well," Eanna grinned at Ron," her mathematics may not have improved, but her determination is mighty".

In fact she was more than grateful to her partner for keeping his sister out of her way most of the week, inventing little jobs for her. She appeared promptly at meal times, was very polite and then disappeared into the bedroom to watch a video on her phone or to draw up her playlist on Spotify. They had a farewell meal in Joe and Sally's on Friday night. Joe was in good form and getting by reasonably with one crutch. The pain was thawing under his eyes.

She returned to his emails. Everything she loved about him infused his sentences. His Machu Picchu one was the last from late on Sunday night. This she hadn't read. She scanned it briefly. Certain words fell under her acute radar, stunning scenery, up with the gods, healing power, temple of the sun, Chakradance, the same words he used as hash tags on Facebook. She smiled and decided she would re -read his emails prior to Macchu Picchu, which would then be the pinnacle in every sense.

From: brendanoconnell21@gmail.com
To: ronoconnell15@gmail.com
September 4 2019 7.00am
Subject Brendan The Navigator in Mira Flores.
Well Ma,

Great to talk to you on WhatsApp this week. I've been bored sometimes in the house, but I've been sketching the streetscapes all week, and watching the paragliders over the clifftop. Just below my window is a small pretty park, where they do Yoga every day at 6.30am. I joined them today. They were quite cool about it all, and just gave me some lovely neat smiles.

No worries on the money front. I still have some savings in dollars and euros. There are cambios on every street corner. Getting around is cheap - just 5 Sol on the Metro into the centre of the city. I've eaten in a lot of tapas bars. I swing my legs at the long counter with the locals. I catch snatches of Spanish. They were discussing the festival yesterday, the feria of San Martin de Porres which was delayed this year due to municipal works. I looked out the open doorway. I heard the music before I saw the procession. About twenty men dressed in white shirts, black waistcoats and trousers were carrying the saint shoulder high. He was a black man who worked many miracles here in Lima in the 16th Century they told me when I asked. Does Grandad have a small statue of him at home? I met Francesco in the Plaza de San Martin (the black man again!) for coffee earlier today. It's such a lovely spring here. Temperatures are around 20 degrees celcius. We sit out comfortably at midday. BTW, he said you're welcome to stay in the house when you come out in the middle of next month.

Now, I simply have to tell you about my nightlife, the Don Quixote bar in Barranco near Mira Flores, the most surreal nightclub ever. They have converted a colonial house into a big bar and café. There are three storeys with different music on each level. I went from Salsa to Jazz to Samba. God, I love the Salsa. I tried chatting up a señorita, but wasn't very successful. She just looked at this worm, then giggled with her girlfriends, eyeing me suspiciously. The walls were a riot of blues, jades, ruby reds, concentric circles and murals of Inca temples. I tried my first Pisco Sour. Google it Ma!

Francesco took me to Las Olivas, one of the shanty towns on Tuesday. OMG, it's just miles and miles of wooden shacks sloping to the sea. They only have electricity from a dynamo. I don't think they have a bathroom, so you can imagine! Some have no running water at all. He took me to visit Father Ernesto who runs the Francis Xavier school for the children. Most of the boys spend their time combing the dumps. They find stuff to recycle and some to sell on the market. The smell is unbearable, but they climb in anyway into the rubbish pile in their bare feet. They only come to school an odd day. I told him I'd like to come back after college, and spend some time there. He said he'd hold me to that, and took my email.

Besos,

Brendan.

PS the sea murmurs prayers to me at night before I fall asleep.

From brendanoconnell21@gmail.com

To ronoconnell15@gmail.com

September 8 2019 12.20pm

Subject Brendan The Navigator goes to Cusco.

Hi Ma,

Flew to Cusco today.

The altitude here makes one feel a bit dizzy. It's weird, but climbing the stairs in the hostel after I arrived was really difficult. All part of the package though I'm told. Got in at 10 this morning and now it's hard to believe it's after midnight. I've just come in from a meal with Theresa, the Spanish girl who's volunteering with me. I met up with her parents, Antonio and Maria and little brother Davide who is ten. She's only seventeen and is doing this solo. The whole family flew in from Madrid two days ago. They're going to fly back to Lima on Thursday after exploring Machu Picchu and the Sacred Valley. Theresa and I will get the local Inca Terra minibus, to Pisac and the IVHA project manager will take us by jeep from there to Chawaytire (our village). It's an hour and ten minutes ride at least over some dirt track roads.

We're two of about thirty volunteers, all starting together. The company put me in touch with Theresa, as we are close in age. Our orientation day is Monday. I've promised to take her to the market tomorrow in San Blaz. She seems so young and innocent. From what I've seen so far, the little hilly cobbled streets are all ringed by the mountains which are magic tonight. The shadows drink down the little houses. The mountain itself is lit up like a galaxy of stars. It makes you feel protected. There's a cool breeze blowing now at this hour, so I wrapped my newly bought Cusco red and blue, woven alpaca shawl around me. I'm sure I'll buy a hat tomorrow. Speaking of hats Ma, you'd be tickled pink at the variety. The women have all kinds: football shapes, saucer shapes, cowboy hats. Their dress is so pretty too. They're all dressed up for another festival today, the festival of Santa Rosa. I got to see another saint being carried shoulder- high. Then I saw something else... wait for it, a bevy of beauties dancing behind her. I could feel the sun on my face and the breeze coming off the mountains. The whole atmosphere was kind of reverential, and the brass band was somber, and then they all got kind of giddy, as the girls started to dance a more modern dance. All the buildings around the square are a mix of old Spanish and Inca. Hard to believe that these buildings were once lined with silver and gold, and that the Conquistadores plundered and massacred the poor old Incas. I must read up more on the history when I get back to Lima. My next email will be after Machu Picchu while I still have Wi-Fi.

Besos,

Brendan.

From brendanoconnell21@gmail.com

To ronoconnell15@gmail.com

September 9 2019 11.00 pm

Subject: Brendan The Navigator in Machu Picchu.

Well Ma,

I finally got there - Machu Picchu. I can see why they wanted to live up there. It really is Earth meeting Heaven. I read something about a cosmic fusion in a poem. Words can't describe how I felt; it was like touching the gods. Most of my journey was by train. It took about 50 minutes to Aguas Calientes. Then I walked about ten minutes up to the summit with some American students. They'd all booked a trip up a mountain called Huayna Picchu over four months ago. It's the one you see in all the photos, covered in lush green vegetation. I didn't know we were getting closer to the Amazon Basin down here. Machu Picchu is a good bit lower down than Cusco. I had an image in my head of you sitting meditating outside the sun temple LoL, maybe doing your Chakradance?

The archaeologists found mummified remains of several women under the temple, so they thought that initially this was all some kind of female tribe that lived here. It appears now that there were hombres like myself, ha ha. The guide met us at the gate. The tour only cost 30 Sol. I'm so grateful to Mr. O'Hara in school for pointing me here. It's some archaeological wonder too. The stones are made to fit into each other like a jigsaw piece, so they just dance or bounce around in an earthquake, and then move back into place. *Cool dudes* those Incas.

There are hundreds and hundreds of steps linking all the houses, palaces, plazas and temples. I wouldn't have minded volunteering on the terraces and planting a few spuds. Tell Grandad, the first spuds came from Peru. I spent about two hours here in total, just imagining what it must have been like. I did some sketches as well. Nobody knows why they left because they didn't write anything down. What a shame to leave no story behind, but we still have our imagination. Maybe we could climb that mountain Huayna Picchu together? We might get a cancellation-you'd never know.

By the way, just to fill you in - the market in San Blaz was so cool. I bought a hat for myself, and a lovely football shaped one for Theresa. She giggled at herself in a small cracked mirror in one of the stalls. The Quechua woman seated on a small rickety chair just cackled at us. She said something in Quechuan, and a man nearby translated "These crazy young people." Tomorrow we have our orientation day, and then we are free in the afternoon. I may not email or whatsapp tomorrow. I should be able to get down to Pisac at the weekends, and access wi-fi from there. You know they have a twenty- four- hour emergency line for any problems anyway- number already texted..

Besos,

Brendan

As she got dressed for school she wondered how his orientation day had gone. Already she was missing not hearing from him. Eanna would be down from Dublin later around 11 or so. She sighed as she stirred her porridge. Today she would be busy at school. She was dividing her time between Rihanna and the new autistic boy in first class called Owen. She found herself missing Grainne, who had moved to Galway. Owen could be a handful, and the afternoons had to be spent in his noisy classroom, By 2pm, the little boy was often to be found asleep at his desk. He required a lot of physical movement, as in ball throwing skills and running around the gym. She also needed to practise making eye contact with him. There was a meeting scheduled with the school psychologist and the class teacher before twelve. Yes school was all buzz, and she loved it.

Somehow she got through the afternoon better than expected. The meeting with the psychologist had gone very well. She'd been given the OT reports to look at, so she knew what kind of games to play with Owen for coordination and eye contact. Rihanna had followed her around on the playground at lunch like a little puppy dog. Owen had become her second shadow. Looking up at the scudding clouds across a diminishing blue sky, she thought of him there in Machu Picchu - hard to believe he was so close to the heavens.

When the final bell of the day rang, she stretched her arms out slowly, unfurling her body from the child's chair she'd been sitting on beside Owen. There was still work to be done for Maureen, (Rihanna's class teacher.) Senior infants' photos taken on Ron's phone were being printed up on the PC as the children filed out the door. She waited discreetly until they had all exited. Now it would take another twenty minutes to get them up and pinned to the notice board on the corridor outside the classroom door. She and Maureen were halfway through pinning them - Maureen handing her the thumb tacks up on the step ladder - when the phone rang in her jeans pocket. She waited until she put the last photo handed to her in place. By then, the phone had stopped. Getting down from the ladder, she pulled it out and checked the number; it was a WhatsApp call. Instantly she recognised the Peruvian code, but oddly not the number. Surely Brendan couldn't be...? Her thoughts were cut off, as the phone rang again. She stiffened involuntarily, as she swiped the green icon upwards. The voice sounded uncertain, hesitant, and the person spoke with heavily accented English.

"Mrs O'Connell?

"Yes,"

she replied, unused to the incorrect title. She was aware of a drawstring tightening the length of her body.

"Mrs O'Connell," the voice continued.

Then there was a heavy clearing of the throat, and a small silence before the male voice continued. "This is Don Miguel Sanchez Rey. I am the managing director of IVHA in Cusco."

Saliva fled her mouth. She was vacuumed, though breathing. He continued on in what seemed like a rehearsed speech.

"Mrs. O'Connell, I'm afraid I have some bad news and some good news for you. Your son Brendan has been in an accident."

Her hands began to sweat ; a wave of dizziness carried her body's shock. Maureen, who had absented herself during the call, but left the classroom door open, brought the teacher's chair into the corridor, anxiously motioning to her to sit down. Her ghosted body reversed into the seat.

"What do you mean accident?"

Her voice suddenly unplugged, was a quivering torrent.

"He was in a bus crash at 8.15 this morning local time. We don't know all the details yet. The good news is, he is alive." The person cleared his throat.

"There were a number of fatalities. However, he has some serious injuries, and is in the acute unit of our best hospital in Cusco. Tomorrow I will be in contact again. Do we have your permission to contact the Irish consulate in Lima on your behalf?"

He paused. She heard herself give an affirmative grunt. The world had departed from her, and decided to take speech as its hostage.

" Expect some phone calls after 8pm GMT. I'm so sorry about this news."

CHAPTER 34

She rang Eanna immediately. He answered on the car phone.

"Hi Ron - just heading into Charlestown now."

Her breathing was coming in charred waves. Sally stood beside her in the kitchen, rubbing her shoulder. Joe sat at the table, trailing his coffee mug round and round in his big hands, looking up at the two women helplessly.

"Everything OK?"

"Eanna, Brendan has been in an accident."

She heard the sharp intake of breath.

"Oh God, when did this happen?"

"Apparently this morning at about 8.15, Peruvian time. He was getting a bus to his new placement in the mountains. I just got a call at school."

There was silence.She could hear him thinking.

"Ron, I'll be there within the hour."

They'd been over and over the details, the scant ones that they had. Apparently more stuff had been added on Facebook via Francesco, whom Ron had befriended in advance of going to Lima. Suddenly she was inundated with more friend requests.

"Joe can befriend them for you if you like, to get more info," Sally said. Ron nodded , screaming silently. She was hanging from a rollercoaster, her wet palms slipping. She rubbed her moonstone pendant repeatedly, until her fingers chafed against the shiny surface.

" God - if there is one- let him come home to us; we'll take it from there. "

"It appears a number of the volunteers were killed and some local people too,"

Joe said now, scanning her news feed, Instagram and Facebook accounts, where the story appeared to have been shared widely. Ron didn't see her father's ruddy pallor peel off him, or his jawline deaden as amateur footage of the crash appeared on Instagram. She didn't observe him hand the phone to Sally, who pushed down a gasp. All she knew was she needed air.

A fog of tears on her path, she ran to the Alder grove. She'd given him his pendant here; he had been angry with her here. They had made up here. She leaned against a small alder tree, unaware she was shivering in a light cardigan. She wouldn't see Orion the hunter tonight. She needed stars.Where the hell were they when you needed them? It was her father's voice that brought her in. He stood at the edge of the copse, calling her hoarsely, waving his crutch uncertainly on the rough grass.

"Love come inside. We will get him home and we'll get through this together."

Meekly she followed him into the cottage..

The accident was on the 6 o'clock news. No names were given, but it was disclosed that a young Irish man had been injured in a bus crash in Peru. His condition was considered serious, but stable. Eanna sat at the kitchen table playing around with a ham sandwich and a mug of tea, Ron refused to eat despite his entreaties.

"He's stable Ron; that's amazing in itself."

He approached her tentatively. Eventually she allowed her ragdoll self to be pulled closer to him. She dropped her head sideways onto his shoulder, as he steered her into the sitting room. He put her phone on silent, scanning for any Peruvian numbers.

"Don't worry," he said to the mute alarm on her face ."I'm just giving you a breather. I'll check it every 30 minutes for urgent messages."

Word had spread. Sally made some cocoa, and got her to sip it slowly putting one of her own large blue cashmere shawls around her shoulders. Joe put more coals on the fire with his one free hand, holding his crutch in the other. He had repeatedly tried Adam, and eventually left a voice mail. Eanna's phone kept ringing. He dismissed some of the calls, and she could hear him answering more out in the small corridor.

"Yes Una, yes that was Brendan they were talking about. We'll definitelykeep you posted."

Then she heard him on to his own mother.

"We don't know any details yet Ma, but he's stable thank God. We'll let you know as soon as we hear more."

John, her school principal was on next.

"We only really know what Maureen told you John. We'll keep you posted. Thanks for the call."

It was heading for 8, and he put Ron's phone back on. The first call was from IVHA. This time, it was Brendan's project manager, whose English was a little better than the man earlier.

"Your son is going to live Mrs O'Connell," he said very clearly

"However ..." here he spoke very slowly, as if every word in the sentence were newly minted."He has been taken to the Clinica Santa Rosa in Cusco. His arm is broken, so he has already been operated on. There is another issue though," and here the man allowed his intended words to fall back into a choreographed slide into his throat before continuing. Ron gripped the moonstone frantically, small dribbles of sweat running down her back, and pooling in the palms of her hands.

"Brendan has been assessed by the trauma team, and for now he has lost feeling in his legs."

The phone on speaker, she barely registered in the periphery of her vision the massive shock on the faces around the firelight.

"We don't know if this is permanent or not, and more tests are needed obviously. I can put you in touch with the doctor by tomorrow."

Eanna took the phone from her when the second call arrived from the Irish consulate in Lima.

"Yes, yes," he said.

"Unfortunately Miss O'Connell isn't available right now. I'm her partner.You can what? You can...? The line isn't clear. Yes I can hear you better now that you're moving around. You will have a liaison person in the hospital in Cusco who speaks good English? And you will send her there ASAP. Yes we will email you our travel plans later on. What about flights? We need to what? We need to check out Latima Airlines." Sally grabbed a pen and paper."Sorry can you spell that? Oh, you'll send on the link, thank you, and a taxi will meet us once we email in advance? Good- how long is the flight time, the most direct one? 19 hours and 20 minutes, and that's the fastest one, cost about €1000 each... I see. So we can email you, and you will let the hospital know then we're coming, and then you'll have the translator in place. I see - thank you."

It was Sally who broke the silence when he hung up.

"Right," she said

"I gather they're going to send this link straight away. Eanna, you make us some more tea, and I'll check the email."

By the time Eanna had brought in the tea tray and a small tomato sandwich for Ron, Sally had clicked on the link. They all stared at her like lost children in a fog. She was the one with the powerful torch; they just had to follow.

"Yes, yes, there's a flight tomorrow morning, but it's 6am. There are two stops: Charles DeGaul and Lima,.You get to Cusco at 19.20 their time. We can make it in the the morning if we leave for Dublin now."

In answer to the unanswered question, who is we? Eanna said,

"I'll go with you Love."

Ron, who had been silent up to now, spoke suddenly and firmly to all of their surprise.

"No Love, you're needed here. Your business is only getting off the ground, and I may have to be gone some time - plus the house is getting to the final stages."

Her eyes held out a hungry appeal to Sally.

"I have no problem whatsoever coming with you Love."

For a moment, Joe looked mildly alarmed before squeezing his wife's hand.

"As you say yourself Sal, you're a good un. We men will be fine here."

"Right, you need to pack Ron," Eanna said.

"Just bring your passport , some euro, an overnight bag with a change of clothes. I can transfer money to you with online banking."

"Underwear, toothbrush, toiletries, nightshirt, T- shirt, sweater, jeans, sandals and a change of shoes," Sally added helpfully. By 10, they were on the road to Dublin Airport, booking two last- minute seats on the flight to Cusco. They were booked into the Skyline Hotel for the night, or at least for what small sleep they might get. It was near the terminal.

Ron settled back into the seat. She'd only flown a couple of times ever in her life. The plane was levelling off. The Fasten your seat belts sign had switched off. Sally beside her had settled into a small nap. She looked across the three rows of the big plane; they were on the second last leg of their journey, the one she didn't plan to take for another five weeks. About two thirds of the plane appeared to be Peruvian. She kept on her large sunglasses. They befriended her anonymity, her desolation. "God," she thought again, "I'm in the clouds up with the gods, and yet I feel so helpless." She stole a glance at her stepmother beside her. Sally played a blinder in Charles de Gaul, using her phone to book them into Hotel de los Viajeros in Cusco.

"It's the best value Love and only two blocks from the centre. He's in the Clinica Santa Rosa which is very central."

"Do you speak Spanish Sally?" she asked suddenly.

"Un poco," Sally replied waving the back of her hand diffidently.

"I bet you speak more than that."

"Actually, I studied it in London; I worked as a lab technician there, and had applied for a post in Madrid. With that in mind, I went to study the language at the Instituto Cervantes by night."

"Did you go to Madrid?"

"I met Sylvie."

Here she smiled – I never forgot my Spanish."

The air hostess stopped at their seat, her trolley filled with foil packed dinners.

"Buenos Dias,"she said agreeably.

Sally stirred in her seat and smiled.

"Buenos dias - tengo hambre.

"I told her I was hungry," she said to Ron, as they removed the lid from the top of the carton.

"I know, I've been practising with that app Duolingo."

They were silent as they ate the beef and carrot stew before them. Ron cleared her throat.

"Sal, are you ok with paying for the hotel? I'll pay you back when we get home."

"No," came the swift reply.

"I've no children of my own Ron. You and Joe and Brendan are family. Sylvie and I couldn't have children."

There was a hard pause. A tight, woven sadness stole into the space between them.

"I never liked to ask you about that."

"I don't discuss it much - three miscarriages and one still-born - he was full term- George."

"Oh God, I'm so sorry Sal."

She took the other woman's hand wordlessly, gently massaging her fingers one by one.

"After the full term loss, I decided no more. I married at thirty, and I was forty- two now. No, no more babies for me, so I served and still do, on the board of several children's charities in Manchester.

Sylvie and I set up three of them: The S & S Foundation, Cope and Braveheart."

"Was S & S for Sylvie and Sally?"

Sally nodded."That was for educational support after school, a bit like Barnardos here. Cope was for young mothers, and Braveheart, a helpline for children from desperate homes. We would encourage them to ring us repeatedly, and work with the police to get them out of there."

"You are one busy lady. How did you find time for us?"

"Your dad and Brendan rescued me Love. I'm quite a wealthy woman, so money is just a tool. You remember that now with your own inheritance."

"Well, I may need the remainder of it now Sal... you know, if we have to...adapt the house and stuff, or pay for treatment down the line."

She could hear the hollowness in her speech rolling down a tunnel in her head.

"Padam, padam," Sally said looking at her.

"Remember, it means step by step in Sanskrit.You told me that. Did you get on to IVHA again?"

"I emailed from Charles de Gaul, and they will send a taxi for us tonight at the airport in Cusco."

"Clinica Santa Rosa? " the taximan said inquiringly when they got into his cab with the cardboard signage IVHA across the windscreen.

"Si," she said in anticipation, a running current surmounting her exhaustion. Driving through the dark Cusco streets, she felt more alert, having eaten an evening meal at Lima Airport.The cool mountain air bore in hard through the open taxi window.

"Lo siento," the taxi man said, depressing the electronic lever to roll it up. The night indigo sky above them blended with a golden patina of lights, showering the pavements, as they approached the historic centre.

"Plaza de Armas," he said suddenly. At their nod, he gestured to his right,

"Catedral".

She glimpsed the lit up windows of the sandstone church she had only seen on Instagram. A mother and child were rolling up hand woven rugs in the square. The child wandered in the direction of a hurrying passerby, offering something in her small fist. The tourist shook his head and quickened his step.

The taxi confidently navigated the warren of small cobbled streets with large square shop front openings in the walls of whitewashed buildings.Wall hangings and paintings could be glimpsed through one doorway. Small restaurants were putting their menus outside on chalkboards.

"Muy turistica aqui," the taxi man said now. Both women chorused,

"Muy turistica."

The density of the old walls suddenly gave way to a broader avenida with affluent three storey balconied houses. She glimpsed a sign for Machu Picchu train station. Then they were turning in the gates of a small white-washed two- storey building with a blue neon sign above it.

"Estamos aqui."

Almost racing in towards the small semi-circular reception desk, she finally stopped, and allowed Sally to inquire what ward Brendan was in. The receptionist, initially puzzled, suddenly smiled in light bulb comprehension.

"El chico Irlandés - por aqui, por favor."

He had refused all pain meds all afternoon. He needed to be awake for them he said. Her heart knotted ; pain cut a cleft in her chest wall at first glimpse of him. She heard Sally's quick intake of breath beside her. He was propped up on three pillows, his white face swamped by the night shadows in the dimly lit ward. She approached him at a run, then stopped at his bed tentatively, and touched the ridged bedspread as if it covered porcelain..

"God, Ma and Sally - can't believe you're both here. Give us a hug - I won't break."

The sound of his voice released her tears from their twenty-hour captivity. She leaned in, aware of the delicacy of his arm cast under the covers. As she disentangled from the feast of his touch, something glinted on the bedside locker. Sally noticed it too. He followed their gaze.

"Me moonstone pendant.When they cut off me trouser legs, they took it out of the pocket.I never got around to fixing the chain," he said contritely. Her only response was a second hug, and kisses that were embarrassingly swampy, he told her later.

CHAPTER 35

The mountains above her had heart, "Pachamama," (Mother Earth), he used to tell her in his emails. After nearly three weeks, this hotel was beginning to feel bizarrely like home. Everyone in Los Viajeros knew their story by now. "Ah Las Señoras Irlandesas - el pobre muchacho." (Ah the Irish women - the poor boy)

The two women's daily routine seldom varied, despite Brendan regularly pestering Ron to at least visit Machu Picchu once. After breakfast, it was a coffee on the sun terrace of the hotel, then a brisk walk to the hospital, stopping often at the markets. Secretly she embraced the surrounding white and lemon walls with dark blue doors and the ubiquitous terracotta rooftops. By now she was trying her Spanish on the smiling gap - toothed ladies with the tall hats and small alpacas in their arms.

"You like photo? You like photo?" they asked repeatedly.

"No gracias," she would say, drawing them into one of her famous smiles.

Others touched her arm repeatedly, courting her eyes. Then they would extend a small stubby hand with a flourish towards their hand woven shawls.

"Que colores."

She would smile again and say, " Tal vez mas tarde." (Later, maybe). Usually she just bought mangoes, grapes and flowers for the patients in the Clinica. Hard to think back to that first day she and Sally met the interpreter and the project manager from IVHA. She had peered in on Brendan before meeting the doctor. Her son lay in a forest of white coats. The consultant, glimpsing them out of the corner of his eye, beckoned to them to wait in the corridor. He appeared outside the door of the ward, and with a smiling flourish of his hand indicated a nearby open doorway to a small office. Inside, a middle -aged woman and a man in his early thirties were waiting.

The lady introduced herself in English as the interpreter. She made all the introductions. The doctor looked from Sally to Ron.

"Madre?"(mother) He pointed to Ron, and then back to Sally.

"su hija?"-Your daughter?- He was looking at Sally full- on now. Both laughed.

"I'm Brendan's mother,"Ron said, holding out her hand, "Encantada."

"Encantada," the consultant echoed, taking it and engaging her eyes .

The energy in the room shifted visibly. The doctor sat behind his desk, and opened an already growing file. He wet the tip of his index finger, flicking through several A4 pages until he came to the two he wanted. He spoke in rapid Spanish after reading the first report.

"Your son has a bi-lateral break in the upper arm, but we're not concerned about that"

the interpreter began. The next report the doctor read slowly with heavy intonation.

"We are however concerned," the interpreter continued,

"about the lack of feeling in his legs. An MRI scan, nerve conduction tests along with electromyography and a spinal tap indicate no physical nerve damage. This does not mean he will automatically walk however. I have consulted with other colleagues in Lima and Massachusetts in the US about Brendan's condition. They believe he has FND- Functional Neurological Disorder." Ron and Sally exchanged worried glances.

" This is not necessarily bad news," the interpreter continued, as the doctor's sentences elongated rapidly."It means we do not understand the workings of the brain. His body is receiving messages telling him it is safer to stay as he is. There is a centre for this condition where there have been many positive outcomes," and here the interpreter paused, unsure how to deliver the next message.

"The centre is in Massachusetts, US, but currently there are no places left on the treatment programme. It appears they are booked out until mid 2020."

Unable to digest the spider web of information, Ron decided to focus on her son for the next week. "Padam, padam" echoed in her brain, serving as a barrier to her mounting fear. Sally said she would pray.

"Do that Love," Ron said softly. She had no update on God's hiding place just now.

By mid-morning, Brendan was sitting up in bed, just beginning to unscramble the story of the crash. He didn't remember everything, but had been told the crash had occurred as the bus driver overtook a car and a van in succession, then, rounded a steep curve at the other side of which was a lorry. A load of prosciutto had just fallen off it and onto the road. The minibus which did not have ABS, jammed on the brakes, swerving into the ravine below. He had no memory of hitting his head, or even the pain in his arm. He did remember coming to and looking for Theresa. They had been sitting together in the front row.

"There was only one seat belt Ma. I was on the inside, and I let her have the outside seat with the belt."

Her fingertips touched the dried up sobs in his chest.

"She didn't make it out of the bus. I got thrown out and the scrub held me. Everyone trapped in the bus died ; it just kept tumbling to the bottom of the ravine.

She squeezed his hand. Sally rubbed his shoulders,

" I told her parents I would look after her. She was only seventeen; it's not fair."

Suddenly he began to shake violently as his eyes held a middle distance.

"Ma, they were all burned." His voice was lost in the Andes, holding inside it the conflagration.The ward was a lung that couldn't find its breath. The other patients looked away. They sedated him .

They began their daily visits to the hospital. The interpreter came again for another consultation - with the psychiatrist this time. Fernando the IVHA project manager returned too, to explain about insurance and 24 hour contact. It was explained that trauma can cause fight or flight or freeze in the body, and in Brendan's case it seemed to be the freeze response.

"A team of experts can help him," the psychiatrist said.

"We just don't know how far they can bring him".

He explained about physical therapy, psychology, the role of cognitive behavioural therapy, even hypnotherapy as a way in to help the brain find its way out of the fear maze.

She bought Brendan a new phone and set him up on Facebook, Instagram and WhatsApp. His face lit up when his friends began to finally video call and text.

"I posted a photo of myself from here on Facebook and Instagram Ma and told them a little of my story so far," he said one evening when the lights had just come on after tea in the ward. She scanned what seemed to be a million comments.

"Hang in there man." "God is good." "You're one tough hombre." "You will make it."

The football team all commented.

"You will get those legs kicking for the county final next year. The team have lost their goalie, but not for long. Love you bro."

Suddenly he paused and lay back exhausted. Small beads of sweat pushed his exhaustion onto his forehead. She wiped them away with a tissue and brought a water bottle to his lips. He drank greedily, and then tried to push himself further up in the bed with his hands clutching the bedposts frantically. She placed both hands under his oxters and began to pull him.

"No Ma," he said tersely, his muscles stiffening.

"must learn to do this for myself."

She meekly let go.

"Have you heard from Dawn?" he asked, suddenly anxious. She shook her head.

"Maybe she's on nights and she's too tired to ring."

" I'm sure she'll ring," she offered lamely.

"It's been nearly a week since we did a WhatsApp video" he said, his voice, shrouded in a fog. He fell silent until the end of the visit.

He rang her hysterical the next morning at 11.

"Dawn has ended us Ma. She's left me. She's left me," he repeated in a kind of manic wind up voice. She could hear concerned voices in the background. Then the line went dead. It took all the following week to pacify him. She stayed for hours at his bedside, just reading or sitting silently with him while he slept. She did a little Reiki to calm his energies, and he slept more deeply the nurses told her. Dawn had returned to Islington, she told him in a very long text, and was going back out with Geoff, her old boyfriend again. She really hoped he would recover well, and was sorry for hurting him like this.

"She said she loved me Ma," he said, his voice hardened into a flat thin line,"but she didn't. How could she just go back to him? She didn't even like him."

How could she reassure him, talk to him of shades of grey ? How could she help her idealistic son navigate these astounding cruelties in his life of barely nineteen years?

Both women had just returned from the evening hospital visit. Brendan's spirits were finally on the rise. He was very popular with the other patients, and he conversed freely making them all wince and grin simultaneously at his halting and grammatically flawed Spanish. Still his legs refused to obey him. Despite several emails to

Massachusetts followed by phone calls from the doctors, no place could be found on the programme. He was placed on a heavy cancellation list. They wrapped up well for the cold night air, and sat before the brazier in the hotel courtyard. Ron always welcomed the sparking of the coals and the release each time of new rivers of light.

"More coco tea?" she asked Sally.

"Yes please. Amazing how we're taking to this tea, isn't it?"

"Only for it, your altitude sickness might never have lifted Sal."

As she poured the tea into Sally's cup, the older woman looked at her.

"You feeling alright Love? it's just you look a little peaky, and did I hear you in the bathroom this morning?"

Ron didn't answer at first. Clearing her throat, she waited until the Quechua girl tending to the fire had gone back into the shadows under the archway.

"Actually Sal, I've missed a period."

"Well that could be stress, altitude, long haul flight."

"Yeah, yeah I know that, but it's been ten days and I feel queasy all the time. I threw up this morning, and before you ask, I didn't eat anything different.

I never even had altitude sickness remember?"

"You're taking precautions aren't you?"

"Yes, yes I am. In fact I can't understand it really."

"Understand what?"

Well, with the barbecue and everything, I was pretty sure I hadn't taken the pill Saturday the day before, but it was definitely missing from the blister pack, so I assumed I must have taken it on Sunday to compensate like they advise if you miss a day. I knew for a fact I was down to the last two in the pack. I was going to take the last one to be sure, but it was just really late and I was too tired I think to make an effort. Anyway I figured I was pretty much covered.

Sally straightened in her chair, put the fingers of her left hand to her bottom lip; her eyes bolted out of their normal calm enclosure.

"So you assumed you were OK?"

Yes, why?

Ron could feel a conundrum rising in her brain which had stayed obligingly undemanding up to now. "What are you trying to tell me Sal?"

Sally took a long sip of her coco tea before replying.

"You couldn't have taken it, because Ailbhe did."

Then the penny behind Ron's shelved worry dropped. She was right; she had missed a day, but why was the second last one removed and not the final one? It was bizarre-made no sense.

"How do you know she took it?" She heard her own question roll in like a vague thunderclap.

"Well... because Eanna got a call from his mother, who found it in her Laura Ashley purse when she was looking for coins to pay the milkman; it was half crumbled, but under Aileen's sharp questioning, she admitted she took your pill out of the pack to keep for later apparently!"

But why didn't she?

"Why didn't she take the last one? It seems she may have been disturbed. Joe asked around and Larry (Laura's chap) met her on the stairs round half nine when he went into the house to use the toilet. He assumed she was coming down from the bathroom.

We didn't want to worry you with any of this."

"God, I told Eanna time and again to take her to the doctor. You know I meant to get a lock for the bedroom door before she came, but we were both flying around like wild things that week."

Sally covered her stepdaughter's hands with her ample ones.

"See, no garnet ring this time love - I'm inflicting no more casualties."

Ron issued her a tight smile .

"On the bright side," Sally continued, Eanna hightailed it to Dublin, and his mum and himself took her to their doctor in Darndrige, who promptly prescribed the pill for her. In fact he said she had a perfect right to have sex, but she must be careful."

Both women fell silent. The only sound was the soft grumble of the traffic on the street below and an insistent crackle from the fire. Sally cleared her throat.

"The chemist is only a block away."

Sitting on the loo, her eyes scanned the small strip in her hand. There was no mistaking the thin blue line, as clear as the mountains above her. She sat there for another ten minutes outside of time. Sally knoocked again on the door.

"You OK in there?"

"Yeah, yeah, I'm coming out now."

"No worries."

They both scanned the strip together until finally Ron spoke.

"Wow, what did Hardy say to Laurel?"

Sally looked puzzled, then said slowly in an American accent ,

"Another fine mess you've gotten us into."

Their laughter released them; it thawed the room, lifting off their every sinew and bone until the guy next door rapped angrily on the wall.

"Not a word at home about this yet Sal," she said, before they turned in for the night.

She shelved the news. Everyone could wait, even Eanna. Truth was, a small seed of resentment was implanted in her which she found hard not to water. He and his mother just wouldn't listen. The Universe certainly had a way of mocking her when all her attention was needed for her son.

Eanna had rung.

"We're doing fine actually," she told him, - churning emotions, sneaky riders in her gut- He told her Joe was returning to the surgeon for an early follow on. His knee had become painful. She would ring him later, poor pet, but now she held it together and the foetus, well the foetus must take a back seat for now.

A week later, Sally told her over breakfast that she had booked a return flight for three days' time, the 5th October. In answer to Ron's frightened look, she said,

"Your dad needs me Love. When are you going to tell Eanna?"

"Not 'til next week, after I meet the gynaecologist in the Clinica." Sally nodded uncomprehendingly. Ron could see she was holding back a lecture by the small series of stressed exhalations over the rest of their silent breakfast. Truth was, there was a gale blowing inside her which she couldn't outrun, and neither could she share it. To distract, she said

"Adam is ringing tonight - says he has news."

"Oh gosh, I forgot about his pregnancy. All OK with them?"

"Apparently so."

Once they'd heard the news, a shocked Adam and Miguel immediately did a video call. Adam then called twice weekly. Brendan adored their calls, hanging on to the staged banter between the two men.

When the call came that night, she was alone. Sally had taken a taxi to the cathedral. She was rediscovering her once unflagging Catholicism.

"Sis have I got news!"

"Is it the baby?" she said, massaging the foetus, whose presence was insisting on being felt.

"No, it's about Brendan."

"Brendan?"

"Yep. We've discovered a clinic in Berkeley - 26 Kilometres from us. It's newly opened up, and they treat FND. The director of the unit is Elizabeth Goulding from Mayo, would you believe? They haven't advertised on social media yet, and their new website won't be up and running for another week or so.

Her heart was on roller blades down the Cusco cobbles as she set the phone down on the bedside locker of her room.

"Ron, you gone?"

"No, I'm here,"

she said to the speaker phone.

"Can they take him?"

"Yes, once he does an interview via something called Zoom."

She had never heard of Zoom, but what kind of magic had the Andes thrown up? The gang in Dublin suddenly gained an absolution.The clinic was called Dowkas (Dochas) meaning hope in Irish.Elizabeth, she mused – Elizabeth - OMG, that's *Alice*. She had opened up a helpline to her mother since their arrival. She was a believer suddenly. Sally found her doing her crown Chakradance on her return from mass. After that, it was all action. Brendan's interview was the day after Adam's contact. He clicked on a link sent from the director's email, and they spoke for 45 minutes on a Zoom call.

"It's a cool platform in the US Ma," he enthused. "She was really kind." Tears ran themselves out of him. Perhaps something extraordinary had begun already, Ron thought patting down her womb. She found herself talking to the foetus out loud when no one was listening

"Well you may have technically been an accident, but I'm not holding that against you. I'm the one with the dicky relationship with the Universe. Me world is always being turned around. "You are welcome, child of The Andes, fruit of Leitrim and Dublin. (For now, the child was perforce an amorphous, genderless, soul extension) I need you to stay calm in there while I focus on your brother." It had been hard to open him up at times. Some days he would be all funny one minute, and then retreating to unusual brittle silences the next. It seemed only Adam and Miguel could release him. She had a code, "Navigator" with her brother on WhatsApp. The San Francisco call would arrive ASAP.

Sally booked a trip to the planetarium outside the city the night before her departure.

"I know your thing about the stars," she said.

Ron beamed "That's me head in the clouds, Ma used to say."

"Well, your Ma is looking after things now. Our boy has been accepted," Sally said.

He had rung to tell them he had received an email that morning. His voice sounded clear, surfing his first real ray of hope.

"This clinic sounds excellent Ma, he said reading from the clinic handbook : psychiatry, psychology, hypnotherapy, occupational therapy, cognitive behavioural therapy, breathwork, massage, physical therapy, meditation and two additional programmes, (introduced for the first time ever in the treatment of FND) Somatic experiencing and Vision Reality, based on the works of Drs. Peter Levine and Joe Dispenza respectively. I guess all that should set me right," he said, in a voice from which the old phantom of despair was already departing.

After she hung up, Ron went quiet and moved over to her bedroom window.

"I will miss it up there with the gods, but Berkeley sounds cool as Brendan says about everything."

"New start," Sally said, "and with a new person too."

"Ah yes, that matter," she said.

She would ring him from the planetarium, she decided. He might be mad at her for not telling him straight off, but he'd get over it. The show was amazing as she and Sally combed the virtual heavens and especially viewed her favourite constellation,Orion himself. "He won't appear here until November," the commentary said. "He will be seen everywhere by then."

"Berkeley," she thought, "I will catch you there, my hunter man."

Before the interval, she signed to Sally she was going outside to make a call. Ascending a small flight of stone steps, she gasped. The Milky Way was strewn across the dark. Its wide band of swaddling white light eased out its back like a large feline above the dark mountain ranges. She inhaled softly before she rang him. He was on the farm drinking tea with the lads.

"I'll just take the call outside by the polytunnels," he said.

"How are yeh? Fantastic news about Brendan - everyone is so hopeful here. The football team are holding a fundraiser by the way."

"Eanna my love," she said softly, sensing his distractedness .

" listen."

She poured her news into the silence.

"You're pregnant?" he shouted into the phone.

"How did that happen?"

Well, looks like a bit of an accident, but with a result we're gonna come to love.

" Oh!"

She could almost hear his catch up thinking on the line.

"Are you there Love?"

He'd gone so quiet, she could hear the concerned whispers in the overhanging eucalyptus leaves around her.

"What kind of ring will I bring out when I come?" he asked, "moonstone or diamond".

Her treacherous heart tripped over the cobbles at warp speed.

"Do you even need to ask?"

She stood there alone for a long time after the call ended. The silent phone nestled in her palm as she looked out at the inky sky with the quarter moon laying on its back. Sun and moon- It was suddenly imperative that she visit the sun, or as near to it as she could get.

CHAPTER 36

"Sit or stand by the ocean - the sun is setting and slowly the sea and sky are turning a vibrant shade of orange. As you inhale, imagine drawing this colour through your entire body. As you exhale, send this orange light into the energy field all around you. Bathe in the orange light. Find your own natural rhythm as you breathe in and out, feeling the vibration of orange. Now breathe the light into your sacral chakra, just below the navel. Feel it pulse with vibrancy and aliveness."

The indigenous music was beginning to build up on the recording. Soft tribal voices were accumulating on the air. She felt deeply on the in-breath into her lower abdomen. She was bringing her breath to her womb. All thinking abandoned, she connected with her belly, where she placed her hands now, drawing in the light at such high altitude. The rhythm of the drums became stronger.

Opening her eyes briefly, the temple of the sun shimmered above her in a gathering glare from a warrior disc of sunlight. She flung her bare arms out to play in the light, as the voice instructed. She adjusted her earplugs briefly, feeling the stability of the recorder in her hip pocket. She was wearing just a light blue string vest and cropped white cotton trousers. She began to gyrate, as the pulsing music and the rhythms inside her joined forces in a growing sensuality.

"Feel your feet on the ground. Connect with the red core of the earth. You might like to imagine you're dancing around a campfire. Feel the pulse in your body. Connect with your legs and feet. Trust in the way your body wants to move and express itself."

There was a heavier beat to the music now.

"Stand under the soft glow of a full moon, and feel the waters flow through your lower belly. Connect to your feminine energy.

Surrender your hips to that movement, cleansing and releasing any stress you are holding."

She felt a kick, subtle at first, then a second one, more intense. A wave of tiredness washed over her. The doctor had said it was unusual to be this tired in the early months, but bloods were clear. Her breasts began to hurt. She opened her eyes and found a low stone wall to sit on. Her gaze was drawn to the terraces below. Above and over to her right, a towering Huayna Picchu extended a protection and an emerging conversation with the heavens. She closed her eyes to focus again on the voice.

"You are dancing in a crystal chamber listening to the voices of the heavenly choir. Above you is an indigo night sky. You emerge now free, swirling in the Heavens."

On impulse, she got up and began to move again.

"A pathway has opened up for you; you are invited to walk it and see where it will lead. You meet your guides, your angels on your path as you come down the mountain, bathed in a fluid evening light."

She was utterly unaware of a growing number of women circling her, each immersed in their own rhythmic dance. That's when she felt the presences, more than one. She could see no faces, just shimmering outlines of light, neither male nor female. Strange unfamiliar voices carried to her on a light wind. Suddenly both breasts stabbed her so sharply, she gasped, bending over. One of the group around her moved hesitantly in her direction, but stepped back as she swayed trancelike gazing at the indigo sky. Suddenly, on the path before her, a brown skinned woman emerged as if from a cliff face, waiting. Behind her was a moving sun, carrying what seemed fluid, genderless, human features. When the woman drew near, Ron felt no fear, just a quiet acquiescence. She carried two infants, one in each hand. It was difficult to determine their gender. Both breasts were on fire now, as she heard a voice.

" hand over anything that is weighing down your heart."

A mist came down on the mountain then, and the woman vanished behind it,carrying the children's receding backs with her. As the recording ended, she stood stock still, opening her eyes, adjusting to the bright glare of the ruined buildings around her. That's when she saw the growing circle of women, each one immersed in their own dance. Seeing she had ceased moving, a woman who appeared to be the group leader tapped each dancing female on the shoulder until one by one they stilled their feet and gyrating bodies. The leader began the applause. Then it grew like a torrent through the women, spreading out to the other tourists moving up and down the steps. The guard at the entrance took up his megaphone and shouted suddenly and unexpectedly 'Bellas Mujeres, Bellas Mujeres" (beautiful women, beautiful women). The words reverberated off the peaks as the assembled tourists took up the cry. Ron felt her cheeks suffused with heat. Her heart lifted to the peaks with a strong double beat. The leader of the women motioned to her to sit down. They all produced rugs from their individual rucksacks and began to sit on the ground around her. It turned out they were a group of women who called themselves "The Free Dancers." They had come from Madrid and incorporated a variety of dances into their routines. Today when they saw her, they recognised at once the Chakradance. They coincidentally had had the same idea as her of doing a dance here in this sacred place. Each drew up their own favourite routine on their recorders, and allowed the rhythms dictated by the music to lead them, Maria, the group leader explained to her animatedly in English.

She conversed with them in broken Spanish. She told them about her son's accident.

"Ah, el pobre muchacho," (the poor boy)

they murmured, with deep kindness anchored in their eyes. She then shyly told them of her pregnancy, realising they were the first ones beyond family to know. She missed sharing her feelings with

Sally who had returned over a week ago now. Visas for Eanna and herself were being expedited, but they had to do a joint interview at the Irish Consulate. He promised to be out by her birthday. Eyeing the women around her, she reckoned many of them to be in their forties and fifties.

"Chakradance is for all ages, though many of us here are mature women as you can see," one of the group who identified herself as Estrella said."We have teenage children and young adults and a couple are grandmothers." She eyed Ron.

"Quántos años tiene usted?" (How old are you?)

"thirty - six next week."

"Ah, Feliz Cumpleaños."

"Digame, ¿ hay algún hombre en su vida?"

(you have a man?) Estrella asked.

She nodded, her tears blocking the sunlight.

"No está aqui. - he isn't here - she said in a lowered tone.

Estrella patted her on the shoulder, misunderstanding.

"Algún dia el vendra (some day he will come.}

Explanations were just too complicated.

By 1pm the women had to return to Aguas Calientes. Ron offered to walk the path with them. Skirting along the edges of the growing crowds, the group walked in single file. She was following the others closely, watching the sign for Salida (exit) when something made her look over to her right. She thought the man might be a Swede or a German, but then he turned. He didn't see her, Someone was pointing out the sun temple to him. She began to shout, and then to run. The Spanish dancers looked behind them in amazement. The security guard was chasing her.

"Por favor Señora, no corer - No running, please Madam - "

He stood frozen by the entrance to the temple, trying to discern where the voice came from. She waved both arms high above her head in a frantic scissors movement. A smile washed over him like a new dawn, breaking up his legion of freckles.

"Te quiero" (I love you)

he said in his Dobbinstown Spanish.

The security man stepped back. The Spanish women stared open- mouthed now. The sunlight glinted off their gold bangles, hitting the old stones sharply.

"Happy Birthday," he shouted. "I thought I'd find you meditating here or dancing."

She permitted her lips to widen in a single straight line. He produced an ivory box from his pocket, and waved it above his head. She moved faster now, wings carrying her heels down the stone staircase. There was a rumble of thunder. A soft curtain of rain washed down the rocks. Breathlessly she hugged him. The women and the other tourists, standing stock still on various levels of the stone steps applauded again. She melted into him, synchronising her wild heartbeat with his calming one. She laid her head gingerly on his sopping chest.

"You weren't supposed to come 'til next week," she said.

"The tide was high," he whispered in her ear.

He removed a ring from the box, and slid it gently onto her finger.

"How could I ignore the pull of the moon?"

THE END

About the Author

A native of Limerick, Mary Moloney has lived many years in Naas, Co. Kildare. She is a former teacher who now practises as a naturopath and herbalist. The Live with Gusto Fund is her first novel.